THE BABY GROUP

Rowan Coleman worked in bookselling and then publishing for seven years, during which time she wrote her first novel, *Growing Up Twice*, published in 2002. She left to write her second novel, *After Ever After*, and now lives and writes in Hertfordshire with her husband and daughter. *The Baby Group* is her fifth novel.

Praise for Rowan Coleman

'Brilliant . . . moving, funny – just the tonic every knackered new woman needs!' *New Woman*

'A fresh, warm and hugely enjoyable read . . . truly brilliant. Her captivating style leaps off the page, engrossing you from the first sentence' *Company*

'A charming tale' *heat*

'Highly enjoyable . . . Coleman tells her story with bundles of warmth and humour' *Spectator*

'Touching and thought-provoking' *B*

'*Growing Up Twice* was a triumphant first novel and the follow-up is just as impressive' *OK!*

'Emotionally satisfying page-turner' *Closer*

THE BABY GROUP

Rowan Coleman

arrow books

Published by Arrow Books 2007

2 4 6 8 10 9 7 5 3 1

First published in Great Britain in 2007 by
Arrow Books
Random House, 20 Vauxhall Bridge Road,
London SW1V 2SA

www.randomhouse.co.uk

Addresses for companies within The Random House Group Limited can be found at:
www.randomhouse.co.uk/offices.htm

The Random House Group Limited Reg. No. 954009

A CIP catalogue record for this book
is available from the British Library

ISBN 9780099492542

Mixed Sources
Product group from well-managed
forests and other controlled sources
www.fsc.org Cert no. TT-COC-2139
© 1996 Forest Stewardship Council

Typeset by SX Composing DTP, Rayleigh, Essex
Printed and bound in Great Britain by
Bookmarque Limited, Croydon, Surrey

For Kate, Steve and their son Oscar
Born 11 August 2006

Acknowledgements

I consider myself extremely lucky to have two wonderful editors working on my books and I want to say thank you so much to Georgina Hawtrey-Woore who has been so supportive and dedicated during the writing of *The Baby Group* and to Kate Elton whose early input was so important to the book. Georgina and Kate, I hope you know how highly I value you both.

Thank you to all of Random House, and especially my heroes in the sales, marketing and publicity departments who have done such sterling work on my behalf for which I am truly grateful.

Thank you also to my agent and good friend Lizzy Kremer, who is a constant source of support, ideas and most importantly laughs – she always keeps me sane.

To my stalwart friends who are always there even if I don't see them often enough: Jenny Mathews (Mrs Basquille), Clare Winter, Lynne Smith, Sarah Boswell, Cathy Carter, Rosie Wooley. Thanks for generating the sales, girls! I miss all of you.

Very many thanks to the dear friends I see every day and who have given me so much support over the last year: Margi Harris, Kirstie Seaman and Catherine Ashley.

My mum has always been extremely supportive of my

career and I don't think I have ever thanked her enough for everything she's done for me over the years, so thank you mum. I love you.

Finally, thank you to Erol, who always makes me smile and laugh and whose dedication as a husband and father I learned to truly appreciate when trying to imagine life without him. It's something I never want to have to experience for real! And to my darling little girl Lily who is a constant source of inspiration and ideas and who lights up every day.

THE BABY GROUP

Conception

Natalie Curzon had been stuck on the Northern line in the half dark on the day she met the man who would completely change her life in the most unexpected way.

She had been feeling sticky, hot and mildly anxious on that unseasonably warm April morning because she knew that she was going to be late for her meeting with the lingerie buyer at Selfridges, a meeting it had taken her and her business partner Alice months to arrange. Natalie didn't want to be late for that meeting; who knew how long it would take to rearrange it?

Firstly she noticed the man looking at her, or rather she felt his gaze as she read over her presentation notes again. For a second or two she kept looking down at the words without reading them and then as she looked up he looked down again, rattling his newspaper to smooth out the pages. Natalie saw him shift slightly in his seat as he studied his paper with infinite care.

Natalie wondered if he had been admiring her. It would be nice if he had, but she remembered only too well the time she had thought that the whole world was admiring her because everybody she passed was staring and smiling at her. In fact, it had turned out that her wrap dress had slipped open at the front revealing a grey and much machine-washed bra to the public at large. The incident had caused her considerable embarrassment and her friends and colleagues much hilarity not least because she was the co-director of a sexy lingerie company. She had never again gone out in public in anything less than her finest underwear.

After giving herself a quick once-over to check that she was fully dressed, Natalie decided she could let herself think he was admiring her. He probably wasn't, he was probably scrutinising the Tube map over her left shoulder. Still, even the possibility gave her a small inner glow. She would have let the moment pass without incident, taking enough satisfaction in a potential unknown admirer and never given him a second thought. But as she looked back down at her notes she sensed the man watching her again.

The second time she looked up he did not look away. Hesitantly, Natalie glanced over her shoulder to see if he really was looking at something else. When she looked back he was still watching her, and this time he smiled. Natalie returned the smile instinctively. He was about her age – perhaps a little older – dressed in a good, dark blue tailored suit. His left hand was bare and there were no telltale tan marks on his ring finger. He wasn't handsome exactly, but he had something about him, a kind of mobility in his face that made him interesting to look at, with his closely shaven pale skin and slightly ruddy cheeks. He had thick, dark, longish hair that curled over his collar and as he held Natalie's gaze she noticed he had very dark eyes, almost black.

'This is a nightmare,' he said lightly, gesturing generally at their predicament. His skin glistened with a light sheen of perspiration that made Natalie worry that her nose was shiny.

'It is dreadful,' she replied with a resigned shrug.

'That's my whole afternoon blown now,' he said, before adding decisively, 'You know, now I come to think of it, what's the point in me going back to the office at all? I'm going to take the rest of the day off.'

'You're probably right,' Natalie replied, thinking he must be someone quite important if he could just take time off like that. She thought about her missed meeting; it had taken her and Alice weeks and weeks of persuasion to get Selfridges to even think about stocking their lingerie range in-store. She looked at the man and wondered if he was going to continue this conversation or let them both slip back into the silence of strangers.

'I might as well take the rest of the day off,' he repeated, almost to himself. He shifted in his seat restlessly, looking as if he couldn't stand to spend another second stuck on the underground train. Natalie sympathised.

'Lucky you,' she said, a touch wistfully. She glanced at the woman sitting to her right who was quite obviously eavesdropping on their conversation to pass the time. Natalie couldn't work out if the man was chatting her up or not. Maybe he was just being friendly, because if he was chatting her up he wasn't being very obvious about it. If she wanted to know for sure, and frankly she did – then she had to try to think of something to say that would elicit a reaction from him that would make his intentions clear.

'I should get back,' she said. It wasn't exactly the alluring and inviting sentence she was reaching for, but it was the only one that came out. She tried again. 'I run my own design company called Mystery is Power with my business partner and best friend, Alice. Lingerie, sexy but very high-class, you know the kind of thing. We're really busy at the moment, but I must admit on a day like this and after being stuck in here it would be nice to be out in the fresh air . . .'

The man looked impressed but not embarrassed or intimidated by the word 'lingerie', and he didn't snigger like a schoolboy. Natalie liked that about him, because it was surprising the amount of fully grown men who did snigger or blush when confronted with the posh word for pants.

'Then don't go back,' he said, smiling with one corner of his mouth. He had a very nice mouth and a pleasant smile.

Natalie sat back in her seat. She wished she could be sure whether or not he was chatting her up. The ambiguity annoyed her slightly. The thing was, she liked him, or liked the look of him at least. She liked the fact that he talked to strangers on a train, that he seemed impulsive and in control of his own life. Of course, that could mean that she was trying to establish a flirtation with a psychopath, but at least that made him more interesting than the average man. She was trying to think of something else to say when he spoke again.

'Come to lunch with me,' he almost commanded, before adding with a tad less certainty, 'if you like, I mean. I know a really nice little Italian quite near to this station.'

Natalie looked back up at him. Now was not the time to be enigmatic.

'Are you asking me on a date?'

'I am,' he said, as if he had only just decided himself. 'Do you mind?'

She smiled at him; he was a strangely appealing mixture of confidence and vulnerability.

'Why not,' she replied, deciding that Alice would approve of her seizing the moment, even if it meant several hundred apologies and an extensive period of grovelling.

'I'm Natalie, by the way.' She held out her hand for him to shake.

'Jack Newhouse,' the man said, taking her hand. His fingers were strong and warm. 'Pleased to meet you.'

'I'm pleased to meet you too,' she said.

And then the train moaned into life and began to ease slowly into the tunnel.

There was no way Natalie couldn't have known that from that moment on, her life was about to take a new and very different course.

Lunch had been good.

Once they were out of the Tube and in the sunshine he relaxed a little more, talking to her easily. He was very charming and there was a spark about him, as if he was brimming with life and energy, that was very compelling.

'This place isn't at all glamorous,' he told her as they made their way into the small restaurant, its walls thick with Artexing and tiny red glass lanterns hanging from the fishing nets that adorned the ceiling. 'But it serves excellent, honest food.'

'I love Italian food,' Natalie said as they ate. 'Well, to be honest, I love food full stop. But especially Italian – somehow I've never quite managed to go to Italy. I keep meaning to, but being self-employed makes taking holiday so difficult.'

Jack looked almost personally affronted.

'That's impossible,' he said. 'You must go, you have to. Italy is the most beautiful, most wonderful, warm, fabulous country in the world. The best food, the best culture, the best-looking people – mostly.'

Natalie laughed at his enthusiasm. She liked the way he approached life, as if he were open to any eventuality. He had an indefinable air about him she couldn't quite quantify. It seemed that, despite his boldness earlier, he wasn't used to seducing women, because unlike some he didn't trot out a parade of hackneyed phrases and clichéd lines. He was very easy to be with and talk to. The conversation flowed so comfortably that they might have known each other for much longer than just under an hour. And the more relaxed with her he felt, the more attracted to him Natalie was.

'My mother is Italian,' Jack said. He paused for a second as if he had just remembered something rather troubling, but then his smile returned and he went on. 'She's a genuine Venetian, would you believe? All my childhood holidays were spent there and my mum and dad live just outside Venice now, they retired there. In fact, I am one of the few men entitled to be a gondolier because you have to be born there to be one, and I was.' He paused again and then added regretfully, 'When I was a boy all I wanted to be was a gondolier.'

'So why aren't you?' Natalie said, smiling at the thought of Jack in a stripy top and straw hat. 'I bet you do a great "O Sole Mio".'

'Who knows, I might be one day,' Jack said and they both laughed, their eyes locking. It was Natalie who, disconcerted by the sudden intensity in his eyes, had to look away first.

'It is an incredible place,' he told her. 'You never tire of just looking at it; even the grubbiest back alley is a work of art.'

'It sounds wonderful,' Natalie said, thinking briefly of her own far less appealing girlhood.

Jack watched her over a small vase of three red carnations, tapping his forefinger impatiently on the table top. He glanced at his watch and Natalie wondered if he had somewhere else he had to be. As much as he seemed to be enjoying her company, he also seemed to find it impossible to be still.

'You're an impulsive kind of woman aren't you, Natalie?' he asked her.

Natalie shrugged. 'I suppose I must be,' she said, feeling the thrill of the unknown bubble in the pit of her stomach. 'I'm having lunch with a virtual stranger after all, and a pretty strange stranger at that.'

Jack laughed.

'Have dinner with me this evening.' Once again it was more like a command than a request, but this time there was no uncertainty at all in his tone.

'Dinner?' Natalie raised an eyebrow; that wasn't exactly her idea of impulsive.

'In Venice,' Jack added, his voice light but his eyes crackling with raw energy. 'Naturally.'

Natalie held his dark-eyed gaze for a long moment and knew without question that as soon as she had caught his eye on the Tube he'd been planning to ask her that question. What she most wanted to know was why. Why had he singled her out?

'Why not?' she said instead, being very careful not to let her nerves show. 'Why ever not?'

Alice would kill her. She could be very reasonable about delayed trains and hectic schedules and even unplanned lunches with attractive strangers, but she would not be amused by Natalie taking off for the weekend with said attractive stranger. It would be the 'stranger' part that would upset Alice, causing her to lecture Natalie at length about potential serial killers and con men and to remind Natalie that she had promised not to get herself into any more silly scrapes after the Paris incident.

But somehow, whatever Alice's warnings and remonstrations might be, Natalie knew she had to go to Venice with Jack Newhouse.

Natalie felt Jack's gaze on her as she watched the sun setting behind St Mark's Basilica. Jack had reserved them a table on the terrace at Cip's Club, at the Hotel Cipriani, situated on an island just across from St Mark's Square. He spoke to all the waiters in Italian. He could have been discussing the waterbus timetable for all Natalie knew, but the rhythm and the tone of the language was certainly beguiling. The animation and sheer joy in his face as he spoke his second language lit him up from the inside.

'This is marvellous,' Natalie said, tearing her eyes away from the impossibly beautiful view to look at Jack, whose skin glowed in the golden light of the setting sun. 'You are a very lucky man to have this place in your life.'

Jack looked thoughtful for a moment, dipping his head.

'It's almost too much,' he said, without looking at her. 'The more joy or beauty there is in your life, the more you have to lose.'

Natalie didn't respond for a moment. Just as she thought she had this man figured out, he would do or say something to throw her. In that second he looked so intensely sad that she thought he might even shed a tear.

'I'd rather have happiness for a little while than never at all,' she said softly.

Then his hand reached across the table, his fingertips stopping a few millimetres from hers. They still hadn't touched each other, not since they'd shaken hands on the Tube. The anticipation tingled between them like a promise. Which was why Natalie put the slight tension she noticed in his jaw and shoulders down to his nervous English genes kicking in.

'Natalie,' Jack said. 'I have to tell you something.'

Natalie felt her own muscles contract. That was the kind of line that usually prefaced a break-up. It would be a record even by her own standards to get dumped in Venice by a man she had only just met. The terrible thought occurred to her that it might be her, and the awful mistake of bringing her here, that had made him feel so low a moment ago.

'You do?' she said cautiously.

'I don't want you to think that I'm this kind of man,' Jack said, gesturing around him with his wine glass.

'What kind of man?' Natalie asked him.

'I don't usually bring women I hardly know to five-star hotels on the Continent for dinner. I don't want you to think I'm a . . . a cad, I suppose.'

'A cad?' Natalie had to choke back laughter.

'Don't laugh.' Jack smiled ruefully, looking down into his wine glass.

'I don't get you, Jack,' Natalie said. 'But I like you. I really like you.'

When Jack looked back up at her his expression was intense.

'You must know that I very much want to take you to bed,' he said. 'But I don't expect it. If you like I can get you a water taxi back to the airport and you'll be home before dawn.' A hint of that smile lightened his mouth once again. 'Or you could stay here with me for the weekend. Like I say, I don't expect it. But I want it. I want you.'

As Natalie steadied herself in an attempt to prevent herself from climbing over the table and throwing herself at him right then and there, a sharp breeze swept in from the sea and rippled through the awning over the terrace, making it clatter like an army of tiny feet racing towards them.

'I'd love to stay here with you,' she said eventually, closing the slight distance left between their fingers. 'But you already knew that, didn't you?'

And when Jack smiled at her it was with a genuine delight that was utterly irresistible.

'Thank you,' he said.

When Natalie woke early on Monday morning, she could hear the rumble and burr of something mechanical. It took her a moment to realise where she was, and then she felt a lovely ache in the muscles of her legs and the tingling between them. She smiled and rolled over, enjoying a luxurious stretch. The last few days had been perfect. That was really the only way to describe her time with Jack. Perfect weather, an incredible city, wonderful food – and Jack. It had seemed that from the moment he had asked her to stay the weekend with him, the tension had drained out of his face and body leaving him totally relaxed. And Natalie allowed herself to be flattered by the thought that perhaps all the contradictions in his character up until that point had been due to the nerves and longing she might inspire in him.

After all, since then he had been a wonderfully easy person to be with. So easy, in fact, that it made Natalie realise exactly how much hard work it was to be with some other people. With Jack she felt she could be the rarest of things – herself. No über-flirt mode, no false confidence, no guarded game-playing. For those few days she had felt closer to this man than possibly anyone, excepting Alice, in her whole life. This must be it, Natalie thought, I'm falling in love and it's happening to me here, in Venice. It was almost stupidly perfect and comically romantic, but just then she didn't care, because every single cynical or guarded bone in her body had been melted by Jack and by Venice.

With her eyes still closed she felt Jack's weight on the edge of the bed and his hand on the curve of her waist. She opened her eyes and smiled at him.

'I'm running us a jacuzzi,' he told her. 'Breakfast won't be here for another half an hour yet. I want to make the most of the last few hours I have until you go back to London.'

'A jacuzzi?' Natalie yawned as he pulled her into a sitting position and then, with one arm around her waist and the other under her legs, he lifted her from the bed.

'I want to make love to you in the water,' he told her as he carried her towards the marble bathroom. 'I've been thinking about it the whole time you were asleep.'

'Have I had any sleep?' Natalie asked, laughing.

'Too much,' Jack assured her. He set her down in the bathroom, then slipping his dressing gown off, he entered the deep, bubbling bath. He held out a hand to her. Natalie took it and stepped in, feeling the warm water rush and churn around her calves as he kissed her thighs.

'I want you *now*,' he said, pulling her down into the water. He turned her around and pulled her bottom towards him and for a brief, fleeting moment Natalie thought about the packet of condoms that were still resting on the table beside the bed. But only for a second, because the next thing she knew Jack was moving inside her and she wasn't sure where she ended and the water began.

Jack Newhouse.

Natalie would reflect on his name several times in the following weeks and months, after it quickly became clear that he had vanished just as suddenly from her life as he had appeared in it.

It was quite poetic really, because when you translated his surname into Italian it seemed to make a lot more sense.

Casanova.

Chapter One

'You could phone your mum,' Alice suggested tentatively, and only because she was safely on the other end of a phone line and she knew that Natalie couldn't throw something at her.

'I am *not* going to phone my mum,' Natalie told her sharply, pressing the palm of her hand against her forehead as she spoke. 'I would rather pull out my own fingernails with my teeth than contact my mother and tell her that not only have I just had a baby when she didn't even know I was pregnant, but I am also unmarried and not in any kind of relationship. I am definitely not asking *her* for any help. She'd be so happy she'd probably drop dead from joy on the spot.' Natalie paused for a moment. 'Actually, perhaps I will call,' she said.

'*Natalie!*' Alice didn't like it when Natalie made jokes about wishing her mother's demise, which was principally why Natalie made them. She was very fond of her friend and business partner, but the two women could not have been more different. They were like chalk and cheese or perhaps more appropriately, considering their business, like soft chiffon camiknickers versus a red lacy thong with diamanté detail. Natalie was well aware that she was the thong; often showy, trying too hard to be sexy and sometimes quite uncomfortable to be around. At least, that was what she had been like before Jack.

If Mystery is Power produced giant pants made out of wee-absorbent paper then that would probably be more her these days.

'You see, Alice,' Natalie went on, 'you don't understand because *your* mother is a nice normal woman who would be interested in her grandchild. *My* mother wasn't even interested in *me* when I was a baby. Plus, she would be so smug. So I'm not contacting her. It's not that desperate yet. It would have to get really desperate for me to contact her, and seeing as I don't even count a giant asteroid about to hit the earth and wipe out humanity for ever as a good reason, I don't think it will ever come to that.'

Natalie glanced out of the window at the leaden March sky that churned over the rooftops of the houses across the street. Winter this year seemed to be dragging on for an eternity and she was counting the days until the clocks changed and the evenings became light again and then finally her aged and cantankerous heating system wouldn't have to struggle to keep the house slightly warmer than the Artic Circle any more.

'She phones the office, you know,' Alice remarked a little bleakly. Alice hated lying, she was terrible at it, whereas Natalie had practically made it her speciality over the years. 'Since you got that caller display she phones the office because you never pick up at home.'

'You know what to tell her when she phones,' Natalie said. Her baby stirred in the carrycot at her feet and she held her breath as she waited for him to break out into the full-blown crying that she had come to know so well over the last ten weeks, but then his face relaxed again and he slept on.

'She doesn't believe that you've been on a fact-finding mission in China for six months,' Alice said. 'And I hate lying to her, I feel sorry for her.'

'You see, she preys on souls like you, innocents who think

the best of people,' Natalie said darkly. 'Feeling sorry for her is exactly what she wants, that's how she draws you in.' She glanced down at her baby son. He looked an awful lot like his father, which was interesting because she had almost forgotten what Jack Newhouse looked like until she'd given birth to his son. Or at least she had tried to forget, very hard.

'And it's not really Freddie I need help with,' she said, an unexpected smile creeping into her voice. 'It's hard and scary and I never exactly know what I'm doing, but somehow we're muddling through. It's more that I need someone to look after *me* now and again. If there was someone to mind him while I had a bath, or watch him while I popped to the shops. If I could brush my hair now and again and put some make-up on I might feel a bit more like *me*. I need to put on some make-up, Alice, I look like crap. I'm fat and shiny and my boobs have gone all enormous and I've got stretch marks. I haven't waxed anywhere in God knows how long. I'm so hairy that if someone caught sight of me naked, God forbid, they might think I was the missing link somehow brought back to life after several million years frozen inside a glacier. Or at least they would do if they hadn't already dropped dead from the hideous sight of my mutated body.' Natalie gave a resigned sigh. 'I know now that I will never have sex again, which is just as well because trust me you don't want to see my . . . well, let's just say it's like Frankenstein's fanny down there. I should have had an elective Caesarean. That midwife who told me natural birth was best for mother and child was so totally lying. I reckon you could drive a juggernaut up there now I wouldn't know it.'

There was a long silence at the end of the phone, and Natalie knew that Alice was mortified.

'Too much information, Natalie,' Alice said eventually.

'Sorry,' Natalie apologised lightly. 'It's just that I've got no one else to talk to. I haven't seen anyone since the day after Freddie was born, except you. No one has visited, not Suze or Phyllis – none of the old crowd. And I know why. They all think I'm mad for keeping him. None of them know why on earth I kept the baby of a man I spent one weekend with and . . . never saw again.'

'What I don't understand is why you didn't want to even tell him,' Alice said. 'If you'd told him things might be easier. You might not be so on your own.'

Natalie knew her determination not to tell Jack Newhouse that he was now a father had worried Alice from the start. But Alice's speciality was preparing for the future. It was Alice who had a five-year plan, Alice who understood the mechanics of achieving year-on-year growth for the business and Alice who pictured the day when Freddie would want to know about his father. Natalie, on the other hand, was barely capable of making a five-*minute* plan, and she found it hard to imagine what the future might hold for her in the next half-hour. Especially when it came to her personal life and *particularly* when it came to how her son was conceived. The thought of any future encounter that might or might not occur between some distant version of her son and his father was simply unimaginable. It was a tactic, in her opinion, that made her new life so much simpler. And it was an opinion that she and Alice fundamentally disagreed on.

'Trust me. He's not the kind of man who wants a baby foisted on him,' Natalie told Alice for the millionth or so time. 'All we would have got from him is money and we don't need that.' She stifled a yawn. 'Alice, the man was a professional philanderer, he had to be. What other kind of man would go to all the trouble of picking me up on the Tube and acting all wonderful and lovely and then whisk me off to Venice for incredible sex?' Natalie paused. Whenever she said out loud what had happened between her and Jack Newhouse it always took her a second or two to believe that it was her that it had happened to, and not some true-life article she'd read in a gossip magazine. 'Anyway, that was all there was in it for him: a conquest, a challenge. And so there would be no point in telling him about Freddie. He didn't call me once after that weekend and I didn't know where to find him. So he's not going to want to know about us now, is he, even if I could get hold of him? And anyway, Freddie's got nothing to do with him. I didn't have Freddie because I'm secretly in love with his dad, or because I'm thirty-six and my biological clock was ticking or any of that nonsense!'

'No one is happier than me that you are enjoying being a mother so much,' Alice said, without bothering to disguise her incredulity. 'But I must admit I was surprised you went through with the pregnancy – it just didn't seem like you.'

'Then you don't know me as well as you think,' Natalie said. It was true that when she had realised her period was late she had thought, 'Right, if I am pregnant I'll just deal with it. I'll get a termination.' And even on the way to the chemist's she was planning who to call, how to pay for it, which credit card to use. During the three minutes she was waiting for the test to show a result she was totally sure she knew exactly what needed to be done. And then when Natalie saw that blue line and knew for sure that there was a baby growing – living – inside her, she suddenly felt as if she didn't have any options any more. She didn't have to *decide* to keep him, because there wasn't any decision to make. She just knew she was going to have the baby.

'I *am* glad you're happy,' Alice repeated warmly. 'And you're right, I did underestimate you. You're a really great mother.'

'And I am happy,' Natalie reiterated restlessly. 'Of course I am, but I'm just a tiny bit bored and lonely, so I was thinking, I might be able to work on the Christmas ranges or something. I could even . . . oh I don't know . . . bring Freddie in to the next marketing meeting?'

'Nope,' Alice said quite firmly. 'No you won't. You told me that on no account was I allowed to let you do any work during the first six months. You made me promise, Natalie . . .'

'Yes, but . . .'

'You said that no matter how much you begged and pleaded I had to keep you off.'

'But I didn't mean it . . .' Natalie pleaded.

'You said you'd say that. You said to ignore you.' Alice was adamant.

'Alice!' Natalie heard another phone ringing in the background.

'Oh,' Alice said breezily. 'The caller display is showing a call from abroad – perhaps it's your mum. Now, if you want to stay in China then I suggest you go and put your feet up.'

'But I'm bored and lonely!' Natalie protested pitifully.

'Go and join a mother and baby group or something,' Alice said and the line went dead.

Natalie looked down at Freddie. A mother and baby group she thought, wrinkling up her nose. She couldn't think of anything worse than sitting around with a bunch of brain-dead housewives going on about married bliss and family life endlessly.

'Fancy game of poker then?' she suggested to her baby.

He didn't seem too keen.

Natalie woke up with a start when Freddie started crying. The house was dark and gloomy and when she looked at the clock she saw it was almost five. She must have fallen asleep where she had been sitting after speaking to Alice, because the phone was still in her lap. That was something she was still trying to get used to: impromptu napping. The health visitor said that she was lucky to be able to nap at the drop of a hat when Freddie was sleeping, and that too many new mums tried to spend all night and all day staying awake. But Natalie didn't like it. It reminded her of the days when she used to drink too much and wake up in places where she didn't remember going to sleep.

Natalie's twenties had been tumultuous, to say the least. It had been a decade filled with a catalogue of terrible decisions that she had then attributed to living life to the full. Living life like an idiot, more like it. Things had improved as soon as she and Alice had become unlikely friends. Alice was the sales rep for a large lingerie company and Natalie was the junior buyer for a small chain of budget-clothing stores based in and around London. They had nothing and everything in common and after several months of talking about every subject in their meetings except for the pedestrian garments that Alice was supposed to be selling, they decided to form a partnership and launch their own lingerie company. It should have failed, two half strangers throwing all their savings and hopes into a business together. But it had worked better than either of them had imagined, because by some amazing piece of good luck Alice and Natalie brought out the best in each other, pushing themselves to peaks of inspiration and hard work that they had never thought possible in their previous incarnations.

Natalie had given everything in the intervening eight years to Alice and to the business, so much so that she had inadvertently straightened out most of her chaotic behaviour and lifestyle choices along the way. She had grown up considerably.

However, there was still room for the occasional and usually highly visible setback, the most recent of which was even now crying to full capacity.

She scooped Freddie out of his carrycot and rocked him against her shoulder.

'Are you wet, hungry or fed up, little man?' Natalie asked the angry baby. 'All three I bet. Let me just switch on the lights and I'll get you changed and fed in a jiffy and after that we've got a whole evening of great conversation and soaps to look forward to! *Yes we have!*'

Natalie flicked on the light switch by the living-room door. Nothing happened.

'Bulb's gone,' she told Freddie, swaying him from side to side as she made her way down the hallway and towards the basement kitchen. 'Naughty bad bulb. We'll just go into the kitchen then, won't we . . . yes, we will, we'll just go into the . . . oh.'

The light at the top of the stairs that led down to the kitchen was also not working.

Natalie carried her crying baby into her study. Nothing. And the light on the base unit of her phone wasn't working either.

'Oh, I know, I need to reset the fuse box,' she told Freddie. 'Silly old Mummy.' But the fuse box just kept tripping.

'It must be a power cut!' she cooed in Freddie's ear as if she had spoken fluent idiot all her life. 'Naughty bad power cut!'

She went to the front door of the house and opened it. There were lights on across the other side of the road. Sheltering Freddie under her cardigan as she walked out on to the steps, Natalie peered up and down the road. There were lights on in both of the houses either side of her too.

'Bastards,' she whispered as she went back into her house and shut the door.

'Not a power cut then,' she said. She looked around the hallway filled with long, dark shadows. No electricity meant no light, no heating, no hot water, no fridge, no TV. It was a disaster.

Natalie took her mobile phone out of her bag, sat at the bottom of the stairs, where the hallway was partially lit by the street lights outside, and put Freddie to one breast. As he quietened and settled into feeding, she set about finding an electrician who was cheap, honest and most of all available – now.

Chapter Two

Gary Fisher looked at his apprentice Anthony in the rear-view mirror and then stole a glance at Anthony's girlfriend who sat next to him in the van. It wasn't Tiffany tagging along on a job he objected to so much, but strapped in a car seat next to her was her and Anthony's five-month-old baby girl, Jordan.

'Look, mate,' Gary said, keeping his eyes on the road. 'You know I don't normally mind you taking time off if you need it. But bringing your girlfriend and your kid on a job, well, it's not exactly the kind of image I want to present to clients – never mind the Health and Safety.'

'I'm sorry, Gary,' Anthony said. 'But there's no heating in the flat, the last tenant never paid their bills and they haven't turned the gas back on yet.'

'And I can't go home,' Tiffany said, looking down at Jordan. 'Mum would never let me see Ant again if I did.'

Gary had to concede that point. Tiffany's parents had threatened to turn her out on the street for even dating a black kid. When they found out that not only did she love him but that she was having his baby they did throw her out and her dad threatened to kill Anthony, and Gary wasn't sure it was an idle threat either. He didn't know Tiffany's parents, but her dad had a bit of reputation in the area as a hard man. Tiffany had stayed with Anthony at his mum's until the baby was born and then Tiffany got offered a flat by the council. Thirteenth floor but not a bad little place; Gary knew, he'd been round to check the wiring.

If it had been any other seventeen-year-old who'd made his then fifteen-year-old girlfriend pregnant and homeless all at once, Gary would have been worried. But he wasn't worried about Anthony and Tiff. Anthony was a good worker and was determined to support his family, and Tiff, who had celebrated her sixteenth birthday seven months pregnant round at Gary's business premises with a cup of tea and a bun, had a good sensible head on her shoulders. She was a steady girl despite her conflict with her parents, and the fact that she was over a year younger than Anthony and hadn't officially left school yet. Still, Gary thought, there was a good chance they'd be just fine, all they needed was a little bit of support now and then and he didn't mind doing his bit. They were good kids.

All three of them.

'They said the gas will be on tomorrow, Gary – this is the last time, I swear,' Tiffany said.

Gary shrugged and pulled the van up to pavement outside Number 42, Albion Road.

'You'd better wait here while we see what sort of job it is,' he told Tiff. 'I'll leave the heater on for you.'

Tiff nodded and the second he opened the van door she started to fiddle with the radio dial, desperate to get it tuned into anything except Gary's favourite, Classic FM.

'Nice house,' Gary said, looking up at the three-storey Georgian terrace. 'Not often you see these still intact and not converted into ten poky flats.'

Anthony said nothing. He didn't say much, Gary had noticed over the time they had worked together, unless something had to be said. It was a quality that Gary admired.

He knocked firmly on the door and after a few minutes a woman in a baggy sweatshirt and jogging bottoms opened it, with a baby on one hip.

'Oh thank God,' she said, smiling readily at him. 'I am so glad you're here. Come in! Don't trip over anything. The lights aren't working, well, nothing's working. I checked the fuse box, it just keeps tripping. I unplugged every appliance but still no joy I'm afraid.'

'Gary Fisher,' Gary said, holding out a hand which Natalie shook with her free one. She had a pretty firm grip for a woman, Gary noticed, and unlike most of his clients, both male and female, she seemed to have a bit of a clue about what she was saying. Her long and, from what he could see in this light, dark hair was tangled and in need of washing. She looked like she hadn't slept recently and she had that kind stale baby scent that hung around a new mother. But she acted as if she was decked out in her best party gear and feeling fantastic, which somehow made her seem quite appealing.

'Natalie Curzon,' she said. 'I bought this house when it was a wreck. I've spent a fortune on getting it restored, *including* the electrics, but not the heating because that still works just about, and I thought it could wait until I had some money again. But anyway, I had a new fuse box in and everything only two years ago by um . . . Coopers? Do you know them?'

Gary whistled through his teeth and shook his head.

'Anthony, get the torches from the van,' he said, as if he were asking the boy to pass him a scalpel.

'Oh God, it's bad isn't it?' Natalie asked him, blinking in the full beam of the high-voltage light that Anthony, on his return, had unwittingly directed right into her eyes.

Gary laughed.

'It might be fine,' he said, with a smile that Natalie could just determine as he took the torch from his assistant and angled it downwards. 'Hopefully it won't be too bad at all. Tell me where your fuse box is and I'll see if I can get the power back on and then I'll do some safety checks – OK?'

Natalie nodded. 'Downstairs in the kitchen there's a pantry cupboard on the left – it's at the back of that.'

Gary and Anthony headed down to the basement taking the flashlight with them, and Natalie sat back down on the bottom stair with Freddie in her arms and looked wanly at her power-cut emergency candle that she had found in the designated place, in the drawer in the telephone table, as soon as she had finished calling out the electrician. It had given her a sense of pleasure and true independence as she marvelled at her own forethought and efficiency. Shame really that the same forethought and efficiency had not stretched to storing away any emergency matches too.

Just then the doorbell rang again. Thinking it would be more workmen, Natalie answered it and found a young girl, tall and pale with what looked like a giant baby in her arms, on the doorstep. She was holding a small torch upwards, shining it directly onto her face.

'I'm really sorry to bother you,' she said. 'Only my boy-friend's in there looking at your electrics? And I'm bursting for the loo – I've not long had baby you see – oh, like you! Would you mind? I brought a torch!'

Natalie blinked at the girl who seemed impossibly thin and healthy-looking to be the mother of the baby and impossibly young to be the girlfriend of Gary Fisher, who must be around forty if he was a day.

'Um, no, I suppose not,' Natalie said, stepping aside to let the girl in. In the gloom that was erratically illuminated by the beam of the torch Natalie thought the girl's baby looked a lot bigger than Freddie, maybe five months old. And only five months after the birth this girl was already wearing straight

24

hipster jeans with no sign that her flat belly had ever once been pregnant. Even with the torch it was too dark to see if the inch or so of exposed tummy had stretch marks, but somehow Natalie instinctively knew there wouldn't be any. In two more months, give or take, Freddie would be five months old and Natalie knew there was no chance her stomach would ever look that way again without surgical intervention – in fact, it had never looked that way.

The girl was watching her expectantly.

'Oh,' Natalie said, tearing her envious eyes off the girl's small firm breasts. 'It's up the stairs, straight ahead. The door with the frosted glass in it but it's dark, so mind the stairs.'

'I'll take the torch,' the girl said. 'Do you think you could manage another one?'

And before Natalie knew it she was holding two babies.

'Unbelievable,' she said to no one especially. 'I'm turning into a crèche.'

Natalie was still sitting on the bottom stair wondering what might be happening to her new best friends in the episode of *Neighbours* she was currently missing, and Gary Fisher was still in the kitchen, when the girl came back.

'That's better,' she said, taking a seat next to Natalie on the steps. She lifted her baby out of Natalie's lap with a 'Hmmph.'

'Oh good,' Natalie said. 'Your baby weighs a ton, no offence.'

'None taken,' the girl said. 'She eats all the time. Before she started on solids she used to watch us eating our tea, her little mouth working all the time. She loves her mashed veggies but I reckon she's dying to get her gums into a cheeseburger!' She brushed Freddie's forehead with the back of her finger. 'It's funny, Jordan is only twenty-two weeks old but I've already forgotten that *she* used to be so tiny. It goes so quick.'

Natalie eyes widened in the dark.

'Not in my house it doesn't,' she said. 'In my house it goes very, very slowly.'

The girl laughed, holding the torch between her knees so that its steady beam cast a wider light. 'Yeah, it can feel like that too,' she agreed amiably. Her head bent over Freddie. 'You are a right little darling aren't you? What's your name, hey? What's your name?'

'Freddie,' Natalie told her.

'Oh that's so sweet – why Freddie?'

Natalie could have told the truth, which was that all the time she was pregnant she had been certain she was having a girl. It made sense to her that it would be a girl. After all, Natalie was a girl, possibly the girliest kind of girl there was, and so *of course* her baby would be a girl. They would be a perfectly matched mother and daughter, Natalie had dreamed, enjoying a completely different relationship from the one she had with her own mother, which barely existed at all outside the occasional phone call filled with bitterness and recrimination. Natalie and *her* daughter would be more like best friends from the very start, going everywhere together and in a few years time choosing each other's clothes and swapping make-up. Natalie had developed quite an elaborate plan for her and little Lucia. There had even been a wedding scheduled somewhere around 2031, the identity of groom unknown and besides not as important as the dressing up.

So the fact that the baby had been a boy had thrown her quite considerably. And it took her almost a week to get used to the adjustment, a week in which he had no name at all. It wasn't that she didn't instantly love him, she loved him with a kind of passion and conviction that she had never experienced before. But she was still catching up to the fact that she had a son, a boy and tiny man that might like football and trains and cars and all sorts of things that Natalie had no understanding of at all.

She supposed that a name would sort of attach itself to him at least sometime before his first birthday. And then a few days after she had got back from the hospital she had been listening to Magic FM in the kitchen when they played 'Don't Stop Me Now' by Queen. Something in the lyrics reminded Natalie of her son's fledgling lust for life that he was already demonstrating on a daily and especially nightly basis, and she decided that until a more suitable name came up she would call him Freddie; after all, he certainly had a great pair of lungs on him.

'All the first-born males in the Curzon family are called Frederick,' she told the young girl instead, for no particular reason other than it was more interesting than the truth. 'It goes back centuries. To, um – Frederick the Great.'

'That's well cool!' the girl said. 'I had millions of names for this one, girl or boy. He wanted to call her Thierry if she was a boy because he's a Gooner, but I said no way is my kid getting a name that's going to get it bullied at school. So we settled on Terry which was bad enough. But luckily she was a girl. I love Jordan, don't you? She so strong and independent and clever too, a real role model don't you think? My name's Tiffany by the way.'

'And I'm Natalie, pleased to meet you.' Natalie shook the girl's hand awkwardly between the babies.

Silence fell in the gloomy hallway as the thirty-six-year-old and the girl who was less than half her age tried to think of something else to talk about. Natalie peered at the face of her watch.

'*Neighbours* is on TV at the moment and I'm missing it,' she said. 'I know it shouldn't matter because nothing ever actually happens in any episode, but since I had Freddie my whole world's shrunk to about thirty-two square metres, do you know what I mean?'

Tiffany looked at Natalie. 'I don't watch much telly, so not really,' she said, making Natalie feel suddenly dumbed down. 'But if you're bored, this is near Newington Green isn't it? Barton Lodge Health Centre's up the road, that's right isn't it?'

Natalie nodded; it was where she was scheduled to take her baby to see the dreaded health visitor, a woman Natalie thought couldn't seem less interested in babies if she had tried.

'They've got a class starting there tonight in a few minutes, at six. Baby First Aid – do you know about it?'

Natalie shook her head. 'I'm not very good at knowing that sort of stuff,' she said. 'It all sounds a bit too much like school for my liking.'

'Well, it's on every couple of weeks,' Tiffany explained. 'I've been meaning to go since Jordan was born but I don't fancy going on my own. People look at me like they think they know everything about me,' she added darkly.

'Because you're so young, you mean?' Natalie asked her, never one to hedge around a subject as long as it didn't involve her personal life.

'Yeah,' Tiffany said, lifting her head a little. 'They think I'm some dumb cow who got herself knocked up to get benefits, or get off school or to try and trap a bloke. But I'm not like that. I was on the pill *and* we used condoms – we were just the unlucky 0.01% that still gets pregnant. I wanted to get my GCSEs this year but it just didn't work out that way. I'm still going to do them one day, hopefully. Anthony and me just want to be together, like a proper family. We're not another statistic on the evening news and it really gets me that all those middle-class rich bitch housewives think they can judge me . . . no offence.'

'None taken,' Natalie said, both surprised and impressed by the teen's force of personality. And then she realised what Tiffany had said. 'Oh, *Anthony's* the father. I thought it was . . .'

'Not Gary?' Tiffany giggled. 'He's ancient!'

'Do you mind. He's about my age!'

Both of the women laughed.

'We could go together if you like,' Tiffany said. 'To the class? Cos I think it's important to know all that stuff, don't you? In case of emergencies or things.'

'Um.' Natalie wasn't exactly sure what 'all that stuff' was, but oddly enough she liked this Tiffany girl and the thought of getting out of the house to somewhere light and warm was alluring, even if it was on a cold and dark March afternoon and only to sit in the back of some boring class.

'I know it's chilly out but he'll be fine all bundled up in a sling,' Tiffany said, thinking she needed to persuade Natalie. 'Jordan loved getting out right from when she was tiny. They like the colours and movement, you know. It stimulates their brain.'

Just then the lights came back on, making everybody squint and blink and Freddie grizzle. Natalie hoisted him up onto her shoulder and bobbed up and down on the step until the grizzling subsided.

Gary Fisher, followed by Anthony, emerged from the basement. He looked pointedly at Tiffany and Jordan.

'I needed the loo,' Tiffany explained. 'And Natalie didn't mind.'

Gary gave her a sceptical look, wondering how she had managed to be on first-name terms with his prospective new client before he was.

'It's fine really,' Natalie told him before adding hopefully, 'Just a fuse then?'

Gary, who it seemed was more comfortable communicating with facial expressions than with words, twisted his mouth into a sideways knot and then puffed out his cheeks.

'Not exactly,' he said on an outward breath, as if he really didn't want to tell her anything bad at all.

'How bad?' Natalie asked him.

The corners of Gary's mouth plunged downwards in a grimace.

'It's pretty bad,' he said, looking as if the whole thing was his fault. 'You don't want to hear this but I have to tell you, it's about as bad as it can get. It was dangerous. You're really lucky that everything shorted without starting a fire – it could have been much worse . . .'

Gary stopped talking when Natalie burst into noisy, messy tears that surprised everyone, including Natalie, who didn't just cry but emitted long, loud, heartfelt sobs that rattled with phlegm on every intake of breath.

'It's all going wrong!' she wailed, starting Jordan off. 'I can't cope with this! How am I supposed to cope with . . . with . . . *this*!'

Inside her head Natalie could hear herself crying, and she could feel the overwhelming wave of anxiety that had gripped her without warning. But there was some integral part of her that was asking incredulously, 'What *am* I doing?'

Internally she realised that things weren't that bad and that of course she could cope with this, she'd coped with far worse in her time. It was an odd kind of split personality that had developed since Freddie was born. The 'normal' her was still there; the capable and excellent-in-a-crisis woman she knew and loved, but she seemed to be trapped inside this other crazy woman who was prone to crying and wailing when she couldn't get the lid off a jam jar, never mind deal with a power cut.

Slowly Tiffany put her arm around Natalie's shoulders. 'There, there,' she said.

'I'm so sorry,' Natalie managed to say at last, calming down a little as she sniffed and wiped her nose on the back of her sleeve. 'I don't normally cry. I've got a business and a mortgage and everything . . . I used to be great under stress. I don't know what's happened to me recently.'

'That little one happened to you,' Tiffany told her, patting her shoulder gently. 'This isn't you. This is your hormones. You're not a nutter, honest. You wouldn't believe the hell I put Anthony through right after Jordan came. It's the same for us all. And the last thing you need is any kind of hassle on top of all that. So don't worry, all right? You're totally normal.'

Natalie looked at her baby's now tranquil face – at least he wasn't upset. A light switched on suddenly might unsettle him, but he didn't seem the least bit distressed to be held by a snivelling, incompetent woman. She found herself smiling at him and then Tiffany.

'I made Jordan cry,' she said apologetically.

'She likes crying,' Tiffany said, patting Natalie's shoulder lightly again. 'It's her main hobby.'

There was a cough by the front door and Gary edged a little closer to Natalie before crouching down beside her.

'I'm really sorry Mrs . . .' Natalie did not feel like filling in the gap so he went on, 'I didn't explain it very well. I mean, yes, it was dangerous, but like I said, you've been lucky. I can patch it up safely for you tonight and then I'll need to come back and start rewiring as soon as possible. I've got a lot of jobs on right now but if you decide to use me then I'll put them on hold.' Gary glanced back over his shoulder at Anthony, who had thrust his hands deep into his pockets and was studying his trainers with infinite care. 'If you liked I could have a word with your husband . . . ?'

Natalie sighed. She suddenly felt terribly tired and didn't want to have to explain herself to the electrician, deciding it would be much less complicated to tell him a small but convenient lie instead.

'My husband works away a lot,' she said. 'In . . . Dubai. He's an engineer.' She glanced up at Gary's concerned face and gave him a watery smile. 'You'll have to deal with me, I'm afraid. I'll try to keep the crying down to the bare minimum.'

Gary nodded, his hands on his hips.

'Well, I don't like to see anyone left in the lurch, least of all a young lady on her own. I can be back tomorrow to make a start if you like. Or if you want to get in a few quotes from other electricians and check my references . . .'

Natalie looked up at Gary Fisher. He wasn't that much older than her, she thought, perhaps four or five years, but something about his turn of phrase and attitude made him seem as if he was from another era, when everybody lived in black and white and a nice cup of tea solved everything.

'Start in the morning,' she told him decisively, with a smile that would have been flirtatious if it wasn't for the appalling condition of her skin and the remnants of lunch that still sat in the corners of her mouth, not to mention her swollen nose and red eyes. 'And thank you *very* much. You're my hero.'

Natalie was charmed to see Gary blush as he bustled back towards the cellar with Anthony to make sure it would be safe for the night.

'The power will have to go off again for a bit,' Gary warned her as he headed down the stairs.

Natalie looked thoughtfully at Tiffany. 'Come on then,' she said. 'Let's go to the baby class thing.'

*

'It must be tough being on your own,' Tiffany said as they headed towards the health centre. 'Haven't you got any family to help out?'

'No,' Natalie said. 'I was an only child and my dad was killed in a car accident when I was quite small and as for my mum . . . she lives in Spain. But it's not help with Freddie that I want, it's seeing people outside the four walls of the house. I'm going barking mad with no one but Fred to talk to all day. It's just really nice to have a conversation with someone my own age – well, half my own age.'

Tiffany laughed. 'You know what you need, don't you?'

'A nanny?' Natalie suggested.

'No, dummy,' Tiff said amiably. 'A baby group!'

Chapter Three

Natalie was disappointed to see that none of the other mothers who had come along to the first-aid class had arrived in grubby tracksuit bottoms and mucus-stained sweatshirts with unbrushed and unwashed hair.

She was not used to being intimidated by other women, especially not the kind who had babies and went to first-aid classes on a Tuesday evening, because she simply didn't know any. For most of her adult life Natalie had never paused to worry about how she looked because she knew she looked pretty good. She didn't care that she wasn't especially thin because in her experience curves were far more appealing than ribcages. And she didn't mind the little bump in her nose or the fact that she was fairly short. She thought the bump gave her face character, and high heels resolved any issues about the length of her legs. As for her dark hair, that had started going grey before she was twenty-five. She simply dyed the silver into oblivion and planned to keep on doing so until she was grey enough to go blonde. Natalie had never been the kind of woman she traditionally pitied and scorned; the kind who was always dieting, always looking over her shoulder in mirrors and always moaning about this or that unsatisfactory little part of herself. Until now.

Now she was comparing herself to a room full of women in

jumpers and finding herself sorely lacking. It was a feeling that was nearly as uncomfortable as the site where her stitches had been, on this hard plastic chair.

'Right, mummies!' The midwife, a scary and oddly hard-looking woman, started chirpily, holding a rather frightening-looking plastic baby up by its neck. 'My name is Heather. Many of you will recognise me because I delivered your babies. I must say it is nice to be talking to your faces for a change!' Heather obviously expected a laugh and looked quite put out when all she got was a couple of embarrassed coughs.

'Um, thank you for coming to tonight's class. I think you will all find it very useful information so please pay attention because it might just save your baby's life . . .'

'Sorry, oops! Oh sorry . . . *sorry* . . . sorry.' Natalie looked to see where the serial apologies were coming from and was happy to see a woman who looked almost as dishevelled and confused as she did, edging clumsily along the row towards the empty seat next to her.

'Sorry,' she apologised to Natalie for no particular reason as she sat down.

Natalie smiled at her and turned back to Heather, who was slapping the plastic baby on the back with gusto.

The apologetic woman rustled and fussed in her seat, rattling a large rummage bag that seemed to be filled with a least ten pounds' worth of small change and several sets of keys until she produced an old envelope and a pen. Natalie couldn't help but glance at her – she was rather diverting.

'I'm taking notes,' the woman said in a low voice, catching Natalie's curious look. 'I've done this three times before but I always instantly forget it. Miraculously my husband has actually got home from work before midnight for once, so I thought I'd pop out and get another refresher. You never know when one of the little buggers is going to stuff a rubber up their nose or swallow a golf ball, do you?'

'Don't you?' Natalie exclaimed in a wide-eyed whisper. 'What, even when they're this small?' The woman looked momentarily confused and then saw Freddie sitting in Natalie's lap, optimistically reaching for the hair of the woman sitting in front of him. Natalie tucked his small questing hand inside hers, prompting him to give a little frustrated whimper.

'Well,' the woman said, smiling indulgently at Freddie. 'You'd be surprised at how tricky they get once they're mobile. It won't be long until this one is crawling and then all hell breaks loose. I've got four children, the fourth is nearly four months old and already itching to crawl. It's all downhill from now I'm afraid!' She chuckled merrily but stopped when she saw that Natalie was not joining in.

'Four children!' Natalie couldn't help exclaiming quite loudly. 'Good God.'

The woman shrugged. 'I always wanted a big family.' She nodded at Freddie, who was endeavouring to lean over his mother's restraining arm and get hold of a hank of that hair if it was the last thing he ever did. 'Your first then?' she asked. 'What an angel. What's his name?'

'Freddie,' Natalie said. 'It's a traditional family name, goes all the way back to . . . well, a long way anyway.'

'Freddie, I like that. I'm Megan by the way, call me Meg. Nice to meet you.' Megan held out a hand which Natalie took with her free one and shook once.

'Natalie,' she said. 'So how do you cope with four – do you have a nanny or an au pair?'

'Ladies!' Heather's voice rose and Natalie realised she was addressing her and Megan. They exchanged glances like two girls caught out in assembly. 'This is not a mothers' meeting, if you didn't come here to listen then you should leave.'

'That's funny,' Natalie whispered to Meg. 'I was fairly sure it *was* a mothers' meeting.'

'Sorry,' Meg said out loud to Heather, tucking one riotous red curl behind her ear. '*Dreadfully* sorry.'

'Me too,' Natalie said, with much less conviction. She glanced at Tiffany who rolled her eyes at her before returning her concentration to Heather, who was now shaking the plastic baby quite hard and shouting, 'Wake up baby!' at it very loudly.

'That would hurt, wouldn't it?' Natalie whispered to Meg, as Tiffany seemed quite absorbed by the lecture.

'I would have thought so . . .' Meg said, vaguely. She bent her head closer to Natalie's. 'So how are you finding it, with your first? I can just about remember that mine was a sort of nightmare and a wonderful dream all rolled up together. I was so glad to have Alex and be a mum at last, and my husband Robert just doted on the pair of us – treated us like royalty.' She sighed and looked wistfully at the strip lighting for a moment. 'It was a lovely time. But it hurt like hell and I slept so little I could barely speak. Actually, I don't think I've slept more than about four hours a night since Alex was born but I seem to have got used to it. I mean, look at me now, I can't shut up!'

Natalie found herself chuckling along with Meg. She was the kind of person who was utterly alien to Natalie's social world, with her wild red hair and a shapeless jumper, that probably hid a lot of lumps and bumps, over that long-worn-out skirt. Absolutely not someone Natalie would have met in the course of her everyday life. Maybe that was why she already liked her; she offered Natalie no reminder of the life it seemed she had left behind for ever.

'I always think it's with your first that you have the most fun,' Meg went on, oblivious to the stony glare that Heather was directing at her. 'Going to all the coffee mornings and clinics, making friends. You don't do that so much with your fourth, people tend to think you don't need any support any more because you've done it so often. Are you in a group?'

Natalie had avoided finding out about anything like that during her pregnancy, partly because although she was not in denial about the pregnancy itself, she most certainly was about how she came to be that way. And anyway, she was determined not to be a mother in the way that everybody else was, in that it was not going to change *her*, that essence of Natalie that made her the woman she was. She would still be *her*, but with a baby. The slight technical hitch with her plan was that every so often she couldn't exactly remember the *her* she used to be, or indeed even far simpler things like her name and what it felt like not to have back pain.

'I'm not really a joiner,' Natalie said thoughtfully, wondering if that was still true. 'And I've never really liked being organised by other people or told what to do. But actually it would be sort of nice to get a bit of advice. And I am a bit lonely being on my own . . . my husband works abroad – and I've got no other family to speak of so perhaps I should give it a go . . .'

She let the husband comment slip out so easily that Natalie realised she had almost forgotten that it was a lie. That was two or possibly three people she had told, or at least implied to them that she had a husband somewhere. Natalie hadn't lied because she was ashamed of her single-parent status. On the contrary, during her pregnancy she'd rather admired her vision of herself: a woman alone and entirely independent, who didn't need any man to prop her up. But it was easier to invent a husband than have to field questions about the baby's father. She didn't want to have to explain to anyone, least of all a lot of very proper ladies in jumpers – and Tiffany – that she most likely got pregnant during unprotected sex in a jacuzzi with a man she barely knew then, and had never seen since, and who still didn't know that he was a father.

Yes, it was far easier to have a husband in the background somewhere. It was a simple lie, and one that as far as Natalie could see was utterly harmless.

'I know what you mean,' Meg agreed with a sigh. 'Life always seems to be full of people waiting to organise you and tell you what you're doing wrong. Robert, my husband for example, love him. Or worse still my sister-in-law, Frances. She's just had her first baby, but you would never have guessed she was a beginner. Apparently I've been getting it all wrong for the last eight years. She organises poor baby Henry like he's a private in the army.' Meg smiled. 'I don't know how I get mine fed and clothed every day, to be honest, but it happens somehow and they seem happy and healthy, so I can't be that terrible at motherhood.'

'*Ladies,*' the midwife interrupted them once again. 'I am not here to waste my or any of these other mummies' time listening to you two gossiping.' She crossed her arms, dangling the plastic baby by one ankle. 'Kindly take your conversation outside.'

'Sorry?' Meg said politely.

'Are you chucking us out?' Natalie asked in disbelief.

'I am,' Heather said.

'Oh dear,' Meg said anxiously. 'I'm *terribly* sorry.'

Natalie looked at Tiffany who seemed to be having a hard time not laughing out loud, and she did not miss the irony that it was her, the grown businesswoman and not the school-girl, who was getting chucked out of class.

'Fine,' she said, standing up and hoisting Freddie up onto

her shoulder. 'I have never been thrown out of anything before in my life,' she lied. 'But if it makes you feel powerful to throw me and my tiny baby out into the night, go right ahead. You do it.'

'Goodbye.' Heather did not waver.

'Outrageous,' Natalie said.

'Sorry, sorry, sorry,' Meg said, as the pair of them edged their way along the row.

'Why is it,' Natalie demanded once they were in the lobby, 'that as soon as you have a baby the whole world seems to think they have the right to treat you like a second-class citizen?'

'Well, perhaps,' Meg said. 'But I think we were slightly in the wrong too, don't you? It's my fault of course. When I actually meet an adult who will talk to me I can't stop. It's like a compulsion. I think I must have a conversation about something other than Barbie or Thomas the Tank Engine and I must have it now!'

Natalie laughed; she hadn't laughed so much since she went into labour. It was nice to discover that she actually could laugh, and better still didn't seem to have stress incontinence any more.

'Oh well, I don't care anyway,' Natalie said. 'It's the perfect end to a perfect day.'

She told Meg the story of her electrical problems. 'They seem like nice enough chaps but it's just the disruption, isn't it? And the not being able to walk around in your pants.'

This time Meg laughed. 'Come to mine,' she offered instantly. 'Come in the morning. I don't live far from here, on the other side of the park – Victoria Road.' She retrieved her old envelope, scribbled an address and phone number on it with half a broken Crayola and ripped it in half. 'In fact, you'll be doing me a favour; the dreaded sister-in-law is due round

40

with little Henry. If there's someone else there she's far less likely to bully me into cleaning!'

Natalie smiled at her second unlikely new friend of the day.

'If you're sure,' she said, looking at the address.

'Positive. We can start our own renegade baby group!'

'She was in a proper bad mood once you left,' Tiffany said, appearing at Natalie's side as the class turned outside. 'I thought I was the one who was always in trouble. That was well funny.'

Meg smiled brightly at the young girl.

'That's a lovely baby,' she said to Tiffany. 'How long have you been looking after her?'

'Since she was born,' Tiffany said, immediately defensive. 'I'm her mum.'

'Oh dear.' Meg looked mortified. 'I'm so sorry. I thought you were her nanny . . . you look far too . . . slim to have had a baby!'

Hastily Natalie introduced Tiffany and Meg to each other. 'I only just met Tiff tonight too,' Natalie told Meg, wanting to put Tiffany at her ease. 'She's my electrician's apprentice's girlfriend and current motherhood guru.'

'Oh how lovely!' Meg seemed to have a boundless enthusiasm for pretty much anything. 'Well, Tiffany, come round tomorrow to mine for coffee. Natalie's got the address. I'd love to have you if you don't mind a messy house – you'd be very welcome.'

Tiffany chewed her lip as she looked at the two older women whose worlds were so utterly different from her own.

'I don't know . . .' she said. Her confidence and composure seemed to wane briefly and her soft, not yet adult features looked uncertain. Natalie had to resist the compulsion to hug her. That was another new thing that had started to happen since Freddie's birth: maternal urges. Of course, Natalie had expected them to come with maternity, but she hadn't expected them to extend past her own baby. Still, somehow she thought Tiffany wouldn't appreciate being mothered just then.

'Come on.' Natalie found herself coaxing the teenager. 'You may as well. You said I need a baby group, and Meg's had four kids so she must know something useful.' Still Tiffany hesitated. 'You can come round to mine with Gary in the morning and we'll go together if you like.'

Natalie was not sure why she was quite so keen to get Tiffany to come with her, except that perhaps for the first time in what seemed like ages Tiffany made her feel like a grown-up again. Not because she was so young, but because she didn't treat her as if at the same time as giving birth to Freddie she had also delivered her brain.

'Well, OK then,' Tiffany said, eventually. 'It's not much fun being stuck in the flat on my own all day I suppose, and I did promise Gary I wouldn't go out in the van with him again.'

'Excellent,' Meg said, and without warning she kissed Natalie on both cheeks and enveloped both Tiffany and Jordan in a surprisingly affectionate hug that made Jordan squeal with delight.

'I'd better get back,' she said happily over her shoulder as she hurried away. 'My husband hates being left alone with the kids for too long – they drive him utterly mad!'

'She's a bit weird,' Tiffany said frankly as they watched Meg rush off into the night.

'Yes,' Natalie agreed. 'But sort of wonderful too.'

All the lights were blazing when they got back to the house, and the radiator in the hallway was creaking and clanking into life. Gary Fisher emerged from the basement just as Natalie shut the front door behind her and Tiffany.

'Learn anything?' he asked her.

'Not a thing,' Natalie said. 'But Tiffany did.'

Gary nodded, his forehead wrinkling with an expression of mild surprise. It was obvious he was amazed that Natalie seemed to get on rather well with Tiffany.

'Well, you're sorted for tonight,' he said, nodding generally at the electric crystal chandelier that sparkled above their heads. 'I'll need to get parts in the morning so I'll be here around ten-ish. I've left you a quote on the desk in there –' He gestured towards the living room. 'You might want to look at it before I buy those parts.'

Natalie, whose arms were aching from carrying the baby for so long, shook her head.

'If it needs doing, it needs doing,' she said, walking into the living room, relieved to see that the baby chair was still on the table where she remembered leaving it. She carefully eased Freddie into the padded seat and he immediately began to cry.

'Um, the thing is,' Gary said as Natalie peered into the baby kit bag, looking for a clean nappy and cream, 'I'd appreciate it if you looked at the quote, Mrs . . . um, Natalie, because I want us to be very clear about what I'm charging you. It's quite a lot. You might need to OK it with your husband . . .'

'Actually, Mr Fisher,' Natalie said smartly, as she produced a nappy and some wipes from the bag, 'I earn my own money, which I am confident will be more than enough to cover your bill so I won't have to ask anyone for permission.' She gave him a sharp smile and snatched up the piece of paper he had left for her on the desk and read it. Freddie's cries reached a crescendo.

The bill was about three times more than she had imagined it would be but she was determined not to be fazed by it. Even if there had been an electrician as equally good and reliable as Gary Fisher apparently was waiting right outside the door at that very moment and who was prepared to knock fifty per cent off his quote, there was no way she would have taken it. It had become a matter of honour to appear to be totally underawed by the cost.

'Oh, is that all?' Natalie said with studied nonchalance. 'Do you want a cheque now?'

'Um, no,' Gary said awkwardly. 'I'm sorry if I offended you, Mrs . . . Natalie. I'll get out from under your feet now. See you tomorrow.'

'I'll see you in the morning, Tiffany,' Natalie said. 'And thank you, Mr Fisher.'

'No trouble,' Gary replied, looking like a schoolboy who was in a great deal of trouble.

Natalie watched her newly appointed electrician and his curious entourage leave with a mixture of irritation and regret. It was nice to have the house full of people and noise again. She didn't realise how lonely she sometimes felt until she was on her own again. Normally her own company and Freddie's didn't bother her at all, but just then she wished she had another adult in the house. Most of her problems were minor: the wiring, the tiredness, and even the nipples that felt as if they had been sandpapered would eventually go away. Natalie knew that and although those things contributed to her weariness, she wouldn't let them get her down for too long. It was that one problem, that one big problem that kept raising its handsome head. What to do about telling Jack, if anything at all.

It was only just past seven and she hadn't eaten anything since lunch, but a sudden wave of demanding exhaustion overtook her, and as Freddie had dropped off Natalie knew she had to try and sleep while she had the chance. As she climbed the stairs with Freddie weighing heavy in her arms, dribbling on her shoulder, Natalie had to stop for a moment as the pure joy and adoration that she felt every time she looked at him threatened to bring her to tears once again. It was impossible for her to regret that weekend with Jack Newhouse, because she didn't regret Freddie. In fact, she rejoiced in his existence minute by minute. But she did regret the storm of emotions that had been battering her psyche ever since she realised Jack had taken her in completely and, what's more, left her pregnant. She was a sensible woman of the world, a clued-up woman. God knows, not only had she been around the block a few times, she'd made some pretty comprehensive maps along the way. So what did it say about her, Natalie Curzon, that she had fallen so easily for what turned out to be just another set of cleverly crafted lines? And worse still, what did it say about her that when she did sleep, Natalie often dreamt about those few days with Jack and would catch herself waking up and wishing they were real?

Mercilessly, with some baby anti-bedroom sixth sense Freddie woke up just as they reached the top of the stairs. As Natalie walked the length of the bedroom floor on a loop, willing her darling to drop off again, she thought how very much simpler it would be to really have a husband like the one she had told Gary she had. A nice, dependable, sensible husband, someone you knew where you stood with, the kind of man that Natalie would normally have run away from at one hundred miles an hour.

As the clock on the bedroom wall turned through midnight and into the early hours of another day, Natalie tried to think what her imaginary husband would be like.

And for some reason he looked an awful lot like her electrician.

Chapter Four

Natalie decided to take cake to Meg's house by way of celebration. She had got herself and Freddie through another night alive and relatively unscathed and she had made a decision to buy cake. Those were two good enough reasons to merit a celebration, Natalie thought. And besides she was looking forward to a social occasion that didn't involve her and Freddie and their house. It wasn't the kind of occasion she would have chosen but, she supposed, cocktail parties weren't de rigueur with new mums. And anyway, just the prospect of getting out of the house had lifted Natalie's spirits. It wasn't until she cheered up that that she realised she had been feeling rather down.

Just knowing that she had something to do the next day had helped her get through what had become another typically gruelling night. And, although it had been filled with crying from both of them, confusion from one of them, regurgitating from the other one and a muddled sleepless small-hours' kind of despair and imaginary-husband related hallucinations, it hadn't been *that* bad.

It was more of a good kind of bad, the kind of bad that Natalie could cope with for the rest of her life if necessary, even if she never slept, ate or had sex again, after all she had done more than her fair share of all three in her time.

She had just about dragged a brush through her hair and

pulled it back into a knot on the nape of her neck when Gary
Fisher and his crew of two and a half arrived, one of whom was
sporting a pink fake-fur gilet over a skinny-rib top that left a
good three-inch gap of her flat tummy showing above her
jeans.

Natalie couldn't help openly staring at her.

'Why are you in such good shape?' she asked her baldly.

'Don't know,' Tiffany said. 'It's probably cos I'm young.'

'Oh,' Natalie said, who had thought up until that moment
that *she* was young. 'Well, pull that top down, you'll catch a
chill.'

Making the decision about what kind of cake to buy was not
quite as triumphant, particularly as there were only two types
in the Turkish grocers, one being Jamaican ginger cake and
the other Cadbury's chocolate mini-rolls.

'Oh I don't know,' Natalie said, scrutinising the two
candidates. 'What do you think?'

'Not bothered,' Tiffany said with a shrug, making Natalie
wonder exactly why it was *she* was so bothered. Natalie
glanced up at her and noticed that she was leaning so far
backwards that she looked like she might unbalance both
herself and Jordan in an attempt to peer around the corner
towards the darker back end of the poky store.

'What are you looking at?' Natalie asked her, forgetting for
a moment her preoccupation with cake.

Tiffany righted herself.

'There's this woman round there just staring at tinned
tomato soup. Not looking, just staring,' she said, keeping her
voice low. 'Like she's in a coma or something.' She bent back
with enviably pain-free ease and looked again.

'Still at it,' she confirmed. 'Like a statue. Do you think she's
all right?'

Natalie half wanted to point out to Tiffany that it was rude to stare at mad people, but after being made to feel so ancient earlier that morning she held her tongue. Deciding to take a leaf out of Tiffany's book instead, she peered round the corner herself. Standing with her profile to them, a blonde-haired, quite presentable-looking woman was indeed staring fixedly at the canned goods.

'It might be a petit mal fit, like you get with some kinds of epilepsy,' Tiffany whispered.

Natalie glanced sideways at her and wished she'd stop surprising her with knowledge and insight, it was quite unnerving. She turned back to the woman.

'She looks familiar,' Natalie said quietly to Tiffany. She edged a little closer, pretending to need a tin of peas, until she could look properly at her face. She recognised her immediately.

'Hello,' Natalie said brightly, making the woman jump. 'How are you?'

The woman blinked as if she had just woken from a dream.

'It's Natalie,' Natalie prompted her. 'I was in the cubicle opposite you at the hospital, you came in the day after me. It's Jess, isn't it? Do you live near here? I live over the road – how are you getting on with little . . . ?' Natalie peered at the bundle in the buggy. All she could see was a glimpse of a tiny blue hat.

'Jacob,' Jess said. 'Absolutely fine.' She smiled at Natalie, who got the distinct impression that Jess had had to force every single muscle into the appropriate position to assume the expression.

'You think that you're going mad, don't you?' Natalie said instinctively. 'One minute you're thinking about fish fingers, the next you're crying or . . . standing about looking all vacant. But apparently it's the same for everyone. Even her.' Natalie nodded at Tiffany who had edged a little nearer. 'And she's young and thin.'

Jess's smile seemed a fraction less fake.

'Oh,' she said, looking suddenly bashful. 'I'm fine – really. I just completely forgot why I came to the shop, that's all!'

'Was it for cake?' Natalie asked her. 'We're, or I should say I'm, trying to buy cake to take to this other woman's house for a sort of informal mums' meeting.' A thought occurred to her. 'Why don't you come along too? I'm sure Megan – that's the woman I'm buying cake for – won't mind.'

Jess looked rather shell-shocked by the invitation and a little bit panicked. Natalie sympathised. She knew that sometimes she had days with Freddie when the thought of doing anything as impulsive as popping out for a loaf of bread seemed impossible. Jess's look of terror made it seem as if Natalie's invitation was to stand blindfolded in front of a firing squad.

'Um . . .' she said.

'Only if you don't have something already on,' Natalie said, with a wry half-smile. 'Like washing Babygros or sterilising something.'

Jess relaxed a little and she almost laughed.

'Well, I suppose I could tear myself away from folding tiny socks . . .' she said. 'Would your friend mind, do you think?'

'Shouldn't think so,' Natalie said, with a nod of her head. 'Now, which do you prefer, ginger cake or chocolate mini-rolls? Oh, let's go crazy and buy both.'

'James, darling, don't chew Gripper's bone – there's a love,' Meg said, swiftly retrieving the dog's toy from the mouth of her two-year-old.

'Why you've even got a dog I don't know,' Frances said,

wiping down Meg's kitchen surfaces with the kind of enthusiasm that Meg found simultaneously intimidating and irritating.

As predicted, her sister-in-law had been cleaning since the moment she had arrived this morning. The first thing she had done was to scrub the kitchen table that had still been covered with the detritus of a typically chaotic breakfast for six. Once that met with her approval she put baby Henry's car seat right in the centre of the table, as if she had somehow created an exclusion zone for him that Meg's unruly and presumably unhygienic rabble could not breach. Then she had started on the floor; she had brought her own mop.

It wasn't that Meg wasn't grateful for the help. She was. It was just that she had asked her sister-in-law round simply for coffee and a chat, and that was partly under duress from Robert. She had not asked her to disinfect her entire house. Worse still, Frances hadn't even asked if Meg minded if she cleaned and mopped and scrubbed, so even though Meg was sure it was unintentional, she found Frances's 'help' really quite insulting. But there was no point in saying anything to her. Meg had learnt that from personal experience over the years.

Frances was incapable of being in the wrong or taking any kind of criticism. Even the slightest hint that you might not approve one hundred per cent of everything she said or did brought out her hackles. Like the time Meg had innocently mentioned that she'd read an article about how long it takes a woman to become fertile again after several years of taking the Pill. All Meg meant to do was to offer some kind of comfort or explanation as to why Frances was not getting pregnant immediately, but instead Frances had taken it very personally, as if Meg had somehow accused her of deliberately spoiling her own chances of becoming pregnant. And Frances was very scary when she was cross, which meant that Meg had somehow found herself apologising abjectly for something she was fairly certain she hadn't done. She had endured the hurt looks and occasional sniffs from Frances for the rest of the night with good grace. It had been harder to keep quiet during Robert's lecture about tact and diplomacy on the way home.

She had done it, though.

Robert always said that his little sister wasn't frightening, just determined. Meg secretly thought that was a polite term for downright terrifying. Even so, she had a soft spot for Frances. She could see that Frances was motivated by the urge to do what she thought was the right thing, even if *she* had the tact and diplomacy of a very angry rhinoceros. So the best thing to do, Meg decided, was to try hard not to be offended and be glad that she had a clean kitchen floor for however brief a hiatus.

Meg noticed that Gripper was attacking Frances's mop just as enthusiastically as Frances had cleaned the floor. She shooed the large poodle out into the back garden hurriedly, hoping that Frances had been too intent on removing limescale from around the taps to notice.

'Anyway, Gripper was Robert's idea,' Meg reminded her sister-in-law, answering what was probably a rhetorical question. 'You must remember, he brought her home one night and said he thought it would be good for the kids to have a pet? I was as shocked as anyone. He'd always said absolutely no pets up until then – I don't know what changed his mind. Alex and Hazel going on and on, I suppose. I have to admit I wouldn't have chosen a poodle myself. I'd have gone for something a bit more cuddly and stupid.' Meg smiled indulgently. 'That dog is far too clever for her own good. Do you know she can open the fridge? But Robert said they don't shed hair so that was that. And the kids love her.' Meg looked out of the back window at her largely unkempt garden where Gripper was making another bid to be the first poodle to dig her way to Australia.

Toodles the Poodles was the name Hazel had given her when absolutely everything she said had to rhyme. But Meg's elder son, Alex, had protested loudly, demanding they give the puppy a proper name, the kind of name that a six-year-old boy could call out in the park. And somehow Toodles had become Gripper which had stuck, largely because Gripper was quite butch for a poodle bitch. Meg always thought she had the spirit of a Rottweiler trapped in the wrong kind of body. Alex said she was a honed killing machine, which was true if you counted socks, shoes and skirting boards as viable victims.

'Well, not shedding hair is *something*, I suppose,' Frances said, producing a large Tupperware container from her seemingly bottomless bag of tricks. 'I just hope you keep on top of its . . . excrement,' she added distastefully. 'It can cause blindness, you know. Now, I made some muffin mix this morning after you told me that you had invited other people.'

Frances managed to refer to Meg's guests as if they were somehow an act of betrayal. 'I knew you wouldn't have baked. I'll just pop it into some cases I've brought with me and into your oven. Is it clean?'

Meg took a deep breath and wafted into the living room, picturing herself as a serene cloud floating over a still ocean until the urge to say something ill-advised to Frances had passed. She decided instead to let Frances discover for herself that the oven was still fragranced with last Sunday's lunch. In fact, if she wasn't very much mistaken, Robert's portion, which she had optimistically dished up, was still decomposing on a plate in there where it had warmed beyond the point of no return. Robert was working a lot of weekends these days.

At least the living room was peaceful, trapping the March

sun and magnifying it into an almost balmy warmth. James lay on the carpet, fixated by his *Thomas the Tank Engine* video, and Iris was fast asleep in the family bassinet. Meg loved to see her fourth baby asleep in the cradle, even if she was already almost too big for it. She remembered when she and Robert had bought it whilst she was pregnant with Alex. Robert had said that they didn't need anything so frilly, silly and most of all expensive for a baby who would be too big to go in it within a few weeks. They should get a cot like everybody else. But Meg had insisted. She said she wanted something that would last for all their children, and that a cot was too big for a newborn baby to sleep in. And as they had been planning to have six children back then she argued that it was actually extremely economical. Robert had given in like he always used to, said he'd just have to close a few more deals, that was all. Meg smiled and felt the memory of those first years pull inside her with familiar happiness. The two of them starting out; united in their vision of the future – a large happy family in a large family house. A dad who provided, a mum who was at home for her children.

Eight years later and they had achieved so much of their dream. A big old house in a nice London suburb. Enough money to send Alex and Hazel to private schools, and for Meg to stay at home with James and Iris. But even though Meg had gained so much, she felt as if she had lost something too – that feeling of unity she used to share with Robert.

They were still a team, Meg told herself, as James launched himself from in front of the TV and into her lap, laughing when he made her go 'oomph'. She kissed her younger son all over his face while he giggled and shrieked for her to stop. She and Robert were the team captains of this wonderful, miraculous family. James, Iris, Alex and Hazel and even Gripper – they were why Robert worked such long hours; he did it for their children and for her. So she couldn't complain that she missed him. She'd just have to live with it.

Just then the doorbell went. Frances came into the living room wearing an apron with 'How to be a Domestic Goddess' printed on it.

'They're here,' she said.

Meg hefted James back onto the floor and went to the door. Curiously, despite her bossiness, Frances was really quite shy and although she might happily come and take over Meg's house without turning a hair, she would never dream of opening the door to people she didn't know.

'Blimey,' Natalie said, holding a Jamaican ginger cake in her hands like an offering. 'You didn't tell me you lived in a mansion – this house makes mine look like a bungalow.'

Meg laughed as she stepped aside to let Natalie, Tiffany and then another woman in, together with three babies in buggies.

'This is Jess,' Natalie said, kissing Meg on both cheeks with chilled lips. Tiffany just nodded at her and Jess held out a hand.

'Sorry for landing myself on your doorstep,' Jess said. 'Natalie found me looking vacant in the corner shop and decided I need rescuing from myself.' She smiled sheepishly. 'She was right. I think I was on the verge of forgetting how to use spoken language.'

Meg smiled warmly at Jess. 'More the merrier,' she said, as she shepherded the procession of mothers, buggies and babies into the kitchen.

'Oh, I've got mud on your floor,' Tiffany mumbled in dismay, looking at the tracks her buggy had left across the sparkling tiles. The fact that she obviously felt so uncomfortable and out of place was very evident.

'Oh don't worry about it,' Meg said breezily with a wave of her hand. 'The dog will be in from the garden in a minute and

54

she'll mess up the whole place! You can park the babies in here, then if they start crying we can just lift them out, can't we?'

Meg caught Frances's eye and hastily looked away again. 'This is my sister-in-law Frances – Frances, this is Natalie, Tiffany and Jess.'

Frances nodded stiffly at the new arrivals. 'I'll make coffee,' she said, turning her back on the group and so excluding herself from having to make small talk.

'Have you actually baked?' Natalie asked, sniffing the air as she took a seat at the table. 'That makes my ginger cake look a bit lame.'

Meg laughed. 'That's Frances, can't you see – she's a domestic goddess.' Everyone laughed except Frances, who remained with her back to the group. Meg bit her lip; she knew she shouldn't have made the silly joke, not about Frances. But she was feeling a bit awkward and shy herself and just wanted to get the conversation going.

'Well,' she said, as Frances lifted little Henry from his table-top haven and put him on a chair instead. 'It is very nice to have some decent adult company again.'

'Hear, hear,' Natalie agreed, raising her eyebrows as Frances carefully set a tray replete with a cafetière, mugs, sugar and even cream down on the table. 'And in a nice clean house,' she added. 'My place is such a tip between me, Freddie and the electrician – it's like Armageddon.'

'Oh that wasn't Meg, that was me,' Frances said, with an icy edge. She pointed at her apron. 'Domestic goddess, see?'

There was an awkward moment as everyone tried to work if Frances was attempting a joke or an insult. Not even Frances was exactly sure.

'So what shall we talk about then?' Natalie said a little chirpily over the silence. 'Feeding? Nappies and their contents? What do you do at this sort of thing? Compare stretch marks?'

The doorbell chimed again.

'Oh, I invited someone else!' Meg said, clapping her palm to her forehead. 'I completely forgot! The neighbours over the road – Jill and Steve?' She looked at Frances. 'They had a little girl recently. I dropped a note in last night; I thought Jill might want to come. That'll be her.'

Frances looked at the five mugs arranged on the tray and slowly got up and fetched another.

'I'll have to make another cafetière,' she said pointedly. 'Megan *never* thinks these kinds of things through.'

But when Meg returned she did not have Jill or anyone who even looked like Jill with her. She had a man with a baby in his arms. A man who just by virtue of his sex immediately reminded Natalie that she had no make-up on again and that her tummy still flopped over the top of her trousers.

'Well!' Meg said. 'This is Steve and little Lucy. It seems that Steve's a stay-at-home dad!'

'Really?' Jess said politely.

'How interesting,' Natalie added, sucking her gut in with the remnants of her abdominal muscles.

'That's cool,' Tiff said in a low voice.

'But you're a man,' Frances said. 'Men can't come to a mothers' group. It's women only, I'm afraid.'

It was Meg who took baby Lucy from Steve's arms and sat the poor blushing man down before giving him back his daughter and pouring him a cup of coffee.

'Of course Steve's allowed!' Meg said as lightly as she could. 'Ours isn't a formal group – it's more of a casual gathering and anyway I think I saw on the local news that Stoke Newington is the capital of stay-at-home fathers, so I'm sure that men are

56

allowed to go to even organised meetings. This is the age of equality, after all!'

Natalie and Jess murmured in agreement.

'But *she* said she wanted to talk about breast feeding and compare stretch marks,' Frances said, nodding at Natalie. 'You can't do that with a man around!'

'Don't worry, *Frances*,' Natalie said, carefully enunciating the other woman's name. 'I *was* only joking. It's just nice to get out of the house. We can talk about football for all I care.'

'I don't have to stay,' Steve said, half rising in his chair.

Three women ushered him back down. One didn't and one teenager stared quite hard at the table top and wished she'd stayed in to watch *This Morning*.

'You'll laugh,' Steve said. 'But I've been wondering and wondering all morning about coming over. Jill said I was an idiot to worry and that of course you wouldn't mind, but I thought – a bunch of girls together – you won't want a man hanging round.' He smiled apologetically at Frances, whose face did not move a muscle. Steve, who had sandy hair and pleasant brown eyes, also seemed to have a treacherous complexion as he flushed perfectly pink once again. 'Jill earns the most money, you see, as a barrister. And I've started working from home as a freelance graphic designer. It made sense for me to give up my old job, it was something I've wanted to do for ages anyway – go solo. I like being a full-time dad, I don't think it's undermining my manhood or anything. I think I'm privileged actually, to be such a big part of Lucy's life so early. So many dads miss out on this bit.'

The women did not actually say 'Ahhhhh,' but all of them thought it. Even Frances was touched.

'Well, good for you,' Natalie said. 'Fancy a slice of ginger cake?'

'Or what about a freshly baked muffin?' Meg added.

And it seemed to be decided without the need for any further discussion that a man was an acceptable member of the group. As Meg came back from fetching a mewling Iris she paused and looked back at the group of people sitting round her table. Natalie and her peculiar mix of confidence and flakiness seemed to make everyone laugh. Jess was pleasant and quietly funny and young Tiffany didn't say two words as she picked at her cake and watched the others talk. Brave Steve with little Lucy cradled on his shoulder was talking about the best winding technique and finally there was Frances, pouring more cups of coffee, refreshing the sugar bowl and wiping rings from under mugs.

Meg was glad they were all there, filling her great big house with voices and laughter, and using up part of her day, helping to take her mind off the things she didn't like to think about.

She had few hours now to shut away her wondering and worrying and not to think at all about her and Robert. Or when exactly it was that they had started to become strangers.

Chapter Five

Jess looked hopefully at the man blocking her way onto the bus.

It had been something of a performance to get Jacob out of the buggy and to fold it down ready for travel. These modern buses were supposed to make it easy for people with push-chairs but there was still never enough room to wheel a buggy on board, not on this route anyway. And for some reason she just didn't get it like other women seemed to. She saw other mums snap their babies in and out of slings in seconds while it still took her several flustered minutes to work out what went where, with her fingers losing any dexterity and even working up an anxious sweat. And as for the buggy, whatever pedal she pushed or kicked or handle she pulled it never seemed to be the right one, she could never get it to fold right down and click neatly into place like it should. The best she ever managed was to get it collapsed and then she had to try to hold it together so that it didn't jackknife out as she tried to make her way down escalators or, as in this case, onto buses.

The other people at the bus stop had ignored her as she struggled to flatten the contraption with Jacob tucked under one arm. Nobody offered to help. Now she had to contend with the man who stood between her and the bus door.

'Excuse me.' Jess's voice wobbled treacherously as she

extended the buggy towards him with an aching arm. 'Excuse me, can you help me please?'

The man looked down his nose at her and crossed his arms.

'I'm not a porter, love,' he said, managing to make her feel as if she was somehow insulting him by asking for his help.

'I didn't think you were,' Jess said, her voice taut as she attempted to fling the buggy onto the ramp. 'I did think you might be a person with an ounce of human decency who might see how difficult it is for me to manage. I was obviously wrong.'

She climbed awkwardly onto the bus, the muscles in her arms aching as she finally managed to clamber past the man. He did not move a single inch to make her life easier and muttered, 'Stupid bitch,' under his breath as she passed.

Jess shoved the buggy into a space behind a seat and made her way down the bus. Jacob began to cry. He was probably hungry, Jess thought, feeling instantly anxious. She had read that if a young baby went too long without fluid it could become dangerously dehydrated in no time. She ran her forefinger gently over the soft spot on his forehead to check if it was sunken, but as she felt the slight depression beneath her fingertips she wasn't sure what constituted sunken, which hiked up her anxiety levels even further.

'Nearly home,' she whispered in Jacob's ear as she looked around for a seat and found none. None of the seated passengers would look at her. A man who was also standing, his leg in a cast, smiled sympathetically at her.

'If I had a seat I'd offer it to you, love,' he said with a shrug.

Jess smiled back at him and held on tight, bracing her legs as the bus lurched forward and swayed her and Jacob dangerously off balance.

It was only a few stops, she told herself. Hardly anything really. It would have been easier to walk it, except that after visiting Meg she just felt so utterly tired with the effort of talking and smiling that she thought she'd get the bus home. Now she wished she hadn't. The experience was hurting her from the inside out.

Somehow before when she used to commute to her job in human resources in the West End, back before Jacob had been born, the hardness of the people around her just rolled off her like raindrops off glass. She never noticed the implicit unkindness and disrespect that everyone showed to everyone else. She supposed she had been just as bad, locked so tightly in her own little bubble that she barely noticed the other humans around her. But since Jacob had arrived in her life all her outer protective shell had been peeled painfully away and suddenly she was vulnerable to every ounce of cruelty or indifference, no matter how slight. And the fact that these people on the bus would not offer her and her baby a seat almost brought her to tears. Jess knew that they were just ordinary people on an ordinary London bus. People who probably worked hard all day for their families and went home in the evening looking forward to kissing their own children goodnight. She understood that. But if these people could be so hard and unfeeling, then what about the next terrorist to get on the next underground train or bus? Or what about Iran? Iran was developing nuclear weapons. North Korea already had them.

All at once the world had become a terrifying place to live in, with danger lurking in every shadow. Worst of all Jess felt as if she was barely equipped to be a mother, let alone to protect her child from the horrifyingly violent and unfeeling world into which she had brought him.

She wanted to be able to just love and enjoy him like his father did. She wanted her relationship with Jacob to be that perfect and that simple, but every single moment of their time together was interwoven with fear. Even when she was laughing, just as she had at Meg's earlier that morning, she felt as if it was merely a fragile front to cover up the truth. No one there knew that her stomach was knotted in a constant contraction of anxiety brought about by an unshakable conviction that somehow, somewhere, something would go terribly wrong.

It had started at conception. Jess had longed to be pregnant again but feared it too, because it filled her with the promise of hope and loss in equal parts. She had been pregnant twice before. The first baby had been lost before the end of the first trimester. It had broken her heart, but eventually she had been able to accept it. But the second, her little girl, was stillborn nearly six months into the pregnancy.

Even now Jess could not bear to think of that grey morning in the delivery suite, with the rain rushing against the window and the faded frieze of bunny rabbits painted around the ceiling. It was the knowing that made it unbearable, the knowledge that every contraction that wracked her body wasn't bringing a new life into the world. Knowing that she was delivering a dead baby, a little girl who had somehow died in the womb. In *her* womb.

Between the waves of physical pain Jess could hear the cries of other children somewhere on the ward. She would always remember the laughter and joy of a family ringing off the walls in the corridor outside, and wanting to scream for them to shut up. But all she could do was to stay as quiet as she could with Lee at her side, holding her hand, telling her she was so brave and how much he loved her, brushing away his tears between reassurances.

What Jess found almost unbearable was that the baby had died without her even noticing her passing. That she hadn't even been able to do that much for her child, to reach inside and try to say goodbye. She felt that she should have known her baby was terribly sick, but instead she might have been asleep or shopping or sitting on the Tube reading the paper when it happened. It seemed such a banal way to lose a child.

It was no one's fault, the doctors told them; sometimes tragedies just happen, but that didn't comfort Jess at all. She always felt it *should* have been someone's fault – and if it was anybody's it had to be hers. It was a feeling that persisted steadily just under the surface of every breath she took and every thought she had had from that moment on.

Almost two years had passed since that morning in the delivery suite, and every day Jess tried as she knew she should to separate her losses from the gain of having Jacob. But it seemed impossible to do, impossible to stop expecting the worst.

Lee had wanted them to stop after they lost the second baby. He said that the doctors had told him there was plenty of time to wait and try again in a year or two. That there was no reason why Jess shouldn't carry a baby full term and deliver a healthy child. But Jess had not been able to wait. She told Lee she wanted to try again straight away. That had been hard for him to understand.

'It would be like putting my life on hold,' she had tried to explain to him one morning. 'Like the next year, or two years would be just treading water waiting for . . . what? There's never going to be a magic time when we know for sure everything will be all right. And I'm still going to be scared, Lee. I'm still going to be terrified even then. I need to try again *now.*'

Lee had sat on their sofa, his head bowed over his knees, and Jess knew he was struggling to find the right words to say and for a moment she wondered how they had ended up together.

She hadn't fallen for him because of his expertise at expressing his feelings and dealing with her in times of tragedy, she reminded herself. She loved him because he made her laugh like no other man ever had, even in bed, and because he loved dogs and hiking and real ale in an ironic way, and he wore his hair in little trendy spikes even though he was slowly going bald and had been since he was twenty-two. When they'd started out in an Islington pub four years ago it had never occurred to Jess to veto him for his ability to manage pain in times of deep despair. So she had to be as patient with him as he was being with her, she owed him that much. After all, when he bought her that first vodka and tonic he couldn't have foreseen that just over fifteen hundred days later they would be having this conversation.

'The thing is,' Lee had said eventually, still staring hard at the laminate flooring, 'I don't think *I'm* ready, Jess. I'm still grieving, I'm still missing . . . her. I . . . I don't think it's right to just . . . replace her.'

Those last two words had almost been the end of them. It *would* have been the end of them if either one had had enough strength to survive without the other. But neither one had. They'd clung on to each other despite everything, and less than a year later Jess discovered she was pregnant for the third time.

When she told Lee he didn't hug her or smile, he just looked at her for a long time saying nothing at all until eventually he rested the back of his cool hand against the heat of her cheek and said, 'It will be all right.'

They didn't tell anyone about the baby until Jess was three months gone. She gave up work straight away, forfeiting any rights she had to maternity leave. Lee said it would be a struggle but they'd manage, and that her health and well-being was what counted. She knew what he really meant was that he'd do anything to stop her from freaking out.

At the twenty-week scan Jess felt as if she was being taken to an execution. She lay on the hospital table completely drained of colour and her eyes brimming with unshed tears. When the technician told her the scan was fine she could hardly believe it. In fact, she didn't believe it.

Whilst Lee's tension seemed to lift then and finally give way to happiness, Jess's fears bound themselves even more tightly around her. And the following months had been just as bad. She'd thought that when she began to feel the baby move that would make things better, because she'd be able to feel him thriving inside her. But instead, when an hour or more passed without her registering a kick, she panicked, convinced that the worst had happened again. Twice the doctor had to come and find the baby's heartbeat for her. He told her that unborn babies sleep just like the rest of us, and that she shouldn't worry. He had become one in a long line of people who told her she was worrying too much, almost as if it was an indulgence that they thought she revelled in. The doctors, their parents, even Lee commanded her to stop fretting so much. But she couldn't imagine a time when she would be able to. She didn't tell the doctor that she had hardly slept for what felt like months and that when she did she woke up with a start, panicking that somehow she'd abandoned her post. That something terrible might happen while she was gone. When Lee tried to reassure her she told him that once the baby was here in her arms where she could see him and hold him, she was sure she would stop worrying. Then at last all the fears and ghosts of the past would be put to rest.

But she was wrong, just as she had known she would be.

From the second the midwife put him in her arms there was a whole new world of worry. Jess was scared that he didn't feed enough. She was worried that he slept for too long, or that he didn't sleep enough. That he didn't seem to poo as much as the book said he should or that he had too many wet nappies. Stupid things that when she asked the health visitor or doctor about them made them smile and look at her as if she was slightly mad.

'It's normal,' the doctor would say.

'He's perfectly healthy,' the health visitor would say.

'It will be all right,' Lee would tell her.

And she'd know that they were right and they had to be right, but she still couldn't shake off this terrible feeling that somehow, somewhere, something was going to go terribly wrong.

'Wake up, darling,' a voice said irritably in her ear. Jess looked up and saw a woman trying to pass her to get to a seat that had somehow become empty. She glanced out of the dirty window. The bus was at her stop.

'Wait please!' she called out, as she struggled towards the bus doors. 'Hold on a minute, this is my stop!'

The bus lurched again, throwing Jess off balance and forcing her to stagger with Jacob in her arms to steady her feet. She watched the front door of her block of apartments slip past. Now she'd have to get off at the next stop and walk back.

'You could have held the bus,' she said to the driver. 'You must have heard me calling you.'

He did not even look at her.

The sky was dark with the threat of rain by the time that Jess finally got the apartment door open. She left the buggy sprawled in the communal hallway half up and half down, not caring whether or not some of the opportunist thieves in the area made off with the vile thing.

She sat down in the gloom of the sitting room and before even shaking off her coat she put Jacob to her breast.

Gradually both of them began to feel better.

'You're not mad,' Jess said aloud to a room that was almost quiet except for the subdued roar of the traffic on Green Lanes that managed to breach even the double glazing. 'You had a difficult time, it will take a while to adjust, that's all. All these people who look at you as if you were a bit weak-minded or silly don't know what you've been through – they don't know how well you're doing.'

She looked down at Jacob suckling and felt two or three still and calm moments pass by with each heartbeat. And then she remembered their visit to the clinic that morning, just before Natalie found her in the shop.

The health visitor had asked her if she had post-natal depression. Jess had laughed. Quite a feat because she had been crying at the time.

'Aren't you supposed to tell me that?' she'd asked before adding, 'I'm just a bit down and tired, that's all.'

'Do you ever feel like harming yourself or the baby?' the health visitor had asked her without looking up from her notes.

'No!' Jess had exclaimed. 'I would never, *ever* do that. He is the most precious thing in the world.' She had hesitated, but Lee was always telling her that talking about her problems would make them better. 'If anything,' she had said slowly, 'I worry sort of obsessively about keeping him well. All the time.'

'Oh well,' the health visitor had said. 'That's OK then.'

'Things aren't all bad,' Jess told Jacob, whose lips had disengaged from her nipple, leaving his small mouth gaping open as he slept. 'At least I bumped into Natalie and met the others. They seemed nice, didn't they? It's good that we've arranged to meet them again next week. It gives me something else to think about. Take our minds off things, hey, Jacob? You'll like Baby Music I reckon, won't you?' She bent her head to him and sniffed deeply. He needed changing. Jess knew she should have done it before feeding him, but his cries and the pain in her breasts had been too persistent to ignore. She knew that changing his nappy now would wake him, and that waking him would mean he'd be crying for hours. But she couldn't bear him to have nappy rash either. What if the health visitor saw that he had nappy rash?

'Sorry, Jacob,' she whispered, carrying him into the nursery and laying him on the changing table. 'I'll be quick.'

Jess had just about undone the poppers on Jacob's Babygro when she heard the front door click open. There was no call of hello. Lee had learnt from experience not to make any noise, on the off chance that his son and girlfriend might be sleeping. Carefully he pushed the front door to and eventually found his small family in the second bedroom.

'What's this?' Jess said, staring down at the baby, a frown drawing her eyebrows together.

'Hello,' Lee whispered pleasantly. 'It's dead at work so I got off early. Good day?'

'Lee, look at this – it's a rash,' Jess said, that familiar edge of panic beginning to sound in her voice.

Lee took a deep breath and looked at his son's tummy.

'Looks like a touch of heat rash,' he said. 'Has he been in his sling or wrapped up too warm?'

'No,' Jess said defensively. 'He hasn't and besides it's cold outside. What *is* it?' She picked up Jacob, who wriggled and began to whimper as his last chances of remaining asleep gradually faded away. Jess rested her palm on his forehead.

'And he's hot,' she said. 'Feel him – don't you think he's hot?'

Lee touched his lips to the baby's forehead. His mum had told him that lips were far more sensitive to body heat than hands and fingers, which were always a bit colder than the rest of the body. Jacob's forehead felt normal to him.

'He's fine,' Lee tried to reassure Jess.

'Is it meningitis?' Jess asked him, panic colouring her voice. 'It might be meningitis. We went on the bus, there was this woman coughing and sneezing . . . Get a glass from the kitchen. Is it supposed to disappear or stay visible? I can't remember – Lee!'

'It's not meningitis,' Lee said firmly, putting his arms around both Jacob and Jess. 'He'd got a bit of a rash, from being so bundled up. He's fine, look at him!' He laughed with sheer joy as he held his amazingly beautiful boy in his arms. 'Just look at him, Jess!' he pleaded. 'He's pissed off, but he's fine. He's got a touch of heat rash. It's nothing to worry about.'

And suddenly Jess's fear subsided and she knew that Lee was right, of course he was right. Jacob *had* had heat rash before. She knew exactly what it looked like. It looked like that.

'I'm sorry,' she said, her shoulders collapsing as she let go of her anxiety. 'I just –'

'Worry.' Lee finished her sentence for her. 'I know you do, but you don't have to. Nothing is going to happen to Jacob.'

Jess let his words sink in for a moment, but still they seemed to have no meaning.

'What do you want for tea?' she said wearily.

'Why don't you have a bath,' Lee suggested. 'Relax for a while and unwind. I'll settle him and order a takeaway later.'

'Thanks, babe.' Jess felt a brief sense of lightening as she walked away from her partner and son for a few precious responsibility-free moments.

'No worries,' Lee said, gazing down at Jacob's angry face.

And he means it, Jess thought to herself as she turned the hot tap on full blast. He's not worried at all.

Chapter Six

Natalie could not stop laughing. There was something about fifteen or so women and two men sitting in a big circle on a dusty floor singing 'Row, row, row your boat' whilst doing the actions with babies who were either asleep or looked utterly bored that was very, very funny and which made her laugh so much she had to stop and catch her breath between fits of giggles. But it was the marching around to 'The Grand Old Duke of York' with babies that couldn't even roll over, let alone march, that made her practically hysterical.

'This isn't a joke, you know,' Steve said, despite chuckling along with her as they marched to the top of the hill and down again. 'It's really good for them, music and singing. It stimulates all of their senses.'

Baby Music had been Steve's idea. Just as everybody had been on the point of leaving Meg's and saying how nice it was and that they must do it again sometime, he had suggested they set a date.

'I'm taking Lucy to a baby music class in that place down by the park, it starts next week,' he said. 'Why don't we all meet there next if you like?' And before Natalie knew it she had been half press-ganged and half volunteered herself for yet another new and strange life experience, and found that she was even a little depressed that she had to wait a week before they were due to meet at the class.

The still so new and yet seemingly timeless life that Freddie and she had enjoyed for the eleven or so weeks before falling into the baby group was, Natalie began to realise, rather small and constricting. Her mostly solitary experience of early motherhood hadn't made her unhappy or especially depressed, but she had underestimated the importance of a peer group in making one feel normal. It was a relief and a pleasure to hear the stories and thoughts and worries of the others at Meg's house, and to know that her experiences were not unique.

So as she had walked home that morning she had found herself wishing that the baby music class wasn't quite so far away, and that there wouldn't be a whole week of sleep-deprived wandering around Stoke Newington trying to avoid Gary Fisher and his apprentice and wondering if it was possible in the twenty-first century for a modern human being to lose the ability to communicate through language.

She needn't have worried, because the week had passed quickly. While she had assumed that contact with the others could not be made until a specific time, rather like keeping an appointment or waiting the allotted number of days after a date to suggest another one, others in the group did not.

Tiffany was the one she saw almost every day of that week. She had tagged along with Anthony the morning after coffee at Meg's house and while Gary had been mid-apology about the girl's presence, Natalie had whisked her off to the kitchen for a chat and a coffee. Gary had stopped apologising for her after that. In fact, he told Natalie in passing as she handed him a mug of tea one morning, he was glad to see that Tiffany had a new friend. Without exception all her schoolfriends had abandoned her as soon as the novelty of a new baby wore off and the reality set in.

Natalie was glad for herself that she had a new friend because, perhaps surprisingly, she liked Tiffany. She liked listening to her stories of the complicated and frankly terrifying school social scene that she was temporarily excluded from. And Tiffany was a mine of information about baby related things, like getting Freddie on to solids and how to help him with teething. She was funny and clever and always seemed relaxed around Natalie, not the shy and acutely self-conscious girl that she had been at Meg's.

It might have been because Tiffany was so mature that they got on as well as they did. Or possibly because Natalie was perhaps a little immature, but either way they had a lot in common.

That Friday Meg had called Natalie out of the blue and asked her if she wanted to meet her for a latte at the French patisserie on Newington Green. It had been a guilty conversation conducted in a low voice and Meg went to great pains to stress that it was not a baby group meeting, just friends having a coffee together. When Natalie jokingly asked her if she needed a password to meet her at that particular coffee shop, Meg confessed that she was feeling guilty for not asking Frances to come. She told Natalie with commendable reluctance that fond as she was of Frances, the advent of their two babies in such close proximity had forced them together on a far more regular basis than she had been used to. Frances seemed to visit her every day. And as sweet and nice as Meg insisted Frances could be, she was sometimes a little wearing.

'Well, you can't like everyone all the time, heh, Tiff?' Natalie had asked the sixteen-year-old as the three of them sat in the café a little while later.

Tiffany had shaken her head and sunk her chin into the zipped-up neck of her parka. She didn't say more than three words the whole time that Meg was there. The girl whose company Natalie had enjoyed so much seemed to have vanished.

When the weekend had come, when other people's husbands and families were home and Gary and Anthony had packed up until Monday, the house seemed very quiet. This time, however, after the bustle of the week and the promise of more entertainment in the days to come, Natalie had been able to enjoy the temporary peace and quiet alone with Freddie.

She did have the strangest feeling though, some hidden instinct that made her feel somehow as if this time was a haven, the quiet before the coming storm.

Now, as Baby Music reached its tumultuous crescendo, Natalie was practically crying with laughter as Meg threw herself into 'Incy Wincy Spider' with the energy and drama of an opera singer, whilst her toddler spun like a top in the middle of the room and Frances frowned with faintly irritated concentration as she tried to get little Henry's tiny fingers to do the actions.

When the four of them made their way outside after the group was finished, Natalie was in the best mood she had been since before she was pregnant. It struck her that when you were out of the world of work and more or less out of touch with your old single or childless friends for the first time ever, finding new friends was almost as challenging and difficult as it could be finding a boyfriend. Natalie was beginning to realise that it had been a stroke of luck that she had met Meg and Tiffany on the day the electrics went wrong. In fact, her dangerous wiring was possibly the best thing that could have happened to her because now she knew Jess, Steve and even Frances too.

Because of them her life had taken on a new and reassuring

dimension. Her universe had shrunk until its limits were pretty much the four walls of her house, an occasional trip to the Turkish grocers and the frequent but usually flying visits from busy Alice. But in the few days since Natalie had met these new people, she had begun to see a slightly different reflection of herself whenever she looked at them.

She was not to any of them the Natalie the rest of the world knew: the complicated, sometimes foolish and always restless woman who had only ever successfully channelled her energies into one thing prior to Freddie, her underwear business. And she was definitely not the woman who got herself impregnated by a philanderer for whom she stupidly harboured some muddled feelings. To them she was sensible, straightforward Natalie. She was Mrs . . . well, whatever. Married to a lovely steady man, with a lovely baby boy and a lovely house. Natalie liked that vision of herself. She felt wrong for liking it, determined as she always had been to be her own woman all her life long and not care if she had a man or not. She did have to admit, though, that in certain circles a husband could be a very useful accessory.

But it wasn't only her imagined home life that Natalie was enjoying, she was heartened by the beginnings of new friendships. For the first time in her life she was comforted to know that she was not unique and that her experience of parenthood was just as challenging and as difficult as other people's. Indeed, it seemed to her that under the circumstances she was making a pretty good job of it, considering that she was a beginner, and despite her inescapably distinctive circumstances she was enjoying every minute of it.

'That floor was very dusty,' Frances said as she came out a little after the others. 'I told the woman. I said she should contact the cleaners and complain but she was very rude . . .'

'I wonder what happened to Tiffany and Jess,' Meg mused,

leaning against the black steel railing that surrounded the pond and looking down at the gathering of ducks and geese that seemed noisily hopeful for some kind of snack.

'Well, I can clear up one of those mysteries,' Natalie said, watching a figure in a long black coat jogging towards them behind a buggy. 'There's Jess now.'

'Has it started?' Jess asked breathlessly as she drew up alongside them, her cheeks flushed and her hair wild with static.

'It's finished, love!' Natalie said with a chuckle. 'You've got the time wrong, you dippy mare!'

Everyone laughed except Jess, whose face fell like a stone.

'Oh no,' she said, with a distinct wobble in her voice. 'I can't believe it!'

'Don't worry,' Natalie said lightly, quickly putting an arm around Jess's shoulders. 'It wasn't that big a deal – you didn't miss much, honest.'

'But we *really* wanted to go,' Jess said, getting quite heated. 'We'd been looking forward to it; it was going to be the highlight of our day.'

Natalie and Meg exchanged glances. It seemed to Natalie that even in her hormonal state Jess was over-reacting just a little.

'I'm so stupid,' Jess went on miserably, apparently determined not to let herself off the hook. 'I can't believe how stupid I am – and now I've missed our meeting!'

'Stop worrying! Baby Music will be there next week,' Natalie said firmly, deciding she needed to rescue Jess from her own distress. 'And as for our so-called meeting, well, that isn't over until there has been coffee and cake, especially cake.' She glanced up at the sky, which was fairly clear for once. 'Who fancies a walk around the park on the way to the café?'

Meg and Frances nodded.

'Can't,' Steve said, 'I've got some work to do. When are we meeting next?'

The five looked at each other and shrugged.

'What we need is a regular date,' Frances said, fishing in her bag and producing a small black diary and a pen. 'How about every Wednesday? We could go to Baby Music first and then have a coffee for half an hour afterwards, which would mean the meeting would be over by . . . midday.'

'Or . . .' Jess began and bit her lip before she could finish the sentence.

'Or?' Natalie asked her encouragingly.

'You might think it's a bit too soon to see each other again, but there's this baby aerobics group on this Friday at the sports centre that I thought might help me get back into shape . . . You exercise with your baby, I think it's supposed to be quite . . . fun.'

Natalie looked at Jess's face. She'd said the word 'fun' as if it was a word from another language. It was obviously something she desperately needed.

'Brilliant idea!' Steve said, making Jess feel quite pleased with herself. 'Count me in.'

'But that's a Friday,' Frances said. 'That's *two* meetings in one week.'

'That's OK,' Meg said. 'We can treat this week as a getting-to-know-each-other week and there aren't any rules, after all. The more the merrier I say.'

'Yes you do,' Frances said, looking down at Henry in his pram with an unreadable expression.

'Aerobics,' Natalie said dubiously. 'Does it have anything to do with leotards because I'm not sure any of you want to see my arse in Lycra.'

'You can see my bottom from the moon,' Meg said with a chuckle that drew a look of disapproval from Frances.

'I think it's time I went,' Steve said, looking a little pink. 'I'll see you there on Friday.'

The four women watched Steve go.

'He's lovely, isn't he,' Meg said.

'He is,' Natalie agreed. 'But I wouldn't shag him.'

'That's it,' Frances said smartly as the others giggled. 'I'm going home. Goodbye.'

'Frances!' Meg called out after her half-heartedly. 'Don't go – come for a coffee.'

'No thank you,' Frances said stiffly over her shoulder as she wheeled Henry rapidly into the distance.

'Did I offend her?' Natalie asked Meg. 'I was only joking.'

'Frances is a funny old stick,' Meg said. 'She's basically a very nice woman but very hard to get to know. I have no idea how she ever let anyone close enough to her to actually marry her, but her husband Craig is lovely and he obviously adores her.' Meg shuddered, possibly against the cold, but probably not. 'I don't think I could be married to her though, it would be like walking a tightrope with no safety net every day.'

'However, you *are* married to her brother,' Natalie said as they set off. 'They're not at all alike then?'

Meg thought about Robert. He must have come home last night after she had fallen asleep. She dimly remembered feeling the weight and warmth of him suddenly materialising next to her in bed and then sometime later when she had got up to see to Iris she had seen his shape under the duvet. He was in the shower when she had been getting everyone's breakfast. He'd been out of the door, shouting his goodbyes down the hallway with his skin still damp before Meg could even offer him a cup of coffee.

'Daddy didn't kiss me goodbye,' Hazel had said wanly over her Rice Krispies.

'He was in a rush, dear,' Meg had said, looking sadly down

the empty hallway to the front door. She knew how disappointed Hazel felt. Robert hadn't kissed her goodbye either. The truth was, Robert did frighten her, but not because he was like Frances. It was because she wasn't sure *who* he was like any more.

'He's like Frances in that he knows how he likes things and he's very focused,' she told Natalie, keeping her thoughts to herself and banishing her worries back to the small hours of the night where they belonged. 'But apart from that they are totally different. Robert's great. A really great dad and a wonderful husband,' Meg went on in a doggedly happy tone. 'We always wanted a big family with lots of kids. I was an only child and it was a very lonely childhood. And Robert – well, you can imagine the kind of home he came from by looking at Frances. His parents were very strict, very authoritarian – still are really. We wanted something different for our children and that's what we've created. I know I'm very lucky not having to worry about going back to work or anything.'

'Lee is great with Jacob,' Jess said as they walked across the park and towards Church Street. 'He's so calm and relaxed with him. When I look at the two of them together I feel sort of out of it. Almost excess to requirements. I think they'd get on fine without me, you know.'

'Rubbish,' Natalie said lightly, picking up the doom-laden sentence and tossing it into the air with ease. 'For one thing, Lee can't breastfeed, can he? And boys always prefer their mum's to their dads. That's a biological fact.'

'What about your husband, Natalie – is he a good dad?' Meg asked. 'What's his name again?'

Natalie froze for a nanosecond. Her tiny harmless lie was just about to double in size. She felt powerless to stop it, and in some ways she didn't want to. She knew she *could* just tell them the truth and she was fairly sure they'd be OK about it.

In fact, they'd probably laugh and be very understanding. But on the other hand, they might wonder why she had lied in the first place instead of just telling them the truth like any normal person would. And if they did that they might not be so keen on being friends with her. And Natalie knew that she needed friends, more especially *these* fledgling friends. As much as she enjoyed her daily conversations with Alice, it was only with these women that she felt her life with Freddie was real and forever, and not just some sort of phase she was going through before everything got back to normal. And on top of that, to be honest, she liked her fictional husband.

'Gary,' she said, plucking the first available man's name out of the air. She might as well call him Gary because in her head he literally *was* Gary, or at least her version of him – the world's first dependable and dull fantasy man ever created in the mind of a woman. 'He's a lovely dad, when he's here and even when he's not. I speak to him every night. He tells Freddie a story down the phone.'

As the others 'ahhhd' Natalie wondered at the lie that had come so easily. She was always one for exaggerating, spinning a good yarn, adding just a little bit of gloss to reality here and there to improve the punchline of an anecdote, but she'd never told an actual, big, massive, get-found-out-and-you're-for-it lie before. Unless you counted not telling Jack Newhouse he was Freddie's father, which wasn't really a lie, but more of an omission.

'He feels bad that he has to work away,' she went on, as if someone else had taken control of her tongue. 'But when he's completed this contract he's coming back for good. We can't wait can we, Freddie?' Freddie, who was fast asleep after the excitement of Baby Music, remained oblivious to his mum's deception and potential insanity.

'He missed the birth, didn't he?' Jess remarked sympathetically.

'Oh no, he was there for the birth,' Natalie said, privately outraged at and full of admiration for herself simultaneously.

'Really?' Jess said. 'Only I didn't see you with anyone except that blonde woman when we were in.'

'Yes, he arrived in the middle of the night I was in labour,' Natalie assured her. 'He cut the cord. We had a few precious hours before he had to go again'.

'Doesn't he get paternity leave?' Jess asked as they reached the café at last.

'Not on a short-term contract.' Natalie winged it. 'Scandalous, isn't it? Now, who's for carrot cake?'

She breathed a silent sigh of relief as she finally directed the conversation away from herself and on to cake. It was dangerous that she enjoyed talking about fantasy Gary so much, because apart from anything else the more she told her friends about him the harder it would be to have to tell them one day that he didn't exist. She'd end up having to invent a mistress that he had abandoned her for, or some kind of tragic engineering accident that left her a fairly young and fairly beautiful widow . . . Natalie stopped herself in her tracks and told herself to get a grip on reality. For a second she imagined how things might have been in a parallel life. She pictured Jack Newhouse holding her hand a she pushed and swore and screamed, and almost laughed out loud at the ridiculous image that was no more real than her fake husband. It was even more implausible, a realisation that gave her a pang of sadness.

Natalie knew it was stupid to miss a man she had never really known and would never know. Except that wasn't quite true. When she looked at Freddie and caught glimpses of his father in his features, she felt as if she knew Jack more now that he was out of her life than the few intense hours he had been in it. She missed not only him – as absurd as that was – but also the idea of having someone to share the joy of her son. She mourned the absence of the other half that had co-created Freddie.

'Gary sounds lovely,' Meg said with a wistful air as she studied the menu.

'Oh he is,' Natalie agreed, snapping out of her reverie and nodding vigorously.

'We're lucky, aren't we?' Jess seemed to need additional confirmation. 'To have found three wonderful men. Really good men are in short supply, you know.'

'That's true,' Meg and Natalie said together with heartfelt emphasis, but for entirely different reasons.

Chapter Seven

When Natalie got back to the house Gary Fisher was vacuuming the front room with a studied concentration that she found oddly endearing.

'I didn't know cleaning came as part of the service,' she said twice before he finally gave up trying to hear her and switched the vacuum cleaner off.

'Oh well, I like to leave a room tidy,' he said a little awkwardly.

'How's it going?' Natalie asked him. It did seem a little surreal chatting to this powerfully muscled man covered in plaster dust while he clutched at the handle of her upright as if it were the very last straw.

'We're making good progress,' Gary said. 'Kitchen's done, half of downstairs.' He smiled and nodded at Freddie. 'How's the little feller getting on then?'

'Brilliant,' Natalie said. 'We had a real laugh today, didn't we, Freddie – and to think I thought I was missing the cut and thrust of the lingerie business!'

Gary blushed deeply at the inflammatory word and looked down at his boots. The two of them stood there for a moment in silence.

'Oh!' Gary said suddenly, his voice seeming loud in the quiet. 'That reminds me, a lady called Alice left you a message on your machine. She said to call her straight away. Something to do with . . . Casanova?'

Natalie sat down on her sheet-covered sofa.

'Oh,' she said. That could only mean one thing.

Jack Newhouse was back in town.

'What did she say again?' Natalie asked Alice nervously for the third time. She found it very hard to believe what Alice was telling her, but she had to, because unless Alice had gone barking mad she was not in the habit of telling lies.

'Like I said we were just having lunch, the first time in months, and then Suze says, "Remember that guy Natalie had the fling with? His name was Jack Newhouse, wasn't it? I remember because she made that joke about his name." So I nodded and she tells me she thinks she's met him, within the last week in London.'

Natalie chewed her lip and looked anxiously at Gary's back as he pulled length after length of old wire out of the hole he had made in her wall.

'But how does she know? It could be anyone, there must be hundreds of men called Jack in London. I bet she never met him! I bet she's making it up, it would be just like her.' Natalie thought about Suze, a pre-baby Friday-night friend who had become conspicuous by her absence soon after Natalie got pregnant, let alone had an actual baby. It did not surprise her in the least that she had scheduled lunch with Alice once she knew that Natalie was not likely to be there. She was fun girl, good for gossip and cocktails but shallow as a puddle and as reliable as – well, as Natalie could be herself sometimes, which wasn't very.

'But are there hundreds of Jack Newhouses who grew up in Venice and have spent the last year in Italy? Because according to Suze that's the Jack she met. Think about it, it's not that

83

weird. You met him near Soho, she met her Jack Newhouse in Soho Square. People move about in the same old small ponds no matter how big they like to think the world is, bumping into the same old fish. And he has got a track record of talking to random women, hasn't he? Well, that's what he did with Suze.'

'He tried to pick her up?' Natalie asked Alice, feeling sickened. It was humiliating, like receiving a second-hand report of her own encounter with him, illustrating so clearly that from Jack's point of view the whole event was horribly routine.

'I'm afraid so, Nat,' Alice said heavily. 'Suze said she was having a fag break when this tall, skinny guy sat down next to her on the bench and asked her if she knew the time. Anyway, he asked her all sorts of questions about herself, told her he'd just got back from a year in Italy, staying with family near Venice . . .'

'Bastard!' Natalie yelled, causing Gary to pause for a second before resuming his wire pulling. She lowered her voice before adding, 'Sorry, it's just that I can't believe this, Alice, I can't believe what you are telling me. Of all the women in London he's got to hit on he chooses somebody I *know*!'

'Maybe it was just the law of averages,' Alice said tentatively. 'I mean, if he chats up enough women in one particular area then sooner or later you were bound to know one of them . . .'

'So what happened then?' Natalie asked her reluctantly.

'He said he had to go to a job interview but asked her if she'd like to go for a drink with him sometime. He wrote down his name and phone numbers on a piece of paper and gave them to her. She said his hand was trembling as if he was really nervous.'

'That's his trick,' Natalie growled. 'That's how he draws

you in, by being all vulnerable and sexy at the same time.'

'It wasn't until after he'd gone,' Alice continued, 'and Suze read his name that all the pieces started coming together, and she thought he could be *the* Jack Newhouse. The one who got you pregnant and then disappeared. She called me and asked me out for lunch. She told me what I've told you and gave me the numbers. She said she thought you could use them.' Alice waited.

'Well?' she said when Natalie remained silent.

'Well what?' Natalie asked her.

'You have to face up to this, Natalie, you know you *have* to. You can't pretend that this hasn't happened.'

Alice paused, clearly waiting for Natalie to agree with her. When Natalie remained stubbornly silent Alice went on anyway.

'You have a chance to contact him now and tell him about Freddie.' Alice finally stated the obvious. 'It's a chance you have to take.'

'Why now – doesn't this just prove what kind of a man he is?' Natalie demanded. 'I haven't seen or heard from him in thirteen months and ten days,' she said, instantly regretting that she had let slip that she knew exactly when it was that she last saw the man she professed to be so uninterested in. She hoped vainly that Alice wouldn't notice, and pressed on with complaining. 'Things are going well, Alice. They are steady and stable. Why should I do anything to change that?'

'Oh, I don't know,' Alice replied, her voice heavy with sarcasm. 'Let me think . . .'

'Alice, this isn't funny!' Natalie exclaimed.

Gary looked up at her this time. She smiled at him and rolled her eyes. Realising that she still had her coat on and that Freddie was still zipped up securely in his warm suit, she tucked the phone under her ear and began to make her way upstairs.

'I don't think it is funny,' Alice said as Natalie moved out of earshot of her electrician. 'But even if you could manage to avoid him for the rest of your life, which seems unlikely, you still have to tell him. Take the moral high ground. I know it's uncharted territory for you, but I think once you've done it you'll feel relieved.'

'Or,' Natalie suggested optimistically, ignoring Alice, 'we could relocate the business to Birmingham. I've always liked Birmingham.'

'Natalie, be serious.' Alice's normally smooth and level tone rose slightly, which was about the only sign she ever gave that she was properly angry and not just annoyed. Natalie didn't want Alice to be properly angry with her. Despite her teasing and ribbing of her old friend it was important to her that Alice thought the best of her. She needed to be in at least one person's good books to feel good about herself, and Alice had always been that person since they had met over women's control-top pants. Although she had suddenly acquired a wealth of new friends, Alice was the one Natalie was certain still to be friends with in a hundred years' time, because Alice loved her exactly the way she was, foibles, tics and all. And even if Alice did sometimes get quite cross with her, Natalie loved her back with exactly the same steadfast loyalty.

'You make calling him sound so simple, let alone telling him . . .' Natalie complained miserably. 'Like I can ring his number out of the blue and say, "Hi, Jack, remember me? No? Oh well, the thing is I've recently had your baby!"'

'It *is* simple,' Alice told her. 'It might be hard to do but it is simple. He is Freddie's father. He has a right to know, just as Freddie has the right to know his father. You haven't even been able to tell him up to now – he vanished after that

weekend, and the way he left things was sort of up in the air
. . . but now you actually have his numbers.'

'I have someone's numbers.' Natalie was insistent. 'We
don't conclusively know if is the same half-Venetian Jack
Newhouse.'

'Natalie, don't stick your head in the sand!' Alice exclaimed.
'It has to be the same Jack. And you have to call him. Think
of this as a sign from above if you like, I know you like those.'

'If it is him, then it's not a sign,' Natalie said. 'It's proof.
Proof that I got myself impregnated by a prick both
figuratively and literally.'

'Nobody's disputing that he behaved badly – but don't you
think that it's time to do the grown-up thing?' Alice sighed.
'You know, the kind of thing a parent does?'

Natalie thought about the last time she had seen Jack.
He had been sitting in the back of a water taxi where he'd
dropped her off at Marco Polo airport. White collarless shirt
unbuttoned at the throat revealing his warm, lightly tanned
and, if Natalie remembered rightly, slightly salty-tasting skin.

'I'll call you,' he had said. Usually Natalie prided herself on
knowing when a man meant what he said. At the time she was
sure he really did mean to call her, she'd been so idiotically
happy at the thought of seeing him again and perhaps even –
who knew? This might be the one romance that didn't drift
apart and might actually turn into something. When he
disappeared without a trace she felt like a fool, but worse than
that it hurt her. It hurt her in the place where her heart was.
She supposed she'd had this ridiculously romantic idea all
along that the man she finally trusted, the man she finally
fell for would be worthy of that honour, or at the very least
want it.

She had been totally wrong. She had to deal with that and
move on.

So as soon as Natalie knew she was pregnant and that the baby had to be his because nobody she'd met since had seemed anything like worth the effort of being with, she never once thought about trying to contact him. She put the prospect of having any kind of real relationship with him in the past, gone and irretrievable even if his baby was slap bang in the very middle of the present, and would be for every single moment of every day for pretty much the rest of her life. What Alice didn't seem to understand was that almost the only way Natalie could deal with Jack Newhouse and all the associated issues he had left her with was if he were far, far away, both in reality and metaphorically. If he was here it would be much, much harder to pretend that she didn't still want him, or at least want that version of him that had taken her to Venice.

But Alice was right, Natalie thought, as she stroked the cheek of her son, which sloped down at exactly the same angle as his father's – she *was* a parent now. Parents didn't put themselves first. Parents didn't do what was easy. They did what was best. And it wasn't best to deliberately keep a child from his father without a really good reason, and Natalie didn't think that heartbreak, jealousy and general bitterness counted.

'You're right,' she told Alice at last. 'I know you're right.'

'I knew you'd see sense,' Alice said, her voice warming again. 'So are you going to call him?'

Natalie sighed. 'I will,' she said. 'I suppose I have to.' She took a pen and pad out of her bedside drawer and wrote down the two phone numbers that Alice gave her.

'Anything going on in the office that I should know about?' Natalie asked, hoping that some complicated distraction might mean that Alice needed her help.

'Not really,' Alice said. 'Selfridges have reordered. The new Web manager is brilliant. That warehouse and supply company she found are doing really well. I'll be biking samples of the winter range for you to OK later on today. Everything is fine with the business, Natalie. All you need to worry about is yourself and Freddie.'

'If only,' Natalie said to herself as she hung up the phone, 'that was true.'

After putting Freddie in his cot she made her way down to the kitchen, hoping to find some more cake. Instead she found Tiffany in Anthony's arms, crying her heart out. She didn't even notice Natalie come in.

Natalie looked enquiringly at Gary, who was pouring boiling water into a teapot that she had forgotten she even had. He pressed his lips together for a thoughtful moment before nodding in the direction of the garden. Natalie followed him outside.

'Sorry,' he said, spreading his hands out, palms up. 'She turned up all upset and I didn't think you'd mind if she had five minutes with Anthony. Apparently she's had an awful morning.'

Natalie was surprised by his apology.

'I don't mind,' she assured him. 'Not at all – but what's wrong?'

It was terrible to admit it, but she felt immensely relieved that some other drama had bowled its way into her day, making it at least temporarily impossible for her to call either of the numbers that Alice had given her.

'Well, from what I can gather, her mum and dad came round to the flat this morning, she was just on her way out to meet you, she said.' Gary raised an eyebrow slightly as if he still couldn't work out what a thirty-six-year-old woman was doing hanging around with a sixteen-year-old kid, which was fair enough, Natalie thought, as she hardly knew herself. 'Well, she let them in of course; she misses them, especially her mum. After all she's only a child herself really, for all the front she puts on. They said they wanted to talk about the baby. Tiff hoped they'd come round to make the peace. She built her hopes up. But it turns out they just wanted to get a look at Jordan. Apparently her dad said . . .' Gary paused, a look of disgust on his face. 'That if she was light-skinned enough to pass for white Tiffany could come back and they'd say no more about it.'

'Oh God, that's awful!' Natalie exclaimed, hugging her arms around her as a sudden chill swept up the lawn. 'Poor Tiffany.'

'The poor kid had to throw them out herself and her dad's a big bloke, determined too. In the end a neighbour gave her a hand. She came straight round here with the baby.' Gary took a step closer to her, lowering his voice even though they were in the garden. 'You don't mind, do you? I expect it's the last thing you need at the moment.'

'Of course I don't mind,' Natalie said. She glanced through the French doors to where she could see Anthony hugging his girlfriend, gently kissing her hair and whispering some con-stant consolation. 'She's very strong to stand up for herself and Anthony against that. Very strong. I mean, I complain about my mum, God knows, but next to Tiffany's parents she'd be up for Mother of the Year. I don't know if I would be able to be as strong as Tiffany.'

'Oh I don't know,' Gary said. 'You seem pretty strong to me, managing here all on your own.'

Natalie glanced at his face, taken aback by the first non-formal thing he had ever said to her. Her scrutiny made Gary look uncomfortable again.

'I don't do badly for a little woman, do I?' she said with a touch of irony.

'I'm just saying, when my daughter was born there were

two of us, more than two really, we had grandparents, aunts, uncles – the lot. But still me and Haley struggled. For about six months we felt like we were walking zombies, I don't know how we did it. So the fact that you are doing it all on your own more or less, your husband away and not really any family about – well, I think that is quite impressive.'

For a moment Natalie was stunned into silence by the compliment. She hadn't expected Gary Fisher to be actively thinking about her and what kind of person she was. But as he had, it was good that his conclusions were positive. People were often irritated, intimidated, annoyed or exasperated by her, but very rarely impressed. It made a nice change, and she was so pleasantly surprised that she had to remind herself not to be disappointed that her fake husband was already married, because this Gary was real Gary, not fantasy Gary. They were two entirely different men, especially considering one of them was pretend.

Natalie stopped that train of thought before she drove herself completely insane.

'So it got better at six months, did it?' she asked him cheerfully, because he looked embarrassed that he had said anything at all. 'What about the terrible twos and threes? You'll have to sit down and go through every year with me up until – how old is your little girl now?'

'Eight,' Gary said, breaking eye contact with her.

'Eight! You're an expert,' Natalie said warmly. 'Will you throw in some parenting tuition with the work you're doing for me?'

'I'm not an expert,' Gary said flatly, his smile closing down. 'I don't see her now.' His head dropped and Natalie wondered if she should give him a hug or something as he looked so sad, but somehow she thought he wasn't the kind of man to appreciate an unsolicited hug from customers.

'Anyway, I'd better get on,' he said. He looked back into the kitchen where Tiffany was now sitting at the table, wiping one eye and then the other with the sleeves of her top pulled down over her knuckles.

'Thanks,' he said to Natalie, who was not quite sure what he was thanking her for, and then he headed back inside. She stayed outside for a moment longer, watching him exchange a few words with Anthony. His apprentice placed one hand momentarily on Tiffany's shoulder before he followed Gary upstairs.

The real Gary wasn't as normal and as average as she had first thought, Natalie realised as she headed back inside to see Tiffany. She couldn't really work him out, which made him suddenly quite interesting to her. She had assumed that he was more or less two-dimensional, the kind of person you can read in an instant, but there was something else there too. Hidden depths as her mother would say, but hiding what?

'OK?' she said to Tiffany as she walked in. She shivered in reaction to the heat of the kitchen after the chill of outdoors. 'Fancy some tea? Gary's made a pot. I think he must have time-travelled here from 1948. Who makes pots of tea any more?'

'My mum does,' Tiffany said, propping her chin on the heels of her hands. 'She makes a pot of tea and she sticks this hideous tea cosy on it and does up a tray with biscuits. Not nice ones, but those horrible pink ones that taste like cardboard. My mum loves those. She thinks she's so . . .' Tiffany searched for the right word, 'decent, but how can she be when she and Dad won't have anything to do with me or Jordan because Anthony's black?' She looked up at Natalie and shrugged. 'I don't get it,' she added weakly.

Natalie sat down and poured out two mugs of dark brown tea; the pungent scent hovered in the steam for a moment.

'We're not supposed to get our parents,' she said eventually. 'I have a theory that it's to aid the evolution of man. Because if we got our parents and wanted to live the same way as they have lived and think and feel the way they do, then the world would never change or move on. It's a good thing you don't get your mum and dad, trust me. By not getting them you've given yourself and Jordan a head start at growing up.'

Tiffany's mouth curled into a small smile.

'Are you saying I'm not grown up?' she challenged Natalie lightly. Natalie looked unapologetic.

'Tiff, *I'm* not grown up and I'm thirty years old . . .'

Tiffany raised an eyebrow.

'OK, thirty-six years old,' Natalie went on. 'I have a son, an actual human life depending on *me* alone to exist, but I still feel the same inside as I did when I was your age. I have another theory . . .'

'Another one, seriously?' Tiff teased. 'You don't look like the theory type.'

'Oh, and what type do I look like then?' Natalie asked her, briefly diverted.

'The mental type,' Tiff said, with another twist of a smile.

'Well, I *am* that type,' Natalie was forced to concede. 'But I do have a philosophical side too. And this theory is a good one. *I* think we all keep growing up until we die. I don't think there's ever a time when suddenly you feel totally confident and in charge and know exactly what to do in all situations. I think we will always be frightened and stressed and unsure and confused pretty much for ever.'

'Oh God,' Tiff said flatly, dropping her forehead onto the table top with a light bump. 'Thanks for that.'

Natalie smiled.

'It's a shame you missed Baby Music,' she said after a while.

'It was hysterical. It's amazing what normal, sane adults will do because it's allegedly good for their kids.'

'Yeah, well,' Tiffany said. 'I don't know about the baby group any more. I mean, it's not really me, is it?'

'What?' Natalie exclaimed. 'What do you mean it's not you? If it's me it's you, let me tell you, because none of that stuff is really me – especially not Baby Music.'

'No, it's different,' Tiffany said. 'I'm a kid living in a one-bedroom council flat in a tower block. Look at your home – look at Meg's! What about when it's my turn to have the baby group round? We haven't even got a sofa. We sit on a beanbag. We have to take turns.'

'No one cares about that stuff,' Natalie tried to reassure her.

'I do, I care,' Tiffany told her. 'It's embarrassing. You're all proper grown-ups with proper lives, husbands and mortgages and all that shi— stuff.'

'Yes, well, that might be true, but we are all mums with babies – that's all we need to have in common,' Natalie persisted. 'And anyway, without your mum around you need the company of old women. It will remind you that being older isn't always wiser.'

'Maybe,' Tiffany replied with a small smile.

The pair sat in companionable silence as Natalie poured out two more cups of tea from her seldom-seen teapot.

'What about your mum, where's she?' Tiffany asked her suddenly. 'I thought most grannies except Jordan's couldn't wait to come and fuss round their grandbaby. Or your husband's parents – don't they come round ever?'

Natalie nipped sharply at her bottom lip for a moment before saying, 'Oh well, you know – in-laws. I was never going to be good enough for their little boy.' She took a large slurp of her tea and glanced about the kitchen. 'Fancy a sandwich?'

'What about *your* mum, then?' Tiff asked, shaking her head to decline the offer of a snack.

'Oh, my mum,' Natalie said, rolling her eyes and preparing to rant. 'My mum is . . .' And then she stopped herself. She had been about to tell Tiffany that her mum was an absolutely terrible mother, not to mention a really bad human being generally which was what she normally told people. But then she realised that next to Tiffany's parents, her mum, with her pathological sunbathing obsession, together with her drinking sangria in the morning compulsion, smoking whilst eating habit and insistence on conducting affairs with highly unsuitable men who only wanted her for her non-existent money, wasn't quite as bad. Even the resentment that Natalie held steadfastly against her for constantly moving her from town to town during her childhood and for never being the kind of sensible, sexless mother that the other kids she never really got time to make friends with had, she still didn't come off as badly as a woman who was racist towards her own grandchild.

'My mum lives in Spain and I haven't seen her in about two years or spoken to her for months and she doesn't even know I was pregnant, let alone that I've had a baby.' The truth just slipped out of Natalie's mouth unbidden and flopped onto the table like a caught fish gasping for air.

'*What!*' Tiffany exclaimed. 'You haven't told her you were pregnant? But why not? I know you think no one ever grows up but *you're* not a sixteen-year-old kid, Natalie – you're married! Why wouldn't you tell your mum about Freddie?'

Natalie considered the prospect of telling the truth about her marital status and for a second time decided against it; the truth in general always seemed to cause such a fuss.

'She never liked Gary . . .' she began.

'Gary?' Tiffany interrupted her. 'Your husband is called Gary too?'

'Yeah,' Natalie said quickly. 'Common name, isn't it?' Tiffany said nothing but Natalie thought she saw an indefinable look cross her face.

'And she made it very difficult for us to get together. She didn't come to the wedding or anything and so . . . well, we drifted apart,' Natalie said, feeling a sudden compulsion to eat a large amount of cake and heading to the bread bin where she had stored her latest bar of ginger cake intended for the next baby group meeting. She cut a large slice and didn't bother to put it on a plate. She sat back down and took two big bites, cupping her free hand under her chin as she munched.

'You should tell your mum,' Tiffany said simply. 'You should give her a chance to do the right thing.'

Natalie looked into Tiffany's pale blue eyes regarding her so seriously and thoughtfully, and felt one hundred per cent stupid.

How could it be that this slip of a girl behaved with more intelligence and integrity than she did? Why did she persist in telling half-truths and spinning fantasies to the people who were becoming the first real friends she had ever made since somehow getting Alice to like her? It was as if she had an instinctive impulse to complicate her life unnecessarily, and to store up trouble in case things got too easy and relaxing. She knew it would only be a matter of time before it came out that she was not really married to an engineer called Gary, and that she was inventing silly stories to avoid revealing the truth about what was, after all, a meaningless one-night stand with a man she tried her best not to think about. And here was Tiffany, her relationship with the woman who by rights should still be nurturing and caring for her in tatters, standing on her own two feet and telling Natalie to give her own mother another chance.

Tiffany was right, her theory that nobody ever grows up

was a rubbish one. If Natalie was absolutely honest she was the only person she knew, excepting some babies, who hadn't achieved emotional adulthood yet.

'I'd better get off,' Tiff said suddenly, scraping her chair back across the tiles. 'Thanks for the tea.'

'That's OK!' Natalie said brightly, finishing off the last of the cake and wiping the back of her hand across her mouth. 'Look, we're going to this baby aerobics class at the sports centre on Friday. God knows what it will be like, I've got this mental image of a load of babies doing sit-ups – but anyway, please come.'

Tiffany still looked uncertain as she pulled on her parka. 'How much does it cost?' she asked.

'Don't know really,' Natalie said. 'Look, come. I can always pay if you haven't got enough.'

Tiffany shook her head. 'No thanks,' she said.

'But you will try to come, won't you?' Natalie persisted, wondering suddenly if Tiffany might feel vulnerable, isolated so brutally from her family and with Anthony out all day working.

'I don't know,' Tiff said, looking weary. 'I'll feel . . . funny.'

Natalie crossed over to her and without thinking put her arms around the girl and hugged her.

'Rubbish,' she said. 'You are a founding member of the group and I for one really like you. Look, if you really feel too intimidated to come out with the rest of the group then I will always do something separately with you. I know you can't be intimidated by me – because you've heard my theories and you know what an idiot I am.'

'That's true,' Tiffany said, her face brightening a little. 'OK, I'll try and come on Friday. It will be a laugh seeing you try and do aerobics.'

*

97

After Tiffany had gone Natalie went upstairs, passing Gary and Anthony who were working in companionable silence in the hallway. She crept into her bedroom and looked down at Freddie sleeping long and sound in his cot, gathering all the reserves of strength he would need to keep her up all night. He was fair-skinned, with ruddy cheeks and a thick thatch of flat, jet-black hair that seemed to perch on the top of his baby head like a wig made for someone much bigger. Natalie smiled fondly at him but at the same time felt a pinch of anxiety in her abdomen.

It was Jack Newhouse's baby who was sleeping so sweetly and peacefully in his cot in her house.

Natalie bit her lip and resisted the impulse to laugh out loud. She'd got herself into some pretty insane scrapes before now. There was that time she'd accepted a lift back to her hotel from an allegedly Swedish guy she had only just met in the centre of Paris. Instead of taking her home he'd tried to kidnap her, but luckily he was the world's least menacing kidnapper and as soon as she started screaming he had pulled over and dumped her at the side of the road in a part of Paris she didn't recognise at all. She had had to pay two prostitutes to take her back to where she was staying.

Until now she had thought that was possibly the most foolish and worst situation she had ever been in. That was until she had somehow ended up with Jack Newhouse's secret baby in a cot in her house while he was somewhere in London, probably even now attempting to seduce yet another conquest. And now she had Jack's telephone numbers by her bed and she knew she had to dial them, because Alice was right, it was a secret that should not be kept from either father or child. Natalie knew from painful experience that the truth, even a difficult one, was easier to bear than years of wondering and false hope. The prospect of making that call, combined with an imaginary husband in Dubai and a set of surprisingly lovely new friends who might all drop her like a hot brick as soon as they found out what kind of a flake she was, more or less topped any sticky situation she'd ever got herself into before.

'Yes, Natalie,' she said to herself. 'I think you've hit an all-time new high in the making a dreadful mess of your life stakes. Congratulations.'

She sat down on the end of the bed and took a deep breath. She picked up the pad with Jack's numbers on it. She thought about how important it was, how critical to Freddie's future that she did the right thing.

She slowly and carefully dialled a number and held her breath as it began to ring. For a second Natalie thought that no one was going to reply and she allowed herself to breathe again.

And then, 'Hello?' a voice said on the other end of the line.

'Hello, Mum. You'll never guess what I've been up to.'

Chapter Eight

Meg sat at the kitchen table, cupping a mug of coffee that had long since gone cold in her hand for several minutes before she realised she was watching Gripper enthusiastically eviscerating James's favourite teddy. Its eyes were gone, its nose was probably somewhere in the dog's upper digestive tract by now and as for its innards, well, they were even now spilling out all over the kitchen tiles; Teddy was well and truly gutted and for the first time in her life Meg thought she knew what it was like to feel that way too.

It was something that Robert had said to her last night, or did it count as this morning, she wondered, as Teddy's head was finally wrenched from his body. Technically it was this morning, Meg decided, because he had come in from work well past midnight.

Meg had waited up for him. She didn't usually, but yesterday morning she had seen a woman on *This Morning*, a relationship counsellor or divorce lawyer or something, declaring that modern women don't care enough for their men. That in these days of 'so-called equality' women expect men to work, bring home the money, do their equal share of the cleaning and cooking, while women are too busy with their own lives to offer the nurturing support that men need. No wonder, the woman said, that husbands got fed up with their battleaxe wives and had affairs with women who were more likely to offer them the attention they needed.

Meg had switched off the TV with a huff, mumbling something about it being utter nonsense as she went about her usual morning routine of picking things up off the living-room floor and dumping them on the bottom stair ready to put away at some future date that never seemed to arrive before everything was back all over the living-room floor. But as she contemplated whether or not it was worth washing the kitchen floor she found herself wondering if there wasn't *some* sense to what the woman said.

After all, Robert worked so hard that they barely spent ten minutes a day together and quite often didn't really see each other at all, as Meg was usually asleep when he came in. And as for any intimacy, well, when she thought about it she realised that that side of things had dwindled almost entirely away. In fact, she was fairly sure she hadn't had sex with her husband since she found out that she was pregnant with Iris. She was so used to him always making the first move in the bedroom that she hadn't noticed that he had stopped . . . making moves. It was because they were both so tired, she told herself, and busy. A new baby is exhausting, and Robert was probably being considerate. But still, the woman on TV was right about one thing, it was important to keep that intimate connection going within a couple. Meg felt sure that she and Robert needed some quality time.

So she decided to wait up for him that night. During the day she took James and Iris to the supermarket where she bought the kind of food she thought Robert might like to eat when he came home late at night: some nice bread, good cheese and hams and an expensive bottle of red wine. Megan had never really mastered what constituted a fine bottle of wine and what didn't, but she knew it mattered to Robert so she bought the most expensive bottle she could find in the shop and hoped for the best.

She thought she had done pretty well at staying awake for so long after she had finally marshalled all the children into bed, including Iris who miraculously still seemed to be asleep as the closing credits of *News at Ten* rolled. But she must have dozed off at some point in front of a late-night horror film, because the next thing she remembered was Robert shaking her by the shoulder and delivering a screaming Iris into her arms.

'You were snoring,' he said, a little distastefully Meg thought. 'And she was screaming her head off. You should have brought the monitor down. It's a miracle they're not all up.'

'Oh,' Meg said, pulling herself up in her chair and blinking. Her mouth was bone dry; she must have been sleeping with it wide open, probably lolling her head to one side. Not exactly the image she had hoped to present to Robert when he came home. She stood up with Iris still crying in her arms and followed him to the kitchen. She wanted to show him what she had done.

'You should feed her,' Robert said, his back to her as he peered in the fridge.

'I thought I'd wait up for you,' she said, putting the palm of her hand on his shoulder. He smelt faintly of pubs, a waft of stale smoke and a tinge of beer rising from his suit.

'I got you some food,' she said, picking up his hand and drawing him towards the table where she had laid out the feast. 'And some wine, I hope it's all right.'

Robert blinked at the table for a moment and then at Meg, who was jiggling a squalling Iris on her shoulder.

'For God's sake just feed her, *please*,' he said as he sat down heavily. 'I'm shattered, I just need some peace and quiet.'

Meg sat opposite him, unbuttoned the top of her nightie and put Iris to her breast. She watched Robert as he poured himself a glass of the wine and then buttered some bread. He seemed pleased with the food at least.

'I was thinking,' Meg ventured, 'it's ages since we've just had some time together on our own.' She looked down at Iris. 'Well, almost on our own. And so I thought it might be nice if I waited up for you.' She paused, not exactly sure how to say what she wanted to say. 'So that we could go to bed . . . together for once.'

'Actually, I'm really tired,' Robert said, dropping the knife onto the plate with a clatter and pushing the untouched food away. 'I think I'll just go to bed now.'

Meg put Iris in her bassinet and stayed downstairs for a few moments longer, carefully covering the cheese and the meat with cling film before putting them away and feeding Gripper a few titbits as she went in the hope that it would encourage her not to raid the fridge again. She wasn't exactly sure what she had expected to happen when Robert came in, she realised, as she went rather hesitantly up the stairs but she supposed she had thought he would be so pleased to see her up, awake and romantically inclined, even if she wasn't that much of an expert at showing it. She had thought that he would at least be . . . friendly. Meg told herself she wasn't being fair. After all the hard work he put in he was entitled to be tired and grumpy. And if he'd stopped out even later than usual to have a drink then he deserved it.

'Quality time isn't snatching a few minutes when both of you are exhausted,' she told Iris in a soft, low whisper as she laid her down in her cot. 'It's about creating time and space to be together. I'll suggest we find an evening. I'll get a baby-sitter. When we're both relaxed and in good moods we'll be just like we always used to be, you'll see.' She smoothed the back of her forefinger along Iris's cheek before creeping out and pulling the nursery door to.

Robert was already in bed, his back facing the door.

Meg slid off her dressing gown and climbed in beside him, feeling rather obvious now in the lacy nightie she had last worn on the romantic weekend break that had resulted in Iris.

'I saw this thing on the telly,' she said conversationally. 'Silly really, about how women should cherish their husbands more . . .'

'Really,' Robert said without turning over, an edge of irritation to his voice.

'That's why I got you the food and stayed up, or tried to. I should have realised you'd be tired . . .' Meg trailed off, looking at the familiar and yet newly alien contours of Robert's back. She reached out and laid her palm flat against one shoulder, feeling his muscles tense at her touch.

'After all,' she said, resolving to keep her hand against his skin. 'We hardly see each other any more, do we? And when was the last time you and I had time to ourselves?'

Robert turned abruptly onto his back, requiring Meg to move her hand quickly out of the way to avoid it being trapped by the weight of his torso.

'Don't have a go at *me*,' he said, with quiet, compressed fury as he stared at the ceiling. 'This is the way *you* wanted it.'

Meg tucked her hand underneath her head as she lay on her side and looked at his profile. She knew he was angry, she knew he was tired, she realised it was pointless trying to resolve any of that now when all he wanted to do was sleep, but still she couldn't let the question that had framed in her mind go unspoken. She knew by asking it she was crossing the border into some place she might not want to go. But still she asked.

'What do you mean, this is the way I wanted it?' she said, feeling suddenly frightened.

'You wanted all this,' Robert said, gesturing sharply around at their bedroom, but meaning, Meg supposed, their house, their life. 'And you wanted the big family and to be a full-time mum . . .'

'We both did, didn't we?' Meg asked him.

'It takes a lot of work to keep this up on my own, Megan,' Robert went on without pausing to answer her and, Meg thought, maybe not even hearing her. 'A lot of hard work. So I'm *sorry* if I'm not home at seven on the dot every evening to eat at a table with my family. I'm *sorry* if I'm out till all hours working my arse off to keep you in the manner to which you have clearly become accustomed but that is just that way it is, because of what *you* wanted.' He rolled over to face away from her again, his shoulders as stiff as bared teeth.

'That's not what I meant,' Meg said, unable to let the unravelling thread of the conversation go, even though she knew that the more she tugged at it the more the fabric of her life might fray and fall apart. 'I didn't mean to blame you, Robert. I do know why you are working all these hours. It's hard for us both at the moment with four small children, but it will get better. And I just thought that perhaps we might be able to make a little bit of time for us here and there . . .'

Robert did not move. He did not even appear to breathe for several frightening moments and then he said, 'I never wanted all this. All I wanted when we got married was you and me, but you kept banging on about how much a big family meant to you, about your dream house and your dream life. Sometimes I wonder if that is all you ever wanted me for, to dish out the sperm and the cash.'

'Robert . . .'

'Because,' Robert went on, 'if we didn't have the kids and this house and a mortgage the size of the national debt then . . .'

'Then what?' Meg asked compulsively.

'Then perhaps I'd have wife I wanted to come home to,' Robert said, his voice hard and angry. For a few seconds longer Meg watched him, waiting for him to turn back to her, to take her in his arms and tell her he was just tired and he'd had a bad day at work and that he was really sorry, he hadn't meant anything he had said. Instead, more than a minute passed before he sat up and roughly pulled his dressing gown on around him.

'I'm hungry,' he said, getting out of bed. He turned the bedroom light off as he closed the door behind him.

That was what Robert had said to her last night, or rather earlier this morning. So yes, she felt that she and James's teddy had quite a lot in common right now.

The doorbell went and Gripper halted her assault on Teddy to bowl up the hallway and hurl herself at the front door, barking enthusiastically at the shadow on the other side of the stained glass. Meg realised that, with much the same excitement as the dog, James would soon be out of bed and downstairs to see who had arrived. At last she got off the chair, her backside numb and her back painfully stiff as she bent to sweep the remnants of Teddy off the tiles and shove them in the bin on her way to answer the door. For one mad, wonderful moment she thought it might be Robert full of remorse and ready to apologise, but then Robert had a key so why would he ring? For a split second she thought about flowers. He might have sent her flowers. But he hadn't been out long enough to organise a bouquet.

She must have slept at some point during the night because she had woken late to hear the front door slam and to find her four-year-old, Hazel, leaning over her dressed in her uniform and school coat.

'Daddy's taking us to school!' Hazel had exclaimed, so

happy that she got a ten minute car ride with her father that Meg almost wanted to cry.

'That's lovely,' she had said. 'Where's Daddy?'

'Waiting in the car. Alex is with him. But I wanted to say bye,' Hazel had said. She was a forthright little girl, she said what she felt and she usually did what she wanted.

'Bye then, sweetie,' Meg had said, kissing her daughter. 'See you at home time.'

No, it wouldn't be flowers. If Robert could wash and dress the children and give them breakfast, a job he never usually had time for, rather than have to risk another conversation with her, then it definitely wouldn't be flowers.

Sure enough, James was already at the door banging his palms against it as Gripper used the little boy's shoulders to prop herself up onto her back feet. Above the noise Meg could hear Iris's irritated wail begin to rise and thicken, proclaiming that she was hungry and wet and generally fed up.

Sweeping boy and dog aside, Meg opened the door.

'You're not dressed!' Frances said, looking at her wrist-watch. 'We're going to be really late.'

'Late?' Meg asked her. Frances tutted and bustled past her with little Henry bundled in a thickly padded snowsuit that made his arms and legs stick out at doll-like angles.

'James is still in his pyjamas, and is that Iris crying?' Frances shoved Gripper out of the way with a firm sweep of her leg. Meg followed her dumbly up the stairs and into the nursery.

'Late for what?' she managed to ask Frances as she picked up Iris and took her to the change table.

'Steve's!' Frances exclaimed irritably. 'It's that baby aerobics thing and we're supposed to be going to Steve's place first – remember? I said that meeting more than once a week would be too much but you were all for it. And now look. We're supposed to be there in ten minutes.' Frances looked around the nursery as if formulating a plan of attack.

'Well, we'll just have to leave this mess for now. I'll dress James while you see to Iris and then have a quick wash. If we motor we should only be about ten minutes late, which is just about acceptable even if you do only live over the road.'

Meg let the tidal force of Frances's voice wash over her and recede before she spoke.

'I'm not going today,' she said eventually.

Frances stopped folding Babygros.

'Not going?' she asked. 'But you have too!'

'I'm coming down with something. I'm really tired. You go, send my apologies, OK?' Meg sat down in the rocking chair and began to feed Iris, noticing how uncomfortable Frances was, being in the same room with her and her naked breast.

'I can't go if you don't go,' Frances said, sitting down abruptly and shifting the starfish-shaped Henry onto her knee.

'Why not?' Meg asked her. 'Of course you can.'

'I can't. You know I can't. They don't like me.'

Meg sank her head into her shoulders. The last thing she needed was to have to support Frances through another of her occasional bouts of paranoia.

'Of course they like you.' Meg forced her voice to sound friendly.

'They like *you*,' Frances said flatly. 'They won't like me going on my own without you.'

'Well, don't go then!' Meg said edgily.

'Are you saying I'm right?' Frances asked her, her tone particularly high and thin. 'Are you saying they don't like me?'

'You said it, not me,' Meg replied. 'I don't think it at all. But in any case I'm not going today.'

'There's no need to shout at me,' Frances said, even though Megan was sure she had not shouted.

'I'm just so tired and . . .' Meg had wanted to say sad, but she stopped herself. Frances would want to know why she was sad and she couldn't tell Robert's sister the truth. She'd have to make something up on the spot, and whatever it was it wouldn't be a good enough to convince Frances that sadness was justified.

Frances was not the kind of person to give sympathy for any minor ills or worries. You needed to have had a leg drop off on the same day your house burnt down for Frances to think you had anything to moan about. A few weeks ago Meg had dared to express sadness about breaking an old and treasured vase that had belonged to her grandmother.

'Well, at least you haven't been killed in a tsunami,' Frances had admonished her. And she was right of course, in the scheme of things an old vase with purely sentimental value was nothing at all. But even so Meg felt she should be allowed to feel a little bit sorry for herself now and again – especially now.

'OK, we won't go,' Frances said, setting Henry on the floor and beginning to unzip him. 'I'll stay and here and help you get this place straight.

'No!' Meg said with much more force than she intended.

Frances froze and looked up at Meg.

'No?' she asked, perplexed.

'Just go to the group, go to Baby Aerobics and have a good time, *please*,' Meg said, knowing she sounded quite rude and feeling both appalled at and proud of herself at the same time.

'Fine,' Frances said, zipping Henry smartly up again. 'Fine, I will go. I know when I'm not wanted.'

'Frances . . .' Meg called out without much enthusiasm as Frances flounced out of the nursery and stalked down the stairs.

'It's just that I don't feel well . . .' Meg tried again, but the front door had slammed shut even before she reached the end of the sentence.

'Mummy?' James's tear-stained face appeared in the doorway. His lip trembling, he approached her, holding out something very small that glinted amber in the light. It was one of Teddy's eyes.

'Teddy's gone!' he wailed, tipping backwards and hitting the carpet with a painful thud. 'Gripper's killed Teddy!'

Meg looked at her little boy lying on the floor, rigid with grief and bawling his eyes out. And she had to resist – with every ounce of her strength – the urge to lie down next to him and do the very same thing.

Chapter Nine

Natalie had expected Steve and Jill's place to look more or less exactly like Meg's, a huge sprawling Victorian mansion, only probably tidier and decorated in more of a contemporary style. She was almost right, except that it was one of three apartments that the house had been converted to in the nineties.

Whereas Meg's house was all quirky little rooms, pantries and parlours, Steve's place was open-plan, polished wood flooring and flat white walls. The main living space included a stainless steel state of the art kitchen at one end and Steve's draftsman's table at the other.

'Livework space,' Steve said, melding the two words into one as he showed Natalie in. 'That's what it's all about these days. Multi-purpose living.'

'Multi-purpose living!' Natalie replied. 'I'm impressed. It's hard enough to find any purpose to living at all when you've only had three hours' sleep and your jeans don't fit you any more.'

Natalie winked at Jess, who was sitting quite gingerly on the edge of a long orange sofa with such a low back and arms that to lean on it would be to take your life into your own hands.

'Look at you,' she said to Jess. 'You look great, not a bulge or a spare tyre to be seen. I want to be you.' Both Jess and

Natalie were surprised by how sincere she had sounded, Jess because she was convinced that she must be the least attractive adult here and Natalie because she had never wanted to be anyone but herself before in her entire existence. Even when her life was at its most difficult and unsatisfactory in her twenties, she had always rather liked being herself.

'You don't want to be me,' Jess exclaimed with a laugh. 'I'm a total neurotic. I had us all up in the night because I thought Jacob was wheezing. I made Lee take us to casualty! Two hours, we were waiting for. In the end the doctors said he was snoring.' She held up her thumb and forefinger. 'I felt about *this* big.'

Jess cringed as she thought back on the events of the previous night, which since daylight had arrived seemed like one of the tangled and backwards stress dreams that she was frequently prone to these days. Except it had really happened.

She had woken with a start and for a while she couldn't understand why. Jacob hadn't been crying and for once she didn't need to visit the bathroom. And then she heard this noise, a long, thin, rattling whistle that was coming from Jacob's cot. There was a beat of silence and then the sound came again.

'Lee!' Jess prodded her boyfriend sharply in his ribs with her elbow.

'What!' he moaned. ''Syour turn.'

'Lee!' Jess elbowed him again. 'Wake up.'

Reluctantly Lee sat up, rubbing the heels of his hands into his eyes.

'Listen,' Jess said intently. She was wide awake now and every muscle in her body was braced for disaster.

'Oh yeah,' Lee said groggily. 'He sounds like a dolphin.'

'He's *wheezing*,' Jess said anxiously, feeling her own chest tighten reflexively. 'Do you remember I told you I had asthma as a kid, it was pretty bad. I had to go to hospital once.' She gripped Lee's forearm. 'I think he's having an asthma attack.'

'He's snoring,' Lee said, flopping back down onto the bed.

'He's wheezing,' Jess said. 'I'm sure of it. Do you know how long a baby can go before getting brain damage if it's not getting enough oxygen?'

Lee sat up again, sighing heavily as he kissed goodbye to any slim chance he had of sleep that night.

'What do you want to do?' he asked Jess resignedly.

'We have to take him to A & E.' Jess was already out of bed with the light switched on as she pulled her jeans up over her pyjama bottoms and reached for a jumper to cover her top half. Blinking in the sudden glare, Lee followed suit, and roused by the shock of electric light Jacob began to cry.

The rest of the night was a blur of street lights and hospital smells and bad instant coffee. Jess had cried when the triage nurse had told her she would have to wait, because she was certain that her baby couldn't wait that long to be seen. With every passing second she imagined something worse that might have caused the noise. It hadn't helped when Lee innocently pointed out that now Jacob was awake he had stopped snoring and perhaps they could all go home?

'I expect you of all people to care about what happens to our son,' Jess admonished him tearfully.

'I do care,' Lee told her. 'I was trying to comfort you. I mean look at him. He looks OK.'

It was true, Jacob was now alert and sitting in his dad's lap. He was looking around him at the busy waiting room, his eyes bright with curiosity at all the strange sights and sounds.

'I don't want you to comfort me,' Jess told him crossly. 'I want you to worry too.'

And then as they had waited, the sleeping drunk who had been sitting opposite them had let out a long loud rattling snore and Jacob had laughed. It was his first genuine laugh and his little shoulders shook as a real chuckle gurgled up from his tummy.

'Did you see that?' Lee exclaimed with delight. 'He laughed! Our little kid laughed, do it again Jakey, go on, son!'

And sure enough as the inebriated man snored again Jacob laughed.

'He can't be that ill, can he?' Lee said as he grinned at Jess. 'Not if he's laughing?' And Jess had been unable to be worried for those few moments as she watched Jacob's face light up with laughter. She got the feeling that as long as he was smiling everything would be all right.

It was then that they had finally been called in to see the paediatrician. They were out again in less than fifteen minutes.

'Well, it's impossible to know for sure if he had a wheezy chest before, but I'd say probably not because it is clear now,' the doctor said after listening to Jacob for a few minutes. 'He hasn't got a cold or a fever, his oxygen levels are good. I don't think he's had an asthma attack. Sounds like he might have been snoring.'

'That's what I said,' Lee said triumphantly, belatedly realising that probably wasn't the best response when it came to staying in Jess's good books.

'Did you have the central heating on?' the doctor asked.

'Yes,' Jess said anxiously. 'But only a bit – I'm worried about it getting too hot or . . . too cold.' She trailed off, suddenly aware of how foolish she must seem. A typical over-anxious, first-time mother, wasting everybody's time.

'Central heating causes a lot of bunged-up noses,' the doctor told her with a weary smile. 'Which in turn causes snoring. You do have a family history of asthma so you should keep an eye on him, but I don't think you have anything to worry about this time.'

'I'm sorry to have bothered you,' Jess said meekly.

'Ah well, better to be safe than sorry,' the doctor replied, glancing sympathetically at Lee. 'And try not to worry so much.'

'The thing is, how are we supposed to know?' Natalie asked Jess after she had recounted her tale. 'How do we know what it sounds like when a baby snores? We don't. We have no precedent. I would have done the same thing.'

'You wouldn't have,' Jess said.

'Well, no I wouldn't,' Natalie admitted. 'But only because you are a proper mum who even thinks to worry about things like that. It never crosses my mind that anything is ever going to be wrong with Freddie. I sort of think he's indestructible.'

'It's official then,' Jess said with a weak smile. '*I* wish I were *you*.'

'I've got us snacks,' Steve said, gesturing at a table of what looked like seeds and possibly pulses. 'I know you like cake, Natalie, but Jill's got us on a special diet. It'll change in about two weeks. We'll only be eating carbs again, or bananas. Or oily fish. She's a big fan of diets, is Jill.'

'Couldn't you tell her that you don't want to go on the diet with her?' Natalie suggested.

'Well, I could,' Steve said with an affectionate smile. 'But she's a barrister. Very hard to argue with.'

When Frances arrived with Henry, Natalie was disappointed to see she did not have Meg, James and Iris in tow.

'Where's Meg?' Natalie asked Frances before greeting her, which a second after she had opened her mouth she realised was probably something of a faux pas, particularly where prickly Frances was concerned.

'Ill, apparently,' Frances said as if Meg was being terribly rude by being unwell.

'Oh dear.' Natalie glanced at Jess. 'I might go and see her later, do you want to . . .'

'She doesn't want visitors,' Frances said, her voice taut with incredulity. 'She told *me* to leave!'

'*Did* she?' Natalie was surprised. Telling someone to leave didn't sound like Meg at all. The woman was patience personified and she was always putting everyone before herself. 'She must be really ill then.'

'Do you think so?' Frances said, seeming to brighten up a little.

'Oh yeah,' Natalie reassured her. 'I mean, you're probably her closest friend. If she spoke like that to you she must be feeling *awful*.'

'Oh dear,' Frances said, her edges seeming to soften as she considered Natalie's comment. 'Poor Meg. She did look awful actually . . .'

'Green tea anyone?' Steve said, producing a Japanese tea set steaming with the aromatic brew.

Natalie wrinkled up her nose. 'Now, Steve,' she said. 'I think we all know a baby group wouldn't be a baby group without one of these.' She plonked the now ubiquitous Jamaican ginger cake on his perspex coffee table. 'And have you got any coffee? I don't mind instant.'

The aerobics class didn't go quite as well as Baby Music.

It was as if everyone was just a little bit off kilter, literally in Natalie's case as she fell over trying to do one of the exercises, landing hard on her back to save Freddie from getting squashed by her weight, a fall which shot an intense spasm of pain up her spine. Steve, she supposed, wasn't quite as relaxed as he was at Baby Music, because he was the only man and despite his best efforts not to care about it, he obviously did a little.

He had been waiting in his jogging bottoms and T-shirt as Natalie came out of the ladies' changing room. She and Freddie had been the first to emerge because she hadn't technically changed, she had just turned up pre-prepared in her loose jersey trousers and long-line T-shirt, not realising that other people were going to bring actual exercise wear to the class. She had expected it to be nothing more than a laugh, just like Baby Music, so when she found Steve clutching Lucy to his chest and trying to look anywhere rather than at the women leaving the previous aerobics class she was privately glad that someone else was as uncertain about this as she was.

'They are all going to think I'm a letch, aren't they?' Steve said under his breath, nodding at the other women who were waiting with their babies for the class to begin.

Natalie laughed. 'Don't be daft,' she said. 'All women think you are fabulous. They all fancy you because you are here with your baby. Ironically a man with his baby is perhaps one of the most attractive sights to a single or indeed married lady.'

'Really?' Steve looked alarmed, eyeing the gradually increasing group of ladies now with some trepidation. 'Jill would kill me if she thought anyone fancied me,' he said with charming anxiety.

'No she wouldn't,' Natalie reassured him. 'We like our men to be fancied. What we do not like is for them to fancy others. That is when you risk wandering into the realm of sudden and violent death.'

Steve laughed, his cheeks pinking up a little.

'Seriously though, Natalie,' he said. 'You're a gutsy kind of woman aren't you, quite like a bloke really?'

'Really?' Natalie said, glancing down at her capacious breasts in mock dismay. 'Is that how you see me?'

'No,' Steve said, now turning a lovely shade of cerise. 'What

I mean is that out of all the girls in the group you're the one who I get the impression has known the most men . . .'

'Oh I see,' Natalie said with theatrical haughtiness as she struggled not to laugh.

'*No*, I don't mean like that,' Steve hurried on, his complexion now more of a deep fuchsia. 'I meant to say that you are a woman of the world, so if you were a bloke what would you think of me? Would you think I was weak for being at home with Lucy, would you think I was failing as a man?'

Natalie attempted to consider the muddled question as she looked at Steve, who now most resembled an overripe strawberry being flambéed.

'I think,' she said after a moment, 'that you are stronger than most regular men. After all, here you are in the middle of a lot of ladies in Lycra, with your baby girl in your arms because you want to give her the best babyhood you possibly can, regardless of stereotypes and what is expected. That takes real guts.'

Steve smiled, his colour calming. 'Would your Gary ever do anything like this?' he asked her.

'Well, he couldn't,' Natalie told him with conviction. 'But only because he's busy building very complicated structures practically with his bare hands and brute strength alone.' She paused and then added before she knew what she was saying, 'But seriously, Steve, I'd give anything to have Freddie's dad with me. Anything.'

It was the unexpected sting of tears behind her eyes that made Natalie suddenly have to turn away from Steve and the other members of the baby group as they finally emerged ready for action from the changing room.

Ever the gentleman, Steve, probably assuming that she was missing her husband, stood between her and the others while she took a second to compose herself. Natalie hugged a wriggly Freddie a little closer to her chest and took a deep steadying breath. Why was it, when she had spent so long rigorously making herself get used to the idea of bringing up Freddie on her own, that every now and then a feeling like that one would overtake her and practically drown her in longing? It had to be because she now knew that Jack was back in London. He was close, really close, but still almost impossibly out of reach.

And so Natalie hadn't been able to enter into the class with quite as much gusto as she wanted to, still shaking off that feeling of loss for something she had never actually possessed.

And as for the others, well, Tiffany looked pale and drawn as she performed the exercises with expertise and grace, her smooth oval face perfectly still, hiding all the fears and insecurities she must be feeling as one so young cut adrift from her parents. Jess looked tired and worn down with worry and a night in casualty. And as for Frances – Natalie thought that Frances was probably born slightly off kilter, never quite fitting in comfortably with anyone around her. Despite her pristine new gym wear which had probably been bought just for the occasion she looked utterly out of place.

As Natalie stepped from side to side without much enthusiasm she contemplated the other and much more pressing reason why she was feeling so jangled and off beam. Because in a bid to avoid telling Jack that she was bringing up his secret love child she had done the only thing she could think of that would mean Alice wouldn't totally kill her next time they spoke. She had told her mother instead, and now that she had she was torn between an oddly comforting feeling of relief and sickening certainty that she was going to seriously regret her decision.

Most disconcertingly, it hadn't been as horrible as Natalie

had expected. She was prepared for smugness, hilarity, scorn and disgust from her mother. But surprisingly she had received none of these things. Instead when she delivered the news in a deliberately light-hearted, this-is-how-it-is-and-I-don't-care-what-you-think-so-there style there had been a long silence on the other end of the phone.

'I see,' Sandy said finally. 'So I'm a grandmother, am I?'

'Yes, at *last*,' Natalie said, rolling her eyes and sighing like a teen as she slipped the pad with Jack's numbers on it under the base of the bedside lamp so she could not see it.

'And how are you coping?' her mum asked her. Natalie had not quite known how to answer the unexpected question. She was waiting and prepared for 'And who exactly is the father and what were you thinking, a woman of your age, having unprotected sex when you should know better?' But certainly not any kind of expression of concern, unless it came with some barbed backhanded insult.

'Um . . .' Natalie considered the question. 'Actually, really well. It's hardest at night with no one to take turns with, I suppose, and I'm exhausted. But I love him so much, Mum, he has changed my life completely and for the better.'

There was another pause.

'If you liked I could come and stay for a bit?' her mum asked her. 'Be someone to take turns with for a while?'

This time Natalie was stunned into silence. It was the fact that her mother had *asked* her that surprised her. She had been fully prepared to have to forcibly put Sandy off with all sorts of excuses once she found out about Freddie. But for her mother to actually ask her opinion about something was new; disconcerting and different. Natalie was surprised by a sudden pang in the pit of her stomach, and when she tried to work out what had caused it she realised it was a simple impulse she had never expected to feel again. She wanted her mum. It was such a jolting and strong sensation that she felt tears in her eyes.

'I would actually,' she said, almost incredulously.

'Fabulous, darling,' Sandy said happily, sounding suddenly much more like her old cocktail-lounge self. 'I'll be over on the first flight! I presume that I need to buy a ticket to London?'

'Yes of course,' Natalie said, already panicking about whether or not she had done the right thing. 'Where else would I be?'

'Well,' her mum said, with a voice as dry as the Gobi Desert, 'I *thought* you might be in China.'

When they left the sports centre Natalie had asked both Tiffany and Jess to accompany her to see how Meg was, but neither accepted. Tiffany said she had to be at a meeting with her teachers and her social worker to talk about what was going to happen with her exams, and Jess said she was desperate to at least try to get some sleep.

'That girl is unreal,' Jess said as they watched Tiff wheel Jordan off down the road. 'Look at how she copes and then look at me. I'm so pathetic. Snoring. I took my baby to *hospital* for snoring.'

'You are not pathetic,' Natalie said. 'You have problems and weaknesses like the rest of us, but at least you face up to your worries and deal with them. At least you don't hide from everything that's going on around you, hoping that somehow everything will work itself out without you having to actually do anything.'

Natalie heard the frustration in her voice as if she were listening to a stranger. Normally she made a point of never letting anything she did get to her because she always said that once a decision or action was taken you could never really

121

undo it, even if you tried. She made a point of facing up to the future that she had a created for herself, whether or not it was something she wanted. Only since Freddie – since Jack if she was honest – she had felt a little less brave.

It had to be the pregnancy hormones, she told herself. After all, they had been present from almost the very first moment she had spent with Jack. It was probably her elevated oestrogen levels that were responsible for how she thought she still might feel about the wretched man to this very day. It must be the hormones that made her teary at the thought of her mother, and now she came to think of it, it was probably because of them that she had told all her new friends she had a fake husband, a fake husband who was gradually taking on a Frankenstein's-monster-like life of his own.

It had to be some internal enemy that was altering her so drastically, because she couldn't allow herself to believe that this confusing maelstrom of emotions would be coming from the rational and sane part of her.

What had troubled her most since Alice had called her to tell her that Jack was back in town was that now instead of being just somewhere, he was *here* in this city, maybe only a couple of miles away from this very spot where she was standing. What Alice didn't understand, what none of her new friends would understand even if she felt able to tell them, was that it was because she wanted to see Jack so much, and wanted to share their son with him, that she was so terrified of seeing him, let alone telling him about Freddie. She could accept his rejection of her because she still hoped her naggingly persistent feelings for him would fade as her hormone levels returned to normal. But what if, as she half feared and half hoped, the very thought of being a father sent him packing to the other side of the world on the first available flight? Perhaps it would be better to tell Freddie that his father had died in a car crash than tell him his daddy didn't want to know him, after all, that was what Sandy had told her about her own father. It was the one lie her mother had told her that she had belatedly appreciated, and the one she had certainly wished she had never investigated. Natalie remembered briefly a wet and freezing February afternoon in Brighton nearly twenty years ago, and the man who had stood on his doorstep telling her in hushed but urgent tones to go away and leave him alone. At least when she had thought he was dead she could fantasise about how much he would have loved her, and how different their lives would have been if he had survived.

But she knew she could never set Freddie up for a meeting like that one, and when it came to it she didn't have any control over what might happen in the future except to try to make the right decisions now. And that would be a first for her.

Natalie looked at Jess's face, so honest and open that you could almost see every minute of her sleepless night illustrated on her exhausted features. Jess who wanted to be her, who thought she was so capable and together. Suddenly Natalie desperately wanted to be able to tell Jess everything about her life, the whole sordid truth. But as they stood in the chill and bluster of that March morning, Natalie realised she had no idea how she would begin to explain just what a mess she had made of everything.

Jess, Meg and the others thought better of her, they might even actually admire her a little bit. She didn't want that to change. She liked being the woman who was the friend of Jess and Meg. She liked that version of herself.

'What's up?' Jess asked her with a smile, cocking her head to one side. 'What awful problem are you hiding from now?'

Natalie laughed and shrugged.

'Oh, just that my mum's coming to stay,' she told Jess with mock heaviness. 'Today.'

Jess laughed. 'Is she *that* bad?' she asked.

'It depends,' Natalie said, reverting to that easy, apparently enviable version of herself who didn't have a real care in the world. 'If you don't mind having a cross between Joans Collins and Rivers as a parent, only minus all their maternal instincts then no – it's not a problem.' She grinned at Jess. 'I spoke to her last night and she sounded almost human, and before I knew it I'd asked her to stay in a moment of weakness. But I know exactly what will happen. She will waltz in, criticise me for getting myself in this situation in the first place and then try to sleep with Gary . . .'

'Gary's home?' Jess said, her eyes widening. 'She'd try to sleep with your *husband*?'

Natalie blinked at Jess for a second or two before her life story caught up with her.

'Oh no, Gary the electrician I meant. It's a very common name,' Natalie said quickly.

'Oh, how confusing,' Jess said. 'So what situation have you got yourself in?'

'Being . . . married . . . to a man . . . who . . . works in Dubai of course,' Natalie said, adding each word to the sentence as it occurred to her. She was fairly sure she had managed to pull the fib off and was trying hard not to think about the further complication she had somehow managed to create for herself in the blink of an eye.

'She can't be that unreasonable, can she?' Jess asked her. 'After all, you can't pick who you love based on their geographical location! And at least you are married. If you knew how much grief my mum gives me about *that* . . .'

Natalie thought about her mother, who was even now winging her way towards Heathrow. 'She *can* be that

124

unreasonable and worse still she's cunning. It's like playing a game of chess with a malicious fox.'

Jess laughed out loud. 'You are funny, Natalie,' she said. 'If she's *that* bad then why on earth did you ask her?'

Natalie looked sideways at Jess. There weren't enough words left in the English language to fully answer that question.

'Well, she is my mother after all,' she said instead with a shrug. 'And in some cultures that's considered to be quite an important thing. Plus she volunteered to get up in the night with Freddie now and then, and I'd give Dracula B & B if it meant I got a good night's sleep again.'

When Meg opened the door she looked terrible. But it wasn't an ill terrible. It was obvious to Natalie that she had been crying.

'What's happened?' Natalie asked her, pushing Freddie's buggy into the hall and then putting her arms around Meg.

'It's all f . . . f . . . falling apart,' Meg managed to tell Natalie. 'It's all . . . all . . . *ruined*!'

A little while later Natalie and a much calmer Meg sat at the kitchen table while James choo-chooed a train around their legs and the babies slept top to tail in Iris's cot.

'That was a pretty harsh thing to say,' Natalie said, when Meg had finished telling her what had happened, keeping her voice expertly neutral so that her son would only hear the tone and not tune into the words.

Natalie didn't like the sound of what Meg had told her one bit. She didn't have direct experience of the end of a serious relationship herself, but she had been there when Alice's marriage to her ex-husband Frank had begun to disintegrate soon after they had launched Mystery is Power. And it was during Alice's divorce that Natalie had realised something that might be worryingly pertinent now. All couples fight, shout and scream and say hurtful things to each other in anger. But they only ever seem to say the really violently cruel things, to vocalise their deepest and darkest resentments that they have been harbouring for years, when one of them is about to leave.

Natalie was certain, however, that Meg didn't want to hear that particular theory just now and after all, she didn't know Robert at all. She had never seen Meg with her husband. She might be completely wrong, and she sincerely hoped that she was.

'But everything he said is true,' Meg said bleakly, pinching her temple for a second as she gathered her thoughts. 'I mean, look at me. I look old and fat and like a mum. I don't look like a desirable woman any more, I don't feel like one. I have to face it, I'm not the kind of woman men look at and want to have sex with – I wouldn't want to come home to me either.'

Natalie looked at Meg. She was tired. Her nose was red and swollen as were her eyes, and she was bundled in three or four layers of mismatched knitwear that probably made her look much bigger and far more shapeless than she a really was.

'Rubbish,' she said firmly. 'You are a sexpot! You've just gone a bit off the boil that's all. You are a very attractive woman. It's just that you insist on hiding somewhere underneath all those jumpers. Never mind quality time for you and Robert – how about some quality time for just you? When you feel good about yourself other people start to feel good about you.'

Natalie tried to ignore the fact that she was doling out the kind of advice that she could do with taking herself. She wasn't sure what was going on with Meg and Robert, but she *was* sure that if anything was fixable it was the way Meg looked, and more importantly the way she felt about how she looked. Natalie knew she could help her with this.

'What do you mean quality time for just me?' Meg asked her.

'I mean that you need to take some time to peel off all those cardies and get back in touch with your inner sexual being,' Natalie replied.

Meg looked worried.

'I reckon,' Natalie continued, 'that when Robert got in last night he was very tired and already in a filthy mood. He took it out on you, which sucks but it doesn't mean that he's spent today filing for divorce or that your whole life is over. I bet you when he gets in tonight he will be feeling really guilty and really sorry.'

'Do you think so?' Meg asked her. She looked so hopeful that for a moment Natalie wondered if she was on the right track; what if her plan wasn't enough to fix things? But she had to try to help her friend, and this was all she could come up with.

'I do think so,' Natalie replied without a hint of caution. 'And when he does I want you to capitalise on that guilt, maximise his bad feelings. Take the moral high ground. Be sweet and understanding and then demand that he makes a date with you for Saturday night. Make him promise to keep it free for you. I'm sure Frances will look after the kids.'

'Robert's very hard to demand things from . . .' Meg said uncertainly.

'It'll be fine!' Natalie said, dismissing the worry with a waft of her hand. 'And when he sees you tomorrow evening it won't be downtrodden dowdy old Meg that's waiting for him . . .'

'Dowdy?' Meg asked her.

Natalie patted her hand.

'Figure of speech – it will be glamorous, sex-kitten, hot-stuff Meg draped over this very table in the finest lingerie that money can buy, except in this case you'll be getting a freebie from me.'

'What?' Meg looked confused.

'I'm going to take you into work tomorrow and sort you out with some sexy knickers!'

'*Ohhh*,' Meg said, as the extent of Natalie's plan dawned on her. 'Oh. I don't know, Natalie. I'm not sure.'

'What do you mean you're not sure? Of course you're sure. We are talking about free shopping here!'

'But will it work?' Meg was disappointingly dubious.

'Of course it will work. Men are not complicated beings. There is no straight man alive on this planet or any other that doesn't go wild for a push-up corset and stockings. God only knows why, but they do, and what's more it will make you feel empowered.' A thought occurred to Natalie. 'In fact, while I'm at it I'll get Jess to come too – there's another girl who needs empowering.'

Natalie was enjoying her latest role as lifestyle guru, not that the irony wasn't lost on her, merely filed away in a mental drawer labelled 'Facts I don't want to face thank you very much'.

'Are you're really saying that silky pants can solve everything?' Meg asked her, the load of worry on her face lightened by the hint of a smile.

'I am,' Natalie told her triumphantly.

'There's just one more thing,' Meg added.

'What's that?'

'I won't have to wear a thong, will I?' Meg lowered her voice. 'I've had *terrible* trouble with haemorrhoids since Iris was born.'

Chapter Ten

With the arrival of her mother looming, Natalie found a long list of things to do after she left Meg's that would delay her having to go home and face up to that particular reality.

First of all she went to see Jess, woke her up to be precise, and asked her if she would like to come with her on her mission to cheer up Meg in the morning, not mentioning that it was also a mission to cheer up Jess too. Natalie had waited guiltily in Jess's baby-clothes-strewn living room while Jess had gone to wash her face and wake herself up.

'God, I'm sorry,' Natalie said when Jess finally returned. 'I can't believe how inconsiderate I am to barge in unannounced. You must think I'm a thoughtless cow. I *am* a thoughtless cow, clearly.'

'Don't be silly,' Jess said, pushing a pile of clothes off what was, it turned out, a stylish azure blue sofa and gesturing for Natalie to sit down. 'Sorry about the mess. Funny thing is that I am not an untidy person. The flat is quite small and normally I like it to be neat, but every now and then I have a sort of go-slow and it all piles up until I can't stand it any more and I have to tidy up in a frenzy.'

Natalie looked around the room; it was modern and light with full-length windows. It was a nice apartment, a proper first home for a young family. The kind of place that made

Natalie wonder how, and more importantly why, she'd acquired her big old place just for herself until Freddie came along. Yes, her house was quite grand now she had renovated it and she was very proud of it, but somehow this flat, this *home*, bought together by two hopeful people looking towards the future seemed far more appealing than her place just then.

'Oh, I don't care about mess,' she told Jess, shrugging off the sensation of jealousy. 'I'm far more interested in getting you to come out on an adventure with me and Meg!'

But like Meg, Jess had not been instantly enthusiastic about the project, which had surprised and disappointed Natalie. She couldn't believe that any red-blooded woman with a pulse would pass up a chance at free shopping, not to mention hot sex. But Jess had looked hesitant and non-committal.

'It will be fun!' Natalie said, feeling her attempt at rousing enthusiasm drop like a lead balloon. 'Remember fun?' she asked Jess.

Jess's smile was wistful.

'I want to come,' she said, her words elongated on a yawn. 'But what about Jacob?'

'What about Jacob's dad?' Natalie replied instantly. 'It's Saturday tomorrow. He'll be at home, won't he?'

'I haven't left him before,' Jess said.

'I haven't left Freddie before either, but we all need a bit of time away from them and any mothers that might be coming to stay. It's not wrong, you know, to have a break. And it will do Lee good to see exactly what you have to cope with on your own all day. Come on, Jess, you need a pick-me-up!'

'You're right,' Jess said, seeming to steel herself at the prospect. 'Of course you are right.'

Technically Jess's flat was on Natalie's way home, but she walked right past her own house and on into Stoke Newington without even a sideways glance.

It was almost dark by the time she headed into the bookshop on the high street, remembering the title of the book that Alice had told her she simply must read several months ago, and deciding that now was the very time to finally buy it. And for a moment on the way back she even considered taking Freddie for a twilight walk around the park, but then decided that no matter how much she wanted to delay going home and seeing her mother she was not prepared to brave muggers and druggies to do it. After all, she would have to go home sometime. Even if she booked her and Freddie into the Ritz for the night Sandy would still be there in the morning, waiting like some shadowy old blinged-up spider.

Natalie chided herself as she walked home; perhaps she was being too harsh on her mother. The woman she had spoken to last night had seemed different. Not too judgemental and even quite motherly at one point. Perhaps it was possible that in the months since Natalie had last seen Sandy she would have grown out the brassy gold highlights, toned down the tan and begun to realise that cleavage is much less alluring when your skin looks like an aged orange crocodile's. It was possible that Sandy might have realised that the years she'd spent dragging Natalie from town to town and school to school as if she were an inconvenient piece of luggage that got in the way of her social life, and telling anyone who cared to listen how hard it was being a young widow on her own, had been a terrible mistake. Perhaps Sandy was planning to try to rectify her failings as a mother before she died of lung cancer or skin cancer or liver failure, or all three. Just maybe, Natalie dared to hope as she put her key in the door of her house, the woman who was waiting for her might be wearing a twinset and letting the grey grow through her hair and chewing Nicorette gum.

After all, if there was a chance she could get Meg into a pair of camiknickers then anything was possible.

'Hello?' Natalie called out as she pushed the door open and eased the buggy over the front step. The hallway was quiet and empty except for Gary's tools which were neatly stacked just to the left of the door, his collection of dust sheets carefully folded beside them. It looked like he had finished early for the day, but then if he had why was his stuff still here waiting to be loaded onto the van?

'Hello?' Natalie went to the bottom of the stairs and looked up.

'We're up here, darling!' The sound of Sandy's voice echoed down the stairwell. 'Your *gorgeous* electrician is helping me with my luggage.'

Her hopes plummeting, Natalie scooped Freddie out of the buggy and hurried up the stairs to the peals of her mum's flirtatious laughter.

Poor Gary was standing by Natalie's bedroom door, the palm of his hand on the back of his neck, looking like a fly caught in a web, utterly powerless to flee.

'Sorry,' Natalie said, hurrying past him into the room. Sandy was laying her clothes out on the bed.

'You'll need to move some of the stuff out of this wardrobe,' she told her daughter without looking up. 'I'll never fit all my things in.'

Natalie looked at the size of her mum's suitcase with dumb horror. It was not an overnight bag.

'Mum, this is *my* bedroom,' she exclaimed, all too aware that she sounded like a petulant teen. 'You are going in the guest room.'

For the first time since she had arrived Sandy looked up at her daughter.

'There he is!' Sandy dropped an armful of clothes with a

132

clatter of coat hangers. 'There's my very firstborn grandson.' She rushed around the bed and before Natalie knew it she had Freddie in her arms.

'Oh look at him, isn't he handsome? He must take after his father – if only we could get a look at his father.'

'Mum!' Natalie hissed. 'Don't be so stupid.'

'I'll be off then,' Gary said, looking longingly down the stairs.

'No you won't, will he, Natalie?' Sandy's commanding tone stopped him in his tracks. 'You'll stay for dinner, won't you, Gary? Let me thank you for all your help. The cabbie wouldn't take euros, Natalie, and as my own daughter wasn't here to greet me I had to rely on the kindness of strangers to get me out of a fix. You owe Gary forty-eight pounds and seventy pence plus tip.'

'Oh God, I'm sorry.' Natalie looked apologetically at Gary. 'I'll get that for you right now.'

'No you won't because Gary isn't leaving now, Gary is staying for dinner,' Sandy insisted, flashing him a capped-tooth smile. 'I'm going to cook paella and bring a little Spanish sunshine into this gloomy old mausoleum my daughter insists on living in, Gary. And you absolutely have to stay because if you leave me alone with Natalie we shall fight and fall out before midnight. It's guaranteed, isn't it, dear?'

'Is it any wonder?' Natalie mumbled, glancing up at Gary. 'Mum, it's Friday night, Gary's probably got something on haven't you, Gary?' she said, surprising herself by the sudden hope that he hadn't. Anything, even sitting through her mother's attempts to cop off with him, would be better than being alone with her.

'Um.' It was obvious that Gary was trying to make up an excuse, but he delayed too long to sound convincing and eventually had to concede that he hadn't. 'Just telly and a takeaway,' he admitted.

'Then you'll stay won't you, Gary?' Sandy all but shouted. 'Dinner with two beautiful women over a quiet night in – there's no contest is there?

'Um,' Gary said again uncomfortably, clearly caught between the desire to be polite and the urge to run several hundred miles away. 'Well . . .'

'Good, that's settled then,' Sandy said, stitching Gary up with the flourish of an expert. 'It's so nice to have a man at a dinner table. It gives cooking real meaning, I always think.'

'Right.' Gary looked down the stairs at his neatly stacked tools. 'I'll just go and tidy up.' And he was gone.

It took Natalie quite some time to persuade her mother to move out of her bedroom and into the guest room. In actual fact she didn't bother to try to persuade her. As Sandy hung things up in her wardrobe Natalie took them out again and relocated them to the other room. Finally, Sandy realised what was happening and admitting defeat wheeled her gigantic suitcase across the hall.

As Natalie sat on a chair in the corner of the spare room with Freddie, watching but not listening to the constant stream of sound that came out of Sandy's mouth, she realised that she should have known that seeing her mother again was always going to be the same, devoid of all emotion or sentiment. But despite everything that Natalie had experienced in her relationship with her mother she felt disappointed, which in turn made her feel like an idiot for expecting anything about Sandy to be different. For some reason, after years of parting and then reacquainting herself with the woman, she still half expected a reunion with her mother to involve hugs or kisses, or at least some sign that the two of them were emotionally connected to each other in some way. Instead, Sandy was acting as if they had last seen each other only yesterday, and that the grandson she had only just found out existed was merely a pleasant diversion. Natalie had no idea who the kindly and concerned-sounding woman she had spoken to on the phone yesterday was, but it was not this woman, not her mother.

On the way down to the kitchen Natalie paused on the stairs and looked back at her mother. 'By the way, Gary thinks I'm married to Freddie's dad who works abroad,' she told her bluntly.

'If you say so,' Sandy said simply, and Natalie knew in this one respect she could trust Sandy. After all, her mum was a woman who built almost her entire life on a series of what Sandy called 'little white lies', from her real age to how much she had in the bank. Natalie knew that Sandy – the original mistress of disguising the truth – wouldn't blow her cover story or even bother to ask why she had one in the first place.

Why, Natalie found herself wondering as she lowered Freddie into his cot, had she invented a cover story in the first place? What exactly was wrong with the bare facts of her life? She was a woman on her own who'd had a brief affair that had resulted in a baby. She lived in the twenty-first century. Nobody really cared about her circumstances, so why did she feel this subterfuge was necessary? Natalie had a stack of reasons and excuses she could trot out blithely to anyone who asked, but the reality was that she was concealing a deeper truth. She had never been very sure, not even when she was a tiny girl, that the real her was good or interesting enough to be loved by anyone, certainly not her father and possibly even her mother. Maybe even especially her mother.

Dinner was amazingly pain-free.

Natalie's mother had been right. With Gary there they did not fight, principally because Sandy was far more interested in Gary than she was in her daughter. All Natalie had to do was to sit back and let her single allotted glass of wine numb her nerve endings while Sandy flirted with Gary. Or rather at him.

Occasionally Natalie considered rescuing the poor man from Sandy's barrage of compliments and innuendo. But it was a dog-eat-dog world and frankly she'd rather not focus her mother's attention back on her. Instead, Natalie used the time to try to collect herself. She felt as if she had been blown in a million different directions and couldn't quite remember where it was she had started out.

This gradually increasing sensation of slipping out of control of her own life had begun the minute that Alice had called her to tell her that Jack was back in town, Natalie decided. Until that moment she had been keeping a tight lid on top of all the unresolved issues and emotions she had concerning Jack, even in the face of Alice's relentless questioning. But it now seemed that Jack was back and there was a very real threat that she wouldn't be able to control what happened next. It was too much.

Natalie could cope with the electrics being ripped out, she almost enjoyed her long nights sitting up with Freddie. She welcomed her tentatively new relationship with the baby group members, and even her mother was manageable as long as she was preoccupied with Gary and half-cut. But the thought of seeing and speaking to Jack made her want to run away and hide in the airing cupboard. She was terrified of seeing him, almost as afraid as she was of not seeing him.

It wouldn't be so bad if she had any idea what he was really like or who he really was. Instead, all she knew about him seemed to be based on lies, on some kind of elaborate performance. He wasn't that sometimes shy, sometimes eccentric man determined to act on uncharacteristic impulse to spend time with Natalie. He couldn't be that man she had talked to more honestly about herself than she had ever done with *anyone*, let alone any man, before. Because if he was that man, then he wouldn't have disappeared without even bothering to call and apologise. The man she had such trouble forgetting didn't really exist. And yet it was that man that Natalie couldn't stop thinking about.

And what galled her the most was that she, a veritable expert in changing the person she was to fit all circumstances, had been fooled by someone playing exactly the same game whilst she – for once in her chameleon-like life – had been simply herself.

If only, Natalie wished, there was some way she could find out what Jack was really like before she had to tell him about his son. If she could just see him again, give herself a chance to let the scales fall from her eyes and examine his true identity, she was sure she would be able to manage her mixed feelings for him. The problem was that she knew, because all the evidence pointed that way, that he was no good, not for her and probably not for any of the many women he must approach on a regular basis, she *knew* that. But she didn't *feel* it yet, because her overriding memory of him was entirely different. It was a memory of a man she thought she could have fallen for, given the chance.

Natalie had barely spoken to her dinner guest when just before ten the baby monitor crackled into life and Freddie began to cry.

'He probably needs feeding,' she said as she pushed her chair out from the table. She was surprised to find that her one largish glass of wine had gone immediately to her head and somewhere in the general locations of her knees. For a moment the corners of the room dilated and then contracted back into right angles as she sat down again unsteadily.

'Bit of a dizzy spell,' she said to Gary and Sandy who were watching her.

'You stay put, love, get your sea legs back. He might just need a cuddle and a bit of a rock,' Sandy said, brandishing the cigarette she had been threatening to light for the last five minutes. 'Oh go on, darling, let Nana Sandy have a go.'

'Nana Sandy?' Natalie blinked. 'Good God.' She exchanged a smile with Gary, who seemed relieved that the glare of Sandy's attention was no longer focused on him. 'I suppose you can have a go, but just for the record if you take *that* thing,' she jabbed her fork at Sandy's cigarette, 'within five miles of my son you will be on the first flight back to Spain. No smoking ANYWHERE in my house, understood?'

To Natalie's surprise, having half expected her mother to choose nicotine over her grandson, Sandy placed the offending article regretfully on the table.

'I'll call you up if he won't go back down,' she said, turning the volume down on the monitor as she went out of the door. 'After all, this is why I'm here, darling, isn't it? To give you a break.'

'Break*down* more like,' Natalie mumbled as Sandy left the room.

'Your mother certainly is a force of nature,' Gary said with a small smile.

'Trust me, there is nothing natural about that woman,' Natalie told him bluntly.

'You two always like that with each other?' he asked her, lifting one eyebrow rather rakishly, Natalie thought. Gary was quite attractive after a glass of wine. Possibly even before it if you liked solidly built, capable-looking men who were a little shorter than average. It would certainly be hard to find a man who was more different from Jack. Whereas Jack was long-legged and lean, Gary was possibly only two or three inches taller than her, with broad shoulders and a muscular torso. He must be little bit vain, Natalie decided, otherwise he wouldn't wear his T-shirts quite so tight, but in Gary she found it quite a charming quality. Jack had a surprisingly fair complexion despite his dark hair and eyes, while Gary's skin was darker, a lightly tanned tone that contrasted well with his light grey eyes. As Natalie's wine swilled around her momentarily empty head she decided she liked the look of Gary. He could be the perfect antidote to almost thin, stringy Jack – a broad, well-muscled, uncomplicated antidote.

'I suppose we are,' she answered with a one-shouldered shrug. 'I haven't really seen her that much since I was old enough to be able to escape her. It was because of Tiffany that I rang her. She made me realise that there was a vague possibility that I didn't have the worst mother on the planet after all. Do you know how Tiff got on with the social worker today, by the way?'

'She's getting it all sorted, I think,' Gary said. 'But it's a lot for her to manage on her own. She says she's coping, but how can she be when she's just a kid herself? Actually, I was thinking that maybe you could keep an eye on her if she needs an older woman to talk to?'

Natalie was surprised and rather touched that Gary had thought to ask her to watch out for Tiffany, even if he did take the edge off with the 'older woman' comment.

'Of course I will,' she said. 'The alarming thing is that technically I am actually old enough to be her mother.'

'You don't look it,' Gary said quietly, instantly redeeming himself from his previous minor indiscretion. 'You look really great.'

Natalie couldn't help but beam at the compliment.

'Well, I think I'm doing quite well as long I remember not to turn into her.' She nodded at the silenced baby monitor.

'I quite like your mother in a way.' Gary, who had visibly

relaxed since Sandy had left the room, leaned back in the chair and stretched his arms over his head, not like the rather formal and shy man she was used to at all. 'She's very . . . ah . . . friendly,' he added, pulling one corner of his mouth down on the last word. Natalie laughed.

'Well, Gary, if I can promise you one thing about my mum it is that at some point before you finish working here she will ask you to have sex with her. That's a given. You are exactly her type: younger, broad, strong and good-looking . . .' Natalie trailed off as she realised her list of compliments had caused Gary's shyness to return.

Natalie was warming rather dangerously to Gary. She hadn't noticed any of those things about him before tonight – in fact, if anyone had asked what she thought about him she would have told them he was nice-looking, in that he looked 'nice'. Nothing more than that. But now as she looked at him she found herself imagining the weight and mass of him under her hands.

'The thing is,' Natalie continued, 'I don't think Mum sees her prey as younger. I worked out a few years ago that she somehow got mentally stuck at her peak, somewhere in her forties I think. And since then whenever she looks in the mirror she still sees that woman, not the wizened old crone she is in reality.'

'She looks all right for her age!' Gary said gallantly.

'Careful, Gary,' Natalie teased him. 'She'll lure you into her boudoir yet!'

The pair of them laughed and Natalie felt quite floaty and mellow. Quite confident and womanly again. She had almost forgotten the still-sore place where her stitches had been, and the fact she was still wearing her stretch, wide-legged trousers from the gym that did absolutely nothing to restrain her failing tummy muscles. In fact, she felt quite good about herself when

Gary Fisher smiled at her, and the spectre of Jack Newhouse that had haunted her all this time briefly diminished.

'It's nice that you stayed,' she told Gary, hearing the drop in the tone of her voice, feeling the flutter of her unmade-up lashes and sensing that she was perilously close to flirt mode. 'Thank you.'

Gary looked down at the table top.

'Thanks for having me,' he said, apparently enormously interested in his place mat. 'Besides, although I'm quite a good cook it's nice to be cooked for now and again. And it would have been a shame if you and your mum had fallen out on her first night here.'

'Oh, there's still time,' Natalie said, glancing at the clock and then back at Gary. The two of them looked at each other across the table, and Natalie thought she must really be drunk because she felt the irresistible desire to lean across the table and kiss her electrician – with tongues and everything.

'So when will you be finished?' she said instead, forcing herself to sit back in her chair and wondering if Gary had noticed her moment of desire for him.

'Another week and a half?' Gary hazarded a guess. 'Maybe even a bit sooner.'

'Oh really?' Natalie was surprised. 'That soon?'

'I'll miss coming here,' Gary told her, tipping his near empty wine glass around and around so that the remnants of the liquid inside circled the bottom of the glass.

'You will?' Natalie said smoothly, almost flirtatiously, finding herself on the edge of that now so familiar precipice, the one she always seemed to climb just before she flung herself into some new, needless complication.

'Yeah, I'll miss this lovely old house. I hardly ever get to work on places like this. It's really great that you've kept it as a house. If a developer had got his hands on it . . .'

And then all at once Natalie was free-falling again, plummeting downwards without any hope of reversing the action she was about to take, even though she knew in the seconds before she spoke that it was doomed to fail.

'But the real question is,' she said, hearing her soft purring voice as if it were an entity entirely detached from her brain, 'will you miss *me*?'

And then she leaned across the table, put her hand on the back of Gary's neck and tried to pull his head, his lips, towards hers.

Gary, eyes wide with fearful mortification, resisted, his neck and shoulders resolutely rigid with horror.

Two or perhaps three seconds of excruciatingly perfect embarrassment passed as Natalie gradually came to her senses and realised too late what it was that she had done. It seemed to take an age for her to remove her hands from Gary's person and sit back down in her chair.

For the first time in her adult life she was glad to see Sandy walking through the door.

'No, it's no good, he needs feeding,' her mother said, stopping short as she entered the room as if she could somehow smell the atmosphere.

Natalie blinked to clear her vision and saw the look of naked terror still frozen on poor Gary's face. She saw her mum trying very hard to stifle a giggle.

'Oh well, thanks for trying, Mum,' she said quickly, getting up from the table with a little stagger. 'I'll settle him.'

Gary stood up too.

'And I'd better be going. Thanks for dinner, Mrs . . .'

'Sandy, darling, and please – stay for coffee. I could use some company.'

Natalie was horrified to hear her mother use almost exactly the same tone with Gary as she just had. Sort of drunken and lecherous with a definite edge of needy desperation.

'Ah no, I really have to go and feed the . . . fish. I've got fish.' Natalie heard Gary mumble a succession of hurried and worried excuses as she left the heat of the kitchen and felt the cool sobering air of the hallway soothe her blazing cheeks.

'I can't believe that I've just made a pass at the help,' she said to Freddie as she lifted him out of his cot. 'I mean, he's not even my type really. I don't even fancy him and he certainly wouldn't fancy me at the moment. The Blob from the Fat Lagoon, that's what I am, little man.' She unhooked her nursing bra and put Freddie to her breast, desperately wishing that she could somehow undo the last few minutes of her life.

What *had* she been thinking? She had not been thinking clearly at all, that was the problem. The wine had temporarily magnified her unresolved feelings about Jack, and for a minute or two there she had wanted somebody, anybody who was not Jack, to want her. It couldn't have backfired worse. When she had touched him Gary had looked as if the thought of her advances had shrivelled his manhood entirely.

'Perhaps it wasn't as bad as I think,' Natalie muttered, settling back in the feeding chair. 'I mean, perhaps I didn't come off as a sleazy desperado, just as a friendly employer.' She remembered her hand on the back of Gary's neck and the mortified look on his face.

'Oh, who am I kidding,' she said to Freddie. 'It wasn't as bad as it looked. It was worse. It's my mother's fault. She's only been here five minutes and already she's turning me into her. She's a witch, Freddie. Your "Nana Sandy" is a witch.'

Natalie looked down at her son who had stopped suckling and was fast asleep, his tiny mouth a newly opened rosebud. 'This has got to stop. I'm not just me any more. It actually *does* matter now what sort of trouble I get myself into. I might not feel like a grown-up but I have to act like one.'

Natalie put the palm of her right hand over her heart. 'From now on I, Natalie Louise Curzon, absolutely promise you, Freddie . . . um . . . Mercury Curzon, here and now, that I will *not* turn into my mother and I *will* break free from the cycle. I *will* be the kind of mother you are not ashamed to have pick you up from school. I *will* buy a faux-fur gilet and a polo-neck top. I will *never* either have sex or attempt to have sex ever, ever again. And . . .' Natalie took a deep breath. 'I will deal with Jack Newhouse in a mature and rational way for your sake. I *will* be a good mother to you, Freddie Mercury Curzon, this I solemnly do swear. I absolutely *will* be the very best mother you can possibly have, considering you've got me.'

Natalie raised Freddie's forehead to her lips and kissed him gently, breathing in his scent as she did so and finding that small oasis of peace that was always present whenever she and Freddie were alone and relaxed like this.

'What I'll do is just go downstairs,' she told her son in a whisper as she laid him neatly back in the cot. 'And act as if nothing happened. Like that time I accidentally had sex with the silk salesman in the stockroom. Then we can both forget about it and everything will all be fine again.'

But just as Natalie was at the top of the stairs she heard the front door gently closing as Gary made his escape.

'He's gone,' Sandy said, appearing at the bottom of the stairs.

'I can see that,' Natalie said irritably.

'The thing is, darling,' her mother called up as Natalie turned on her heel, deciding that now was a good time for the oblivion of sleep, 'if you're going to have a fake husband it's probably not a good idea to try to get off with your real-life electrician. Do you see?'

Natalie would have happily slammed her bedroom door shut, except for the fear of waking Freddie.

Somehow a really quiet and careful push did not achieve nearly the same satisfaction.

Chapter Eleven

It had taken Natalie a long time to leave the house the next morning. It wasn't because she wasn't ready in time. Despite only getting to sleep just before three, she was up at seven again and in the shower shaving her legs, plucking her eyebrows and washing her hair with enjoyable thoroughness, knowing that there was somebody else in the house to see to Freddie should he wake early after his busy night. Natalie decided that today was going to be fun because it was the first day she had been out anywhere without Freddie since his birth, and as much as she loved him she knew she would relish her few hours of freedom. Indeed, she thought, as the first signs of spring seemed to take the edge of the cold, she felt like a butterfly escaping from its grungy cocoon and spreading its glorious wings in the sunlight.

Dressing had not been quite so freeing, though, and she had approached her wardrobe with considerable trepidation. After all, today was a Saturday shopping trip to town. Such an expedition was not to be undertaken in jogging bottoms or milk-stained sweatshirts. She had to wear proper clothes, clothes with seams not necessarily containing Lycra. But would any of her proper clothes still fit her? That was the question that had threatened to dent her determination to enjoy the shiny new day, that and the prospect of having to buy clothes one, possibly even two, sizes bigger than she was accustomed to.

It was possible, Natalie supposed, that her pre-baby figure had not been as magnificent as she remembered it, but even if she was looking back with rose-tinted spectacles she was still finding it hard to feel quite the same love for her physical self these days. No wonder poor Gary wanted to run a mile from her literally heavy-handed advances.

As the thought popped unbidden into her head, a wave of excruciating embarrassment passed over Natalie. Still, she had vowed to herself and to Freddie that she was going to put the incident behind her, move on and be a proper adult. And this time she was determined to do it.

She had been here before, well not exactly – she'd never made a freakish rebound-from-a-relationship-that-barely-even-happened pass at a handyman before – but she certainly had embarrassed herself now and then at wholly inappropriate moments. Like when two years ago at the funeral of a long and trusted warehouse employee she had (fraught with grief, she later argued) asked a slightly younger but extremely good-looking man back to her place for drinks and perhaps a little fooling around.

Yes, it *had* been embarrassing that the young man had turned out to be Bob's grandson, and yes, the whole of the warehouse staff were scandalised for several months, even if they all laughed about it now at Natalie's expense. She had accepted it with good grace, knowing her punishment for such a heinous crime was that she was doomed to be teased about the incident until the end of time itself or when Bob's grandson turned twenty-one – whichever came first.

That *surely* had to be worse than lunging at Gary. Except that unbelievably her motives weren't quite as honourable as they had been with Bob's grandson. Because it wasn't so much that she wanted Gary – or at least she didn't think it was – no, she was certain that it had a lot more to do with the fact that she wanted to forget the spectre of Jack Newhouse.

Natalie forced herself to remember her promise to Freddie again. She might want to forget Jack but she could not. She had to face him. Just not today. Today was going to be a fun day, she reminded herself, even if it killed her.

She opened her wardrobe doors and looked at the row of neatly hanging clothes from another lifetime and wondered which of them might possibly fit her. She was determined to pre-select exactly the right garment. She was resolute that she would not try on anything that she would have to take off again because she could not get it over her thighs. Subsequently it took her several minutes to select, perhaps optimistically, a pair of wide-legged trousers and a top that didn't have buttons with the potential to gape over her cleavage. She held her breath as she gingerly pulled on the trousers, and discovered after the brief celebration of doing them up that it was probably a good idea to try not to breathe out ever again. The stretch top was better; Natalie was pleased to see that her deepened cleavage actually looked quite fetching in it. A hip-covering long jacket followed and then she examined herself in her full-length mirror. On the highly unlikely off chance that she might meet the love of her life whilst out on her mission to save the sexual lives of Jess and Meg, she thought she would not scare him off completely. At least not with her clothes on, anyway, and as she had sworn to never ever take them off in front of a man again she didn't have to worry about that.

So she was feeling relatively good about herself by the time she found her mother in the kitchen.

It all went downhill from there.

As she walked in Sandy hung up the phone quickly without

bothering to say goodbye to the person on the other end of the line.

'Who was that, your dealer?' Natalie asked her, only mildly interested.

'Just a friend . . . from Spain who is watering my plants while I'm away,' Sandy said slowly, as if she were considering telling Natalie more.

'And?' Natalie asked her.

Sandy thought for a moment and then shook her head. 'And I've asked them to drop the crack off at the back door, is that all right with you?' she quipped with a sunny smile.

'Ha, ha,' Natalie said mirthlessly, and then a frown slotted between her eyebrows. 'You are joking aren't you, Mum?'

Sandy tipped her head on one side and examined her daughter. 'You look well,' she said as Natalie poured herself a coffee.

Natalie took a deep breath and counted from ten backwards and then forwards for good measure. But still she could not stop herself from asking the inevitable question, 'What do you mean, *well*?'

Sandy looked perplexed. 'I mean you look . . . well,' she said, gesturing with her unlit cigarette as she sipped her coffee. 'What else would I mean?'

'You couldn't just say "nice", could you.' Natalie felt her insides wind up a notch tighter with every word. 'Or even "good". You have to say something cruel.'

The rational part of Natalie's brain was telling her that she was being a little hypersensitive, not to mention a touch unreasonable but when it came to her mother Natalie seldom heard the rational part of her brain.

'I'm sorry, dear.' Sandy spoke gently, as if Natalie was still about six years old. 'I really don't see how "you look well" is cruel. I mean it's not as if I told you you look fat is it?'

'*Well thank you very much!*' Natalie bellowed at her mother.

'What have I done?' Sandy said guilelessly. 'And anyway, I thought you said your weight problem never bothered you,' she added.

Natalie sat down on a kitchen chair with a thump and began counting backwards from one hundred until she realised there was no number high enough to calm her fury.

'Right,' she said bitterly. 'That's it. I can't go now.'

Sandy looked deeply perplexed.

'What on earth do you mean?' she said. 'Honestly, Natalie, what kind of mother are you going to be if you can't take a joke – you are far too highly strung for your own good . . .'

'Joke!' Natalie spluttered in amazement. 'And anyway I am NOT highly strung.' She forced herself to keep her potentially hysterical tone in check. 'In any case I am not going out and leaving my infant son with you. It would be like leaving a bunny rabbit in a cage with a crocodile. I'm going to give Freddie the chances you didn't give me and one of those is the chance to grow up without being totally messed up by you!'

Sandy took a deep drag on her cigarette before remembering it wasn't lit and dropping it on the table.

'You are being ridiculous,' she told Natalie. 'And I know why – you are under a lot of pressure, love. Hasn't it occurred to you that I of all people might be able to understand what you are going through? We are a lot alike, you and I . . .'

'We are not alike,' Natalie said, her voice so low with barely restrained fury that Sandy did not register it.

'You're frustrated being stuck in here day after day!' Natalie's mother went on. 'Go out and have a break. After all, I brought you up, I'm sure I can manage a baby for a couple of hours.'

'Brought me up!' Natalie exclaimed. 'Well, yes, if you call checking me in and out of a record number of hotels, schools and caravan parks for fifteen years bringing me up – then I suppose you did!'

'Not this again.' Sandy sank back in her chair and dropped her head.

'I'm not having you do the same thing to Freddie as you did to me,' Natalie said, slamming her palms down so hard on the table that they stung for several seconds.

'I don't know what you think I did to you, Natalie,' Sandy said, leaning across the table. 'But I can tell you that what I *did* do was my very best. I was only a kid when your dad got me pregnant. A single mother back then didn't have a lot of options – not like today – but at least I kept you. At least I didn't put you up for adoption.'

'I wish you had,' Natalie said under her breath.

'Well . . .' Sandy bit her lip, and waved her hand across her face, unable to find anything to say. Natalie knew she had got under her mum's usually impenetrable defences and at once felt a mixture of triumph and guilt.

'Whatever you think of me as your mother,' Sandy managed to say after a while, 'you have to acknowledge that even I can't ruin a baby's life in the few hours you'll be out.'

Natalie stared at her until she felt the glare of her anger dull a little. Was it possible that her mum was actually trying to be nice? On this occasion perhaps had she jumped the gun just a fraction?

'I haven't left him before,' she said awkwardly, not sure how to climb down from her habitual attack mode.

'He will be fine,' Sandy reassured her on a deep breath. 'He was up so much of last night that I doubt he'll wake up before you get back but if he does, nappies and creams are on his change table, there's a bottle of milk in the fridge, to be warmed to room temperature, and I've got your mobile number.' She offered a conciliatory smile. 'And I'm not taking him out so the chances of me forgetting where I've left him are really small. It will be OK, Natalie. Please trust me. If you won't let me help you, then what's the point of me being here at all? I want to help, please let me do this for you.'

Natalie looked at her mother for a long time. In the morning light, without the benefit of her potions and make-up she looked old, almost frail. The dark roots at the base of her hair had begun to show through, and the shadows under her eyes looked deeply ingrained in the paper-thin skin. She had a smoker's mouth, circled with an aurora of tiny radiating lines, and jowls that had given up the fight against gravity long ago.

She was fading, Natalie suddenly realised with a shock. Her mother wasn't immortal after all.

She had hoped that the point of Sandy being here might be that the two of them would reach some understanding at last, find that connection a mother and daughter should surely have. But perhaps her mother was right. Perhaps Sandy's sole useful purpose could be to give her a few hours off here and there. Maybe expecting anything more was asking more of her than she was capable of giving. And then at least they would have *something* between them.

'You'll take care of him properly, won't you?' Natalie asked her mother seriously.

'Of course I will,' Sandy said. And for once, Natalie was surprised to find, she believed her.

It was clear to Natalie that Meg and Jess hadn't spent quite so long agonising over what to wear on their shopping trip as she had. Meg, because she was wearing what she always wore, a baggy old skirt and shapeless jumper, and Jess because in her jeans and jacket it was plain as day that she had shed any extra baby pounds she might have had quite quickly. Natalie tried hard not to feel jealous of Jess, concluding rather churlishly that it was only because Jess worried too much and didn't eat nearly enough cake.

'You managed to persuade Robert to spend a bit of quality time with the kids then?' Natalie asked Meg as they stood at the bus stop on Newington Green. She was scanning the horizon for a black cab on its way to the West End to begin a day's work, in the hope of being able to avoid travelling on a bus.

'Well, no actually, I didn't.' Meg grimaced. 'He said if I wanted him to be home by seven tonight then he had to go to the office for the morning.' She didn't mention that that morning's short and stilted conversation was more or less the only communication they had had since he had said . . . what he had said. Meg had found it absurdly nerve-wracking enough to pluck up the courage to ask her own husband if he might be able to keep Saturday evening free for them to spend together, but the fear he might repeat those cruel words to her had almost prevented her from approaching him at all. And then she made herself remember, she was his wife. They loved each other. What she needed to do was to remind him of that, and that would be impossible if she couldn't even *speak* to him. He had looked surprised when she asked him to be home by seven, telling him she had a special night planned for them. Some other expression had passed fleetingly over his shadowed features, one that Meg had been unable to read. But he had told her he would be back for dinner, he had promised.

So Meg was putting her faith wholly in Natalie's conviction that a pair of sheer camiknickers would sort the whole thing out, and was hoping for the very best. It was exactly how she was going to reveal her sexy new look to Robert that was worrying. She'd never been especially good at being seductive. Still, she'd cross that bridge when she came to it and pray that Natalie was right about those pants.

'Who's got the kids then?' Jess asked.

The bus stop was nearest to her flat and every few seconds she glanced up at her kitchen window and thought about going back. From the moment that Natalie had persuaded her to come out with her and Meg she had been looking forward to a few free hours, imagining that somehow they would be hours free of the constant gnawing fear she held so tightly in the pit of her stomach. But if anything that feeling had intensified from the moment she left Jacob in Lee's arms at the front door, both of them looking as if they hadn't got a care in the world. It was that that Jess found difficult to accept. In her mind's eye she could see the appropriate level of parental anxiety stretched out between her and Lee on a sliding scale of percentages. She thought that the right balance would be for both of them to worry about Jacob equally, fifty per cent each. But instead, Jess felt as if she were obliged to take on the worry almost a hundred per cent. It was bizarre to admit, but true, that if Lee could even just look like he wasn't coping quite so wonderfully then she would have instantly felt better. But he never did, instead he always looked so easy and natural with Jacob, and Jess was sure she never looked that way, because she rarely – if ever – felt it.

'The kids are with Frances,' Meg said. 'Poor little beggars. But the worst thing is I had to tell her this massive lie so that she wouldn't feel left out. You know what she's like.'

Natalie and Jess exchanged glances – they were starting to know.

'What was the lie?' Jess asked.

'I told her I had women's problems!' Meg said, partially covering her mouth with her hand like a naughty child. 'That I was seeing a private gynaecologist.'

'Well, it's halfway true,' Natalie said, spotting a black cab approaching from the other side of the green, and waving her arm frantically to catch the driver's attention. 'You do have women's problems. Woman's biggest problem, in fact – man.'

'Now,' Natalie told the others as they stood outside the Soho-based head office of Mystery is Power. 'We should be all right, there shouldn't be anyone in the office. My partner, Alice, has got this big thing about work-life balance. No one is allowed to get into work before nine or to stay after six, and especially not at weekends. So just in case anyone sees us, we're dropping by to pick up a . . . book I left in my desk drawer.'

'But why, if there was someone there it would be all right, wouldn't it?' Jess asked Natalie, looking sceptical. 'I mean, you are the boss, right?'

'Yes,' Natalie said. 'Yes I am. It's just that Alice is slightly more of a boss than me, and besides I promised not to come near the office until Freddie was six months old. Alice takes this work-life balance thing very seriously. She'd murder me if she caught me.'

The others looked a little bemused and not surprisingly, Natalie thought.

What they didn't know was that Alice blamed her divorce on the business. In recent months she had come to the conclusion that she would rather have the business than her husband, but still she knew that if she and Natalie had not been working twenty-hour days in the start-up period of Mystery is Power, she would probably still be married to Frank. She sometimes told Natalie that she was relieved it was just a business she had created and not a baby, because she was certain that Frank would have been as jealous and resentful of a child as he had been of her career. But whether or not the divorce had been the right thing in the end for Alice, she was determined that the business would not be responsible for anybody else's family problems. As a result she and Natalie made sure that all employees divided their home and work life equally, and Natalie had to admit that creativity and productivity seemed to be running at peak capacity because of that policy. One of the things that Alice was most strict about was maternity leave. She insisted that new mothers concentrate wholly on their child without having to worry about what was happening at work, safe in the knowledge that they would have a job to come back to. Natalie was no exception.

Alice would also want to know if she'd spoken to Jack, and might wonder where her imaginary husband had come from, Natalie thought, but she didn't share that with her blissfully ignorant friends.

'Goodness,' Meg said. Natalie and Jess looked at her. She was transfixed by the mannequin in the studio's display window who was posed on all fours, presenting her behind in one of Mystery is Power's more risqué numbers. 'Oh dear – I'm not entirely sure . . .' Meg began.

'Oh, don't be silly, I wasn't going to get you to try on anything like that,' Natalie lied. She slid her key into the front door of the office and turned it. 'Now, follow me, ladies,' she said. 'Your journey of awakening begins here.'

'Well, that's very nice,' Meg replied tartly as she followed Natalie. 'As long as it doesn't involve anything with tassels.'

'Come on, Meg, come out!' Natalie coaxed. 'It's only us girls here. Come and give us a twirl!'

Meg had been in the changing cubicle the fitting models used for a good five minutes longer than was necessary to put on something so skimpy.

'I'm really not sure,' Meg said dubiously.

'This has *got* to be the one,' Natalie told her through the curtain. 'I hand-picked this for you with my expert eye – I know it will make you look and feel like a sex bomb!'

'Well . . .' Meg said hesitantly. 'It certainly is better than that PVC number you tried to force me into, I think a layer of my skin came off with that one.'

'Yeah, sorry about that,' Natalie said cheerfully. 'I always think it's best to start with the totally outrageous and that way you might be brave enough to try something much more risqué than usual. You see, I knew that the red bra with the nipple holes I gave you to try wasn't really *you*.' She winked at Jess. 'But it pushed your envelope, so to speak, and actually, come to think of it, it could be very handy for breastfeeding. I'll have to get Alice to flag that up in the marketing material: the multifunctional nipple-hole bra – genius.'

'Please let us see, Meg?' Jess said. She was a little tipsy from the champagne that Natalie had managed to root out of Alice's office, and she was hopping up and down in a full-length, ivory, lace negligee set designed for brides on their wedding nights. It was a full-blown affair with yards of chiffon and handmade lace that made Jess look a little bit like a child playing at dressing up, particularly as when she had told Natalie and Meg that wearing it was probably the nearest she'd ever get to wearing an actual wedding dress, Natalie had fashioned her a veil out of some netting they used for window dressing and attached it to Jess's head with a blue-trimmed garter.

'If only Lee could see me now,' Jess had said as she looked in the mirror, her eyes bright with laughter. 'He'd run about two millions miles. God I look a sight!' But still, she had yet to take it off.

'Come on, Meg.' Natalie tried to catch a glimpse of the woman through the crack in the changing-room curtain. 'Reveal yourself to us. We are your friends. You can trust us. And just remember you are *wo*man, alluring enticing *wo*man full of mystery – and what is mystery?'

'Power!' Jess called out obligingly, her garter headdress slightly askew.

'Exactly, mystery *is* power but only if you reveal your hidden delights eventually otherwise it sort of loses its edge, what with all the waiting around. What *are* you doing in there?'

'I'm *thinking*,' Meg said. She looked at her reflection in the mirror, trying to work out if the expression on her face was more horror or amazement, because she was feeling both. It was as if someone had taken her head – the head of a careworn middle-aged mother of four – and stuck it on the body of a nineteenth-century Parisian prostitute, the kind that would be having a bath in a painting by Renoir. Her body, she thought in astonishment, actually looked pretty good: soft and voluptuous and potentially even quite inviting. That stunned her, but on the other hand she had never thought when she married Robert that the sensible-shoe-wearing, fresh-faced girl she was then would have to get up like a hooker only a few years later to try to attract the attention of her husband. That was the part that horrified her, the part she wasn't quite sure she could reconcile herself to. What if Robert took one look at her and thought she just looked like a sluttish piece of mutton dressed up like a tarty lamb? Or worse still, a fetid hunk of sheep carcass masquerading as mutton?

But then again he had said that the normal her, the everyday her wasn't the kind of wife he wanted to come home to. That was exactly what he had said, as clear as day. And when he'd said she wasn't the kind of wife he wanted to come home to, he hadn't been merely attacking her domestic skills. What he had meant to say, but had not been either brave or cruel enough to put into words, was that she was not the woman he wanted any more. There was not a single atom of her being that he still wanted to be near.

Meg stared hard at her reflection. So was this the sort of

wife he wished for, she wondered? Would this packed-in, pushed-up flesh be enough to make everything good again? It seemed impossible.

'Please come out,' Jess begged. Meg smiled at the sound of her. Jess might have been a little tipsy but even so she had looked truly happy and genuinely relaxed for the first time since Meg had known her, as she watched her trying on the pretty baby blue gingham matching set that Natalie had found for her and the rather more racy crimson number she would also be taking home. It was as if the underwear had brought her out of herself; maybe Natalie was right about pants holding the key to everything. That was until it was her turn and Natalie had handed her the PVC basque and the nipple-hole bra.

Natalie was right about one thing, though: after those two ensembles, this corset with a layer of black chiffon silk slicked over baby-pink satin seemed much more her style than she could have ever imagined.

Meg took a deep breath and opened the curtain.

'Wow,' Natalie said, and she didn't appear to be laughing. 'You are hot.'

'Is it really wow or is it desperately sad?' Meg asked her. Natalie drew back the curtain for Jess to see, and Meg had to resist the impulse to cower in the corner. She hated feeling so exposed.

'Flipping Nora!' Jess said. 'You look incredible. You've had four kids and you look like . . .'

'Like a ripe peach,' Natalie said thoughtfully.

'Or a rose in full bloom,' Jess added, her head tipped to one side.

'Bloody gorgeous,' a male voice said from the doorway.

All three women shrieked and the one in her pants raced back into the cubicle and dragged the curtain shut. Natalie turned round to find Gregory, their head designer, standing there, looking like Christmas had come early.

'I keep telling you we need models like that,' he said. 'Real, sexy women, and anyway what are you doing here?'

'Gregory!' Natalie yelped happily, momentarily forgetting poor Meg. She rushed over to kiss him, calling out over her shoulder, 'Don't worry, Meg, it's only Gregory and he sees half-naked women every day of the week. He's become immune to it, a bit like a doctor really, haven't you, Gregory?' She nodded enthusiastically at him.

'Yes,' Gregory said loudly as he disentangled himself from Natalie's embrace. 'You've seen one half-naked woman, you've seen them all.' Then, lowering his voice, he added, 'I think that's the woman I've been looking for all these years, can you get me her number?'

Natalie smiled indulgently at him.

'She is fabulous, isn't she?' she said. 'But that's not the point. That woman is married with four children.'

'Not necessarily a deal-breaker,' Gregory said, smiling at Jess. 'This one looks as if she's about to get married.'

'I'm Jess,' Jess told him, sticking out a lace-garnished wrist. 'I am not married. I live in sin.'

'Who doesn't?' Gregory said with a shrug. 'Any chance of some of that champagne?'

Eventually Meg re-emerged fully clothed, if a very bright shade of pink. She even managed to shake hands with Gregory although she could not look him in the eye, and he could not stop looking at her with that predatory fixation that had lured more than one model into his lair. Natalie considered telling him to lay off her friend, that Meg was far too good and decent for an old Lothario like him, but she decided not to. It was good for Meg to feel the full heat of another man's desire for her. It would remind her that she was actually very desirable.

'Let's open Alice's last bottle of champagne and celebrate,' Natalie said, already easing the cork from the bottle.

'Celebrate what?' Jess asked, holding out her glass.

'Womanhood, of course. And a night of unbridled, more or less married passion ahead of you two ladies, courtesy of Mystery is Power.'

'You are so sweet, Natalie,' Jess said. It was a compliment that wasn't often, if ever, aimed at Natalie. 'Here you are fixing us up – it must really make you miss your . . .'

'Anyway, why are you even here, Greg?' Natalie asked the designer, hoping Jess would see her interruption as a kind of 'I don't want to talk about it' reaction and leave the subject of absent husbands alone.

Greg smiled steadily at Meg.

'It must have been fate,' he said. 'That and because Alice wanted to meet me here and go over our winter collection before the big presentation on Monday. Believe it or not, we do miss you being around. It turns out you really do make a positive contribution to the company after all!'

'Oh ha, ha. Who says men can't be bitchy,' Natalie said and then she realised what Greg had said. 'Hold on, Alice told you to meet her . . .'

'Here,' Alice said, appearing in the doorway, her arms crossed.

'Now, Alice, I can explain . . .' Natalie began bracing herself for the full stay-away-from-work lecture.

'Don't be an idiot,' Alice said. 'I'm not cross, you dummy – it's great to see you and you've brought some friends!' She smiled unquestioningly at Jess, still in her bride's nightie, and shook Meg's hand.

'Actually I've seen you before,' Jess hiccuped as she took Alice's hand. 'I was on Natalie's ward when she had Freddie, my baby's about eight hours younger than him.'

161

'Oh, well, nice to meet you properly,' Alice replied. 'I haven't had a minute to visit Natalie while we've been getting the new collection ready, so it's good to know there are some sane people keeping an eye on her.' She smiled at Jess. 'Or insane, anyway.'

Alice embraced Natalie, and pulling back examined her friend's face. 'You look great,' she said. 'And you've lost a lot of that baby weight.'

'I knew there was a reason I loved you,' Natalie told her. 'Your comforting lies.'

'I'm just glad Natalie's got some friends to hang out with and keep her out of trouble,' Alice said with a laugh as she sipped from the glass of champagne that Natalie handed her. 'Otherwise she just keeps pestering me day after day to let her come back to work!'

'Yes, we were saying before,' Jess said, rather reluctantly removing her garter headdress. 'How hard it must be for her with her husband away. I don't know what I'd do without Lee, not that he is technically a husband . . .'

'Her husband away?' Alice repeated the phrase, as if she needed a moment to absorb its meaning.

'Oh well, I do miss him, yes of course I do, but not to worry!' Natalie said quickly, grinning fixedly at first Alice and then Greg. Greg would be a little slower to pick up on the lie, but he'd probably go with it because it wouldn't be entirely out of character for Natalie to have actually got secretly married in the last few of months. It was Alice she was worried about, moral, high-minded, straight-as-a-die, truth-telling-fanatic Alice.

Alice's smile was unreadable.

'And where is he working now?' she asked Natalie sharply. 'China?'

'Dubai actually,' Natalie said.

Alice raised her eyebrows and took a sip from her glass.

'Poor old you,' she said lightly. 'And poor old Freddie too. I'd bet he'd love to see his dad.' She tipped her head to one side so that her straight hair fell over one shoulder. 'Can I have a quick word with you in the office, Natalie? About the collection?'

Natalie followed Alice into her office. She winced when Alice firmly shut the door behind her.

'Guess what,' Natalie put in quickly before Alice could speak. 'My mum came to stay! I phoned her and invited her over like you told me to. She's been here since yesterday and we've hardly fought at all! Well, not while we're in separate rooms or asleep.'

'Really?' But Alice was only momentarily distracted. 'And have you spoken to Jack?' she said, sitting on the edge of her desk and crossing her arms. 'What about Jack?'

Natalie chewed the inside of her mouth. 'What about Jack? Well, I was about to call him when you'll never believe what happened . . .'

'Natalie,' Alice interrupted her. 'Come on, this is me you're talking to. Just exactly how did you go from deciding to tell Jack he is the father of your baby to inventing a fake husband?'

'Did I mention my mum is staying?' Natalie said wanly.

'Natalie!' Alice's voice was full of frustration. 'You know that I love you, don't you?'

Natalie nodded. 'I love you too,' she replied.

'And since you've been on leave I've realised exactly how much stuff you do around here, stuff I didn't really appreciate before.'

Natalie brightened a little. 'Really?' she asked.

'Yes! Knowing all those journalists, and buyers, and writing all the presentations. It's been hard work to keep up your standards, which by the way is meant purely as a compliment and not as an invitation to come back to work yet.'

'Thanks!' Natalie said. 'But if you're complimenting me why does it still sound like you're cross?'

'I'm not cross,' Alice said crossly. 'I'm worried about you! What I'm trying to say is that you are a good, kind, generous person, not to mention my best friend. And you are obviously a clever person, otherwise you wouldn't have helped make this business work so well. But yet you still seem to think and act like a half-brain-dead teenager who's got pissed on a bottle of Thunderbird! What's all this about a husband, and what about Jack?'

'The husband thing was sort of a random comment,' Natalie explained. 'The electrician asked to speak to him and I don't know, I sort of flapped and before I knew it I said he couldn't because my husband worked abroad. And then I mentioned it to one person and another and it snowballed! It's too late to take it back now. Did I tell you I'm in a baby group? We meet once or twice a week to do activities. We did Baby Aerobics yesterday and every time I threw Freddie in the air he laughed his head off. Proper deep little chuckles. I swear he's got the laugh of a fifty-year-old man who smokes fifty a day and drinks whisky.'

Natalie was hoping to distract Alice with some baby talk, but it was a faint hope.

'It's not too late to take it back,' Alice said firmly. 'They seem like nice, *normal* women to me, even the one got up like a young Miss Havisham. And if you want nice normal friends then you'll have to try really hard to be a nice normal person too. Tell them what happened – your life will be much better, I promise you. Otherwise I know you. You'll end up hiring an actor to stand in for your imaginary husband.'

'Oh, I hadn't thought of that . . .' Natalie began, only half in jest.

'Nat!' Alice exclaimed. 'You need all the friends you can get

– when are you going to get it into your thick head that you are a good person, a great person in your own right? You don't need a fake husband for real people to like you.'

'I do *know* that,' Natalie said, feeling a little cornered. 'I didn't mean this to happen.'

'Well, sort it,' Alice pressed on. 'And what are you going to do about Jack?'

'Well, you must admit it is a hard thing to do,' Natalie said, all trace of humour gone from her voice as she remembered what she had to confront. 'He'll think I'm phoning for another wild, sex-fuelled fling and instead I'll be about to announce to him the birth of his son.' Natalie looked at her hands: her weeks-old nail varnish was chipped and her nails bitten down, her skin looked dry and neglected. 'And . . . well, things are good with Freddie. I love him so much, Alice. It's great being able to love another person that much and be fairly sure that he loves me back, even if it is just for the milk and the midnight chats. We get along really well together. Jack will spoil everything, I know he will!' Natalie was dismayed to hear the strength of her emotion thicken her voice.

Alice's face softened and she dropped her crossed arms to her sides. 'I'm sorry, Nat. I've been bossing you around, telling you what to do without thinking about how all this must make you feel. It must hurt you very much.'

'It doesn't hurt me.' Natalie reacted defensively. 'I'm not hurt. I'm worried.'

'You liked Jack,' Alice ventured. 'I know you said you weren't bothered when he didn't call you after Venice, and you said he wasn't important when you discovered you were pregnant. But I saw you, the way you acted, the way you looked when you got back after that weekend. It's a cliché, but you were glowing, Natalie, you looked so happy. You were different too, you were more you and not one of the many made-up versions of you you think you need to hide behind. When he didn't call, when he disappeared, I saw how much you were hurting. You can hide it from that lot out there, but not from me. You still feel something for him, don't you?'

Natalie hung her head and nodded slowly. 'It's hard not to really,' she said with a shrug.

Alice slid off the desk and put her hands on Natalie's shoulders.

'Darling,' Alice said affectionately. 'You have to get past this. All I want is you to be able to look in the mirror one morning and see the person that you really are, not the person you think you are.'

'Huh?' Natalie was confused.

'You think you are a devil-may-care, responsibility-shirking, part-time femme fatale who will constantly be entangled in some kind of complicated situation because you can't help but attract trouble,' Alice explained in a matter-of-fact tone.

'Hey, less of the part-time,' Natalie joked weakly. 'And anyway, I am well aware that all I am now is a full-time milk cow with my sex appeal stuck on repulse mode.' A brief image of Gary's fear-struck face darted across her memory.

'Now, that's not true,' Alice said. 'What you really are is a vibrant, clever and successful businesswoman, a great friend, a generous funny sweet person . . .'

'Vibrant?' Natalie interrupted. 'I don't like the sound of vibrant, it makes me sound like I've got bad taste . . . how about attractive, or handsome – even handsome is better than vibrant.'

'. . . who, as it turns out,' Alice continued, 'is a natural and happy mother. You are better than you think you are. You are so much *stronger* than you think you are. That's why you have to sort out all these distracting messes you're in; the affair you had with Jack is over – it's gone.'

'God, tell it like it is, Alice,' Natalie exclaimed.

'But,' Alice continued firmly, 'the son you had because of it is here to stay. You have focus on a real, straightforward life. Maybe then you'll start to be happy.'

'But I am happy!' Natalie protested, waggling her fingers by way of demonstration. 'Look at me, I'm virtually hysterical.'

'You could be happier than you know,' Alice said sagely.

The two women regarded each other for a long moment and then Natalie said, 'I love you, Alice, but sometimes you talk an awful lot of bollocks.'

Natalie was only half listening as Jess and Meg chatted away happily over a chicken Caesar salad and bowl of pasta. She was looking around the small Italian restaurant, gazing at the fishing nets that hung off the ceiling and the thickly Artexed walls and thinking about the first time she had come here. It was the day that she had met Jack Newhouse and he had brought her here for lunch.

She hadn't intended to bring her friends here. As they had wandered out of Soho and onto Oxford Street the three of them had been in high spirits and more than a little tipsy.

Natalie was glad that Alice now knew all her shameful secrets and, despite everything, she felt that sharing her fake husband with her oldest friend and confessor had eased the problem, as if just talking about it was the equivalent of actually doing something. So she decided to give herself the rest of the day off from thinking about him at all, at least intentionally. It was harder to reign in those unconscious thoughts that seemed to pop into her head unbidden at any moment, but she would try.

Jess had phoned home just as they were leaving Mystery is Power and looked relieved when Lee told her that Jacob was fine, lying on the floor on his play mat batting the mirrors on his baby gym. He told Jess to take her time and enjoy herself, but as she hung up the phone she looked uncertain.

'All OK there?' Meg asked her.

'Fine, absolutely fine,' Jess replied. 'Which is great. It's just . . . I suppose I'm jealous really. That Lee finds it all so easy.' She shrugged and shook her head. 'Stupid, I know.'

'Not stupid,' Natalie said. 'Not *especially* rational but not exactly stupid.'

'And . . .' Jess hesitated. 'Well, I've had a great time today, I really have, I've felt happy and relaxed. But sometimes I worry that if I'm not worrying, if I'm off duty, that's when something bad will happen.'

'Now that is stupid,' Natalie said mildly.

'And at least you know they are both fine,' Meg said. 'So let's make the most of this time, shall we?' Her smile was fleetingly obscured by a frown. 'Poor old Frances. Oh dear, I do feel terrible that I'm out having fun while she's got all my children, who are a handful at the best of times.'

Natalie put a sincere hand on her arm. 'If you feel terrible call her and get her down here, the kids as well,' she suggested mischievously.

'You're right,' Meg said. 'I don't feel *that* terrible.'

'Who fancies Topshop then?' Natalie asked her friends, shepherding them determinedly past Marks and Spencer.

'Topshop?' Jess asked uncertainly. 'I can't remember the last time I was in Topshop. I started to feel like I was a bit old for it.'

'Which is exactly why,' Natalie told her, 'we should shop there.'

Natalie loved expensive clothes. She was never happier than when handing over her credit card to pay for one tiny garment that could have bought an entire branch of New Look, but still she loved Topshop. Specifically Topshop, Oxford Street, London. She supposed it might be because she had grown up with it; it had always been there through her teens, her twenties and even now, as that big number that began with an 'f' and ended in a zero was looming just a few years away, she still got a buzz out of shopping there. It was true that she could no longer get away with a lemon yellow puffball miniskirt and that the shop staff all looked as if they needed babysitters but whenever she had time to spare she'd spend it in Topshop if she could, getting her eardrums blasted by the in-store music and searching for something, anything, to take home.

'Because,' Natalie explained to her friends as she rifled through the discount rack, 'while you shop at Topshop you are still technically a young woman. Our challenge now, ladies, is to find and purchase a garment that we would genuinely wear on a daily basis. Scarves, hats, earrings, and hosiery of any kind do not count. It must be a fashion item. And if we each succeed then we may claim our right to eternal youth for another season. Go forth and seek your Topshop treasure.'

How Meg managed to find what had to be the world's last remaining gypsy skirt on the discount rack Natalie would never know, but find it she did. Even though the elastic-waisted monstrosity was exactly like a dozen other skirts that Natalie had seen her friend in, she supposed it was a fashion item of a sort, it was something that Meg would regularly wear and it did come from Topshop, so technically she had completed the challenge. Jess breezed it by buying a short black denim miniskirt that she looked far too good in and Natalie scraped in with a dark red V-neck top that she hadn't realised, until the others pointed it out to her, was almost exactly like the one she was wearing.

'Doesn't matter,' Natalie said as she looked down at her chest and then into the bag. 'What matters is that it is a fashion item from Topshop. Ladies, it's official. We are all still hip with the kids.'

As they had wandered and talked, heading back towards Charing Cross Road, and as it had become clear that Jess and Meg were following Natalie's lead she had begun to get the strangest feeling in the pit of her stomach. The kind of feeling she usually only experienced when she was about to go on a first date or make an important sales presentation to prospective buyers. As they walked she had focused on the raw-edged sensation and tried to assess what might be causing it. Life was certainly pretty fraught at the moment, that was true, what with enforced lack of sleep compounded by her dear mother in residence, a faux-husband lie to remember at all times and the Jack Problem. That was it, of course. The Jack Problem.

Natalie had been so busy trying not to think and not to worry about what would happen when she finally saw Jack that she hadn't noticed where their aimless strolling was taking them. She had brought herself and her friends back to the restaurant that Jack loved, the place where they knew him by his first name and brought him complimentary desserts. A place where he could definitely be considered as a regular, the very definition of which meant that when he was in town he was often there. He might, she had suddenly realised, even be in there right now.

Perhaps it was *because* he was in there that her treacherous feet had brought her here. Perhaps she had been thinking so hard about not thinking about Jack that some primordial force within her had homed to where Jack would be waiting.

The thought had stopped Natalie in her tracks outside the Italian Kitchen. For a second before Meg had pushed open the door to the busy trattoria Natalie had had to pause to catch her breath, bracing herself against seeing him and having to take those first steps towards finding out exactly how this mess would resolve itself. She heard her blood pounding and felt her intestines contract as adrenaline surged through her system.

But of course Jack wasn't there.

The anticlimax left Natalie feeling utterly drained and secretly rather foolish. For a few brief seconds she had convinced herself that fate or her amazing psychic powers were going to take the dilemma out of her hands entirely, but of course she wasn't just going to bump into Jack; fate would not be that kind to her, of all people, and considering she had just bought a top almost identical to the one she was wearing she didn't imagine that her intuitive skills were all that finely honed, either.

So when the same waiter who served them last time, but who did not remember her at all, sat them down at a table near the kitchen she was so exhausted by the release of tension that she was only able to smile and listen as Jess and Meg talked. Neither woman was entirely relaxed either, Natalie realised, Jess always keeping one eye on her watch and Meg glancing down at her bag of underwear every few minutes with a look of quiet trepidation.

With a sense of almost peaceful detachment Natalie looked at the table in the window where she and Jack had had lunch and tried to go back to that moment, that seemingly incon-sequential moment that was only meant to be a fun diversion, and wondered what it was that had brought her here. At what point exactly had she made the decision that had altered her own existence so wonderfully and so completely? She tried to pin it down, but she couldn't. It might have been when she caught Jack looking at her on the Tube, or perhaps in the restaurant over lunch when she saw the light in his eyes as he talked about Italy. Technically it was probably when she idiotically decided to have sex with him without using a condom, but the romantic part of her didn't want it to just be about that. There was no one decisive moment, Natalie concluded. It was everything, every passing second of those few days.

It was almost as if she'd lived an emotional lifetime in that weekend. It would be a lie to say she regretted it, because it would mean she regretted Freddie and that certainly wasn't true. She rejoiced in him: it was as if his birth had reconnected her to the planet she was so often perilously close to drifting off again. Perhaps if she was able to look at what had happened in a purely philosophical light Natalie would see that Jack had given her this marvellous gift, the best possible gift. But she didn't feel especially philosophical about Jack. She felt a lot of things, but philosophical wasn't one of them.

'You're quiet, Natalie,' Meg said, interrupting her thoughts. 'You didn't get into trouble with Alice for giving us free stuff, did you?'

'Mmmm?' It took Natalie a second to register the question. 'Oh no!' she reassured her. 'Alice was fine about that. We just had to catch up on some business stuff. Alice is a sweetie really. She is sort of like the mum I never had. She's always telling me where I'm going wrong and what to do about it, and I'm always ignoring her and getting it wrong anyway. As opposed to my real mum who is always telling me where I went wrong before I do anything, and then getting drunk.'

'I don't think you get anything wrong,' Jess said, a touch wistfully. 'You look like you've got your life completely sorted to me!'

'Well, it is a trial being perfect, you know,' Natalie said, wondering what Jess would say if she knew exactly how

172

messed up Natalie's life was. Part of her almost wanted to confess then and there just to make Jess feel better about herself, but she didn't seem to have the energy. She emptied a second tube of sugar into her coffee.

'I'm just tired, I suppose. I frequently forget that the human body isn't meant to rush about on only four hours' sleep. Last night is catching up with me. Mum said she'd take turns at night but it turns out that I can't sleep when he's awake, so it's easier for me to be with him. I'm not complaining, at least I got to go out today with you two – it's been fun.'

'Is your mum's visit as bad as you expected?' Jess asked her with a wry smile.

Natalie shrugged. 'I honestly didn't think she would be any good at that night-time stuff when I asked her to come over. I didn't think she'd be good at anything grannyish. I really only did it because Tiffany made me realise that even my mother is better than some people's. I mean she nearly gave me an aneurism on the way out this morning, but still I feel surprisingly good about leaving Freddie with her. Mostly because I've locked the vodka in the coal shed.'

Meg and Jess laughed and Natalie smiled, beginning to feel a little more like her old self again. Or at least the version of her new self that she was when she was around these women. She put her sudden drop in spirits down to tiredness and dear Alice banging on about doing the right thing. Yes, it was just the lack of sleep and the glass or two of champagne and being in this place that had her thrown her off kilter.

Alice had said she had to get a grip on reality, and Alice was more right than she knew. Because even Alice didn't know how much Natalie still thought about Jack, how much she still dreamt about him, both sleeping and waking. Soon he would have to be contacted and she would have to see him, possibly on a regular basis, for more or less the rest of her life, and before that happened she had to try really hard to fall out of love with him. The problem was, time was running out, and Natalie hadn't worked out exactly how she was going to do that, because if Jack going off and leaving her in the lurch with his love child didn't put her off him, it was going to take something a hell of a lot worse to do the trick.

Espadrilles, maybe. She never had been able to bear a man in espadrilles.

By the time they had paid the bill and were putting on their coats, Natalie had almost convinced herself that the very fact that she had not bumped into Jack in the restaurant *was* down to fate, after all. It was fate telling her that Alice was wrong and she was right not to have contacted Jack about Freddie, and that nothing would come of it except more complications and possible misery. Alice wanted her to have a less complicated life. Well, Jack not knowing about Freddie, at least until she had got this stupid crush over with, was far less complicated all round. Jack out of her life was much better for her than in it and that was a decision backed up by no one less than God.

However, Natalie was about to find out first hand that God really is extremely partial to moving in mysterious ways.

'We're bound to get a cab if we walk towards the British Museum,' she was saying, happily at one with the cosmos.

But then she walked out of the door of the Italian Kitchen and right into Jack Newhouse.

'I'm so sorry, I . . . . Natalie!' Jack took a step back as he recognised the woman he had collided with. 'God.'

Neither of them moved or spoke.

Natalie stared up at Jack standing right there in front of her, in all his Technicolor glory, blinked a couple of times and then seeing out of the corner of her eye an amber light approaching at speed yelled, 'Taxi!'

Chapter Twelve

Inevitably the cab sailed past Natalie and her friends, utterly oblivious to her plight.

'Oh,' Natalie said, rather sheepishly as she watched it go. 'Missed it.'

She made herself look at Jack in the most casual and off-hand way she could manage. If looking like a petrified rabbit caught in the headlights of an oncoming juggernaut qualified as nonchalant in this sort of situation, she succeeded.

'Jack!' she managed to say, dismayed to notice that he actually looked better than when she had last seen him, as if the past year had somehow roughed him up a bit in a good way. His smooth, light skin was now tanned, which made his dark eyes look even more intense, and his hair was much shorter, shaved almost right to his head. He was thinner, almost slight, and not at all the muscle-bound god that her electrician was, for example. But still, looking at him here in the flesh made her heart beat faster.

It took every ounce of precious energy she had left to haul her emotions under some semblance of control.

'Natalie, well . . .' Jack said her name again, and looked once in both directions as if searching for an emergency exit. He refocused on her reluctantly, and smiled stiffly. 'It's been a long time, how have you been?'

'Oh well, you know,' Natalie said. 'I'm busy. Very busy.'

Jack maintained his rather stiff smile as he looked at her, making her feel like some mildly amusing exhibit at the zoo. She could feel the almost molten interest of her friends at her shoulders, like red-hot laser beams boring into her back. She knew they were waiting to be introduced to this man, but she decided to ignore them. She was afraid of introducing him. She had absolutely no idea *how* to introduce him, especially not to those two. Perhaps something like, 'Meet Jack; an expert in meaningless one-night stands and begetter of love children extraordinaire!'

Jack's false smile dropped for a moment. 'You look really well,' he said. It didn't help that it was exactly what Natalie's mother had said to her that morning – that platitude that meant nothing.

'Do I?' Natalie attempted to sound unimpressed, but instead managed only incredulity. There was a breath of silence as the two looked at each other, both seemingly trying to navigate the least painful route out of the situation. For Natalie the choice of direction was easy. She realised that the longer she stood there staring at Jack Newhouse, the more chance there was of everything going terribly wrong. She wasn't ready for that particular conversation, especially not here and now and in front of Jess and Meg. The direction she most wanted to go in was the opposite one to Jack, and preferably at high speed. Still, she could not let this moment go. A happy coward she may have been once, but that was before she made her vow to Freddie, a vow that required a brave woman to keep it.

'Actually, Jack.' Natalie steeled herself. 'I'm glad I ran into you. I had heard you were back in town and I was going to call you and see if we could meet up for a drink or dinner maybe?' She was all too aware from the frankly appalled look on Jack's face that she sounded as if she were asking him out on a date.

'Well, of course that would be great but . . .' Jack took another step back from her, obviously struggling to tag an excuse onto the end of that 'but'. 'Well . . . I can see your friends are waiting for you so shall I call you?'

Natalie forced herself to persist. 'I don't suppose you still have my number, do you?' she asked him bluntly. He did not reply. 'So let's arrange it now, shall we?'

'Now.' Jack repeated the word with an edge of worry. 'Now, you say . . . Look, Natalie, I don't know if you're still upset about what happened or not, but I hope you'll believe me when I say that I am sorry.' Jack looked hopeful that his apology would get Natalie off his back and out of his life.

'Don't worry, Jack,' she reassured him. 'I'm not some vengeful bunny-boiler, I'm not even trying to pull you. I don't think of you in that way at all. I just thought it might be . . . useful to catch up.' It was a blatant lie, but one that made Natalie feel a little more comfortable in this acutely uncomfortable situation.

She realised she had to handle this carefully. If she was too demanding he'd run a mile from her. 'I just thought it might be nice?'

Jack looked at her thoughtfully as he considered her proposal. This was not what Natalie had expected, this period of pondering. She had expected either a quick no or a resigned yes. This apparent indecision was even more insulting than when he had seemed keen to run away from her.

'I've got somewhere to be right now,' he said, probably meaning a date. He glanced at his watch and then looked at Natalie again. He was genuinely unsure whether or not to meet her, she realised with horror. It was a difficult decision for him; what she couldn't understand, when she had told him outright she was not after him, was why.

Then quite suddenly he smiled at her, a deep, genuine smile that lit up his taut face and made Natalie's treacherous intestines back-flip with joy.

He took a step closer to her, and she could feel his hot breath on her cheek. For the briefest moment she closed her eyes and wondered how it was possible that any single human being could have this kind of effect on another, the kind of effect that Jack Newhouse was having on her right at that moment and without even touching her. She could sense the heat of his skin even beneath the two or three layers of clothing he was wearing. It was insane how much she just wanted to forget everything that had happened, grab him and hold his body next to hers. It was pure unadulterated madness, and if all it was was some chemical or biological reaction that her free will had no control over, it wasn't fair. It simply was not just.

'I do feel bad about the way we left things,' Jack said, his voice low. 'And believe me, it's not like the real me at all.'

Natalie looked up at him then; his dark eyes seemed honest and open, but she'd seen that look before. Little did he know that he had turned her world upside down, and still less did he know that she was about to do exactly the same thing to him. She just wished the thought of it gave her more satisfaction.

'Good, because actually, Jack,' she said, 'we do need to talk . . .'

'I'm staying at a friend's place while she's abroad,' Jack interrupted her. Natalie heard the 'she' and tried to look unmoved by it. At least he was not staying at her place while she was in the country, which was something. 'It's on Willoughby Street, opposite the British Museum. How about dinner tonight? Not here I suppose . . . somewhere in Soho? You probably already have plans.'

Well, Natalie thought, if he was trying to flatter her he was doing a good job, and she supposed she did sort of have a date.

With her baby. She toyed with the idea of saying she did have a date tonight and that they'd have to make it another time, but she didn't, for two reasons. First, she really wanted to see Jack again alone, whatever the circumstances, and secondly her promise to Freddie meant that playing games with Jack was not the way to go about it.

'No,' she said, praying her mother would be up for a bit more babysitting. 'I can make it – what time?'

'How about I book somewhere and you call for me at eight?' Jack asked her. 'Number two Willoughby Street. The top bell.'

Natalie nodded. 'OK.'

'Good, see you then,' he said, beginning to walk away.

'Jack!' Natalie stopped him in his tracks before he'd taken two steps. 'Jack, you will be there, won't you?'

Jack frowned and she knew the pleading tone of her question must confuse him, not to mention Meg and Jess. But still she had to ask it because if he wasn't there, if he stood her up, she didn't know if she'd have the strength or the will to try to face him again.

Unbelievably he paused once more before answering. 'I will,' he said, and then he turned his back on her and disappeared into the crowd of Saturday shoppers.

For quite some time Natalie just stood there and looked at the place where he had been.

'Who *was* that man?' Jess said. 'You're not really going to meet him on your own, are you? What about Gary?'

Natalie laughed, amused by the scandalised look on Jess's face. 'He was someone I spent a few days with just before I met Gary,' she said, mingling half-truths so easily that momentarily she quite forgot that there was no Gary, at least not one she was married to. 'It was a very intense affair. He fell instantly for me and he wants to see me again.'

'Are you sure about that?' Jess asked her, looking puzzled. 'No offence, Natalie, but he didn't seem *that* keen.'

'That's his way of hiding his keenness,' Natalie told her. 'Anyway, it doesn't matter because I'm only going to see him to tell him about Gary and to let him down gently.'

'Are you sure it's a good idea?' Meg asked her with some concern. 'Seeing an old flame while your husband is away?'

'It's fine,' Natalie said. 'I am completely in control of the situation. I'll tell him about Freddie the minute I get there, of course I will.'

'And Gary,' Jess said.

A preoccupied Natalie looked blank for a moment.

'Your husband, Natalie!' Meg said, laughing nervously.

'Oh yes, and Gary,' Natalie said a little vaguely. 'Of course I'll tell him about Gary too.'

Chapter Thirteen

Meg wasn't used to an empty house. When she went in even Gripper was absent, a sure sign that she was holed up somewhere chewing the head off something she shouldn't. Meg closed the heavy front door behind her and listened to the house as if she might be able to hear fragments of her own life echoing in the shadows. But everything was perfectly still.

'Gripper!' She called for the dog as she walked through the ground floor, flicking on every light switch she passed and turning on the TV for good measure, even though she had no intention of watching it. '*Gripper* – whatever you've got, drop it!'

She walked into the kitchen and switched on first the kettle and then the radio, intent on filling the quiet house with noise. As she sipped a much-needed cup of tea, Meg looked at the Mystery is Power bag that Natalie had given her, sitting on the kitchen table. It was gone three o'clock and Robert had promised to be back by seven. All the food was prepared and just needed to go in the oven, so she had a whole afternoon, if she wanted it, to pamper herself in readiness for the evening. She couldn't remember the last time she had properly got ready for a date, and for some reason the thought of doing it now made her feel foolish. It was the amount of effort it required, she realised. Farming out the children, prising herself into underwear she would never normally go near. Was it really necessary to go to those lengths just to have dinner with her husband? To try to smooth out some of the furrows that their relationship had turned up recently, shouldn't she just be able to talk to him without the need for all this effort? But then she remembered she had tried that and worse still she remembered, with a contracting knot of pain in her chest, what he had said to her.

Meg knew she just had to try, really try to get one thing right between her and Robert. She felt sure that if she could just do that then the rest would follow on, reconnecting them piece by piece, like pulling up a misaligned zipper. She had to show him how much she loved him and that she was still there for him, still the woman he had married and the wife he wanted to come home to. Somehow she had to make him see that, because if she didn't . . . Meg couldn't face the thought of what might happen then.

Jess closed the flat door behind her as quietly as possible. She could hear the murmur of the TV in the living room and sure enough Lee was on the sofa watching the football, his feet up on a stool and a cup of tea balanced precariously on the arm.

'Hey babe,' he said, keeping his voice low. 'How was it?'

'It was great,' Jess said, willing herself not to mention the position of the cup of tea or the number of times she had asked Lee not to balance drinks on the arms of the sofa. She was determined not to spoil her seduction technique with nagging.

'I brought home something to show you later,' she said. The soft tone of her voice made Lee look up at her.

'Oh yeah?' he said, a slow grin spreading across his face.

'Yeah,' Jess smiled as she walked round the sofa to kiss him. 'And I . . .'

It was at that moment she saw Jacob. He was fast asleep on the sofa, lying on his tummy, and from the angle that Jess saw him, his nose and mouth were obscured by the very edge of a cushion.

'Lee!' Jess reached across and knocked the offending cushion to the floor. Kneeling down by the side of the sofa she stared at her son, holding her own breath until she was sure she could see the steady rise and fall of his back. She glanced up at Lee, who was fixated on the TV screen again.

'I can't believe it – we've let in another goal! Bloody hell . . .' he moaned, sitting back in the sofa.

'Lee,' Jess said. 'You know you're not supposed to do that, don't you?' She was trying her best to rationalise the anger and fear she was feeling. She knew there was no harm done, Jacob was fine. And she knew that Lee had been sitting right next to him, but just the thought that he would do something so thoughtless and foolish, something he must know would upset her, chased any idea of seduction right out of her head.

'Lee! Did you hear me?' This time the tone of her voice made him look up for entirely different reasons. Huffing out a sigh of displeasure, Jess scooped Jacob off the sofa and into her arms. Immediately he began to grizzle and nuzzle at her chest in search of milk. On her way to the armchair she deftly turned off the TV with the toe of her boot.

'Oh *what?*' Lee exclaimed in dismay. Jess ignored him.

'You never, *ever* put a baby to sleep on his tummy,' she said, her voice taut. 'You never, *ever* put them to sleep on the edge of a sofa and you certainly NEVER, EVER let them do it with a cushion practically on their *head!*' Jess unhooked her maternity bra and put Jacob to her breast, trying to reconcile her rising frustration and fury with the relief of having Jacob suckling in her arms again. 'You know that, Lee,' she added.

Lee did not reply.

'Lee!'

He shrugged and stared at the blank TV screen as if he could somehow still determine the fixtures. This was one of the most difficult things about Lee. He hated confrontation but he was also rigidly stubborn and hated to back down, a combination which whenever they fell out resulted in him acting like a sulky teen and Jess berating him as if she were his mother.

'But I was right next to him, babe,' Lee eventually said. 'I hadn't left him. I wasn't going to leave him. You didn't have to worry, I was watching him!'

'You were watching the football!' Jess countered. 'A troop of naked strippers could have abseiled past the window and I bet you wouldn't have noticed them!'

'I bet I would have,' Lee said with a smile, trying his best to lighten the situation. He failed.

Jess looked down at Jacob. Her son looked impossibly fragile to her, so delicate and easy to break that sometimes she even found it difficult to put him down in his cot for fear of hurting him. She couldn't understand why Lee didn't see him in the same way, or why he was prepared to take even a calculated risk with his safety.

'It's just you *know* all that stuff,' Jess went on, the threat of tears thickening her voice. 'And you know what I've . . . what *we've* been through to get him, Lee. I just don't understand why you wouldn't look after him as carefully as you possibly could.'

Lee sat still for a moment longer and then got up from the sofa and crossed the room in one stride, kneeling at the foot of the chair and resting his arms on either side, encircling his small family.

'I'm so sorry,' he said, looking Jess in the eye. 'You're right – I didn't think. Or rather, I thought if I was next to him it would be OK. But it was wrong of me to do that, it was wrong for Jacob and it was wrong for you. It was great to see you come in looking happy with a smile on your face. I don't want you to think you can't leave him with me. I promise you that from now on I'll always put him on his back in his cot and do everything by the book, I swear. Do you believe me?'

Jess looked into his eyes. They were such steady and honest eyes. She knew that he wouldn't intentionally do anything that might upset her. He just didn't think sometimes. He just didn't see disaster lurking around every single corner the way she did. And that probably made him the normal one in the couple.

'I do believe you,' Jess said with a small smile. 'Unlike your promise to stop balancing mugs of tea on the arms of the sofa.' The two smiled at each other.

'I tell you what,' Lee said, his voice softening. 'I'll stop doing that if you show me what you brought home from the shops.'

Meg tied the cord of her dressing gown tightly around her waist and fed Gripper another piece of aromatic crispy duck. She looked at the kitchen clock. It was five past nine.

She had phoned Frances just after she got in to check on the children and see how they were doing. They were doing exactly what Frances told them to, of course, because that was the way Frances ran her house, with military precision. Even so, Meg could hear Alex and Hazel laughing at a game of Mousetrap they were playing with Craig, a game they were reluctant to be dragged away from to say hello to their mother. James, separated by Frances's stringent TV-viewing rules from his beloved *Thomas the Tank Engine* video after only half an hour, was building happily with Duplo, and Iris had had her bottle at the same time as Henry and now the pair were napping side by side.

'Are you sure you don't mind having them for the night?' Meg had asked her sister-in-law, because she felt she should. Frances, who was always more than ready to help her out in any way she could, somehow had the knack of simultaneously seeming just a touch resentful about being put upon even when volunteering her assistance freely. In this case Meg had actually asked her for what was really quite a big favour, and so the mixture of guilt and gratitude that she instinctively felt was required from her by Frances was a tricky one to gauge.

'If you think it's too much,' Meg went on, 'I could come and get them and put them to bed here and I'm sure Robert and I would have just as nice a time.' Meg half wanted Frances to say, 'Yes, please come and get them' because she missed her children in the same constant way that she did whenever they weren't in the same room with her. But love them as she might, even she knew there was little hope of any kind of romantic dining going on with all four in the house. At least two children at any given time would be demanding something from one of them.

'Nonsense,' Frances replied smartly. 'They are absolutely fine here. You shouldn't have asked us to have them if you weren't sure that we could look after them.'

Meg bit her lip,. It really was quite amazing how regularly she managed to unwittingly offend Frances.

'I just hope Iris doesn't keep you up all night,' she said wanly.

'Organisation, Megan,' Frances said. 'That is the secret, one you have never seemed to master.'

Meg had had dinner ready for exactly seven on the dot so that she could serve it the moment that Robert walked in the door. She really had thought he would be on time, because punctuality was one of his big things. He could not bear lateness; he often said people who were habitually late were basically telling you that your time, the precious moments of your life, was worthless.

But he was very late now. Meg was used to him coming home at all hours when he hadn't specifically agreed to be in at a certain time. But he had never done this before, not ever.

Just before seven she had put on her new dark green top that had been sitting in her drawer with the label still attached to it waiting for a special occasion, and the Topshop skirt with a pair of heeled boots. It seemed silly to put on boots when she wasn't going out; but she didn't think she looked fully dressed without them. She hadn't put on her underwear at that stage, because it seemed impossible to breathe out at all once you were in it. Instead she had planned to pop upstairs just before dessert and surprise Robert after the lemon sorbet, although she was not exactly sure how. She had hoped a couple of glasses of wine would have helped her wing it.

At a quarter to nine Meg had reluctantly tried his mobile number, reluctantly because she didn't want him to think that she was nagging him. It rang for a long time before his voicemail picked it up. She hesitated before leaving a stupid and clumsy message. 'It's me, Meg. It's nearly nine and I just wonder if . . . you are OK? Are you coming? Can you call? I hope you're OK.' Meg looked at the telephone for a long moment after she put the receiver down, half expecting him to ring back immediately. When he did not she decided she simply had to revise her plans. He was probably stuck in a traffic jam somewhere, with his phone completely flat.

Instead of allowing herself to get upset, or worse still give in to the impulse to cry, she would move directly to phase two of the evening. She went upstairs and put the underwear on, wishing she had a silky satin dressing gown, like the negligee in Natalie's collection, instead of the chunky towelling one she slipped on over the ensemble.

She waited, her whole body poised, leaning towards the moment she would hear Robert's key in the lock. But even as she waited she knew he wasn't coming, at least not for another twenty or so minutes. She knew this because Gripper seemed to always know exactly when Robert was going to come through the front door, no matter what time of the day or night it was. And at almost exactly twenty minutes or so before he appeared she would stop whatever she was doing and go and position herself by the front door, getting ready to greet the leader of the pack.

But Gripper was nowhere near the front door. She was asleep under the kitchen table, full of aromatic crispy duck.

Jacob had cried for about an hour after Jess had finished feeding him. She had put him on her shoulder and rubbed his back until she heard a bubble of air pop out of his mouth and felt a warm wet spurt of excess milk dribble down the back of her neck, inevitably missing the muslin cloth she placed on her shoulder. But still he cried.

She walked him unsuccessfully up and down the living room for a long time until Lee took over. Standing in front of the TV he swayed Jacob from side to side as if he was on the deck of a boat in a stormy sea, and for a while Jacob stopped crying, only to start up again the moment Lee stopped moving.

'Try singing,' Lee had suggested when he handed the baby back to Jess. Jess tried singing but it seemed to make Jacob cry even harder which made them both laugh, despite their frustration.

'Try stroking the bridge of his nose,' Jess said as she transferred Jacob into Lee's arms once more. 'I heard it makes them want to close their eyes while also soothing them.' As she watched Lee tenderly stroking her son's nose she thought of the contents of the Mystery is Power bag again. The bellows from Jacob's healthy and strong lungs reassured her, and the sight of Lee handling him so tenderly and carefully made her feel happy. For a few precious moments she felt an incredible kind of high and a sensation of peace simultaneously.

And suddenly the peace became literal as well as meta-phorical. Jacob was asleep.

'You've done it!' Jess whispered, putting her arm around Lee's waist and looking down at Jacob. She kissed Lee's shoulder.

'Let's put him in the cot and then I think it's time that you and I had a little lie-down ourselves.'

'Crikey,' Lee said happily.

By a quarter to ten Meg was beginning to realise why womankind gave up bones and stays in favour of Lycra at the first opportunity. While in the lamplight of the bedroom she secretly thought that she did look rather fetching, visualising what her soft white torso would look like underneath the corset made her wince, as she could picture long red welts mirroring the garment's construction printed into her ample flesh. Every few minutes she would go to the top of the stairs and peer down at the front door. Gripper still wasn't there.

Meg rather wished that she didn't have quite such a reliable indicator as to Robert's imminent arrival. It robbed her of the balm of hope and made the waiting seem all the more futile. After what seemed like an age divided between sitting on the edge of the bed and chewing her bottom lip while looking at her knees, and leaning over the edge of the banisters hoping to get a sight of Gripper, nose on paws by the door, Meg noticed that the digital alarm clock on Robert's side of the bed now read 23:04.

Even the resolute optimist in her had to admit that the evening had been ruined. He wasn't here, he hadn't come. He hadn't even called. But Meg still believed that it had to be due to circumstances that Robert couldn't control, because, she told herself, even if he were about to leave her, the man she had married would never be intentionally late. Even if he had planned all along to tell her over dinner there was no hope for their marriage, she was certain he would have been on time to deliver the bad news. She tried not to take his absence personally. She did her best to excuse his failure to call and let her know what was going on, and as she lay down on the bed and closed her eyes for a few minutes she told herself there was nothing to be gained by crying about something she wasn't sure had even happened yet.

But all the same there were tears on her pillow as she drifted off to sleep.

'Babe,' Lee said admiringly as Jess posed rather self-consciously in the door frame in her new underwear.

'What do you think?' she said, tilting her head to one side and cocking a come-hither eyebrow. She didn't have to ask. What he thought of her was highly visible as he waited on the bed.

'I think come here,' Lee said, kneeling up and holding out his arms to her. 'Right now.'

As Jess slid into his arms and felt the dry warmth of his palms sliding down her back and across her bottom she felt happy. More than happy, she realised, as she buried her face in Lee's neck. She felt like herself, like the woman he had met in that pub in Islington. She felt like his partner, his girlfriend and his lover again. She felt just like that woman she had once been; that woman who knew how to be happy.

Meg opened her eyes and realised that she was not dreaming. Robert really was there on the bed, kissing and nipping at the tops of her breasts with a hungry mouth.

'Robert?' She only managed one word before he covered her mouth with his, moaning in the back of his throat as his hands ran down the length of her body.

'God, Meg,' he whispered with urgency as she helped him struggle out his own clothes. And then she felt the weight of him, his skin next to hers; the bite of the corset digging into her flesh under the pressure of his body; the strength of his fingers gripping her thighs.

For a moment Meg felt sure she had to be dreaming, because this man who was intent on freeing her breasts from their constraints was not Robert. The passion and hunger she saw in his eyes were not like him at all; she felt as if she were being somehow wonderfully devoured and as she began to believe in his desire she felt herself ignite too, and rise to meet and mirror his excitement. Layer after layer of her daily life seemed to slip away: the erratic mother, the disorganised housewife, the woman who was always keen to please but never quite sure that she did enough.

For a few intense moments Meg felt utterly powerful, an omnipotent goddess holding the dreams of all men in the palm of her hand. She cried out, experiencing the shock of orgasm just moments before Robert climaxed himself and then collapsed, his face falling into her shoulder.

For several moments she listened to him breathing and then he rolled off her and drew her into his arms, pressing her back against his chest and kissing her hair.

'I love you,' she whispered happily.

But Robert was already asleep.

*

'It doesn't matter,' Jess said, stroking Lee's back with the palm of her hand. 'Honestly.'

'It does matter,' he said. He was sitting up in their bed, his forehead in his palms. 'It does bloody matter. I don't get it. I mean, I want to. I want you so much . . . it's never happened before.' He looked at Jess over one shoulder. 'You do know it's not you, don't you, Jess?'

'Of course I do,' Jess said. She wasn't sure how to react, whether or not she should seem really upset or try to shrug it off. 'Look, we're both shattered. And stressed and . . . just come here.' She put her arms around Lee's shoulders and pulled him back down onto the mattress. Once he was lying next to her she rearranged his arms so that she could fit in the crook of his shoulder, her cheek on his chest. She wasn't sure whether she should tell him that being in his arms like this was what she loved best of all.

'He's asleep and we're in bed. Just to be here with you is bliss,' she said.

Lee hugged Jess closer to him and kissed the top of her head.

'But I really wanted to . . .' he started again.

'Me too,' Jess said. 'I'd almost forgotten I had a sex drive.'

'You do know, don't you,' Lee said again, 'that it's not because I don't love you.'

'I do,' Jess repeated her response. 'I do know that you love me and I love you too.' She sat up a little and looked down at Lee. 'I really do love you.'

His smile was puzzled. 'You look like you've only just realised,' he said with an edge of uncertainty.

'No, that's not it. I've always known, it's just that in the last few weeks with all the worry and stress of having Jacob I'd sort of forgotten exactly how much. But even if we haven't quite . . .' She smiled at him. 'I feel better somehow anyway. Natalie must have been right about the power of a pair of sexy pants!'

Lee laughed. 'Damn, and I thought what you needed was the healing force of my penis.'

'Lee!' Jess laughed, punching him lightly in the ribs.

'It's good to see you laugh again,' Lee said, sliding a few inches down the bed so that his eyes were level with Jess's. 'Actually it's quite a turn-on.'

Unable to sleep, Meg eased herself out of Robert's arms and picked up his hastily discarded trousers that were lying crumpled on the floor. As she held them by one leg, a few loose coins and his mobile phone fell out of the pocket. She picked it up, realising that it couldn't have gone flat because the display had lit up as it hit the floor.

Meg looked at the screen. It was displaying a text message. He must have forgotten to close it after reading it. She saw the letters on the small screen for a split second before she actually read the words. Some intuitive part of her warned her just to put the phone face down and walk away right then, but it was a warning that came too late. She had read the text already before she realised what it meant.

I'll miss you tonight. Think of me when you are with her. Lx'

Quickly Meg closed the text and put the phone down on her dressing table. She looked back at the bed where Robert was sleeping soundly. She thought about that exciting, unfamiliar look in his eyes as he had made love to her and then she thought about that text.

'Think of me when you are with her.'

That was what it said.

Chapter Fourteen

Natalie arrived on Willoughby Street at seven forty-two, a full eighteen minutes early. She had tried very hard not to be early. She had, in fact, tried actively to be rather late. But despite her efforts, fate had conspired for her mother to be unusually compliant, not to mention sober, a taxi to be stopping right outside her house just as she opened the front door and the usual Saturday-night traffic nowhere to be seen.

Willoughby Street was a very short street. More of a dead end than a proper street, Natalie thought resentfully as she hovered on the corner. Willoughby Close, they should call it, or Avenue. It most certainly was not a street. A street would have offered a far greater opportunity for walking up and down, uncertain of your next move. Almost the only door on Willoughby Street, apart from the side entrance to a comic-book shop, was the main entrance to the flat where Jack was staying. A door just waiting for her to approach it, almost indecent in its obviousness.

Well, at the very least she could not be early, she decided, as she set off with a plan to take a brisk mind-clearing walk around the block. But her plan failed almost instantly as she found herself entering the Museum pub on the corner. She circumnavigated several tourists enjoying the authentic British pub experience and asked at the bar for a Virgin Mary.

'Sure you don't want the vodka in it?' an authentic Australian barman asked her with a jaunty smile.

'Oh, I want it,' Natalie said. 'I really, really want it but I can't have it. I'm breastfeeding and I try to keep my baby's alcohol intake down to three or four units a day.'

He didn't bother her again after that.

As she sipped her drink Natalie realised that she was utterly unprepared for this moment.

She also realised that there was never going to be any time, at any point in the future, when she would be prepared for it. It was unpreparable for, if such a word existed, which she was fairly sure it didn't. The thought, though, gave her a small sliver of comfort, a sense of friendly fatalism. What happened next was entirely out of her control. All she had to do was remember her promise to Freddie, not let her feelings cloud her judgement and make sure that she behaved with dignity and integrity.

It was the last part that she had worried about the most as she got ready earlier that evening.

Inevitably, Sandy asked her where she was going.

'Out,' Natalie said automatically. Sandy had been standing outside smoking several cigarettes in quick succession after an extended period without her nicotine hit. She had talked to Natalie between puffs through a five-centimetre gap in the French doors.

'I just thought that as you are asking me to look after your son for the whole day, the very least you can do is tell me why,' Sandy said, hugging herself as if chilled, even though it was a fairly mild evening.

'Why do you think that?' Natalie said, rooting through her make-up bag for her eyeliner. 'You came here to help me look after your grandson so I could have a break. I'm having a break.'

'Actually, that wasn't the only reason I came back. I have a life too, you know, in Spain. Things I'd like to talk to you about.'

'Look, Mum.' Natalie paused, sitting at the breakfast bar, her compact hovering in mid-air, her eyeliner pencil millimetres from her lids. 'I can't do this now. I'm really, really grateful that you've had Freddie for most of the day and I know I'll have to pay for it with emotional pain for the next ten years or so. But I have to go out tonight, it's important. Now please come in and stop smoking for five minutes. You're no good to me at all if you spontaneously combust.'

Sandy took one more deep drag of her cigarette before reluctantly stubbing it out with the toe of her slipper and coming in. She stood at the end of the breakfast bar watching her daughter carefully outline her eyes.

'You look lovely,' she said after a while.

Natalie nearly poked her eye out. 'Pardon?' she said, dropping the pencil, which rolled off the marble counter and clattered onto the floor.

'You do,' Sandy said. 'You look really lovely . . . are you meeting a man?'

Still stunned by the unprecedented compliment, Natalie was almost tempted to tell her mother everything. The urge to unburden to Sandy the truth about the momentous occasion that she was about to embark on was so great that she nearly couldn't resist it.

But this was still Sandy she was talking to. Still the woman who told a boy she once brought home from school that she had written that she loved him over a hundred times in her secret diary.

Just because at that moment she wasn't half-cut and spouting a load of rubbish, it didn't mean that she wouldn't revert to type at any moment. Her seemingly spontaneous compliment was probably just a cunning trap to try to lure Natalie into divulging information that could later be used against her. All Natalie had to do was to think of how her mother had behaved around Gary (while quietly editing out her own behaviour on that front) to remind herself what Sandy was really like. No, it was too dangerous to trust her with anything so important.

'Not a *man* man,' she said cagily. 'A business contact. Alice asked me to step in. She's got the collection to sort out for the show and it's just a one-off meeting. A business dinner, that's all. I won't be long. You will stay sober until I get in, won't you?'

Sandy sighed. 'Well, don't stay out too long,' she said. 'I can't promise anything after ten o'clock.'

Natalie tasted the thick and tangy tomato juice on the back of her tongue as she watched the clock behind the bar, waiting for what seemed like an aeon for it to be eight o'clock. At last the hour hand clicked into place and she knew that every second that passed now made it one more second that she was officially late. It was a small gesture of rebellion, but one that made her feel a little better nevertheless.

She stood. She straightened her shoulders, she lifted her chin and made her way to the place where Jack was staying.

'This is the moment,' she said as her finger hovered over the buzzer. 'This is it.'

Despite being prepared for not being prepared for any-thing, it turned out that what Natalie was least prepared for happened the minute that Jack opened the front door of the apartment.

He kissed her. And not just on the cheek.

He planted a kiss full on her lips. Not with tongues or anything overtly sexy, but a mouth-to-mouth kiss, after which

Natalie could have done with some mouth-to-mouth resuscitation.

'Hello, Natalie,' Jack said, as she tried her best to look nonchalant and unconcerned, as if attractive men threw smackers her way on an hourly basis. 'I'm here.'

'You are indeed,' she said, catching her breath. 'Sorry I'm late, traffic you know.'

'You're not late,' Jack said as he stepped out into the evening and closed the door behind him. 'You're right on time – what were you doing, waiting by the door watching the clock?' He laughed but Natalie didn't. And then Jack didn't.

'I booked Alistair Little,' he said as they left Willoughby Street. 'Is that OK?'

Natalie nodded and they paused on the pavement, caught in the difficulty of the moment. One thing was certainly clear. The instant easiness and spontaneous rapport that had once existed between them was now quite gone.

'Well, then, shall we?' Jack asked her.

They walked side by side on Great Russell Street, with that awkward gait of two people who did not know each other well enough yet to be able to walk comfortably down a street together. And it wasn't surprising, considering that for most of the time they had spent together prior to this moment they had been horizontal.

'Looks like the weather is improving,' Natalie said.

'Mmm,' Jack replied. Small talk too, it seemed, would take a little while to find its flow.

The evening was clear, but an earlier shower had left a mirrored slick on the streets and roads, reflecting the lights of the city as they walked, not quite in step. Natalie kept her head down, watching the toes of her boots as she went, trying hard to think of how she was going to say what needed to be said. She decided that there was almost no way to say it, or at least

198

only one way, which, though utterly obvious, seemed impossibly hard.

'I've missed London while I've been away,' Jack said suddenly, picking up her hand and tucking it through his arm as if he was determined to move their stilted reacquaintance on. 'I suppose loads of famous people, poets and writers and such have probably said it a million times better, but it's so full of life. Chock-full to the brim with millions of heartbeats. Of course, it's not as beautiful or as romantic as Venice, or as glamorous and slick as New York, but it has just as much style. It's got this collective spirit. It's . . . indomitable. Makes me feel glad to be alive.' He stopped for a second and looked down at Natalie. 'Glad to be here with you. It's good to see you, Natalie. It's good to be walking next to you down the street and I'm sorry if I've been a bit odd or awkward since we bumped into each other. It was just that I didn't expect to see you there, I wasn't prepared.'

He smiled at her and Natalie couldn't help but return his smile, even though she wished she knew what it was he had to be prepared for. His smile, she noticed, was not quite the same smile that had charmed her as she sat beneath a Venetian sunset all those months ago. His face was even leaner now, his eyes less uncertain and more intense. It was as if he had lived through many experiences in the twelve or so months that had passed since she had seen him last. She would have been glad if this new, unknown experience that was etched on his face hadn't suited him, but unfortunately it did. Never storybook handsome, Jack somehow looked stronger, more comfortable within himself – despite the tiredness in his eyes. He looked stunning; not a word that Natalie normally applied to men but the only one she could think of when it came to Jack Newhouse. Stunning.

So as Jack opened the door of the restaurant for her she

prayed to any passing god who might be listening, any guardian angel with nothing much to do in the vicinity, and just to be on the safe side the cosmos in general, to please, please help her deal with her attraction to this man. Because it seemed likely that only divine intervention was going to stop her from doing something she would undoubtedly live to regret.

Natalie wiped a tear from under her eye.

She could not stop laughing.

'It's not funny!' Jack protested, although he was laughing too. 'So there I was sitting next to this woman and she's saying, "And I hear that Jack Newhouse thinks he a dead cert for the job. Do you know him? I don't know who he thinks he is but he's not even been in work for the last year. He knows nothing about how the markets are now. I heard he's a totally arrogant prick. Have you heard that?"'

'Why didn't you tell her that she was *talking* to Jack Newhouse?' Natalie asked him.

'Well, because it was the interview waiting room and it started off being quite funny, and then just got more and more awkward as the conversation went on. I mean, after she had called me an arrogant prick I think the moment to come clean had passed, don't you?'

Natalie shook her head, her shoulders trembling with mirth.

'What happened?' she asked him.

'I was praying that she would get called in before me,' he said with a fatalistic shrug. 'But of course she didn't. The secretary comes out and it was just me and this woman sitting there and the secretary smiles at me and says, "Mr Newhouse, you can come through now."'

Natalie's eyes widened. 'What did you do?'

'Well, I sat still for a second or two, I mean, it sounds stupid now but I really didn't want to embarrass this woman. She seemed pretty nice other than the vicious insults she had hurled at my good name, and a lot of what she said about me was true except for the arrogant prick thing – besides, I think she found me rather attractive.'

Natalie rolled her eyes and sat back in her chair, eyebrows raised.

'I was being ironic,' Jack said. 'Anyway, "Mr Newhouse?" the secretary prompts me again and then it's too late to do anything. I see the realisation of who she has been talking to dawn on the poor woman's face.' He grimaced at the memory. 'So I got up and said. "Really nice to have met you."'

'And what did she say?' Natalie asked.

'If my memory serves me correctly and it should do because this was only last week, she said, "Oh shit."'

'Poor her!' Natalie said, knowing what it felt like to be mortified in public.

'Not that poor. It turns out she was right, my current knowledge of the markets is out of touch and besides they didn't feel I'd fit into the company ethos of work, work, work after my . . . well, anyway she got the job.'

'Oh good,' Natalie said without thinking.

'Good!' Jack exclaimed good-naturedly. 'Actually it *was* good. I'm going to work at a much smaller place now. Running investments for rich private clients, you know, only millionaires and royalty may apply. It's a really nice firm, all good people and they are into the whole life-work balance thing. Which is good. I've realised recently life is too short to spend most of it chained to your desk.' He glanced down and added casually as he looked back into Natalie's eyes, 'Now that I'm back in London for good.'

They smiled silently at each other as the waitress set their coffee down. Natalie wondered how this had happened; the evening hadn't gone like she had planned or imagined at all. How, when she had so very many important and serious things to say to Jack, had the last two hours sailed by filled with delightful, entertaining but ultimately meaningless chat? It was as if they had been making love in that jacuzzi in Venice only last week. Actually no, it was different from that. It felt as if they had never been to bed together; as if they were two very different people from the pair who had met on the Tube over a year ago; as if this was a first date. At least, Natalie reminded herself, that was how it felt to *her*, not Jack, even if he was looking at her with what might have been a twinkle in his eye.

She knew she should tell him her secret now, but selfishly, childishly, dangerously, she didn't want to. She was curious to see if that twinkle in his eye might ignite into something more.

If this was what Natalie had wished for, this time to spend with Jack to see if all the months that she had fought her feelings for him were based on nothing more than a pleasant daydream, she hadn't expected to feel this way. What she had hoped for was confirmation that he was nothing more than a self-serving, narcissistic, egocentric seducer of women. But his warmth and charm were intact, if anything even magnified since the last time she had seen him. And what's more, whether it was real or imagined, when she was with him she felt comfortable in her own skin. Relaxed and together on the very night when she should have felt her most nervous and terrified.

'You look thoughtful,' Jack said, watching her as she sipped her coffee.

'You look lovely,' Natalie said out loud before she even knew it.

Jack shook his head, briefly running his palm over his short hair.

'Oh Jack, I'm sorry,' Natalie said hastily, seeing his acute discomfort. 'It just came out. I didn't mean it, it's just the wine and I don't know why I said it. I was trying to be funny I suppose.'

Jack laughed loudly, making Natalie start. Well, at least he thought it was funny even if she didn't.

'No one's said anything like that to me for a while,' he said with a sheepish grin. 'Actually no one's said that to me ever! And it's been an . . . eventful year. It's taken its toll, so what I'm trying to say is that it's nice to receive a compliment.'

Natalie watched him. He seemed to mean every word he was saying and yet she knew that he had been chatting up Suze only a few days ago. A man who doesn't think he has what it takes to attract women doesn't try to chat up strangers in the street.

'It's been eventful for me too,' she said quietly.

There was a long pause and then both of them spoke at once.

'The thing is . . .' Natalie began.

'There is something you deserve to know,' Jack said simultaneously. They both laughed nervously.

'After you,' Jack said, with an incline of his head.

Natalie thought about Freddie and how any other topic of conversation would be wiped clean off the board once she had told Jack about him.

'No you go,' she said. 'Please.'

Jack nodded, took a breath and began.

'That day that I met you I had . . .'

Natalie's mobile phone purred into life in her bag, vibrating noisily against her keys.

'I'm sorry,' she apologised, thinking immediately of Freddie. 'Do you mind if I take it? It might be . . . important.' She trailed off her excuses and her heart stopped when she saw it was her home number calling.

'Mum?' she said as she answered the phone. She could hear Freddie crying, screaming in her ear. 'Mum!' she repeated.

'Now, I don't want you to worry,' Sandy began, speaking loudly to be heard over the baby.

'What's *happened*?' Natalie's tone was urgent.

'Nothing much, I nearly didn't call you at all but then I thought you'd just get cross when you came home and found out so – anyway, hardly anything at all. Freddie just had a little accident, that's all.'

'What!' Natalie exclaimed. She glanced at Jack and then stood up, walking out into the cold night air. 'Mum, is he OK?'

'He's fine! A bit upset but fine. I was changing his nappy and he – I didn't realise he was so mobile, Natalie – the wipes had run out so I went to get a packet from your drawer and in the two seconds my back was turned, he rolled off the table. Cracked his little head on the corner of the drawers. Now, I'm sure he's fine, he cried his eyes out and he's alert and awake – but he has got a lump the size of an egg on his forehead. But I'm fairly sure he isn't concussed.'

Natalie heard the familiar gasping snuffle that Freddie did when he was gathering his strength for another great howl. Just as it broke with an ear-shattering crescendo she told her mother, 'I'm coming home – now.'

'Are you OK?' Jack asked her when she got back inside the restaurant. 'What's happened?'

'My bloody mother,' Natalie said as she sat down, hearing the tremble in her voice. Then, perhaps more than at any moment since Freddie's birth, she wanted not to have to tell

Jack about Freddie but for him to simply know, so she didn't have to explain the way she was feeling. If only he had always known, and they had had a year of evenings like this, in each other's company, there to support each other. It was a pointless and childish wish, trying to conjure a different past that had already long been spent in other ways.

'My mother has had an accident at home, started a . . . pan fire. Nothing serious she's just a bit shaken, so I need to get back. I'm sorry, Jack.' As Natalie stood up so did he.

She found her wallet in her bag but Jack put his finger on her wrist and said, 'No, this is on me, I insist. Look, Natalie, I admit I didn't want to see you tonight. But I am glad I did.'

He called over the waiter to alert him to the cash he had left on the table, telling him to keep the change. As they emerged into the night air Jack spotted a couple across the street emerging from a cab. He sprinted over and reserved it for her.

'I'm so sorry,' Natalie said absently as he opened the door for her. 'This isn't how I planned it at all.'

Jack held her forearm for a moment as she was about to get into the cab. 'I'd like to do this again sometime.'

Distracted, all Natalie could think of just then was the sound of her son crying.

'Well, we'll have to,' she said, as if the reasons were obvious.

'Then I'll call you,' Jack said. 'I do still have your number.'

'OK,' Natalie said and then the cab door was shut and the car was pulling away from the kerb.

Freddie had stopped crying long before Natalie got home, Sandy told her.

'Oh my God,' Natalie said as she removed the damp piece of kitchen towel that Sandy had been holding to his forehead. 'Oh my God – Mother, what did you do to him?'

She peered at the lump that was just over her baby's left eyebrow. It was purple, pink and tinged with a greenish blue all at once and looked dreadfully sore.

'It's a bump,' Sandy said, pouring herself what she assured Natalie was her first drink of a very long day. 'All kids get scrapes and knocks and bumps. It's the way they hurl themselves around.'

'Not eleven-week-old babies, mother,' Natalie said sharply. 'Funnily enough, when they can't walk or talk or swing from climbing frames it is generally considered to be the responsibility of the adult to keep them bump-free.'

'It was an *accident*,' Sandy said, sipping a large vodka over ice. Natalie didn't think that her mother was drunk, but she didn't like the fact that as soon as she had arrived Sandy started drinking.

'Anyway,' Sandy went on after taking a gulp from her glass, 'how many times have you left him for a couple of seconds while you've popped to get something?

'Never!' Natalie exclaimed. She looked at her son, who was sitting up in her lap playing quite happily with her string of freshwater pearls. His eyes were bright and he seemed otherwise perfectly well cared for. Accidents did happen and Natalie knew he wasn't seriously hurt. And she knew that if it had been her who had been looking after him when it happened she'd have felt terrible and mortified, but she'd have been much more able to get past it because it would have been her mistake, her responsibility. But it hadn't been her, it had been her mother.

'When I called I didn't mean for you to leave your date,' Sandy said, refreshing her drink.

'I wasn't on a date,' Natalie snapped back.

Sandy sighed, her bosom rising and falling with the effort. 'Look at him – he's fed, he's clean and he's happy.' She smiled, tucking one chin into another. 'I had a lovely time with him, Natalie, it was a great day. And that bump – well, it was just an accident.'

'Story of your life really,' Natalie said, sweeping her son up and carrying him to her room. Once upstairs she laid Freddie on the bed and looked at his bump again. It wasn't quite as big and terrible as she had first thought. In fact, despite Sandy's alarming assessment on the phone, it was hardly more than the size of a thumbnail. And as she gently applied some arnica cream to it she supposed that many grandmothers wouldn't have even bothered telling their daughters that such a minor injury had occurred. Her mother had told her because she knew that either way Natalie would be angry with her, and she had probably reasoned it would be better for her to be just angry with her about the bump, without adding withholding information to the charge.

And in a strange sort of way, maybe her mother had been that guardian angel she had prayed to earlier that evening. After all, Sandy had saved her from what was becoming a confusing and unpredictable situation. Her intervention had given Natalie breathing space to consider what she had once only wondered about and now knew for sure. Jack had done something more to her than get her pregnant in those few days.

He had got under her skin, inside her heart and her head. Perhaps if she hadn't had Freddie the feelings would have gradually ebbed away, or perhaps not. But either way she had been struggling with them ever since she met him, and one thing was certain: if she was going to have him back in her life in any capacity, these emotions were not helping.

And as for Jack? Natalie had thought that towards the end of their evening that he might have wanted her too, if not nearly in the same way. He hadn't been pleased to see her, he'd almost run a mile when she'd bumped into him and she had more or less had to press-gang him into agreeing to meet her, but eventually he had clearly made up his mind to enjoy the evening as best as he could, which might very well have included sleeping with her. If her mother hadn't called she thought that perhaps over brandy Jack would have asked her to go home with him. One more night, no strings, no promises, that was what he would have offered her.

The truly frightening thing was, she was sure that if it hadn't been for her mother's intervention, she would have accepted.

Chapter Fifteen

When Meg woke up in the early hours of Sunday morning it took her a second or two to work out why. It was still quite dark outside and all the children were still at Frances's house. And then she felt Robert's breath in her ear and his hand sliding around her waist over the mound of her belly and finally cupping one breast. Everything that had happened last night came back to her all at once.

'Good morning,' Robert whispered in her ear.

'Is it morning?' Meg asked him sleepily. Robert rolled her onto her back and easing his weight on top of her, kissed her for a long time. It was a tender kiss, a gentle and loving one, and Meg longed to let herself fall into it without any reservation, but she couldn't, there was one small tight part of her that held back. Robert didn't seem to notice.

'It's just gone six,' he murmured as he pulled back from their kiss. 'But I couldn't wait any longer. I have plans for this Sunday. I want to make love to my beautiful and sexy wife, make her a great breakfast in bed and then go and fetch my children and spend the day with my family.' He bent his mouth to her neck and kissed her below her jawline. 'Sound good?'

'We haven't done that in the longest time,' Meg said wistfully. 'Spent a whole day together.'

Robert stopped kissing her and looked into her eyes.

'I know,' he said. 'And I know that's partly my fault. I've let work rule my life and it's got me stressed and made me . . . cruel. Meg, I didn't mean what I said to you the other day. I was just angry at some work stuff and I took it out on you. It was wrong, really wrong.' The smile that followed was sweet; he looked boyish and young again with his hair all tousled and his face creased with sleep. 'Can you forgive me?'

Meg looked up at him, colourless in the dawn light, and smiled.

'Course I can, silly,' she said, because she wanted to.

She really wanted to believe that from now on everything was going to be all right. And maybe she could pretend that she hadn't seen what she had last night.

If she could just do that, then maybe everything would be perfect.

Natalie lay wide awake until 7.30 a.m. on Sunday morning, a time when she felt it was finally appropriate to get out of bed. Freddie had been asleep since four, but try as she might she could not force herself into unconsciousness. Jack and Freddie and what was going to happen, not to mention what might not happen, and a whole series of jumbled and disjointed thoughts spun around and around behind her eyelids whenever she attempted to close them. So she decided it was better to stay awake, stare at the ceiling and try to imagine a Sunday morning with her fake husband instead.

He'd bring her breakfast in bed. Coffee, orange juice, croissants and eggs. Then while she ate he'd feed the baby, sitting in bed next to her. They would watch the morning news and because it was Sunday they'd be going to some-body's parents' house for lunch. Either his fake mum and dad's, whom Natalie envisioned as a nice friendly old couple

210

who lived in a thirties semi in Tottenham. Or her fake mother's place, an elegant Victorian villa, where her fake mother lived with her cat, taught piano and went ballroom dancing every other Thursday afternoon. Then after lunch they'd go for a walk around the park, and in the early evening when the baby was asleep they'd make love in the living room on the sofa. They'd be sitting hand in hand watching the *Antiques Roadshow* when, suddenly overcome with desire for her, he'd reach over and kiss her, his hand cupping her breast and then . . . It was at that point that Natalie felt it was appropriate to get out of bed.

Fake-husband fantasies might be distracting but they were also dangerous, especially when they concerned your real-life electrician.

What she needed, Natalie thought as she showered, was a distraction to get her through this day, this sort of no-man's-land of a Sunday where everything was still up in the air and unresolved. She couldn't go round to Meg's, where she hoped marital bliss was in full swing, and she knew Jess and Lee had the grandparents coming. Alice would be working on the collection with Gregory, and Natalie didn't think that Frances – as intrinsically good a person as she was somewhere underneath all those prickles – was the kind of distraction she was looking for. That left Steve, who she knew was playing footy with his mates in a bid to keep in with his manhood, and Tiffany.

That was what she would do today. She would go and visit Tiff and Jordan and see how they were getting on. If there was one person who put her own self-inflicted troubles into perspective it was Tiffany.

And as for Jack, well, it was out of her hands, at least for now. He had said he would call her.

Of course he had said that once before, and she had still been waiting for that call a year later.

211

Meg wondered how she would feel at this moment if last night hadn't ended the way it had, if all she had done was fall asleep in Robert's arms.

She decided that she would have felt utterly happy, content and secure in the strengthened foundations of her marriage. Erasing the two minutes that prevented her from feeling like that, however, was harder than she had hoped. Instead, she was left with this peculiar mix of happiness and anguish; the joy of seeing him here now playing with his children, and the fear that despite how it looked and how it felt, it could all be just a fragile veneer in danger of shattering at any moment.

She sat on the bench and watched her family playing frisbee.

Alex and Hazel kept shouting at her to come and join in, their cheeks ruddy and their eyes bright as they raced around on the grass trying to throw the frisbee to each other before a leaping Gripper caught it. But Meg said she had to watch over Iris and anyway she wanted to watch as Robert scooped up James and hurled the giggling infant into the air only to catch him just in the nick of time, with a whoop and a shout of delight from her son.

Her husband had been true to his word when it came to his plans for the day.

They had made love again that morning, not with the same passion and intensity as the night before, but this time somehow seemed more poignant. He had been so gentle and so tender with her that for the first time in a long time Meg felt *truly* cherished. She wished she could be certain that it was a feeling based on reality and not artifice.

Breakfast in bed had been scrambled eggs on toast and a cup of tea, and then just past eight they had left to pick the children up from Frances.

Robert, possibly the only man on earth to be able to stop his sister's blunt questions and unintended rudeness, had engulfed Frances in a bear hug the minute she had answered the door, and thanked her profusely for giving him and Meg the break they needed. He promised to have little Henry for her and Craig in return any time. Frances had gone pink and glowed with pleasure at her brother's gush of gratitude.

Meg knew how much the thanks and approval of her older and always more successful brother meant to Frances, and she was torn between delight that Robert had so expertly extricated them from Frances's home in order to spend the day together, and feeling sorry for the woman who could be brushed off after a doubtless sleepless night caring for five small children with nothing more than a few platitudes. Did Robert mean to manipulate Frances, Meg had wondered. Did he mean to manipulate her?

If there was one thing she could be certain about, it was that he did love his children. The four of them, five if you counted Gripper nipping at their heels, were now tearing around and around a great old oak tree, Robert with his arms raised in a monster pose, the children squealing and giggling with delight. At last Robert caught James, tucking him under one arm and then hooking the other round Hazel. All three tumbled to the ground in a muddle of laughter and mud.

'Attack!' Alex commanded Gripper. 'Attack the monster!'

And with uncharacteristic obedience Gripper pounced gleefully on her master and began a dogged attempt to literally lick him to death.

Natalie didn't like to think of herself as small-minded and reactionary, so when she saw the four or five kids in hooded tops as she approached Tiffany's tower block with Freddie she was determined not to automatically think badly of them.

They were probably perfectly lovely, ordinary young men out for a nice sociable skateboard or something. No, she absolutely would not judge them until they had at least mugged her for her mobile.

But she did jump out of her skin when one of them stopped her in her tracks, shouting, 'Hey, Missus! Hold up!'

Natalie spun round, expecting to find a 'piece' pointed right in her face. Instead it was the stuffed blue puppy that Freddie had taken to that confronted her.

'Dropped your kid's dog,' the boy said with a wide toothy smile.

'Oh thank you terribly,' Natalie said idiotically.

'No worries, man,' the boy said, winking at her as he loped along to catch up with his friends. But even despite that motiveless act of kindness, Natalie was ashamed to admit that she was relieved when Anthony finally let her into the flat.

'All right?' he asked her.

'Super,' Natalie said because she was sure Anthony didn't really want to know. 'You?'

'Yeah, good,' he told her. 'I'm off out. Derby match on at the pub. Meeting Gary for a lunchtime pint. He's Spurs, poor bloke.'

'Smashing,' Natalie said, wondering what on earth Anthony was talking about. 'Well, have a good time.'

Anthony nodded farewell as he closed the door behind him.

Tiffany appeared in the doorway of the living room in a pair of drawstring pyjama bottoms and a vest. 'Hiya,' she said and she shook a jar of Nescafé at Natalie. 'Coffee?'

'Please. Do you mind me dropping round?' Natalie asked Tiffany as she lifted Freddie from his buggy and followed her into the kitchen. 'Is it too early for you young people? I know it's only eleven but I've been up for hours and I waited and waited to call you.'

*

Tiffany had sounded uncertain when Natalie had phoned and invited herself over.

'Are you sure you want to come here?' she had asked.

'Why not?' Natalie replied. 'I mean, unless you've got plans or you're busy or something.'

'It's just that this place isn't . . . it's not really sorted yet. There's no sofa and no decent mugs and we have to pour a bucket of water down the loo to flush it until Ant gets round to fixing the cistern.'

'You should have got yourself a plumber, not an electrician,' Natalie joked, but Tiffany didn't laugh. Natalie could hear her discomfort in the silence.

'I don't care about flushing loos and matching mugs,' Natalie said. 'I want to see you and Jordan, not a three-piece suite.'

'It's just . . .' Tiffany paused as she searched for the right words. 'When someone else is coming over I look round at this place and I see that my life isn't as sorted as I make out.'

'Whose life is?' Natalie said, feeling a pang of empathy for the teenager. 'If you don't want visitors that's fair enough, I am sort of forcing myself on you. But I have to say if I do come – I'll bring cake.'

Tiffany chuckled. 'Well, OK,' she said. 'As long as it's not that awful ginger cake again!'

'I'm glad you came, I'd have been bored here on my own with Jordan.' Tiffany smiled at Natalie and handed her a milky coffee where she was sitting on the beanbag, made the way a little girl might like to drink it. 'My school mates don't keep in touch much any more. I suppose they think I must be boring now. They're right, probably.'

'You'll make new friends when you start college – I wanted

to find out how you'd got on when you saw the social worker and your teachers about your exams,' Natalie said, as she took a sip of the coffee.

Tiffany nodded.

'Yeah, it was good I think,' she said. 'My teacher reckons if I catch up over the summer holidays I can take them in September when they do the retakes. My coursework was mostly up to date and it still counts, so I just need to finish that.'

'Still sounds like a lot to do, though.'

'Well, I'm getting help at home from my form teacher, Mrs Gough, in the holidays. She's really nice, because she doesn't have to help me and I can't pay her or anything but she says she wants to see me do well. I'm lucky, I know so many nice people.' Tiffany looked out of the window at the sky. 'And if I do well enough in the exams then I can go to college. They even have a free crèche for students.'

Natalie nodded. 'God, you take it all in your stride, don't you? Let me think, what was I doing when I was sixteen?' She had a brief flashback of standing on her father's doorstep in the rain. 'Sunbathing, playing spin the bottle and kissing boys, that was all I was doing. And look at you. You're a mum, making your own home, you're getting more qualifications than you can shake a stick at and you look so capable, Tiffany. I'm very proud of you. Nothing scares you.'

Tiffany's smile faded and she looked down into her coffee cup for a long time.

'Lots of things scare me,' she said. 'I keep thinking what if I can't pass the exams? What if Anthony and me break up and I'm on my own? What if I never talk to Mum again?' Her voice cracked on the word 'Mum' and she paused. 'I wish all I was doing was sunbathing and playing spin the bottle in the park. That's what I *should* be doing. I mean, I love Ant and Jordan, so much. I really, really do but sometimes I just wish things were different – easy.'

Natalie laid Freddie on the play mat on the floor and struggled up off the beanbag. She went over to Tiffany, putting her arm around her. 'You miss your mum, don't you?' she asked her simply. 'You hate her, you're angry with her and she really hurt you but you still miss her. Because she's your mum, right?'

Tiffany nodded. 'When I was poorly or sad, or I'd hurt myself my mum would always be there. She'd always have room for me in her arms no matter what she was doing. She'd cuddle me and say, "Mum's got you, you're all right now." I know I shouldn't have gone behind her back, and maybe I was too young to be having sex but we were being careful. I didn't try to get pregnant. And the really bad thing is that I know if it had been a white boy I was pregnant by she would have been OK in the end. She would have taken me in her arms and told me, "You're all right now."' Tiffany dropped her head onto Natalie's shoulder and Natalie felt the young girl's shoulders trembling under her palms.

'I bet she misses you too,' she said.

'But it will never be all right, will it? Because I can't and I don't want to change the colour of my baby's skin. I'm proud of her and Anthony. So nothing will ever be all right again with me and Mum, and I act all strong, Natalie, but sometimes I just want my mum.'

Natalie held onto her tightly.

'Do you want to go and see her? I'll come with you if you like?' Natalie offered.

Tiffany looked up at her. 'She'd make mincemeat out of you,' she said with a watery smile.

'Well, then, let her try,' Natalie said with kamikaze

217

bravado. 'I happen to be world-class negotiator, not to mention a champ at judo.'

'Yeah, right,' said Tiffany.

'That is one of the things I don't like about you, Tiffany,' Natalie said gently. 'You always see right through me. But seriously, do you want to go? We could go today – unless the whole family will be round for Sunday lunch?'

Tiffany looked thoughtful as she sat up.

'Dad will be fishing on the canal until at least four, that's when we have Sunday dinner, and Dan will be round his girlfriend's. It will be Mum on her own at home. She says it's her peace day with everyone out of the house. Could we go?' She looked at Natalie questioningly as they heard Jordan stirring in the bedroom, with little hopeful hiccupping cries.

'We could,' Natalie said.

'But she won't change her mind,' Tiffany said, shaking her head. 'About Anthony or Jordan. It's too late.'

Natalie took her by the wrist and pulled her to her feet.

'It might be,' Natalie said. 'But there is always the slight possibility that it might not. And that is worth finding out, isn't it?'

Tiffany's family home was a smart 1950s semi with its pebble-dash painted cream and the front garden turned into off-road parking. A jaunty basket of red geraniums hung either side of the front door, and identically planted window boxes sat outside all the front windows. It didn't look like the house of a woman who would punch the friend of her estranged daughter at the least provocation but still, Natalie was nervous as they approached. She had no idea where she got this reckless campaigning spirit from when it came to sorting out her new friends' lives. If she could only confront her own problems with as much direct action as she demanded from Tiffany and Meg, she might have resolved them by now. Perhaps she shouldn't have brought Tiffany here, but when she saw her face this morning as she talked about how much she missed her mum she knew exactly how Tiffany felt. She had been missing her mother for years, even when the woman was living under the same roof as her. If there was a chance for Tiffany to get back some sort of relationship with her mother, Natalie wanted her to take it. Any chance, even the slightest, had to be worth the risk.

'We'll go round the back,' Tiffany said, her voice lowered as if they were committing some kind of stealth operation. 'She'll be in the conservatory listening to the radio.'

'Roger, over and out,' Natalie said as she negotiated Freddie's buggy through the narrow alleyway and past the wheelie bins. Sure enough, on the back of the house was a large Victorian-style conservatory, and sitting with her feet up and her eyes closed was Tiffany's mother.

Natalie had imagined her as a big woman, with meaty arms and maybe a couple of tattoos, but this woman was as slight as her daughter, fashionably dressed, her long brown hair carefully kept. As Natalie observed her she reckoned that if it came to it she could take her on in a fight.

Putting the brake on Jordan's buggy, Tiffany went over to the conservatory door and pushed it open. Her mum didn't stir.

'Mum?' she said softly and then again, 'Mum?'

The woman opened her eyes.

'Tiffany,' she said, sitting up. 'What are you doing here?' She looked at her daughter and then at Natalie who was standing outside beside the two buggies.

'You'd better come in,' she said stiffly.

Natalie was staring at a plate of pink wafer biscuit a few minutes later.

So far it had all gone rather well in that there had been no shouting or throwing of things. She noticed that Janine, as she had been instructed reluctantly to call Tiffany's mother, didn't look at either her daughter or her granddaughter as she bustled around the kitchen they were sitting in, finding plates for the biscuits. Worst of all, Natalie noticed that Janine kept glancing up at the kitchen clock every few seconds, obviously keen for Tiffany to be gone.

Finally she sat down and managed to look her daughter in the face.

'Your dad will be back before long,' she warned coolly. 'You know how angry he gets.'

'And what about you?' Tiffany asked her. 'Are you still angry with me?

Natalie looked at Tiffany, a vulnerable girl who was so obviously in need of a reassuring hug and wondered how her mother could resist putting her arms around her and doing just that. And it wasn't just Tiffany's age that made her seem so fragile, Natalie knew that. Only yesterday she had felt just the same as Tiffany did now, wishing with all her might that she and Sandy could have that strong mythical bond mothers and daughters are supposed to have. Perhaps that's was why she was so interested in trying to get Tiffany and her mother back together. She was almost the same age as Tiffany when things went wrong between her and Sandy, and they had never been right since.

Janine looked enquiringly at Natalie, who had lifted a fretful Freddie out of his buggy and plonked him on her lap. He immediately picked up a teaspoon and shoved it in his mouth.

'Are you her social worker then?' Janine asked Natalie bluntly.

'Who, me?' Natalie replied. 'No, I'm a friend. We go to baby group together. Anthony is helping rewire my house.

220

He's doing a really good job, he's a good kid. Hard-working, responsible – you don't meet many like that at his age.'

Natalie hadn't actually met any other seventeen-year-old boys since she was seventeen (if you didn't count poor old Bob's grandson), so she had no idea what they were like. Still, it seemed like the right thing to say.

'I see,' Janine said, with a nod at Tiffany. 'You brought her here to interfere with our private business.'

'No, Mum I . . .'

'She brought me for moral support,' Natalie said firmly. 'And because a couple of hours ago she was crying on my shoulder over how much she missed her mum.'

'Well,' Janine said, looking down at her lemon gingham wipe-clean tablecloth. 'Well, she had her chance, she made her choices.'

Natalie was about to speak again when the look on Tiffany's face stopped her.

'I'm doing my GCSEs in September, Mum,' Tiffany said in a small voice. 'I'm getting help in the holidays and I'm going to college next year, like I always planned.'

There was silence.

'Jordon's doing really well,' Tiffany went on, smiling down at the gurgling baby who was happily gnawing on her buggy book. 'She's got two teeth now, another one on the way I think. She crawls everywhere and since she's been on solids she's growing so quickly, sometimes I think she'll . . .' Tiffany trailed off; her mother was looking at the clock again.

'I suppose we'd better go then,' Tiffany said.

'You better had,' Janine agreed.

As Tiffany rose from her chair Natalie put a hand on her wrist and she sat back down.

'Is this really what you want, Janine?' Natalie asked.

Janine looked at her. 'I don't see how it is any business of yours,' she said.

'It's not, except that I can't imagine this is really how you want it to be with your little girl. Why are you punishing her for doing nothing more than thousands of other girls her age do every year, and not half so many deal with so well? You've brought her up to be this amazingly strong and resourceful girl, she must have learnt her mothering skills from you and she's a damn good mother. You look like an intelligent woman, and I know because Tiffany's told me that you two were very close. Do you really want to destroy your relationship with your daughter and granddaughter over a non-existent problem? Is it really worth it?'

Tiffany gasped and stared at her mother as Natalie braced herself for a barrage of angry abuse. But Janine didn't move. A few seconds ticked by on the clock, the only sound to break the otherwise total silence.

'I miss her too,' Janine said, speaking about her daughter in the third person. 'I wonder how she's doing, how the little one is. I know that boy is taking good care of her, people tell me. But it's her dad. He won't have it.' She shook her head, hopelessly. 'He's stuck in his ways and stubborn. I said to him maybe we could try to get to know the boy, get along with him, maybe meet his family. But like I said, he won't have it. He's an ignorant old fool.' She looked down at Jordan in her buggy for the first time, and was rewarded with a gap-toothed smiled.

'She's beautiful,' she said, acknowledging Tiffany at last. 'You're doing well. A first baby is hard to manage.'

'You could still see us,' Tiffany said, her tone so hopeful Natalie felt her eyes prick with tears. 'Dad doesn't have to come. You could come and see us . . . you wouldn't *have* to tell him.'

Janine looked at her daughter and shook her head. 'I can't

go behind his back,' she said, with finality. 'You know I can't. We've been married twenty-eight years. We trust each other. He's not a bad man, just a stupid one.' Her smile was bitter as she looked down into her teacup. 'You know, I think it was the shock that did it – when you told us you were pregnant. I just don't think that he ever, *we* ever, expected it would be our little girl. Always so good, always worked hard at school, never out later than you were supposed to be. He still saw you as the little girl who used to sit on his lap and read with him not so long ago. He was shocked and hurt, Tiffany. He latched onto the first thing he could think of to try to break you and Anthony up and to keep you as his little girl, pregnant or not. But you didn't choose him, you chose Anthony. And that hurt him.'

'I didn't mean to hurt him,' Tiffany said. 'But how could I choose? I love Dad but I love Anthony too and he loves me, Mum, he really does.'

Janine nodded slowly. 'Yes, it does look that way, that's for sure,' she said thoughtfully. 'I think if things had happened differently, maybe when you were a bit older, he would have been fine with Anthony. But he's said what he's said now. He's made his stand and he hates to admit he's in the wrong, you know that, Tiff. Once his mind is made up it's impossible to change it.'

'But I miss you, Mum – I need you,' Tiffany pleaded, her voice breaking.

Janine looked at Tiffany, her eyes brimming with tears, but she did not make a move to touch her.

'Dad'll be back soon,' she repeated, her voice trembling. 'You'd better go, love, hey?'

Tiffany scraped her chair back and hurried out of the house as fast as she could with Jordan in the buggy, as Natalie strapped Freddie into his. Janine sat perfectly still, her elbows resting on the kitchen table as she held onto the teacup she had yet to drink from.

'He's the most precious thing in my life,' Natalie said to her, nodding at her son. 'I'd never let anything stand in the way of being his mum. I can see how much you love her, Janine, don't lose her for ever.'

When she got outside she found Tiffany sitting on the front wall furiously wiping away her tears with the sleeves of her jumper.

'I told you it was too late,' she said when Natalie stopped beside her.

Natalie shook her head. 'I don't think it is, I think you really got through to your mum there and anyway, whatever happens you tried, and that's important. It really is. I'm proud of you.'

'Will you stop being proud of me,' Tiffany said with a loud sniff as she stood up and defiantly shook her hair off her shoulders. 'It's getting to be embarrassing.'

'Come on,' Natalie smiled. 'How about you come back to my place, I'll cook us lunch, we'll eat a load of cake and watch my *Dirty Dancing* DVD. It never fails to cheer me up.'

'What's *Dirty Dancing*?' Tiff asked her.

'For both your sake and mine,' Natalie said, slinging an arm around Tiffany's shoulder, 'I'm going to pretend I didn't hear that.'

The children were filthy so when they got back from the park Meg and Robert gave them one big midday bath, a fun-filled hour that saw the bathroom covered in mud and Meg and Robert wet through. Once Alex, Hazel and James were dried and dressed and packed off to watch a video before lunch Meg found herself alone again with her husband.

'Just being with you and the kids has been great,' Robert

told her, drawing her body against his in an embrace so tight that she could hear his heart beating. He kissed the top of her head. 'I feel like I've been away for a long time and now I've finally come home.'

Meg looked up at him and perhaps the searching expression in her eyes surprised him because he dropped his arms from around her and took half a step back.

'Have you?' she asked him intently. 'Have you really come home?'

'Of course I have.' Robert smiled. 'Back where I belong.'

Chapter Sixteen

Natalie found a Post-it note stuck to the telephone in the hallway when she and Freddie got back with Tiffany and Jordan.

Jack called at 12, it read, in her mother's characteristically undisciplined scrawl. Natalie looked at it thoughtfully. It was highly unexpected. If she had expected him to call her at all she had not imagined it would be today. And apart from anything else it meant that he *did* still have her phone number. After more than a year he still had the phone number he had never attempted to call after they had first met.

What did that mean, Natalie wondered. Did it mean anything at all? After all, she kept numbers on her mobile phone for ever, names of people she could barely remember any more and hadn't spoken to in months. But even if the fact that he had held onto her number was of no significance, he had still called her back unexpectedly quickly.

That had to mean something, but Natalie had no idea what. She looked at the entirely inadequate Post-it note.

'Typical,' she said out loud.

'What is?' Tiffany asked her, unwinding her long pink scarf from around her neck.

'Typical of my mother to not acquire details,' Natalie said, waving the Day-Glo orange paper at Tiffany. 'For example –

am I supposed to call him back or is he calling me back? And what *tone* of voice did he have when he called? Short? Disappointed? *Confused*? Now I'll never know. Like I said – typical.'

'Really?' Tiffany said wearily as she hefted Jordan out of her buggy. 'That's a very atypical thing to typically get wrong. I don't know anyone who writes on a phone message how the person sounded – and anyway, who is this Jack guy?'

'Oh, no one,' Natalie said, tucking the Post-it note into her pocket and wondering if her mother was in the house. It was quiet, there were no tell-tale signs of her paraphernalia scattered around the hallway; the stupidly high-heeled tan boots were gone, her white coat with the imitation fur, leopard-skin collar was not hanging on the end of the banister and her gold fake Gucci handbag had disappeared from beside the phone. It looked like she'd gone out.

It occurred to Natalie that she probably should have asked Sandy what she was doing today, maybe even have had *lunch* with her. After all, so far she had spent the minimum amount of time with her mother. But if she'd gone out it showed that she wasn't exactly sitting around pining away, waiting for her only daughter and grandchild to return. Typical, Natalie thought sullenly to herself, aware of yet unable to repress the irrational thought.

'If this bloke is no one, then why do you care whether or not he's confused?' Tiffany asked her reasonably.

Natalie looked up at Tiffany. 'Because I am a naturally caring, empathetic person, of course,' she said, loading Freddie onto one hip and picking up her shopping bags with her free hand.

'You do that a lot,' Tiffany observed.

Natalie swung round and looked at her. 'Do what?' she asked.

'Say something that is obviously completely mental but with such authority that people don't tend to question it. I've noticed, that's all,' Tiffany said with a shrug. 'It's quite cool.'

Natalie examined Tiffany's face and wondered just what else the young woman had guessed about her.

'Yes, well,' she said. 'Come downstairs and help me peel potatoes. How's that for authority?'

Once in the kitchen Tiffany installed Jordan and Freddie on the rug by the window where they ignored each other happily, Jordan lost in her mission to chew through her rubber teething ring and Freddie striving to move just one single millimetre closer to Blue Dog, who was tantalisingly out of his reach.

'Actually, now I come to think of it you are very mysterious,' Tiffany said, after a few minutes of companionable peeling.

Natalie blinked. 'Who, me?' she said. 'Mysterious? I am not.'

'You are,' Tiffany said, arching a finely plucked eyebrow. 'I think I know why too.'

Natalie looked up sharply at the teen.

'What? What is why? What?' She had had more coherent moments.

'You can tell me, you know, if you want to.' Tiffany brandished the peeler at Natalie as she spoke. 'You've been really kind to me and I am good at listening if you want to talk. I wouldn't judge you.'

Natalie put down the potatoes she was midway through peeling and wiped her damp starchy hands on a tea towel.

'What do you think I have to tell you?' she asked Tiffany cautiously.

Tiffany's smile was full of sympathy. 'It's nothing to be ashamed of, Natalie. If things aren't as good between you and your husband as you are always saying they are and if you're splitting up, is it because of that Jack bloke who left a message? Have you been having an affair and now he wants you to leave your Gary and marry him and is that why you want to know whether or not he's confused?'

Natalie spluttered all over the pre-prepared baby sweet corn.

'I hope you're not planning to take a GCSE in revealing denouements,' she said, scandalised. 'That is most certainly *not* what is going on.'

'I reckon it is,' Tiff went on confidently, 'otherwise how do you explain that you have no photos of your so-called husband anywhere and that you don't wear a wedding ring?'

Natalie stared in horror at Tiffany. 'Next you'll be telling me it was Professor Plum in the library!' She snorted in what she hoped was a suitably derisory fashion. Tiffany had just picked a few very large holes in her story, which so far nobody else, including herself had noticed.

'Look, Tiff, you've got it all wrong,' Natalie assured her.

'What then?' Tiffany asked her steadily. 'What's the mystery?'

Natalie looked at Freddie inching his way along the mat on his tummy. She thought about her son and Jack, and she thought about what was about to hit a very large high-speed fan at any moment anyway, and that soon all of her new friends would inevitably know the shocking truth about her. Actually it wasn't the truth that was shocking, the truth would have been quite mundane. It was the unadorned silly web of lies that she had got herself tangled up in that was shocking; the kind of complicated nonsense that normal people would probably put down to borderline personality disorder. Sometimes Natalie wondered if she *was* a bit mad, chasing her tail over a fib that now was only to save the dignity she had never had too much of in the first place. The sane thing would be to simply tell Tiffany the truth right now.

And so she said, 'Don't be such a plank, honestly. The photos of my Gary are in my bedroom, my wedding ring is at the jewellers being buffed and Jack is just a friend I had a bit of a falling-out with, that's all. Now shut up, Miss Marple, and peel.'

Some habits, it seemed, were hard to break.

'Natalie,' Tiffany persisted, perhaps sensing Natalie's split-second wrestle with the truth. 'The way you act, I sometimes wonder if you've got a husband at all or if you made it all up!'

Natalie looked up sharply from the chopping board.

'But how did you . . . ?' She stopped herself when she realised from the expression on Tiffany's face that she hadn't known, she had only been teasing.

'What, you mean . . . ? Tiffany spluttered. 'You mean you haven't got a husband. You mean you actually *did* make one up?'

'No!' Natalie protested. Tiffany raised a highly sceptical eyebrow. 'Well, yes, OK then, except when you put it like that all blunt and matter-of-fact it makes me sound mad and totally unhinged and I'm *not*.' She paused, struggling to rationalise the irrational. 'I didn't mean it to get so out of hand. It sort of slipped out when Gary was banging on at me to get the quotes checked by my husband and it grew from there. I know I was stupid, but I didn't know any of the group that well then and I wanted to fit in. Besides, I wasn't exactly ready to tell you the truth about me and Freddie, I wasn't sure if any of you were ready to hear it without running a mile.'

Tiffany seemed frozen to the spot by her words.

'Well, say something then!' Natalie begged her. 'Shout at me, tell me what an idiot I am. Stomp off and tell the others if you like, but please don't remain rooted to my kitchen floor until the end of time looking so horrified!'

Tiffany thought for a moment and slowly shook her head.

'You muppet,' she said.

Natalie shrugged – she couldn't deny it.

'I know,' she said. 'I know I am. Look, I'm planning to sort it out, I really am.' She spread out her hands in a pleading gesture. 'Will you just keep it to yourself until I can tell the others myself, please? I will as soon as I get the chance.'

'Course I will,' Tiffany said, pouting a little. 'Just because I think you're a nutter doesn't mean that I'm a snitch. And anyway you're my friend, weirdly even my best friend right now – so of course I won't tell.'

Natalie's smile was one of relief.

'You're one of my best friends too,' she told Tiffany happily.

'So,' Tiffany said as she resumed peeling. 'Do you want to tell me about you and Freddie now?'

Natalie looked at her young friend and found herself giving in to an irrepressible urge to giggle.

'Why not?' she exclaimed. 'Why ever not?'

The phone must have started ringing again just as Sandy was coming in through the door because she picked it up before Natalie could get to the extension in the kitchen and brought it downstairs with her.

'Jack, *again*,' she said, leaning towards Natalie so that she could take the handset from where it was wedged between her left ear and shoulder. 'He seems keen!'

Natalie took the phone, noticing that her mother was laden down with shopping bags from Argos to Zara; she must have been into the West End.

'Hello, dear, I'm Nana Sandy – oh, what a lovely little girl,'

Sandy said to Tiffany who was sitting on the rug playing with the babies after lunch. 'I must show you what I've bought . . .'

'Jack,' Natalie said, as she left the kitchen, pulling the door to behind her. She sat on the stairs up to the hallway. 'I didn't expect you to call . . . so soon I mean.'

'Well,' Jack said. 'You left in such a hurry. I just wanted to see if everything was OK. Your house hadn't burnt down or anything?'

'Oh no,' Natalie said with a half-baked chuckle. 'No . . . no.'

It seemed that despite Jack's speed to call her, the awkwardness they had managed to shrug off last night had returned with a vengeance.

'Natalie, last night was really . . . nice . . .' Natalie thought she could hear a 'but' waiting to be tagged onto the end of the sentence. 'Look, can I see you again – no real reason, no agenda . . .' Jack said. 'Just because . . . we never got a chance to finish our conversation, did we?'

'No, we didn't and we really do have to, Jack,' Natalie agreed, determined to put an end to this situation.

'Can you come over tonight?' Jack asked her. 'To the flat where I'm staying?'

Natalie paused, but he couldn't have known it was because she wondering if she could get away with asking her mother to babysit again when she hadn't even asked her to have lunch with her.

'Or if you want I'll come over to you, I still have your address.'

'No, no,' Natalie said hastily. 'I'll come to you. Eight?'

'I look forward to seeing you then,' Jack said.

'Wouldn't bet on it,' Natalie said as she hung up.

'You're sure you don't mind?' Natalie asked Sandy as she sat expressing milk at the kitchen table. It was an odd sort of progress, when it came to the mother-daughter relationship, but Natalie had never imagined that she'd be able to sit, milk-heavy breast in hand, squirting it into a contraption that most resembled a medieval torture device whilst her mum cooked herself pasta. 'I know it's a day and two nights in a row, and I know I haven't exactly seen you very much since you got here, but this *is* important.'

'This Jack fellow,' Sandy said, testing her tomato sauce.

'Yes,' Natalie said, screwing the top on one bottle of milk and transferring it to the fridge. She then began on the other breast. The last thing she wanted was for any breast milk leakage to occur before she had told Jack about Freddie. 'He's an Italian buyer, we're hoping to distribute Mystery is Power through him on the Continent.'

'He didn't sound Italian,' Sandy observed.

'He speaks very good English,' Natalie told her, slipping off her nursing bra under the sleeves of her top and exchanging it with some difficulty for an underwired black number that was now slightly too small for her.

'Well, I'm here,' Sandy said. 'If you ever want to talk.'

'Thanks, I'll bear that in mind,' Natalie said, pulling her black chiffon shirt down over the bra and then undoing a couple of buttons, not, she told herself, because she wanted to look sexy but because if she didn't they would ping off anyway. She paused by her mother, considered kissing her on the cheek and instead bent to the baby chair that was positioned safely in the middle of the rug.

'See you later, buster,' she said, planting a kiss on Freddie's nose. 'Try not to let Nana Sandy drop you out of any first-floor windows.'

When Jack opened the front door to the flat he looked different. Dressed casually in a T-shirt and combats, he looked younger, less formal and forebidding then he had done in his suit. With his face taut with tension, a little gaunt even, Natalie thought that without the moonshine and frisson of yesterday he should not be the kind of man to get your heart racing. No wonder Suze hadn't accepted his invitation for drinks. He wasn't her type at all; come to think of it, the way he looked right now he wasn't Natalie's type either. But it didn't mean, she realised regretfully, that when she was confronted with him, a shadow of stubble on his jaw and perhaps the evidence of a late night around his eyes, she didn't still love to look at him, she didn't admire every contour of his face.

'You're here,' he said, this time with a weary smile.

'I am, right on time,' Natalie observed.

Jack nodded and stepped back to allow Natalie into the communal hallway. The flat on the top floor, he told her, and he led the way up the stairs.

Once inside the tiny flat Natalie slipped off her coat and handed it to him, closing her eyes for the briefest of seconds as she became suddenly aware of the close proximity between them.

'Come through,' Jack said. He led her into a rather small sitting room, where a real coal fire was burning in the grate and the walls were lined with shelves filled with what seemed like hundreds of books.

'All Minnie's,' Jack said. 'She loves to read. Especially the steamy stuff. I told her I'm not sure it's good for her at eighty-three, but she says it should be prescribed on the NHS. She's touring Europe with her toy boy right now. He's seventy-four.'

The two virtual strangers stood in the small room, looking around at almost anything except each other. Natalie could feel the pressure of all the unspoken history they had created between themselves in their short acquaintance steadily building towards a thunderous climax.

'Look, Jack, there's . . .'

'Natalie, the thing is . . .'

They both spoke at once.

'Please sit down.' Jack gestured to a chintz-covered wingback chair by the fireplace.

'I need to tell you something a bit . . . massive,' Natalie said, twisting her fingers in knots as she spoke. Jack didn't really seem to hear.

'Natalie, the reason I asked you here was because, well, I have to be honest, I didn't really want to see you again, but then there you were standing in front of me and it made me think about that weekend we met. I just wanted to clear the air between us. It seems like the right thing to do, because I want you to know that the reason it didn't go any further wasn't because of you – it was me, you see . . .'

'Jack.' Natalie stopped him in his tracks. 'You're going too fast. You don't have to tell me what happened last year – it really doesn't matter any more, what matters is . . .'

'It does actually matter.' Jack was insistent. 'To me at least – will you let me explain, please?'

Natalie wanted to say no, she wanted to say that what she had to tell him was absolutely, positively the most massive thing that he was ever likely to hear. But somehow she couldn't bring herself to do it, partly because listening to his excuses for not being in touch would delay the inevitable a few minutes longer, but also because she thought her news deserved top billing.

'OK,' she said with a shrug.

Jack nodded decisively. 'Wait there.'

He returned with two glasses and a bottle of wine. He poured out the first glass and handed it to Natalie. She looked fondly at it and wished she could drink it in one, but she knew from recent experience that any chance of her behaving with dignity and integrity would fly out of the window if she did, so instead she simply held it – like a talisman. Or an arsenic pill, just in case things got really bad.

'So.' Jack sat down opposite her on a low settle, his long legs folded awkwardly as he leant forward, resting his elbows on his knees and cupping his wine glass between his palms. He looked like he'd eaten too much of the wrong side of the magic mushroom from *Alice in Wonderland*.

'Right.' He took a breath and looked into his glass as he spoke. 'Here we go. The day I met you was rather an unusual day,' he said. 'It was a day when I did things I would never normally do, behaved in a way I would never normally dream of. I was in shock, I suppose.'

Natalie didn't know she was biting her bottom lip until she felt the sharp pain. She realised she was afraid.

'In shock?' she asked him. 'Why?'

'Well.' Jack looked uncomfortable. 'It's still hard for me to talk about – I still find it a bit embarrassing. It's stupid, I know, but I think it's because men never normally discuss these sorts of things, least of all with women . . . I don't know how to tell you this but . . .'

'Is it that you are gay and only realised after spending the weekend with me?' Natalie asked him abruptly.

'God no!' Jack exclaimed. 'I would have thought that you of all people would have known I wasn't gay.' He looked rather offended.

'Well, are you married then, have you got kids and you fancied playing away for a weekend and you regret it terribly – is it that?'

Jack looked at her.

'It's so strange that we don't know each other better when

I feel like I've known you for years,' he said. 'And anyway, I'm not the sort of man who would cheat on his wife if he had one, which I don't.'

'Jack, please, just tell me what I'm here for,' Natalie implored.

'OK, I will,' he said. 'The day I met you I'd just found out I was going to die.'

'Die?' Natalie couldn't comprehend what he was saying. 'Like be dead?'

'Yes.' Jack smiled fleetingly. 'Like be dead. I was on the Tube on my way back from my consultant. I'd tested positive for cancer for . . .' Jack blushed, clearly struggling to muster the words. 'Um, for testicular cancer, that's cancer of the . . . er . . . ball . . . area.'

'Christ,' Natalie said, because nothing else seemed appropriate, and because of all the things she had expected him to say that was not one of them.

'I heard him say "You've got cancer" and I didn't hear much after that,' Jack went on, looking into the fire. 'Except that it was stage two cancer, and that it had spread from my groin into the lymph nodes in my belly which would kill me if left untreated. It's a strange thing to be suddenly faced with your own mortality, Natalie.'

He watched her for a few seconds in the flickering firelight. Natalie felt glued to her seat, unable to move a muscle, not even her face. Cancer?

'So I was sitting on the Tube, stuck in that tunnel, and I could almost hear the wasted seconds of my life ticking away. And all I could think was, "This is it." I was going to die. I'd never do the things I wanted to do with my life, took for granted I'd be able to because I'd always thought I'd live for ever. Take a balloon ride across the Serengeti, gamble my shirt in Vegas, be a husband one day, be a father. I was scared shitless. More than that, I kept thinking I had to make every last minute of my life important, make it count for something.' Jack looked back into the fire and smiled as he remembered that morning. 'And then I saw you, sitting opposite me on the train. I remember you looked a little pink from the heat and you had a couple of buttons undone on your top.' Jack was almost shy as he a flickered glance in that direction. 'Like you do now and your hair was all kind of wild and I looked at you and I thought, "Oh God, what if I never have sex again?" '

Natalie sat back a little in her chair.

'So I just happened to be in the right place at the right time?' she said, finding her voice at last. 'If another woman had been sitting there who looked halfway shaggable you'd have picked her up?'

Jack sighed and took a long, thoughtful sip of his wine.

'I don't know,' he admitted. 'Maybe. I didn't have anything planned. I didn't really know what I was doing or who I was being. All I knew was that I didn't want to go back to the office and waste more seconds of my life on spreadsheets and meetings. I wanted to *do* something, *feel* something! I didn't plan to take you to Venice. It just sort of happened. When I started talking properly to you at lunch I suddenly really wanted you to see the city. And I wanted to be the one to show it to you. I was being selfish, Natalie – I wasn't thinking about anything apart from what I wanted and on that day at that time I wanted you. I wanted a distraction from the truth.'

'I see,' Natalie managed to say.

'I didn't want to tell you all this,' Jack went on. 'I didn't ever want to have to see you and look you in the eyes and talk to you about my gonads, or rather the lack of them. But then I did see you and seeing you made me think.' He looked directly at Natalie for a second. 'That time we spent together was really special.' He smiled ruefully. 'I mean, I didn't just imagine it, did I? You felt it too, right? Otherwise that would be seriously embarrassing, almost as embarrassing as talking to you about my gonads.' Jack laughed but Natalie couldn't see the funny side.

'It was special,' she said quietly. 'It really was.'

'I couldn't believe what was happening. I couldn't believe that this woman, the first woman I'd ever picked up on the Tube, was so great.'

The first woman. Natalie pondered. Maybe she had been the one to start him off on his serial conquests, among whose victims Suze might have been included. She didn't know if the thought made her feel better or worse.

'Everything about you was so great,' Jack told her. 'Your sexiness, your laugh and most of all your openness. It was so refreshing to meet a woman who wasn't into game-playing or pretending to be something she wasn't. You made me forget everything my consultant had told me and for those couple of days I felt like I'd never have to think about it again. And then you had to go back to London and I realised . . .' He trailed off, his face full of uncertainty again.

'What?' Natalie asked him.

'Reality set in,' Jack said quietly. 'I was about to undergo surgery to remove my testicle and lymph glands, followed by a long and difficult treatment that would mean I'd feel really ill for a long time, and very likely lose all my hair. I had to face up to that. I knew I couldn't keep running away and pretending that everything was fine, not this time. There was no more time for distractions.'

Natalie said nothing. She couldn't rationalise what was happening. She had been right all along. Jack really was a completely different man from the one she thought she had met that day on the Tube. But he was completely different in a completely different way from what she had imagined. He'd told her all she'd had to do was to be sitting right in front of him to be whisked off to Venice. He could have chosen almost any woman to distract him from his illness. The randomness of it all stunned her. Consciously or not, she supposed that up until that moment she had always believed that she and Jack were meant to be together, if only for that weekend. That Freddie was meant to happen. And yet if he had got on a different train, or even the next carriage, everything that had happened to her in the last year would have evaporated into thin air. It seemed inconceivable that her life could be thrown so arbitrarily into total disarray.

'I got back to London the day after you left,' Jack said, when it became clear Natalie wasn't going to speak. 'I had a hospital appointment where they talked through my treatment with me, explained about the surgery and the three cycles of chemotherapy that would follow. They told me I'd be feeling like shit for the best part of a year. Look at me, I'm not exactly Mr Universe to begin with – I don't jog or train with weights or anything, but I'd always thought that I could if I wanted to one day – and then to find out that I wouldn't even have the strength to lift a coffee cup. Funny really. Like a bad joke.'

But Natalie was about as far from wanting to laugh as any woman could possibly be. Instead, tears were standing in her eyes as what Jack had been telling her finally began to sink in.

'I was alone here in London, there wasn't any family or really close friends here that I felt I could ask to care for me, so I decided to go home, to my mum and dad to have my treatment in Italy.' Jack sighed. 'Look, Natalie, I want you to know that if it hadn't been for the cancer I would have called you. I would have wanted to see you again and maybe things might have been very different. And now . . . well, that's what I wanted you to know. I know that we've missed our chance, our moment has passed and it's too late to go back, even if we wanted to. But it matters to me that you know why.'

Natalie blinked and a single tear rolled down her cheek and onto the back of her hand. She was crying for Jack and for herself, but most of all for Freddie. She was crying for her baby who would lose his father before ever really knowing him.

'And now?' she asked him, her voice unsteady.

'Now?' Jack asked her.

'How . . . how long have you got left?' Natalie forced the sentence out with difficulty, feeling as if with each word she spoke her heart was suffering another tiny tear.

Which was why she didn't expect Jack to laugh out loud.

'Oh God,' he said. 'About another sixty or seventy years. I'm not dying, Natalie – I'm cured!'

Natalie burst into uncontrollable tears.

'Oh no, oh God.' Jack stepped towards her as if to embrace her and then thought better of it, his arms hovering before dropping heavily to his sides. 'I'm so sorry, I keep forgetting that other people know as little about it as I did when I first found out. If I had really listened properly to my consultant at that appointment, I would have known then it's ninety per cent curable. I was in the lucky ninety per cent.'

Natalie shoved him back so hard that he fell back onto the settlee with some astonishment.

'You bastard,' she said, her voice low with fury.

'What?' Jack looked confused. 'Weren't you just crying a minute ago because you thought I was dying?'

'You total and utter arrogant bastard,' Natalie said, feeling the tumult of emotions she had been experiencing throughout this evening reaching boiling point in her chest and distilling into one hundred per cent proof rage.

'*Did you even think about what effect your game-playing*

would have on me?' She hurled the words at him. 'You used me. You made me feel all these things, made me trust you and want you and all the time you were playing this *game*!'

'I wasn't,' Jack insisted. 'Not all the time. I just didn't want to . . . I couldn't tell you the truth.'

'Why, because you'd finished needing your *distraction*?' Natalie asked him.

'No, because I didn't want you to know that I was about to be castrated,' Jack shouted. He took a breath and lowered his voice. 'At least that's what it felt like. I didn't want you to see me as a pathetic invalid. I still don't.'

'What if I didn't care about that? What if I thought that the time we spent together was the best time of my life, and that I wanted to be with you even if you were bald and sick and one testicle down?'

'Did you really feel like that?' Jack sounded surprised.

'I don't know,' Natalie said furiously. '*Nobody asked me!*'

'I didn't think it was fair . . .' Jack began, looking utterly confounded by her reaction.

'So you were being all noble,' Natalie said scathingly.

'Well, yes, actually.' Jack clambered to his feet and stood opposite her. 'I did think I was being noble!'

'Well, your nobility was sod-all good for me, Jack,' Natalie told him, her voice low now but no less fraught. She knew that this was her moment at last, and she knew that all chances of her meeting it with dignity and integrity were long gone.

'While you were swanning off being all noble, Jack, I was left wondering what had happened. You could have at least told me that you were being noble, you could have at least told me . . . *something*!'

'Natalie,' Jack said, looking shell-shocked and confused all at once, 'I didn't expect any of this. All I wanted to do was to get things straight between us.'

'Don't worry, we're going to,' Natalie told him.

'What do you mean?' Jack asked her cautiously.

Suddenly Natalie made a grab for her bag, pulling out her wallet and flicking it open to reveal Freddie's photograph. She thrust it in Jack's face.

'What's that?' he asked her, peering at the photo.

'Did they cut out your brain at the same time as your testicle?' Natalie returned sharply.

'What do you mean?' Jack looked again at the photo. 'Oh God, you've had a baby.' He sat back with a thud on the low settle.

'Of course, how foolish of me.' He shook his head. 'Here I am trying to let you down gently . . . I should have known you would have moved on, met someone else – started a family.' He thought for a moment and as Natalie waited she could almost see him doing the sums in his head. He looked up at her. 'You moved on pretty quick,' he said, looking gratifyingly offended.

'Oh, you idiot,' Natalie seethed. 'I told you I had something to tell you too, didn't I? Not that you listened.' She took a breath. 'While you were in Italy being noble with your very curable cancer I was here on my own. Pregnant.'

There, she had said it, but as she looked at Jack she realised he still didn't understand what she was saying. 'About nine months after our weekend in Venice, Jack, I gave birth to a baby boy. To your son.'

Jack's jaw dropped.

'Congratulations, Casanova. You're a father,' Natalie told him.

Chapter Seventeen

Natalie had never thought she would be so glad to be awake rocking a screaming baby at five forty-five a.m. on a Monday morning. But she was more than glad, she was ecstatic because at least that meant that the worst weekend of her life was finally over and she could get back to her unreal life, the life where everybody liked her and she was in control.

The first thing Jack had said once the penny had finally dropped was, 'Are you sure he's mine?'

Natalie snatched back her photo of Freddie and held it close to her chest.

'I'm going,' she said, turning on her heel and looking for her coat.

'Natalie, wait . . .' Jack followed her into the tiny hallway, crowding her out with his presence.

'I didn't mean to say that, it's just a lot for me to take in. I didn't expect to find out that I had a kid!'

'No.' Natalie looked up at him. 'Join the club.'

'Look, I need some time to think,' Jack said. 'I need time to get my head around it.'

Natalie opened the front door and turned back to face him.

'Don't bother, Jack,' she said. 'I don't need you.' The words felt as painful as if her mouth was full of shards of broken glass.

'I don't want you. You've got your whole life ahead of you now, and so have Freddie and I.'

'Freddie?' Jack looked confused.

'That's his name,' Natalie told him.

'Oh. Right.'

'We don't need or want you. We release you. Forget you ever met me or knew about him. Stay out of our lives, please.'

She waited for what seemed like an age for him to say something; to say that he did still want her and that he did want to get to know his son. But Jack's gaze fell to his feet and all he said with a shrug was, 'OK. OK then.'

'Goodbye, Jack,' Natalie said as she shut the door on him for ever.

When she got home all she wanted to do was to find Freddie and hold him in her arms. She raced upstairs and then she stopped just outside her bedroom door.

Her mother was in with Freddie and she was singing to him. She was singing 'Fly Me to the Moon' and not in a drunken sort of way, either. She had a nice voice, smoky and soothing, a voice honed on a thousand fags and countless vodkas.

Suddenly Natalie remembered something: her mother always used to sing Sinatra to her when she was little. In the bath, with bubbles in their hair, they'd sing this song together and Sandy would say that one day they would fly to the moon, just the two of them on the back of a magic bird and, once they'd got there, eat all the cheese two girls could possibly want. How could she have totally forgotten something that now seemed so vivid? Could it be because it was a happy memory? Did it suit Natalie to believe that she had never been happy with Sandy?

She pushed open the door a crack and watched as Sandy

dropped a soiled nappy into the bin and then cleaned Freddie with a wipe.

'Nana's going to get it right this time,' she cooed to the baby. 'No leaving you on your own again, even for a second, you wriggle monster you! I don't know, you'll be all over this house before she knows what's hit her. Mummy's going to have a terrible time trying to find period-style stair gates, I tell you.' Natalie watched as her mother bent down and blew raspberries on Freddie's tummy, conjuring his wonderful gurgling laugh. 'There's a good boy,' she said. 'There's a lovely good boy, aren't you?'

Then Freddie peed in her face.

Natalie clapped her hand over her mouth as the stream of liquid arced upwards and hit her mother dead centre between the eyes.

'Ugh!' Sandy exclaimed, screwing her eyes shut, and for a second Natalie forgot everything except this wonderfully silly tableau.

'Mum!' she said, pushing the door open. 'Are you all right?' She handed Sandy a muslin cloth that was hanging over the end of the bed.

'A bit damp, love,' Sandy replied, chuckling as she dabbed at her face. 'He's a real marksman!'

'Go and wash your face, I'll finish here,' Natalie offered. She stood well back as Sandy passed and then went over to where Freddie was lying on the change table, clearly delighted to be nappyless.

'Hello, baby.' Natalie looked down at him, resting the palm of her hand lightly on his tummy. 'Remember I promised you that I was going to be the best possible mother you could ever hope for?' she asked him. He kicked his legs enthusiastically in response. 'Well, we know where we stand now, darling. We've got nothing left to worry about except us. Except you and me.'

Natalie took a deep breath and made herself smile. 'And we're going to be fine on our own.'

'Not quite on your own,' Sandy said, appearing in the door frame with a damp but clean face. Natalie tried her best to hide her distress, but even her dissembling skills weren't quite up to strength this time.

'What's happened, love?' Sandy asked her.

Natalie picked Freddie up and held his cheek to hers.

'Oh, Mum,' she managed to say through the threat of tears.

'Come on.' Sandy opened her arms and for the first time in twenty years Natalie went to her mother's embrace, and let her hold both her and Freddie.

'I'm here, love,' Sandy said. 'I'm here for you.'

Natalie had cried for a long time, not in a dramatic or noisy wailing way. Not the easy come, easy go hormonal tears that had become such a familiar part of her life recently. She cried because she was in pain. She had just sat down on the edge of her bed with Freddie in her arms and her forehead resting on Sandy's shoulders and the tears had fallen. Sandy hadn't asked her anything more and she hadn't volunteered anything. Eventually Freddie had dozed off and sometime after that Natalie's tears stopped.

'I'm sorry,' she said pulling herself into an upright position suddenly aware of being vulnerable around Sandy. 'It must be tiredness, and the business meeting didn't go as well as I hoped.'

Sandy looked at her sceptically.

'You don't have to tell me anything . . .' she said, clearly hopeful that Natalie would relate everything that had led to her daughter's misery.

Natalie thought about telling her the whole story, and a large part of her wanted to. But then she realised she still couldn't. This moment between her and Sandy, this closeness, was new and most welcome. But Natalie didn't know if it was real or temporary, some kind of glitch in their difficult relationship that might vanish all too soon. She sensed it was a fragile connection between them, and she didn't want Sandy to destroy the one good thing that had happened that night by opening her mouth and putting her foot in it. Besides, she didn't know that there was anyone in the world she felt ready to tell what had happened between her and Jack that night, not even sweetly understanding Tiffany who had listened without judgement to the truth about her and how Freddie was conceived. Somehow in the space of less than an hour she had ricocheted from thinking that Jack might still possibly want her, to finding out about his cancer, to listening to him tell her in so many words that he didn't want to know about his son. It had turned out to be the worst-case scenario she had feared all along, but instead of being able to face it head on she felt as if she'd been played like a pinball through a machine.

'I'm tired,' Natalie told Sandy, nodding down at sleeping Freddie. 'I think I'll join him. But thank you, Mum.'

Sandy smiled. 'Glad to be of help,' she said, leaning over and kissing Natalie on the forehead. 'Goodnight, love.'

Things seemed to go depressingly quickly back to normal between Natalie and her mother after that. When Natalie, in need of a glass of water after feeding Freddie, found Sandy sitting in the kitchen just after one in the morning half-cut and with a drink in her hand, she realised that one tearful hug did not mend everything. It was a spectacularly awful sight that turned out to be even more visually disturbing than the drunken stupor that Natalie was accustomed to. Although the stupor usually involved drooling and Richter-scale snoring, it could at least be ignored. Awake though, and, in Sandy's own words, 'more than a bit squiffy', she was much less easy to avoid. Sitting under the harsh kitchen lights in her short nightie, legs akimbo, she looked like a too scary reject from a horror film featuring the zombie-nympho-undead.

Natalie was depressed further to have been right not to trust her mother with any details about what had happened with Jack. And she was stung that Sandy had felt the need to turn to the bottle so soon after they had had, in Natalie's eyes at least, something of a breakthrough.

'I feel awful,' Sandy slurred, topping up her tumbler to the brim.

'If drinking makes you feel so bad,' Natalie suggested before she thought she might actually commit murder if her mum groaned, passed wind or burped one more time, 'then why don't you stop? It can't be good for you at your age.'

'Nonsense,' Sandy said. 'A little drop here and there never hurt anyone.'

'Fine, drink yourself to death,' Natalie replied, struggling to remember why on earth she had thought they could ever be close.

'You'd like that.' Sandy narrowed her bloodshot eyes at her. 'Then you'd have all my money and all your problems would be over.'

'You're right, of course,' Natalie said sweetly, deciding to decamp back to the relative sanctuary of her bedroom. 'That would be lovely if only you had any money. Goodnight, Mother, no need to tell you where the vodka is.'

Natalie had fumed back upstairs, bitter and resentful that the one glimmer of light to have sparked from her dire encounter with Jack had vanished the moment her mother was relieved of babysitting duties. She clearly loved the drink more than Natalie and Freddie which, Natalie told herself hotly, should be of no surprise to her. To think that for a second there she had thought that Freddie might actually be bringing them closer together!

It had been a long and miserable night, there had been nothing good to watch on TV, and Freddie didn't really sleep, he was in a fretful and restless mood. So all she had to think about in the empty hours of her nocturnal confinement was the look on Jack's face as she had left the flat.

It had been blank, absent of any emotion at all. There was nothing that Natalie could have even hoped to interpret. She had a nagging sense that she had done something wrong, that she could have handled the situation a little better. Perhaps getting very angry with a man for having a traumatic and life-threatening disease had not been her finest moment.

When Natalie thought about what Jack must have gone through she felt a panicky feeling fluttering in her chest, an echo of the intense fear and grief she had felt those few terrible minutes when, listening to his account of events, she had still thought that Jack was going to die. If he had died she would have been devastated, Natalie realised. Did that make things better or worse? Worse, judging by how things were going, she concluded.

And maybe she shouldn't have just sprung Freddie on him the way she had. Yes he had been secretive and deceitful but so had she. If she had really tried hard she could have found Jack, she could have tracked him down and informed him of her pregnancy. But she didn't, partly because in some respects she was old-fashioned and genuinely shy and couldn't quite bring herself to phone the man who had so overtly rejected her, and partly because of reasons that were almost identical to Jack's she supposed.

How could she ask a man she hardly knew to be part of her pregnancy, let alone a father? It seemed unjust. She had assumed that Jack would react badly and leave her, anyway.

The only difference was that whereas he had underestimated her, she had been right about him.

It was that look in his eyes when she told him that she and Freddie didn't need him that she couldn't get out of her head. It wasn't blank, she had been wrong about that. It was a look of relief.

There might have been the slimmest of reasons to hold onto her feelings for him until that moment. There might have been *some* oblique possibility that things could have worked out between them. But if there was then the expression on Jack's face had extinguished any such hope.

Finally Natalie knew that she had to get over Jack Newhouse. She had to do whatever it took.

Now at least the sun was up and the seemingly endless night was finally over.

Monday was a proper day; it was a day of action and outdoors. A day where she felt she could legitimately rejoin the human race as the single, messed-up, largely in denial and mainly dysfunctional person that she was.

Besides – and Natalie had never thought this phrase would lift her heart – it was baby group day. She was going to Jess's house for lunch and then Frances had booked them in at a baby swimming class in the afternoon. All she had to do was to pretend she had never tried to snog Gary, forget that Jack had ever existed and tell her new friends that she was not the married lady and mother-about-town that they thought they knew. She was actually a compulsive liar with potentially the most complicated life of the lot of them. Still, life was full of challenges.

Her first challenge began when Gary arrived exactly at nine a.m., letting himself in with the key that Natalie had given him and finding her in the kitchen still in her pyjamas, a little behind schedule in transforming herself into her weekday super-self due to her exceptionally wakeful night.

Gary had seen her in her large and utterly sexless pyjamas on several occasions but this time Natalie felt more than a little self-conscious to be bra-less and pantless under the thick brushed cotton.

She had hoped that the moment that she had fancied Gary would have passed with the fleeting insanity that the glass of wine had brought on, and the mess of intense emotions that Jack had stirred up in her again would have put paid to any attraction she felt for him. But bizarrely she seemed to be even more drawn to him. It was as if Jack was a raging inferno and Gary was a smooth cool lake. A smooth cool lake with rather powerful forearms and muscular shoulders. Natalie felt bad for thinking of the poor man like this. She had to hope that the condition would wear off, because muscled hunk-of-meat men had never been her type.

Charming, funny, erudite and sophisticated men were supposed to be her type. So why had she fallen for a skinny, no-good wastrel and why did she now fancy her solid and stoical electrician? Gary had barely spoken ten words to her, let alone made her laugh and laugh at some witty urbane aside. But then again neither had he got her pregnant, made her fall in love with him and then, after appearing to be amazingly brave and courageous, spoiled it all by happily exiting from her and her child's life ASAP.

And, after all, today was the first day of her moving on with her life. And what better way to move on than into the arms of a man as different from Jack as he possibly could be? It was just a shame really that he seemed to find her repulsive.

'All right?' Gary greeted her, looking at her left shoulder as he spoke. Natalie rejoiced that at least she didn't have to battle against his sweet-talking charm.

'I'm fine – you?' she replied breezily. 'Good weekend?'

Gary shrugged and his eyes met hers for a moment that, if Natalie wasn't so sure that her present feelings towards him were illusory, would have been electrically sexy.

'Oh you know, the usual,' he said. 'You?'

'Same,' Natalie said. 'Tea?'

He had another tight T-shirt on today. He looked good in it, like he had one of those six-pack things that pop stars in boy bands had. It was the sort of muscular tone that Natalie had never really been drawn to, until the thought of licking that rock-hard stomach suddenly popped into her mind. Yes, she might well be unfortunate enough to think of herself as recovering from being in love with Jack, but Jack wasn't here, and Jack wasn't ever going to be here so it couldn't do any harm to admire Gary in this way. It wasn't as if anything was going to happen.

'Please,' Gary replied. 'And one for Ant too, he's unloading the van.'

Natalie didn't answer him immediately because, despite her silent warnings to herself, just at that moment she wanted to run across the kitchen and rip off that tight T-shirt, lick his nipples and shove his hand up her top.

'Two sugars each, that's right isn't it?' she said instead.

Gary nodded. Natalie decided she had to confront this. She had to get the whole failed-kiss attempt out of the way and then maybe all these other strange feelings she was having would go too; the last thing her already fragile self-esteem needed was to develop feelings for yet another man – even if they were only lustful – who did not want her.

Confronting the botched-kiss attempt would be like aversion therapy, she thought, although she had absolutely no idea what aversion therapy was. Still, she had to do something to break the spell.

'Gary?' she said, after a moment of two of consideration.

'Mm?' Gary glanced up at her. He really did have quite intense eyes, sort of hazel and in their own way very . . . compelling. She took a breath, closed her eyes, opened them again and hoped to see the slightly stocky, not especially tall, sweet but charmless electrician she had hired recently.

Natalie opened her eyes.

No, safe Gary was not there. It was still his German porn-star doppelgänger who was standing in her kitchen. She pressed on.

'Um, about Friday night . . . you . . . when I tried to . . . anyway, I'm really sorry and . . .'

'Friday night?' Gary cut her off with the question. 'It was nice, thanks. Look, don't apologise for your mum, she's a bit full on but harmless, honestly.'

Natalie looked at him for a second.

'Actually I meant when I . . .' Bravely she tried to exorcise her lust demon again.

'Don't mention it. Forget about it, honestly. I'll go and help Anthony unload.' And he was gone.

Natalie stared at the space where he had been standing. He obviously wanted to pretend it hadn't happened. Which meant he wasn't the least bit interested in her sexually, and that when he was looking at her he didn't see a German porn-star housewife waiting to be serviced. He saw a slightly podgy woman in her jimjams still wearing the remnants of yesterday's make-up and probably a bit flushed in the face.

Natalie should have felt relieved. She should have been able to purge her urges for him now that he had made it brutally clear that the whole incident was just a horribly embarrassing hiccup he was happy to forget about. But the contrary part, the difficult, complication-creating part of her that Alice had spent so long trying to retrain, wasn't so sure. Still smarting from the wounds that Jack had left her with, Natalie wanted to know why this man didn't fancy her either. And she wanted to know what she could do to change his mind.

After all, there was no chance she'd ever be with Jack now – so what did she have to lose apart from her dignity?

And she'd lost touch with that particular asset months ago.

Chapter Eighteen

'So? How'd it go?' Natalie asked Jess as she unwrapped the now obligatory Jamaican ginger cake and slid it onto a plate. On her and Freddie's brisk walk over to Jess's she was fairly sure she had boxed up the horrors of the weekend and filed them away in the darkest corners of her mind. She'd spent too long agonising over Jack Newhouse, she had decided. It was time to move on, to leave that complicated and confusing part of her life behind. If she concentrated really hard on putting a spring in her step and a toss in her hair she could almost believe what she wanted her friends to believe, that she was happy.

Jess's smile was shy.

'It was good actually,' she said. 'I must admit I didn't think it would be. I thought you and your rants about knickers was just you being . . . you. But the underwear did make me feel confident about my body, which did make me relax and even though there were one or two little glitches it was worth it in the end. It was so nice to feel that close to him again. Like a proper couple, well, you must know?'

'Oh well, if I did I've forgotten,' Natalie said deliberately ambiguously. It was her new resolution not only to tell the baby group the truth, but also to try not to tell them any more lies.

Meg came into the kitchen with Iris on her shoulder. 'James looks like he's starting a cold,' she said, looking exhausted. 'Poor little thing couldn't sleep, he was up all night grizzling, usually a sure sign he's coming down with something. Combined with Iris in full flow I've had a right old night of it.'

Natalie saw Jess looking anxiously at Iris and then at Jacob, who was sleeping apparently germ-free in his baby chair on the kitchen table. No doubt Jess was praying that her baby didn't pick up James's threatened cold, either directly or via Iris.

'Jess was just telling me that I have single-handedly saved her sex life,' Natalie said, hoping to distract Jess from her worries. 'So I'm ready now for your gratitude.'

Meg smiled. 'Oh it was wonderful, probably the best sex I've ever, ever had.'

'*Really?*' Jess exclaimed, with a wide-eyed laugh. 'Meg!'

'I told you . . .' Natalie said smugly. 'I knew all their marriage needed was the Curzon touch. I could be a lifestyle guru! I could teach arguing couples everywhere how to come together, couldn't I, Meg? Hey?'

But Natalie's smugness was abruptly curtailed when Meg burst into violent tears.

At Natalie's direction, Jess shut the kitchen door as Meg sat down at the table and wept.

'What happened?' Natalie said, taking Iris from her arms.

Meg told them the unedited details of the night and Natalie and Jess went from cursing the inconsiderate husband, to oohing at Meg's surprisingly frank description of the sex part, to swearing quite virulently when she told them about the text she had found on Robert's phone.

'What did you *do?*' Jess asked Meg, her eyes wide with horror.

'Did you beat him over the head with a blunt instrument?' Natalie asked her, feeling at that moment genuinely moved to violence by what in her eyes was a clear cut case of adulterous-guilt sex (not that she wanted to tell Meg that just yet).

'I didn't *do* anything,' Meg said, wiping at her steady flow of tears with the piece of kitchen towel that Jess had handed her. 'I couldn't think what to do. I mean, a few minutes before I'd been so happy, we'd felt so close. I just thought there was bound to be an explanation, it was bound to be something to do with work and nothing to do with me at all. So I just put the phone on the table and I lay down in bed next to him and waited for it to be morning.' Meg sat up a little in her chair and smiled weakly at her two friends. 'And yesterday he was so lovely, like the old Robert again, really loving and attentive. He brought me breakfast in bed and came with me to pick the children up from Frances's; he even told her we couldn't stay for lunch. We took Gripper out and had lots of games in the park. It was wonderful. So I didn't say or do anything because, after all, it *might* be nothing at all, mightn't it?'

Natalie and Jess exchanged glances.

'I suppose it's possible,' Natalie said, sounding as if she thought finding Elvis alive on the moon was far more likely.

'But you have to talk to him,' Jess said. 'You have to.'

'But why? Why do I?' Meg asked her. 'If I confront him and he tells me outright that there is someone else, what will I do? After all, it's not as if he's leaving me. I don't want to be divorced. I don't want to be a single mum with four children. If I don't know for sure then I don't have to do anything, do I?'

'You can't go on not knowing,' Jess said. 'It will just eat away at you, the not knowing. It's better to face the truth even if it's not what you want to hear. You can't live a lie – can she, Nat?'

'Not technically the best plan,' Natalie said after a while, feeling like a dreadful hypocrite. She wanted to say to Meg that single motherhood wasn't that bad really, even if sometimes you felt lonely, bitter and regretful not to mention hurt, battered and bereft. And that with your friends around you, you could do just as well if not better on your own. But she couldn't say any of that because she had abandoned her own admittedly comparatively cushy single-mother status in favour of a fake husband. She understood where Meg was coming from – if she'd felt the need to invent a husband for such a flimsy reason, she could see why Meg would be so keen to hold onto a terrible real-life spouse. But then again Meg didn't want to keep Robert just for appearances's sake. She loved him, she absolute adored him. It was written all over her face.

'Look,' Natalie said. 'I can see why you don't want to confront him. And I think you're right not to, after all it might be nothing at all!' Meg smiled so hopefully at her that for a moment Natalie felt intense guilt at offering her friend what she was certain was false encouragement. 'What we need to do is find out more, build a case. Can you check for other texts, receipts, stuff like that . . .'

'I can't *spy* on him,' Meg said. 'That would be wrong!'

Natalie was on the point of despairing when Frances marched into the kitchen, pushing the door open with such force that it banged against the wall.

'What would be wrong?' she demanded. 'What are you doing here anyway? We are all waiting in there! Tiffany said Natalie had something interesting to tell us and besides, Steve's brought gluten-free poppyseed muffins!'

'Yum,' Jess said, trying hard to sound enthusiastic but only managing sarcasm.

'I haven't got anything interesting to tell anyone,' Natalie put in hastily.

'Well, those sandwiches that Jess apparently made are going curly at the edges,' Frances added accusingly.

'Anyway, why are you waiting and for what?' Natalie asked her. 'There isn't exactly an agenda. Eat the delicious *home-made* sandwiches!'

'This is a baby *group*, which means the group of us meet all at once,' Frances snapped back, shooting Jess a disapproving look for good measure. 'I don't think it's a good idea to have a splinter group, Megan,' she added, talking directly to her sister-in-law. 'You know how funny some people can be.'

'Don't you mean you?' Natalie said under her breath, but Frances didn't hear her, she was too busy examining Meg's red and swollen face.

'Are you *still* ill?' Frances seemed to be affronted by the very idea.

''Fraid so.' Meg nodded, forcing an apologetic smile. 'James has got it now and it will only be a matter of time before the rest of them go down with it.'

'Well, come on then,' Frances said, nodding towards the living room. 'Join the *group*.'

'Let's go through,' Meg said as Frances walked out of the kitchen. 'She hates to feel left out of anything. I think it goes back to when she was at school, you know what girls are like. Poor Frances was a bit of an awkward duck and she never really had any good friends. I won't think about Robert just now. I'm tired and I honestly think I'm getting this cold. I'll think about it when I feel better. I mean, if I'd never seen the text I would be feeling so happy today, as if everything was going right again.'

'OK, but I don't think you can be in denial about this, Meg,' Jess said kindly. 'I think you have to know. There are some instances in life when you have to face the truth however much you are afraid of it, don't you think, Nat?'

Natalie nodded. 'Jess is right,' she said.

'Jess – are you going to be mother?' Frances called out pointedly from the living room.

Natalie shrugged. 'Look, don't worry, I've got a plan to sort this out once and for all.'

'A plan? What kind of a plan?' Meg looked worried.

Natalie patted her firmly on the shoulder.

'Simple,' she said. 'We'll go undercover.'

Steve stood by the edge of the pool, a multicoloured bath towel wrapped firmly around his middle. He was surprisingly hairy, Natalie noticed, surprising because he was light-skinned and sandy-haired with the kind of pale lashes and brows that in a certain light made him look as if he didn't have any at all. Yet his chest was covered with thick darkish-brown hair that thinned into a line that headed in the general direction of his navel. Odd the things you didn't know about people until you went swimming with them, Natalie thought. And drawing her own towel a little tighter round her middle she sucked her tummy muscles in as far as they would go, which was not nearly as far as she wanted.

'Lucy looks so cute in that outfit,' Natalie said as she approached Steve, nodding at the baby who was sporting an all-in-one pink and white striped suit.

'The one thing I regret about having a boy is the lack of opportunity to dress him in pink frilly stuff,' she went on, smiling at Lucy. 'Well, I suppose I could still dress him in pink frilly stuff, he wouldn't know the difference, only I don't want to give him any ammunition to hurl at me later in life.'

Steve, who was regarding the water with a look of mild terror, did not reply.

'Are you OK, Steve?' Natalie asked him.

'I'm fine,' Steve said, looking sideways at her. 'It's just . . . well, I don't know, I feel a bit odd.'

'Odd!' Natalie exclaimed. 'Why? You're not still worrying about being the only man in the group, are you?'

'No,' Steve said, a flush of pink colouring the bridge of his nose. 'This time it's the . . . garb.' He gestured at his half-naked torso. 'It's just I'd never do Baby Music or Aerobics or have tea with you lot in my pants, would I? It feels strange you seeing me almost naked.'

Natalie laughed. She was aware that it probably wasn't the right thing to do, that laughing at a man who was concerned about his female friends seeing him in his Speedos was probably tactless and potentially psychologically damaging. Still, she had had a very emotional and stressful weekend and his worries, as endearing as they were, somehow broke then tension.

'There's no need to get hysterical!' Steve said, looking rather alarmed. He watched a couple of the other mothers file in with their babies and climb into the water. Tiffany and Meg appeared, Tiffany long-legged and resplendent in her school swimming kit and Meg in a maroon number that had no underwiring support at all and was obviously manufactured before the invention of Lycra.

'It's just, *you* are worried about *us* looking at *you* – what about *you* looking at *us*?' Natalie enquired.

'Natalie,' Steve said, 'I just wouldn't. I don't think of you girls in that way at all. I'm a married man.'

Natalie shook her head and grinned. 'Well, most of us are mostly married!'

'I don't mean I think you'll *fancy* me,' Steve said. He lowered his voice and leant his head a little closer to Natalie. 'It's just – well, I haven't been swimming for a while and it looks like I've put on a few pounds since the last time. These trunks are a bit snug shall we say?'

Natalie pressed her lips together for a long time, waiting for the bubble of mirth in her chest to disperse. It wasn't fair to laugh at Steve's anxieties, she told herself sternly. She would never have laughed at any of her female friends if they had been worried about what they looked like in their swimmers.

'Steve, this is a swimming pool,' she began to reassure him. 'Nobody looks at another person in that way at a swimming pool, especially not . . .' Natalie had been about to say you, but as she had been appraising his hairiness only a few moments ago she thought that probably wasn't quite true. 'Especially not men,' she finished instead.

'We women don't judge men by how they look naked. In fact,' Natalie added, a glint of mischief forming in her eye, 'we don't even see your nakedness, it's an evolutionary thing, left over from primeval times. It's designed to stop the female of the species running a mile when the male gets his kit off. So you see, we ladies are blind to your near nudity.'

'Is that true?' Steve asked her dubiously as Meg and Tiffany joined them.

'Absolutely,' Natalie assured him. 'Didn't you see that documentary on it? That posh bloke with the bushy moustache presented it.'

Natalie smiled at Jess, who was joining the group along with Frances. 'You saw that documentary about how women never look at men's bits in swimming pools for anthropological reasons?' Jess blinked at Natalie. 'Steve's worried we're going to ogle his package,' Natalie told her, with a covert wink.

'Goodness me,' Frances said disapprovingly. 'This is why men don't belong in baby groups. It's simply not natural.'

'Ohhh,' Jess finally cottoned on. 'I absolutely did see it. I saw that, Steve – it's true.'

'Really? Oh well, then,' Steve said, dropping his towel. 'That's all right then.'

It was during the cheers, wolf whistles and ripples of applause from Steve's fellow group members – all bar Frances – that Natalie found out something else she didn't know about Steve. He blushed all the way down to his knees.

Once in the water Meg finally began to relax. James, definitely snuffly but in good spirits, was in the free crèche and despite her other worries she was resolved to enjoy this rare time she got to be with Iris alone.

It seemed that Iris was a true water baby, revelling in the depth of the water around her and the sense of weightless freedom she had to be feeling. The baby chuckled delightedly as Meg, carefully supporting her head, whooshed her gently through the water as she followed the teacher's instructions.

Meg loved to hold Iris close to her in the pool and feel the warmth of her baby's skin against her through the coolness of the water. She had her father's eyes, dark and intensely inquisitive, her gaze roaming over the intricacies of the ceiling's various air-conditioning vents and valves. But despite that, Meg felt that her fourth child was more like her than any of the others.

Alex was a mini-version of his father: strong, determined, a natural leader whom other children wanted to befriend. Hazel was perhaps the most physically like her with her red hair and heart-shaped face, but she too had a confidence and zest for adventure that Meg had never had. Meg had always been a homebody. Even as a child she had never been happier than when surrounded with the familiarity of home, much preferring the tranquillity of her own garden to the prospect of holidays by the sea, never really seeing the appeal of the big wide world. Perhaps it was because she was an only child, so comfortable in her own environment that to venture out of it seemed like a pointless exercise. Hazel definitely didn't take after her mother.

James looked like his grandfather, Meg's father. He was the only one of the four to have fair hair and a round face, and she couldn't be sure yet but she was fairly certain the sweet, shapeless nub of his nose would broaden and lengthen just like her father's, and one day he would be a very handsome young man. It was difficult to know what his personality would be like when fully formed, except that he already had an unswerving dedication to the things he loved. Like poor old Teddy, who on Sunday evening Meg had spent a long time trying to sew back into some semblance of his previous self, as if by rescuing Teddy she was somehow salvaging herself at the same time. James had been delighted when she had presented him with the misshapen toy this morning and it seemed that he was still devoted to it, despite Teddy being much less plump than he used to be and now possessing only one eye, one ear and no nose at all.

No, James was not the sort of child to cease to love a toy just because it had been mauled beyond recognition, and Meg admired that about him.

When Meg watched Iris, however, she felt as if she were looking into a mirror.

Iris was almost always cheerful, largely even-tempered except when she was hungry or tired. And although she was still so young she didn't cry or get angry if James snatched a toy from her, instead she'd break into a wide gummy smile and look pleased simply because James was pleased. And most of all Iris liked nothing more than being at home, with the noise of her brothers and sister around her, familiar toys within reach and even the odd curious lick from a friendly poodle. She was a family girl, a homebody, Meg thought as she swooped her gurgling daughter up into the air and down again. Just like her mother.

Prompted by the instructor, Meg let Iris cling on to her

forefingers and took a step away from her so that she could kick and float freely in the water, but as she did that the joy evaporated from Iris's face and she began cry. Quickly Meg pulled her baby to her breast and put her arms around her, suddenly feeling the overwhelming urge never to let Iris go, never to risk letting her out into the world where one day inevitably somebody would be unkind to her, where one day she would feel lost and wish with all her heart to return to the safety of her home and her childhood.

As Meg began to make her way out of the pool, cradling Iris close to her, she thought about Robert and the threat of hurt that had hung over her since she had discovered that text. But he had been so lovely with her since they had made love, so gentle and even tender. And she had watched him with the children yesterday, seen the way he looked at them and at her. It was a look filled with love and pride and satisfaction. An expression that couldn't be fabricated, she was sure. She climbed out of the pool and wrapped a large towel around both her and Iris, feeling her daughter's rapid heartbeat fluttering against her skin.

Whatever that text meant it had nothing to do with her and Robert's marriage, Meg decided. It was nothing that would threaten the life that she and her husband had built up together.

It was simply impossible, because Meg knew, she was absolutely certain, that Robert would never do anything to jeopardise that which he held most dear. And so she had nothing to fear by agreeing to Natalie's foolish scheme of going to spy on him tomorrow morning. If anything, all it would do would be to prove that she was right.

Chapter Nineteen

It was late when Natalie finally got home, gone ten, which was why she was surprised to see that Gary's van was still parked outside.

She stood at the top of the stairs down into the basement and listened. Her mother had music on and was obviously cooking. Somehow she had conned Gary into staying for dinner again, probably with God knew what nefarious intentions, but Gary, who was no fool, couldn't have minded too much because he was still here, after all. Perhaps that was why he didn't fancy her, Natalie thought irritably, perhaps he liked his women wrinkly and sun-dried. In any event, Natalie was not in the mood for either of them just at that moment. Not her mother's drunken flirtation or Gary's inexplicable sexiness. Instead, she unbuckled poor exhausted Freddie and lifted him out of his buggy, deciding to take him upstairs to see if he was hungry. She needed to get her head around what had happened and to work out the extent of her rersponsibility for it.

When she had come up with her wild plan yesterday at Jess's flat she could never have guessed in a million years that it would end the way it had. What she had seen Meg go through this afternoon had certainly put her own problems into perspective, because even though what had happened with Jack had devastated her and knocked her right off her feet, she knew that one day she would recover from it.

She didn't think Meg would ever be able to recover from what she had been through today.

At first their expedition had been quite fun when Natalie, Jess and Meg met up that morning to implement the master plan that Natalie had conceived at yesterday's baby group. They decided they were going to carry out their 'mission' and then go for a late lunch on Upper Street. They planned on picking an especially snooty Italian where their children would annoy and frustrate the mostly childless diners.

They had been laughing in the cab because three women, three babies in buggies and one two-year-old were not the most ideal grouping when it came to a spot of espionage. They had joked about getting some camouflage gear or dressing James up as a pot plant.

'It's OK,' Natalie said when the cab dropped them off on Upper Street close to Robert's head office. 'In fact, the kids are perfect cover. We are a bunch of mothers out shopping. We happened to be passing and you, Meg, thought you'd drop in so James could say hi to his daddy.'

Meg's smile rapidly faded into an anxious grimace.

'But Robert hates me turning up at work unannounced,' she said. 'He says it's frowned upon by management. And anyway, he won't be there. He told me he's driving out to Surrey to meet clients and won't be back until late.'

'He doesn't have to be there, trust me,' Natalie said. 'In fact, if he's not there that's all the better. You can pop into his office on the pretext of leaving him a note, and have snoop at his emails and rifle through his drawers while you're there. Meanwhile, Jess and I will introduce ourselves to any available co-workers and find out if any have names beginning with L, and if they do whether they look like a cheap whoring tart or not.'

Meg's face looked anxious and full of uncertainty, and for a moment Natalie had wondered if it wouldn't be better for them to turn around, go back to Meg's, drink tea and convince themselves that nothing was going on. After all, Natalie more or less lived her life by the 'it will be fine in the end' principle even if the end never quite seemed in sight. Who was she of all people to force Meg into confronting something she didn't want to? Particularly when in her own very recent experience, facing the truth was not nearly as rewarding as it was made out to be.

'Come on, Meg,' Jess said before Natalie could suggest they retreat. 'Like you say, it's probably nothing to worry about. And you dropping into the office doesn't have to mean anything. It's just you taking some friends to meet your husband. After all, you're walking past the door, you're married to him, and you've borne him four children. I think you have a right to pop in, don't you?'

Meg steeled herself.

'I do,' she said. 'I do have a right to pop into my husband's office. Of course I do.' She smiled at the other two. 'After all it's no big deal, is it?'

The offices at Pharmacentric weren't designed to be pushchair-friendly. It took a few minutes to get them all through the turnstiles and past the security guard before they even approached the single and quite cramped lift.

'I think we've blown our cover,' Natalie joked in an attempt to dispel the tension in the lift as it lurched up to the third floor. 'I think that guard guessed we're not Russians using the babies as cover to smuggle out some secret microfilm that we plan to take with the miniature cameras hidden in their dummies.'

And they were actually laughing when they rolled the buggies out of the lift, even Meg. She smiled at the extremely glamorous middle-aged lady who was sitting at the reception desk opposite the lift.

'Hello, Yvonne,' Meg said warmly. 'How are *you*?'

Natalie had noticed that Yvonne's genuine smile at seeing Meg had seemed to fade fleetingly, as if something that had just occurred to her clouded her pleasure as she returned the greeting.

'Meg,' Yvonne said warmly. 'Little James, isn't it? – and the new baby! We weren't expecting you. Robert's not in the office at the moment.'

'Oh? *Isn't* he?' Meg did a rather bad job of feigning surprise. 'Silly me.'

Yvonne's smile seemed frozen for a second, and then as if remembering her manners she stood up and peered over the reception desk. 'Look at her,' she cooed at Iris, who was fast asleep in her buggy. 'She's absolutely beautiful, and still so small . . . Four months is she now?'

Natalie remembered thinking it was strange that Yvonne seemed so touched by how small Iris was and had not commented on how much she had grown and how time had flown since her birth, because that was almost the stock response for any given person meeting any given baby. It was surprising too that Yvonne wasn't smiling as she admired Iris.

'I is big,' James said, drawing himself up to his full two feet and puffing out his chest. 'Like my daddy.'

'You are, darling,' Yvonne said, sitting back down on her chair, this time mustering a smile for James. 'You are a lovely, big, strong, handsome boy, who's going to break a few hearts one day I don't doubt . . .' She glanced at her watch.

'Well, lovely to see you again, Meg,' she said, obviously meaning it as a farewell.

'A-hem,' Jess coughed melodramatically and waggled her eyebrows at Meg, looking so comical that Natalie had to turn her face away from her and stifle a giggle in her hair.

'Don't forget that thing,' Jess urged, nodding at Meg. 'You know, the thing that was the reason why you had to pop in?'

Meg looked blank, like an actor who had just forgotten her lines in front of a full house.

'That note you wanted to leave in Robert's office,' Natalie prompted her pointedly. 'If he wasn't in when you popped by? Remember? You said you wanted to leave a note in his office?'

'Oh yes!' Meg said, going a bit pink. 'Sorry, Yvonne – do you mind if I pop into his office to leave a note on his desk? A few bits and pieces I'd like him to bring home, if he ever comes home that is!' Meg laughed, but even though Yvonne chuckled along with her she seemed unable to look her directly in the eye.

'Of course,' she said. 'Go ahead.'

Meg left Iris and James with Jess and Natalie as she went into Robert's office.

'I've heard a lot about this company,' Natalie lied shamelessly to Yvonne. She had no idea what Pharmacentric did, only that Robert was in some kind of sales. 'Do you enjoy working here?'

'Oh yes,' Yvonne said, seemingly very interested in the movements of the lift while maintaining her professional charm. 'It's a good bunch of people.'

'I heard that Robert's PA is excellent, I'm looking for a new PA for my business. I was thinking about trying to poach his – what was her name again?'

Yvonne looked a little puzzled.

'Brian,' she said. 'Young Brian, he's a graduate trainee, keen to get into sales. Robert's training him on the job.'

'Oh, that's right,' Natalie said, exchanging a look with Jess, who seemed to be on the brink of a fit of giggles. 'Brian, Brian the Brain I've heard Robert calls him.'

'Does he?' Yvonne looked nonplussed. 'I've heard Robert call him a lot of things but never that.' Yvonne dipped her head back to her computer screen, where she was inputting some information.

Natalie and Jess exchanged a frenzy of facial expressions over Yvonne's head which could have been loosely be interpreted as:

'Go on then!'

'No you go on then!'

'Ask her!'

'*You* ask her!'

'Do you need potty?' James asked them both. 'You got funny poopy faces. Want to sit on pot-pot?'

'No thank you, James,' Natalie said, her voice vibrating with repressed laughter. 'I'm fine on the pot-pot front.' She raised her eyebrows at Jess and added heavily, '*I've* got guts of steel. Never been known to back down from a challenge.'

Jess rolled her eyes and after a second's thought, addressed Yvonne directly.

'Now I come to think of I used to go to school with someone who works here,' she said, struggling to keep a straight face. 'Have you got a Lucy?' Yvonne looked blank. 'Oh wait I mean Lorna . . . or . . . Laura or possibly Linda . . . I mean, I don't remember her name exactly, only that it begins with an L and I heard she works here now?'

'Lynne, Lynne Sisely – is that who you mean?' Yvonne looked uneasily at the lift doors when she said the name.

'That's her,' Jess said, catching Natalie's eye. 'Lynne – what's her job here again?'

'Lynne's a sales manager. Does all the head office liaison.'

'You should pop in and say hello to her,' Natalie told Jess. 'Is Lynne in her office?'

Yvonne looked stricken.

'No, no she isn't.' She looked at her watch and back at the lift doors. 'Meg seems to be writing him a very long note, I wonder if she . . .'

The lift bell pinged. Natalie was certain that Yvonne held her breath for the two seconds it took for the doors to slide open, revealing a couple of young men in suits.

'Here I am!' Meg reappeared, reaching out her hand to James as she smiled at Yvonne. 'Sorry I've been so long, it took me ages to find a pen would you believe? Well, we'd better be off. Lovely to see you again, Yvonne.'

'And you, Megan,' Yvonne said. She suddenly reached across the desk and laid a hand on Meg's forearm. 'It really is lovely to see you again, and your children. They are so beautiful.'

'Thank you.' Meg looked about, confused by the unexpected rush of affection from Yvonne.

'So?' Jess asked her once they were crammed into the lift. 'What did you find out while you were in there?'

'What do you mean, what did I find out?' Meg asked her.

'All that time you were "looking for a pen",' Natalie prompted Jess. 'Did you check his emails?'

'Or look in his desk?' Jess added.

'No!' Meg sounded shocked. 'I really was looking for a pen.'

Natalie and Jess groaned in unison.

'Look,' Meg said as the slow and rickety lift rumbled to a stop on the ground floor. 'While I was in there I was thinking, what on earth am I doing? I'm being crazy. I've just had the most wonderful weekend with my husband in ages, he even came home early last night. He put the kids to bed and we had a Chinese and a bottle of wine on the floor in front of the TV, just like when we were first together. The truth is we've had a rough patch and maybe I don't know all the reasons why, but if we're through it and if we're fine then maybe I don't need to know. Things are really good at the moment so why would I, based on hardly any evidence at all, rifle through his desk looking for proof of an affair? It would be wrong, like a violation of our relationship. I did decide one thing when I was in his office – I was looking at a photo of us on holiday last year when Iris was still a bump. We're a unit, a team, and Roberts deserves my trust and respect. The more I think about it the more I'm sure it's nothing to worry about. When he gets in tonight I'll just ask him about it like a woman who has a good relationship with her husband can, and he'll have a perfectly good explanation . . .'

It was at that moment that the lift doors slid open. What the three women and assorted infants saw revealed before them like a tableau in Greek tragedy took some moments to absorb.

For a microsecond Natalie thought that the couple locked in a wet and passionate kiss as they waited for the lift to come were guilty of poor taste and nothing more.

But then she turned and saw the look of frozen horror on Meg's face, and she realised that the couple were not just people.

The man had to be Robert and the woman, if Natalie's guesswork proved correct, was the infamous Lynne Sisely.

The lift doors shut again without Robert or his friend seeing them.

'Who was the lady Daddy was kissing bye-byes to?' James asked his mother innocently.

Instinctively Natalie slid her arms under Meg's elbows and supported her friend as her knees buckled beneath her. If it had been possible for Meg to collapse in that small and airless space, Natalie was certain that she would have done so. She would have lain on the floor and screamed her head off if it had not been for the lack of floor and her children. Instead she gripped Natalie's wrist tightly in her fingers, until the flesh around them went white, and she stood her ground.

'What do we do?' Jess asked Natalie. 'Do we go up again?'

'Yes,' Natalie began. 'I think we should go up and wait . . .'

'No,' Meg said, her voice quiet but strong. 'No, we don't go up. We go out.'

'Are you sure?' Natalie asked her. 'Maybe you need a little time to collect your thoughts . . .'

But to Natalie's amazement, Meg took a deep breath and let go of her wrist. Reaching out, she pushed the 'doors open' button.

This time Robert and Lynne were not entangled when the doors opened and Robert's eye met Meg's.

Natalie seemed to remember everything that happened in the seconds that followed as a series of stills – almost like a photostory on the problem page of a tabloid newspaper.

Robert's face grew ashen the moment he recognised his wife and children standing in the lift in front of him, and in that same moment he dropped Lynne's hand and took a step away from her.

Meg advanced out of the lift, just like, Natalie thought as she remembered the scene, Queen Boudicca about to face down thousands of Roman soldiers, defiant even in the face of certain death.

Lynne Sisely looked for a moment as if she was going to make a run for the stairs but her face hardened and she didn't move. She was staying to fight her corner Natalie realised, and at the same time resolved not to let Lynne get in the way of anything Meg and her husband had to say to each other.

'Darling,' Robert said, his voice shaky. 'What a lovely surprise.'

'I saw you,' was all that Meg managed to say, her voice tight as if her throat was constricted by some external pressure.

'Yes, I know, I was supposed to be in Surrey, wasn't I? But the clients just cancelled. So inconsiderate – but at least I'll be home early; we can all have dinner together, hey, James?' Robert addressed his son, who, perhaps sensing the crackling tension in the air, had retreated behind Meg's long skirt and didn't seem terribly keen on coming out any time soon.

Robert walked forward and made an attempt to kiss Meg but she shook him off, barely managing to suppress her emotion.

'James,' Jess called lightly as she took the handle of Iris's buggy and guided it, along with her own, towards the door. 'Help me with Iris's pram and you and I can look at the sweet shop next door. We might find you a lolly. We'll wait for Mummy there.'

It seemed that the lure of a lolly was all that could persuade James to tear his eyes away from his parents and follow Jess as she made a hasty if haphazard exit.

Natalie did not move except to position herself and Freddie at Meg's shoulder.

'Meg.' Robert's face looked so full of tender concern that for a moment Natalie thought it was Lynne who was going to clock him one. 'This isn't what it looks like.'

'I saw you kissing her,' Meg said, her tone now taut, edged with disgust but clear. 'Groping her. Tell me, how is that not what it looks like?'

Robert seemed to struggle to catch up with the turn of events.

'Meg I . . .' Possibly he thought that he would be able to explain himself. But Meg had other ideas.

'When you came home hours late on Saturday night you had spent the day with her, hadn't you?' She wasn't so much asking him as telling him. 'You got out of her bed and into mine, didn't you? You had sex with me, knowing you'd just been *fucking* her.'

The alien sound of Meg's voice swearing seemed finally to make Robert understand how serious the situation was. His face blanched white and Natalie could see genuine panic in his eyes. Was it losing Meg that concerned him or was it just being found out? She couldn't tell.

'Look, we need to talk,' he said eventually, 'but not here, not like this – let's go home . . .'

'Why?' Meg said as if she couldn't hear his pleas. 'Why, Robert? Don't you have enough? What about your children? Did you give them a single thought while you were doing this? I just can't . . . I can't believe this is happening to us . . .'

'I needed someone who was there for *me*,' Robert began with a determination to be heard.

Meg looked from Robert to the highly coloured Lynne, and Natalie guessed that in that nanosecond she had pictured them in each other's arms and she couldn't bear what she saw.

'I can't . . . I just can't.' Meg began to head for the door.

'I don't love her!' Robert said as he followed her. 'I love you.'

Natalie blocked Lynne's attempt to follow Robert with Freddie's buggy.

'Oh dear,' she said to Lynne with an icy little smile. 'He doesn't love you, apparently! You wait, he'll be saying he was using you for sex next.'

'He doesn't mean it,' Lynne said, watching her lover chase after his wife. 'He told me he loved me, loads of times.'

Robert had caught Meg by the door, grabbing hold of her forearms.

'It's you that I love, Meg, it's you that I want. This thing with . . . her, it was nothing, it was just sex, I promise you. I

277

thought it might be love but then on Saturday night I realised it was you I love, you and our children – I always have!'

'Usually I hate to say I told you so but in this case I'll make an exception,' Natalie said to Lynne. 'That *was* all you were to him – sex.'

'Just sex!' Meg shouted, looking as if every word she was speaking was causing her physical pain. 'Just sex? How can you say that it's *just* anything? It's everything, Robert! It's years of trust and love and intimacy ruined, all ruined, and if you realised on Saturday night that you loved me how come you are still managing to fuck her on Monday lunchtime?'

Robert was speechless for a second or two, and then he seemed to realise where he was. He was standing in the foyer of his office building with a street full of shoppers walking by outside and a couple of security guards and God knew how many CCTV cameras watching his wife screaming abuse at him.

'Look, I'll come home with you,' he said levelly to Meg, as if she was being needlessly hysterical and he was the sensible one. Both Natalie and Lynne gasped as Meg turned around and shoved him so hard that he staggered backwards and fell over, sprawling at her feet.

'Don't bother.' Meg looked down at him. 'Don't bother coming home now or ever. It's too late.'

Natalie watched her walk out of the building and she saw Robert staring after her, sprawled on the floor, finally calculating what he had risked and probably lost.

She looked at Lynne, whose skin was blotched and angry. She looked older than she probably was, haggard and worried. She looked like a woman who was tired of being alone and who thought she had finally found someone to love her, even if he was never there when she woke up in the morning. If

Natalie hadn't hated her quite so much she might even have felt sorry for her. But she did hate her, very much.

'He is leaving her for me,' Lynne said to Natalie. 'He *said* he loves me.'

Natalie took a step closer to Lynne and looked her up and down.

'I'm not a perfect person, Lynne. I've been around the block a good few times. Even had more than one boyfriend at once on occasion. But I tell you one thing I have never done. I've never, ever gone after a man who's married, let alone one with children. I've never been so pathetic and so desperate that I'd want to break up a family and do that to another woman.' Natalie leaned even closer to Lynne's face. 'If you know what's good for you, you'll pull yourself together and have some self-respect. You are pitiful.'

Lynne took her eyes off Robert and glared at Natalie.

'But I love him,' she told her with complete conviction.

'Then I feel sorry for you. I really do. You've wasted your love on someone who won't ever love you back.'

'Just who do you think you are?' Lynne shouted at her furiously.

Natalie smiled at her serenely. 'A better person than you,' she said. She wheeled Freddie's buggy over Lynne's toes as she left. 'And it's not often I get to say that.'

When they got back to Meg's house it was time for the older children to be picked up from school. Meg had asked for some time to get herself together and had gone up to her room with Gripper closely at her heels. Natalie thought it was best to leave her to herself for a while to let the events of the day truly sink in. She and Jess would be there when Meg needed them.

Jess volunteered to go and fetch Alex and Hazel.

'I can go if you like,' Natalie said as Jess zipped up her jacket in the hallway, but Jess shook her head.

'I don't know what to say to her,' she said. 'I can't get my head round it. You should stay with her. You always know the right thing to say.'

'Do I?' Natalie said thoughtfully. If it was true it was news to her.

'Well, better than me,' Jess said. She had started to unfold her buggy again. 'I realised something today. I was a bit jealous of Meg, because she seemed to have it all, didn't she? This house, no money worries, four healthy children and a husband who earns big bucks. But she doesn't have the one thing that I have got, the one thing I couldn't have coped without over the last few years. She doesn't have a partner she can truly trust. We're luckier than we realised, aren't we?'

'Lee is a good man by the sounds of it,' Natalie said with a smile. 'Listen, you can leave Jacob here if you like. I might as well watch him along with James, Iris and Freddie – that way you'll have one less child to manage on the way back and two free hands for road crossing.'

Jess looked down at the half-erected buggy for a few seconds and then back up at Natalie. 'It's stupid, I know,' she said awkwardly. 'And trivial, considering everything that's happened not to mention probably pointless considering he's been with them all day, but I'm worried about Jacob catching their cold. I mean I'm worried sick.' She caught her lip in her teeth.

'He's not been ill yet,' she went on. 'Not properly. And I fall to pieces if he cries a lot or has a bit of heat rash. I don't know how I'll cope when he's really ill. I know I can't avoid it but it terrifies me, Natalie. What if I can't look after him, what if he gets really ill and . . .'

Natalie realised what Jess was about to say and tried her best to make light of her fears.

'That won't happen, Jess, honestly. Babies are really strong,' she said. 'They are much tougher than we think. They don't just die!'

The moment she said the last word in that sentence, Natalie knew by the look on Jess's face that she absolutely did not have the knack for saying the right thing.

'Oh, Jess, I'm sorry, what have I said?' Natalie reached out and touched Jess's arms. 'I was only joking, or at least trying to – are you OK?'

Jess sat down heavily on the stairs. 'I've lost two babies,' she said bleakly. 'One to miscarriage and one was stillborn. They both just died, Natalie, and nobody really knows why. No reason, they said at the hospital. No reason? So babies *do* die and they die for no reason, I *know* they do.'

'Oh, Jess,' Natalie said. 'I can't believe how thoughtless I was.'

'You didn't know.' Jess offered the empty platitude.

'It must have devastated you,' Natalie said, the final facets of Jess's sometimes fragile personality slipping into place. 'It must have made your pregnancy with Jacob very frightening.'

Jess nodded and rubbed her eyes with clenched fists.

'At the hospital after I had delivered my little girl they brought her to me. They wrapped her up in this soft white blanket and put her into my arms. She was tiny, but so perfect. I looked at her and I couldn't understand how someone so beautiful, so perfect looking could just die. Her little face was so pale and still, like a porcelain doll's, and I wished and wished for her to open her eyes. I never got the chance to look into her eyes.'

'Oh, Jess,' Natalie whispered.

'Sometimes I'll wake up in the middle of the night with a start and for a few seconds before I tune into Jacob's crying or realise that I need the loo I'll see him lying like that in his cot,

281

pale and still. I have to go and hold him, wake him up even, until I can make the nightmare go away.'

Natalie knelt in front of Jess on the tiles in the hall and put her arms around her.

'I shouldn't be telling you this now,' Jess said apologetically. 'Not when Meg needs us. But I've wanted to tell you all for some time now. I just didn't know how to; people feel awkward and embarrassed when they know, they stop looking me in the eye for a while.'

'Of course you should tell us,' Natalie said. 'And it's no surprise that you feel so frightened and so anxious about Jacob's well being. You'd be strange if you didn't fret about him, especially after what's happened to you. But I look at you, Jess, and all I can see is an amazingly courageous woman.' Natalie brushed the hair back from Jess's face and tilted her head upwards. 'You have been brave enough and strong enough to face some truly terrible ordeals, and you've come through them with a partner who loves you and a happy healthy baby boy. And don't you think that if you are courageous enough to survive that then you owe it to yourself and to Lee and Jacob not to falter now? Sometimes you have to be just as brave and courageous to be happy.'

Jess gave Natalie a watery smile. 'You are a very wise person,' she told her.

Natalie sat back on her heels, and shook her head. 'I'm so not,' she replied, a little embarrassed. 'I just want to see you happy and relaxed, enjoying your lovely boy.'

Jess nodded as she stood up and kicked the buggy so that it clicked shut. 'I'll leave Jacob here with you,' she said.

'Are you sure?' Natalie asked her. 'I mean, I can go if you like and you stay with the babies?'

'No, you're right, it's getting cold out there and it would probably be just as bad for him to be out in this weather. I'll go and get Alex and Jacob alone.' She smiled. 'I need some fresh air to clear my head anyway.'

'Have you remembered the password?' Natalie asked Jess as she held the front door open for her. She was referring to the secret word that Jess had to give to be able to collect the children from school.

'Yes, Armageddon,' Jess said. It had doubtless been meant as a joke when Meg had thought of it months ago. But as her world seemed to be coming to a violent and destructive end it didn't seem very funny any more.

Natalie laid Freddie down in his cot and rocked him, watching the two bright points of reflected light in his eyes in the darkness until finally he couldn't fight sleep any more and his lids flickered shut.

The last couple of days had been nothing like she had envisioned. For one thing she had had no chance to get her own pointless secret off her chest and tell the baby group the truth about her and Freddie. But she thought of the look on Jess's face as she told Natalie about her lost babies. And she thought of Meg as she had left her, shell-shocked and utterly powerless to change what was happening to her life. And Tiffany's face as her mother had asked her to leave. Those women had all been through something awful, something that it would be impossible to recover from without the utmost strength of will.

All that had really happened to her was that she'd met a man and they'd spent a few great days together that had turned out rather differently from how either of them had expected. Perhaps she had spent the intervening months between then and now building their encounter into something much more significant and important than it really was, because she had needed that crutch of expectation to keep her going. At least she now knew where she stood, and a bruised heart and hurt pride were small prices to pay for the precious legacy that would bring her a lifetime of love and happiness: a son who had maybe made her a better person than she had ever been. In comparison to her friends *she* had hardly suffered at all.

Yet if there was any tragedy, any victim, in what Natalie and Jack had stumbled into, it was Freddie. Poor little Freddie, who didn't have a clue as to what was going on around him.

But at least he felt safe and secure and loved, Natalie was sure of it. And if she could keep him feeling that way from this moment on until the day she died, at least she'd be doing something right. She'd be doing her best for him.

That was something she *could* get right.

Chapter Twenty

With Freddie settled, Natalie went to the top of the stairs. She couldn't hear any noise coming from below so she ventured down slowly, stair by stair, until she reached the hallway. The tiles felt cold against her bare feet. She peered out of the window. Gary's van was still parked outside. He really must genuinely like her mother. Unless of course she had paralysed him with her crippling venom, leaving him powerless to fight her off. Or more likely got him so drunk that sex with an OAP seemed like a good idea.

The kitchen door opened and a swell of Latin-American music followed by her mother's cackle floated upwards.

'Nonsense,' Sandy was saying as she was coming up from the kitchen. 'You simply have to stay for another coffee. I wouldn't ask you, Gary, but I get nervous being in this big old house on my own. Now, I'll just find some more whisky to give those coffees a little kick and . . . Oh, it's you.'

Sandy appeared at the top of the stairs in a brightly coloured kimono-style dressing gown, a lit cigarette in one hand, a tumbler of something amber-coloured in the other and to complete the look, her ratty and ancient hairpiece that she persisted in jamming onto her head despite the fact that it had stopped bearing any resemblance to the actual colour of her hair about fifteen years ago. She was dressed to kill, and not just by scaring people to death, Natalie realised.

Her mother on the pull was the very last thing she needed to confront.

'I told you not to smoke in the house,' Natalie said quietly. Sandy giggled.

'Gary said you'd say that, but as I said to him, if you and young Fred aren't in, what harm can it do? I didn't hear you come in – sneaking up on me now, are you?' She tottered a couple of steps closer to Natalie on her heeled slippers. 'He is ever so lovely, you know. We've just been talking and laughing all evening. I can't get him to have a drink, mind, and he keeps trying to leave but I think I'm in there, so no hard feelings.' Sandy slapped one hand on Natalie's shoulder, her blurred features looming in Natalie's face. 'Be a love and stay out of the way,' she said, finishing off with a loud hiccup.

Natalie had *never* been in the right mood for one of her mother's special harlot performances. Not even as a young girl when Sandy had still seemed genuinely glamorous and pretty to her did she enjoy her mother's company when she was in seduction mode. But if there had ever been a time when Natalie was the furthest from being able to tolerate Sandy's narcissistic foolishness, then this was it. Today of all days Natalie could not stand her a second longer.

She plucked the cigarette out of Sandy's hand, opened the front door and threw it out onto the street and pushed the door shut again. Then before Sandy could protest she snatched the glass out of her hand and emptied it in one burning swallow that told her it was the cooking brandy she'd had at the back of the cupboard for at least three years.

'You cheeky madam . . .' Sandy began, her reactions somewhat delayed by cheap booze.

'When I *say* you can't smoke in my house I *mean* you can't smoke in my house, not ever,' Natalie said, her voice full of pent-up fury and frustration as she regarded her mother. 'Just look at yourself, Mother.' Natalie put the glass down on the hall table and now taking Sandy's shoulders, directed her to her reflection in the hall mirror.

'Can't you see what you look like? Don't you have any sense of reality any more? You can't think you look good like that, you can't. You look ridiculous, Mum, you look . . . awful.' Natalie stared at her mother's reflection but Sandy seemed to be numbed to what she knew were hurtful comments. She just shook Natalie's hands off her shoulders and staggered a few steps until she was a safe distance from the mirror.

'You're just jealous,' Sandy slurred.

'Jealous!' Natalie exclaimed. 'That's a laugh!'

'You've always been jealous of me,' Sandy persisted. 'Even when you were little girl. You couldn't stand me having any fun. You hated the fact that men were interested in me. The moment Mummy got any interest you'd start attention-seeking. What you never realised is that I am more than just your mother. I am a woman too.'

'You were never *anyone's* mother!' Natalie heard herself shout, and dimly realised that Gary must have heard it too. She didn't care. 'A woman who drags her daughter from town to town latching onto whichever lowlife will tolerate her until he gets bored with her – that's not a mother. All you ever cared about was you. Always looking for the next man, always telling me that this was The One. How many of them were there, Mum? Twenty at least, must be. You didn't care about what happened to me. I was just the burden you would have got rid of if you'd had the guts!'

'I loved you,' Sandy began shakily. 'I always put you first. If your father hadn't . . .'

'Don't you talk to me about my father,' Natalie said angrily. 'He's nobody, some man you barely knew – and all I

287

was to him was some dirty secret he hoped would never get out.'

'I loved him,' Sandy said.

'You've never loved anyone but yourself,' Natalie told her bitterly.

'I love you!' Sandy replied, close to tears. 'You must know I love you.'

'I've never known it,' Natalie replied, her voice like ice. Why did Sandy do this to her? Just when she felt that things were improving between them her mother would do something, say something, that made Natalie feel as if they were strangers, continents apart, and as if she were split into two. As she spoke she was aware that the sound of her voice was cold and indifferent – she knew she must appear hard and uncaring, when the truth was exactly the opposite. But she could not bring herself to reveal her still raw and bruised feelings to Sandy, she could not trust her mother to understand or to care enough. The more Sandy pleaded with her the further Natalie wanted to be from her, and the more she hated herself for it. Hated herself and the chemical reaction that turned her to stone, impervious to her mother's tears.

'It was different then, in the seventies and even the eighties,' Sandy said. 'To be an unmarried mother with no dad around. People looked at you differently. Like you were just a stupid tart.'

'They weren't far wrong, were they?' Natalie said cruelly.

'You can talk,' Sandy shot back.

'You're right, Mum, can't think where I picked that up from.'

Sandy seemed to bite back her retort. 'It was hard, Natalie. I tried my best. You were never an easy child.'

Suddenly Natalie found that she was crying. The tears were running down her cheeks and she could not stop them.

'Do you know why I don't call you?' she asked her mother. 'Why I didn't tell you about Freddie? Why I didn't tell you what really happened to me on Saturday even though I wanted to, even though I was desperate to? Because I keep hoping that one day you'll change or I'll change and that somehow we will fit together properly. I keep hoping that one day I will actually be able to feel close to you. I even thought that Freddie might change something between us. But he hasn't. You're the same as you always have been, Mother. And that's why I don't call you. Because I can only keep hoping when you are not here.' Natalie shook her head, desperate for Sandy to react in *some* way. 'Don't you realise that? Don't you care?'

Sandy's face looked horribly tired and haggard in the harsh hall light and her hairpiece had slipped to one side.

'I'm sorry, Natalie,' she said, as if Natalie had been trying to talk to her about the price of eggs. 'I'm a little bit drunk. I think I ought to go up now. I'll see you in the morning, dear. Say goodnight to Gary for me.'

Natalie stood perfectly still until she heard her mother's bedroom door close and then she sat on the stairs and put her head in her arms and wept.

She wasn't sure how much time had passed when she noticed Gary's boots in her field of vision.

'Um, you OK?' he said.

'I seem to be doing a lot of sitting on steps blubbing,' Natalie said, taking a deep breath and wiping her face on her sleeve before looking up. Gary looked like a man caught between the horror of having to deal with a weeping woman and his general sense of decency.

'Is it the hormones?' he asked her hopefully as he manfully made the decision to sit on the step next to her.

Natalie shook her head, and took a few deep breaths to steady herself.

'You probably heard,' she said, forcing a watery smile. 'Mum and I had a bit of a tiff.'

Gary's large hands rested on his knees and he looked at them for a long moment before using one to pat Natalie's shoulder a couple of times.

'I heard,' he said, returning his hand to his knee. 'Look, I'm sorry I was here at all and that I let her get so drunk but she sort of got me cornered and I don't know, I never used to think I was the pathetic type but I couldn't seem to get past her. I kept thinking you were bound to come home soon and rescue me. But you were a long time.'

Natalie glanced sideways at Gary and realised that he was quite traumatised by the evening himself. She found herself chuckling.

'It's not funny,' he said. 'I kept thinking that wig thing was going to leap off her head and get me in the jugular.'

'I'm sorry to laugh,' Natalie said. 'I don't know why I am. It's been a horrible day. My friend Meg caught her husband with another woman. I was at her house. The husband came back and it got pretty messy.' Her smile disappeared as she thought about everything that had happened at Meg's house. 'It took a long time to calm her down. Her sister-in-law turned up and threw us out, otherwise I would have stayed the night and then you would've been in trouble.'

Gary's brow furrowed.

'That's horrible,' he said. 'I know what that's like.'

Natalie looked up at him. 'Do you?' she asked.

He nodded and she saw in his face the echo of a past pain. 'It takes a lot to get over it. I'm not really over it now. I mean, I don't miss my ex any more. But it's my girl. I've got access rights but she moved away. I can't find my daughter, I

290

think she's gone overseas. I haven't seen her in years . . .' Gary took a deep breath. 'I'm worried that she thinks I don't love her.'

Natalie looked at him then and this time it was her hand that rested on his shoulder.

'That's awful,' she said.

Gary shrugged, the muscles of his shoulders moving under her palm.

'Keep looking for her, Gary,' Natalie said. 'Because even if you don't find her, one day she'll be big enough to come and find you, and if you can show her that you wanted her and you really tried to find her it will mean a lot to her. It will mean everything.'

'I'll never stop trying,' Gary said with a sniff, glancing away from Natalie and perhaps brushing a tear away. 'Look, let's not talk about me. I don't usually like to talk about it. I'm not good at talking about . . . stuff.'

'Me neither,' Natalie said. 'Not real stuff anyway. I'm very good at talking about nothing in particular, or making things up off the top of my head. But when it comes to talking about anything that is actually important and serious I turn into a total moron. I never seem to be able to make it happen in real life the way I see it in my head and then people get upset and cross and storm off and I'm always the one to blame somehow, even when they are quite clearly in the wrong just as much if not even more so than me and . . .' She stopped herself before she said too much, and shrugged. 'I'm babbling. Babbling is also one of my fortes.'

He looked sideways at her and then took a breath. 'The other night when you nearly kissed me . . .'

'Oh, look, don't feel like you to have to start talking on my account,' Natalie interrupted him hastily.

'I like you, Natalie,' Gary said. 'Have done since I first saw you, even though you were all covered in crap and looked awful.'

'Oh thanks,' Natalie said, with a small laugh. 'You charmer, you.'

Gary blushed. 'I'm not good at that sort of thing either,' he said.

'I like that about you,' Natalie assured him, leaning just a little closer to him so that her bare forearm almost touched his. Gary continued looking steadily at his intertwined fingers.

'I mean, you've got something about you, you're very attractive, a sort of . . . womanliness,' he said, obviously struggling to form the compliments.

'Are you saying I'm fat now?' Natalie teased him gently, unable to resist.

Gary shook his head. 'You know that's not what I'm saying. What I mean is for all your brashness and self-confidence you've got this vulnerability – a sort of fragility. Sometimes when the fronts drop you look like you need someone to put their arms around you and protect you.'

Natalie didn't speak. She couldn't. Somehow Gary had managed to encapsulate exactly how she was feeling at that moment, and the urge to have his arms around her overtook any challenge she had set herself to kiss him simply as a diversion.

'It's obvious you're not completely happy at present,' Gary went on. 'And I know it's because you miss your husband.' He managed to look her in the eye. 'So what I'm saying, Natalie, is that you shouldn't lunge at any old bloke you happen to find to try to get back at him when he's not even here to know about it. You're worth more than that. If you miss him that much you should tell him to come home, tell him to pull his socks up before he loses an amazing woman and maybe even his son. Give him the chance to do the right thing. Marriages are worth working at.'

Natalie looked at Gary steadily. 'You are an amazingly perceptive and lovely man,' she said. 'And far, *far* too nice and kind to get involved with me and my car crash of a life but . . .'

Gary blushed deeply and Natalie thought she saw the whole of his body tense at her words.

'What I wanted to say was that if you hadn't been married I'd have kissed you back,' he said. 'But I make it a rule not to get involved with married women. I *know* how much it hurts people and besides, the last thing I need is angry husband on my case.'

Natalie froze for a second as she digested his words.

'Look,' Gary went on. 'I'm sure he'll come to his senses if you talk to him. I'm sure he would come back if you asked. Think about everything you've got. Your little boy, this house – it's too much to throw away over an electrician. Even a hot one like me.'

'Gary.' Natalie was getting that familiar feeling in the pit of her stomach. The feeling she got whenever she was about to do something utterly insane that was bound to have all sorts of consequences she hadn't thought of until after they'd happened. How could Gary be so right and so wrong about her at the same time? She didn't know, but one thing she did know was that she didn't have a husband at all, angry or otherwise.

'Yeah?' Gary asked her.

'I'm not married,' Natalie told him.

'Pardon?' Gary looked at her blankly.

'I haven't got a husband in Dubai. I made him up because . . . well, it seemed like a good idea at the time. You were right about Freddie's dad, about how I feel about him. But he's never coming back. I'm on my own, I'm not married.'

Gary and Natalie looked at each other for a long moment.

'Right,' Gary said.

'I'm hardly ever that honest with anybody,' Natalie said. 'I pretty much never tell the truth.'

'So why now?' Gary asked her, his voice low.

'Because it's been a horrible day, and because I think I'm sort of changing, maybe even growing up. And I'm realising that I don't need to pretend I'm someone I'm not for people to like me – at least I hope not.' She bit her lip. 'And because I feel lonely and vulnerable and worried about what's going to happen next, and you are a nice, decent man so I thought I should tell you everything first.'

'First?' Gary asked her, warily.

'Yes,' Natalie said, aware that with her make-up spread across her face, her jogging bottoms on and hair that hadn't been brushed all day she must look only slightly more appealing than her mother. 'Before I try to kiss you again.'

Gary blinked at her and before Natalie could lean forward he held her shoulders, and stopped her in her tracks.

'Don't kiss me,' he said, looking into Natalie's eyes. There was a second's silence. 'Let me kiss you. I'm old-fashioned that way.'

Chapter Twenty-one

Meg could not sleep.

She wanted to sleep, she longed for the oblivion of sleep more than anything, but she had to stay awake because Iris was poorly. Her nose was blocked, her head was hot and she must have been feeling very uncomfortable, the poor little mite, because as soon as Meg tried to put her down in her cot she became distraught again. So Meg had no choice but to walk her up and down the hallway, taking one step over Gripper on the way to the kitchen and one step over her on the way back towards the foot of the stairs; it felt like she had been making the trip for hours, and as she checked her watch she realised it was almost four in the morning. Gripper had been lying with her nose on her paws pointing at the front door for several hours now, which Meg had found disturbing. Normally it would be a sign that Robert was about to arrive, but she was certain that was not going to happen. Perhaps the dog sensed what was going on. Perhaps she was pining for what had been lost.

'I've made some camomile tea,' Frances said, keeping her voice low. 'And some toast. You need to eat.' Meg looked at the kitchen table. Frances had turned the butter out into a butter dish, made the tea in a pot and even found a napkin which she had folded next to the plate and knife she had set out for Meg.

'You should go home,' Meg told her. 'What about Henry?'

'Henry will be all right with his dad for one night. Besides, you need me here now to look after you. That's what friends are for.'

Meg could not say that actually she would do better without her sister-in-law. Just having Frances here, despite how sweet and supportive she was trying to be, was exhausting. At least with Natalie or Jess, or even Tiffany and Steve, Meg would feel free to crumble, to dissolve in her misery. But with Frances in charge there was simply no room for self-pity.

'You'll get through it,' Frances told her stoutly. 'You have no choice. Giving up isn't an option, with four children to care for you can't put yourself first.'

Meg felt it would be impossible to explain to Frances, whose whole life seemed to have been built on those stoic foundations, that what she wanted more than anything was to give up and give in. That just for now, just for a little while, she wanted to be able to surrender to the agony that was wracking her body. Somehow, feeling the full intensity of the pain she was in would give her a cruel kind of comfort.

Frances took Iris from Meg and nodded towards the table.

'You eat, I'll walk,' she said. 'She must need to sleep soon. She's been crying for hours. It's not like her – she's probably sensing how unhappy you are.'

Meg sat down at the table, trying to shrug off Frances's comment which was probably meant harmlessly enough but somehow felt like an accusation. She obediently poured the hot golden liquid into her mug, laced her fingers around the cup and felt the warmth seep through the ceramic and throb against her palms.

'You realise that if I had known anything I would have told you, don't you?' Frances asked her as she paced. Meg nodded – if she was sure about one thing it was that Robert hadn't told anyone else in his family. His parents, upright and ultra-conservative, would probably disown him once they knew.

'I can't believe that this is happening,' Frances added. 'I honestly can't believe that he would be so stupid. If Mother and Dad find out that will be it, you know. They'll be finished with him.'

Meg laboured over buttering her toast. She wondered if it was that Frances, like her brother, simply wasn't capable of facing the real issues that his affair had created, or if she really did believe that parental approval was the most precious thing at stake here.

'It can't be kept from them,' Meg said. 'They will have to be told.'

Slowly and very carefully Frances sat down at the table opposite her. Iris was sleeping at last.

'He was in a terrible state when he arrived at my house,' Frances whispered across the table. 'Really shaken up, Meg. He felt awful.'

'*He* felt awful? Probably only because he'd been caught,' Meg replied, tasting the bitterness of her own words in her mouth. 'Trust me, I saw him with that woman and whatever he was feeling it wasn't awful.'

'I know it's a horrible thing to have happened,' Frances went on. 'And I know you must be feeling pretty low at the moment, but these things don't have to mean the end of a relationship. I know you haven't just instantly stopped loving Robert . . .'

'Frances!' Meg cried loudly, clapping her hand over her mouth as she heard the pitch of her voice. She went on in a ragged whisper, 'Of course I still love him, of course I do – that's why I feel as if my guts have been ripped out of my body and dragged through broken glass. That's why I feel like I want to die. It's not me stopping loving him that's the problem. He doesn't love me any more. He can't. If he did he would never have . . .' Meg trailed off.

'He says it was just meant to be sex but that it all got out of hand and that the woman started to expect more from him. He knows he's been foolish, an idiot, but he says that he'll finish it for good if you say you'll give him another chance.'

'You mean he hasn't done that yet?' Meg asked Frances, feeling the spark of her anger rekindling into a fierce flame in the pit of her belly. 'You mean he's hedging his bets? Keeping his options open?'

Frances looked exasperated.

'He still loves you, Meg. You and the children mean the world to him.'

'He was fucking her for months, Frances.' Meg pushed the plate of toast away so hard that the plate spun and tottered on the wooden surface. 'I think he was even with her on the day I gave birth to Iris.'

Meg knew that Frances would be appalled at her language, but she said nothing about it. Instead she took a breath and tried again.

'It hasn't been easy for him either. He felt excluded from the family, excluded from you. He says you stopped paying him any attention.'

Meg furrowed her brow and glowered at Frances. 'This is not my fault,' she said quietly.

'I'm not saying that it's your fault,' Frances replied hastily. 'All I'm saying is that there were reasons for what he's done. If he hadn't been unhappy here he would never have had an affair.'

Meg found that her foot was tapping against the tiled floor. Her fury was burning brightly now. It was new to her, this constant fury; she didn't think she had ever felt anything like it before in her life. But if it was at all possible she liked feeling it, preferred it at least, to the alternative – the excruciating sense of loss.

'He could have told me how he felt. He could have said that our four children were taking up too much of my time. He could have said he wasn't happy. We could have talked about it, perhaps worked it out. But he didn't do that, did he?'

'Perhaps he found it too difficult to talk to you,' Frances offered. 'Maybe if you just sat down and talked you'd be able to work it out now . . .'

'For God's sake, Frances, why can't you understand what he's done to me?' Meg stood up, scraping her chair back across the tiles. 'Why can't you see what your precious brother has done? He was having an affair while I was pregnant with his child. He was sleeping with another woman while I was *giving birth*. He had sex with her and then with me on the same day! He's not only betrayed our marriage, he's betrayed our children – each one of them. You say he doesn't love her. Well, I wish he did, because otherwise he's ruined all this – and for what? For his cock!'

Iris was crying again and Meg reached across the table and took her out of Frances's arms.

'You're *his* sister,' Meg said. 'I think you should go to him.'

Frances pressed her lips into a thin blue line, looking as if she were losing patience with Meg.

'I understand that you are upset, Megan.' She spoke slowly and deliberately as if she were addressing a lobotomy patient. 'But you are being unreasonable and short-sighted here . . .'

'Oh fuck off!' Meg suddenly shouted at her. 'Just fuck off, Frances, fuck off to Robert and listen to his excuses.'

Frances sat still for a moment, her expression frozen.

'You shouldn't have spoken to me that way,' she said eventually. 'I expect an apology.'

'An apology! You should be the one apologising for your bastard scum of a brother – he is the one who has caused all this – not me!'

'Megan!' Frances looked at Meg as if she didn't recognise her. 'I've been here almost all night for you . . .'

'I don't want you here for me,' Meg told her. 'I don't want your pep talks and your excuses. Just go, go and leave us alone. We don't need you. *I* don't need you, you're not my friend, Frances. I put up with you because Robert said I had to. But I don't have to any more so just . . . leave.'

Meg watched as Frances's skin blanched white. On one level she instantly regretted her words, but she was still far too angry and too hurt to be able even to attempt to retract them. Frances stood up.

'Very well,' she said, steadily. She collected her coat from the coat rack and Meg watched her as she opened the front door. The first grey streaks of dawn were rising in the sky. Frances paused and looked at Meg.

'I know you put up with me,' she said. 'I know you don't really like me very much, that you think I'm bossy and difficult. But you've been the nearest thing to a friend that I've ever had. I *hate* him for what he's done to you. I honestly hate him for it.' Suddenly Frances's voice caught with unshed tears. 'I just want things back the way they were.'

She drew up her collar around her ears and hurried off into the dark morning.

Meg closed the door and held Iris close to her, soothing the baby until her cries subsided again.

She knew exactly how Frances felt.

She would have done anything to turn the clock back to that night she had spent with Robert. To have not seen that text or needed so much to know what it meant. Perhaps if she had just gone to sleep that night instead of picking up Robert's

300

trousers, that would have been the turning point. Perhaps that night he would have realised he didn't need anyone else. He might have come back to her then without her having to know that he had left.

But it was too late. She couldn't undo what had been done.

It would be morning soon and then she would have to get dressed and get on with it, just as Frances said. She'd have to face the new day, uncertain of what the future might hold but ready to deal with it, whatever it was.

But until then, in the few shorts hours until the emerging dawn turned into daylight, she could be as pathetic and as miserable and as scared and as devastated as she wanted to be, as indeed she was.

Until the day began, she could mourn the death of her marriage.

Chapter Twenty-two

Natalie woke up with a start as if she'd just remembered something urgent she had to do and then she realised. She'd already done it. Or, more precisely, she'd already done *him*.

She rolled over, looking at Gary in the half light of the early dawn. He was not asleep either; his eyes were wide open, looking up at the unfamiliar ceiling of her home office. In the heat of the moment she had thought it would be the most appropriate place for them to spend the night.

'What are you thinking?' she asked him. 'And I don't mean that you have to tell me something wonderful or romantic, I just wondered what you were thinking.'

Gary turned and looked at her. 'I'm wondering if I should be here,' he said, simply.

Natalie nodded. 'I don't think you being here is bad,' she replied after a moment's pause. 'Because we both wanted what happened to happen and what happened was really nice and neither one of us wants anything else to happen that the other person doesn't want so really when you think about it everything that's happened is fine.'

'Pardon?' Gary asked her, with a hint of a smile.

Natalie smiled back and stretched out. She had been worried she'd feel self-conscious about her post-baby body, after all this was the first time that she had had sex with anybody since Freddie was born. She was worried that it would feel different, that she would feel different and that it might possibly hurt. Everything had changed 'down there' since the stitches – it even looked totally different, as she had discovered with the aid of a compact mirror one morning. She was nervous and tense as the crucial moment approached but she didn't have to worry about being inhibited, in fact the opposite had rapidly become true. The heat of Gary's desire for her had been so urgent and frankly so obvious that it had been impossible not to feel desirable. Somehow the combination of his solid muscular mass and her soft pliant body had worked wonderfully well. And when he was inside her she quickly forgot her worries about any pain or discomfort. For a time she forgot everything.

So although she was certain the feeling would not last, just for those few hours Natalie had gloried in her flabby tummy, her stretch marks and enlarged breasts. Gary had made her feel something she hadn't felt since well before Freddie was born. He made her feel like an individual again, a separate person whose purpose stretched beyond that of merely being a baby-support system. Natalie hadn't realised until that state of self had been returned to her just how much she had let it slip away; she hadn't really missed it until she got it back.

'What I'm saying is I needed last night, more than I realised actually. I'd really started to fancy you a lot, which is odd because you're not my usual type, but I was starting to get quite heated and anyway,' Natalie smiled wryly, 'it was a great night. I don't regret it at all so don't worry about me. I know your work here is nearly finished and you'll be moving on. I don't expect you to fall in love with me or marry me or any nonsense like that.'

Gary watched her, saying nothing for a moment or two.

'Maybe it's not you I'm worried about, Natalie.' He smiled

sideways at her. 'I get asked out now then on dates, mostly ones my mate's wives have set me up on. Women can't stand to see a man of a certain age single, it drives them mad! But nothing's ever come of them. I never click with anyone, I haven't got all that talk some women like. But I liked you as soon as I saw you.' Gary paused. 'I thought you were married but you're not. Which makes you a bit mental but also available. I'd like to see you again, Natalie.'

'I like you too,' she said, in an attempt to dodge the issue. 'I really do.'

'So do you really want me to just go when I finish the job, or would you like to see me again too?' Gary asked her with some effort.

Natalie drew a circle on the sheet with her fingertip as she considered what he had just said. The bald truth of the matter was that if she did see him again it would be for all the wrong reasons, and she couldn't do that to him.

'Gary, last night was important to me but I . . . I think I've treated you unfairly. I wanted you to take me to bed, I wanted you to put your arms around me like you said and make everything go away and you did for a while. But more than anything I thought that if I . . . if we spent the night together it would help get me over Freddie's dad. And it couldn't, no matter how wonderful it was, because all the feelings I had yesterday were bound to still be there this morning. I can't just dump them in one night. I have to let them sort of wear away. And I can't see anyone while I'm waiting for that to happen. It's not fair.'

'Can't I decide if it's fair or not?' Gary asked her.

'Any minute Freddie will be up,' Natalie said. 'And worse still my mother will drag herself from her pit and want to know what's going on. If she catches you here my life will be pure misery until the day I can finally get her to leave again.

Actually it will be pure misery anyway, but she'll have more ammunition and I can't have that.'

'I think you're a bit hard on her, you know,' Gary said, sitting up in bed, accepting the change in subject with good grace. He was aware, Natalie realised, that she had chosen not to directly answer his question, but he seemed at the moment quite content to let it pass.

'Are you joking? You spent the evening with her!' Natalie cried.

'Yes I did,' Gary said, looking faintly puzzled as he spotted his boxers on the back of the desk chair. 'And yes she is a drunk, scary, over-the-top kind of woman. The sort of woman you wouldn't choose to be your mother. But, well, you'll hate me for saying this, Natalie, but you and she aren't that dissimilar.'

Natalie looked at him, horrified.

'I actually do hate you!' she told him, although his words were not exactly a revelation. For as long as she could remember she had been hiding from the fear that she would inevitably turn into the woman she frequently loathed, and the weird thing was that the more she fought against it, the quicker it seemed to be happening.

'She talked about you a lot last night,' Gary said. 'She really loves you, you know, and she's ever so proud of you.'

Natalie looked at him as if he were mad.

'Don't be silly,' she said flatly.

'She is. She told me.'

Natalie sat up too, drawing the covers up under her chin, and feeling the chill of the morning air raise goosebumps along her spine.

'She has never once said that to me. Not once.'

'Well, she said it to me, so don't you think you should try a bit harder?'

Natalie shook her head. 'No, no I don't think I should,' she said bitterly. 'I think she should.'

She felt the warmth of Gary's palm on her back and she resisted the temptation to lean on it. It would be all too easy to lean on him for support, but she had to get through this part of life on her own two feet. Only then would she be truly ready for whatever the future held, even if it was the possibility of ending up like her mother.

'That piece of information didn't exactly have the effect on you I thought it would,' he said.

'It's just that she can say that to you, the man she was planning to stun into paralysis with her spider venom and then bind up in her web before eating you. But she can't say it to *me*. And that makes me angry.' Natalie shook herself as if she could physically dissipate the anger she was feeling.

'Look, don't worry about me,' she said, summoning a smile. 'I'll be fine. It's enough that you had sex with me and fixed the wiring, you don't have to solve my family problems too!'

'Glad to be of service,' Gary said wryly as he reached for his boxers, and sitting on the edge of the sofa bed he began to pull them on.

Natalie watched him in this oddly touching and vulnerable moment and before she knew it she had flung her arms around his shoulders, pressing her bare breasts into his back.

'You are a nice man, Gary,' she told him.

'Nice?' Gary said. His tone was casual but Natalie had felt all the muscles in his neck and shoulders contract when she had touched him.

'Yes, nice,' she replied. 'Don't underestimate the sexiness of being a nice and decent man.'

Gary shrugged. 'Nice,' he said with some resignation.

Natalie looked at him. He seemed like such an easy person

to be with. This had been a rarity in her previous relationships, not that she could count Gary as a relationship. Nor for that matter could she count many of the men in her life as relationships. For a second Natalie got a glimpse of what life with a man like Gary could be like. Relaxed mornings talking about nothing especially. Friday nights in, watching TV and eating Chinese. Saturday mornings shopping in ASDA. Great sex every now and then, and more importantly a steadfast, warm and loyal friendship. For a second it didn't seem like too terrible a prospect.

'I wish things were simpler,' she said wistfully.

Now fully dressed, Gary knelt on the sofa bed and leaning forward, kissed her briefly on the lips. He looked into her eyes.

'I'll be back later on today to clear up and settle the bill,' he said.

'Oh, you old romantic,' Natalie replied, laughing.

'I could try to be romantic for you,' Gary said, standing up. 'But you don't want that, do you?'

'No,' Natalie said regretfully as she closed the door softly behind him. 'I don't suppose I do.'

Chapter Twenty-three

Natalie was trying hard not to notice Tiffany staring at her.

'Cake, anyone?' she offered, passing a plate of Jamaican ginger around the rather subdued table.

'Jill says she'll put you in touch with a divorce lawyer if you want,' Steve told Meg. 'She says she knows a woman who can get you anything you want and more besides in settlement.' He was very careful to avoid looking at Frances, who sat straight-backed at the end of the kitchen table, all too aware of her unspoken status as a potential spy in the camp. She wouldn't have come to this meeting except that Meg had asked Jess to phone her and make sure she did. She told Jess to say she was sorry for what she said last night, and that she'd hate to lose Frances too. So Frances had come to the meeting, and Meg thought it had to be a true testament to their friendship that she had done so.

'It hasn't come to that yet, surely,' Frances said, but everyone ignored her.

'I don't know what I want,' Meg said flatly. For now at least it seemed that the tears and anger had evaporated into a more manageable numbness. From this position of emotional paralysis Meg supposed she should begin to try to imagine what the future would hold, even if it seemed impossible to visualise the next ten hours, let alone the next ten years. As the thought crossed her mind she had a sudden vision of herself ten years from now, trying to manage four teenagers alone. It was a terrifying vision.

'I don't know what I want,' she repeated.

'Well, the house for starters,' Natalie said. 'And half of everything else, at least.'

'It's too soon to be talking about this,' Jess said, reaching out and laying her hand on the back of Meg's wrist. Meg looked at Jess's hand but she didn't seem to be able to feel it.

'It's not too soon,' Steve said regretfully. 'Jill says she knew about this one guy who as soon as his affair came out emptied all the joint bank accounts and moved all his assets into his girlfriend's name. He fleeced his wife good and proper. The poor woman was left with almost nothing. She says you need to talk to a lawyer now, maybe even today.'

'No she doesn't,' Frances said from the other end of the table. Nobody looked at her. 'Look, Robert is at my house, I know exactly what's he's doing and he's not doing any of that. The only thing he's doing is wondering why he's behaved like such a fool. He's devastated, Megan. He'd do anything to try to turn the clock back.'

'Shame he didn't think about that when he was practically chewing the face off that woman the other day,' Natalie said sharply. 'He is the one who is responsible for the end of this marriage and he'll have to live with it.'

'He is fully aware of that,' Frances said. 'But there is more to think about than houses and assets – there are the children . . .'

'He wasn't giving them much thought while he was carrying on with her, was he?' Jess felt compelled to say. 'He was with her when Iris was being *born,* Frances. Defend that.'

Frances kept her features perfectly level.

'I do not defend him,' she said. 'I'm only saying . . .'

'Look,' Natalie said. 'We're here for Meg, not Robert. If you can't support her then you'd better go.'

'I support them both,' Frances said, and when no one replied she began to rise slowly from her chair.

'Wait!' When Meg spoke everybody looked at her. 'Don't go, Frances, you're right,' she said.

'Pardon?' Natalie looked confused.

'She's right,' Meg told the group. 'It's too soon to think about lawyers, it's too soon to make up a list of what I want from my marriage. I need time to think about what's going to happen to me and the children. I need to decide if I really want this to be over.'

'*What?*' Jess said, looking around at the others for support. 'Of course it's over, Meg. You can't go back from this! Can you?'

Meg shook her head and looked at Jess. 'I don't know,' she said, with some emphasis. 'But I need to be able to think about it for the children's sake and for mine. Frances understands that, and if the rest of you can't then perhaps you should be the ones to go.'

Natalie, Jess, Tiffany and Steve exchanged glances.

'We're here to support you, whatever you want,' Natalie said.

'Even if I take Robert back?' Meg asked her.

Natalie nodded. 'If that is what you choose, Meg. But please promise me you won't make that decision based on the fear of being alone. Because you'll never be alone. You'll always have your friends. And you are a stronger and more capable woman than you realise.'

Meg raised her head and looked at Natalie.

'Were you married in a church, Natalie?' she asked her suddenly.

'Er, no,' Natalie said, noticing Tiffany was staring hard at her again. She was clearly waiting for Natalie to make the confession that she had assured Tiffany she would make days ago. Surely the girl realised that it still wasn't the right time, that right now no one wanted to know about her non-marriage. 'It was a package-holiday thing, on the beach. It was lovely. Gary looked great in white trunks.'

'I bet he does,' Tiff said under her breath.

Natalie frowned at her and looked at Meg. 'Why do you ask?'

'I got married in a church,' Meg said. 'I don't go to church a lot and I'm not exactly religious but that ceremony meant something so special to me. When I spoke those vows I meant them absolutely. Marriage is not always supposed to be easy. It's *easy* to let things go wrong. It's *easy* to lose your way and make the wrong decisions and most of all, it is *far* too easy to just give up when things seem too hard or too painful. Robert had sex with someone else, he lied to me and betrayed me, and the thought of being able to get over that and to carry on being married to him sickens and appals me.' Meg paused, closing her eyes for a moment as she fought to compose herself. 'But not being able to do it terrifies me too. I have four children who love him. And *I* love him. If he was leaving me and didn't want to come back then I wouldn't have a choice. But I do have a choice, and it's one that I owe to my children and myself to think very, very carefully about. When I took those vows I meant them, every word.'

Everyone else at the table sat in silence for a second. They had never seen Meg look so serious but more than that, so strong. In her weakest and most vulnerable moment she seemed to be more determined and more certain than ever.

'But, Meg, it's Robert whose broken the vows,' Jess reminded her tentatively.

Meg looked levelly at her. 'Yes,' she said. 'Yes he has, but don't you see? *I* haven't – yet. I haven't broken them. And I will have to think long and hard about whether or not I am going to.' She suddenly looked so tired and young, like a little lost child.

Natalie, who was sitting next to her, put her arms around Meg's shoulders. 'If that's what you want,' she said.

'But do you understand why?' Meg asked each of them

'Yes, we understand,' Tiffany said, when nobody else seemed to be able to speak.

They all sat around the kitchen table until morning turned into afternoon, each forgetting or choosing to ignore their planned trip to the second Baby Music class. It seemed impossible that only a week ago the world had seemed so different.

In near silence, Frances remarked, when she glanced out of the window, that Gripper was digging up the newly emerging daffodils by the fence.

Meg seemed unperturbed.

'So what about *EastEnders* then?' Natalie tried. 'Who'd have thought that *she* was a lesbian! Seriously, everybody is a lesbian these days in soaps. I don't mind; I'm all for lesbians, but I think they should have few more gay men, don't you? Even it up a bit?' She looked around at the blank faces. '. . . Or is that just me?'

'Um,' Steve said.

'Really,' Frances muttered under her breath in disgust.

'Hadn't thought about it much, I have to admit,' Jess told Natalie apologetically.

'Sorry.' Natalie grimaced. 'Sometimes I just get compelled to say what's in my head and quite often it's extremely stupid.'

'Why aren't I surprised?' Frances said loud and clear, arching one eyebrow.

Natalie was about to open her mouth in response when Steve spoke.

'That's what Jill says about me,' he said cheerfully. 'She says, "I love you, darling, but you never think before you open your mouth." I always know if she's about to tell me I've done something wrong because she always starts with the phrase "I love you, darling, but . . ."' Steve smiled. 'She read about it in this American book on how to have a successful relationship. Apparently it's supposed to diffuse the build-up of anger, because it's so much better to disagree in an "atmosphere of love". For example, as Jill said to me only this morning, "I love you, darling, but I do wish you wouldn't pass wind audibly."'

This time the whole group laughed.

'She reckons it's that bloody book that will keep our marriage on track,' Steve went on, happy that he had single-handedly lifted the mood.

'Maybe you could lend it to me then,' Meg said with a watery smile. 'I need all the help I can get.'

Steve blushed to the tips of his ears. 'Oh God, I'm sorry, Meg . . . Jill's right about me, isn't she? I don't think.'

There was silence except for the ticking of the kitchen clock and the distant sound of Gripper's daffodil excavation.

'Anyway,' Jess stepped in, smiling at Tiffany 'How are you, Tiffany – how are things going?'

Tiffany shrugged and stirred a third spoonful of sugar into her coffee.

'I'm going to take my exams in September.' She glanced up at Natalie, the first look she had given her all morning that wasn't a glare, and even smiled. 'Natalie came round to my mum's with me the other day. I thought it was a washout, a total waste of time – Mum didn't want to know. But yesterday she came round while Dad was out at work. We had a cup of tea, talked about things, what's on telly, gossiped about

Mum's neighbours. Not anything real or important. She didn't mention the reasons why she hadn't been before or why Dad didn't know she had come now. But she came and we sat and talked and she even held Jordan on her lap for a little while and kissed her before she went. It wasn't a big reunion or anything, she never said she was in the wrong – but at least she came.' Tiffany smiled tentatively. 'It might be a start, you know? It'll be hard and there will be more shouting, but it's like Meg says, things that are worth having don't come easily.'

After that everyone seemed more relaxed. The baby group members settled back into discussing their babies, what new clubs they might join, which ones they wouldn't go back to in a million years, and although Natalie was as resolutely chatty as the rest of the group, she couldn't stop thinking about what Tiffany had said. Because it was the teenager and not Meg who had clarified the notion in her mind.

Things that were worth having didn't come easily, that was what she'd said.

Just as it would seemingly be so easy to have Gary in her life, it felt nearly impossible to bring her and Freddie to a point where they could have Jack in theirs: where Freddie, no matter what had happened between Natalie and Jack, could have his father.

At some point during their last meeting, Natalie wasn't sure why, she had become utterly furious with him, consumed with a rage that had incinerated all her common sense in one solar-strength flare. It was when he told her that he wasn't dying, she remembered. Was she angry with him for not dying? she wondered anxiously. And then she realised it was not that. For the short time she had thought she was going to lose him without ever really having him she had been devastated. And it was such a terrible and horrific prospect to face that when he had laughed at her and told her everything was going to be fine she had snapped.

What had exactly followed then was muddy and confusing, but Natalie knew she hadn't prepared him at all for the news about Freddie. She had literally flung it in his face; it was a selfish, vengeful act, designed to shock and scare him as much as he had shocked and scared her.

She had promised Freddie she would do the right thing by him, but she had already failed. There was only one thing she could do now to try to rectify the situation.

She had to go back and see Jack again.

And this time she'd take Freddie with her.

Chapter Twenty-four

Frances was the last to leave. Steve had gone first, leaving Meg the solicitor's number on a piece of paper he attached to the fridge door by a Teletubby magnet.

'Just in case,' he said. 'Jill says you should be prepared for everything.' He thought for a moment and dropped a hand on Meg's shoulder. 'And *I* say you're a bloody marvellous woman and you shouldn't accept anything but the best. Promise me you won't, Meg.'

Meg smiled up at him. 'I won't, Steve,' she said. 'That's the last thing I want.'

Jess had gone soon after, when Jacob woke from his nap and wouldn't stop crying.

'See you all at Tiff's,' she had to say quite loudly to be heard over his yells.

They had been discussing when to hold the next meeting, and Frances had put into words what the rest of them were reluctant to say.

'Well, it's my turn of course, but I hardly think considering my current guest that it is an appropriate venue.'

'And it's not fair to keep turning up at Meg's all the time,' Steve said. 'I bet she's sick of the sight of us.'

'Well, Jess and Steve have already held a group and we know Natalie currently has workmen in, so that leaves . . .'

Frances stared pointedly at Tiffany, who instantly retreated back to the shy and awkward girl she often was around the other members. Her cheeks flushed pink and she sank her head between her shoulders.

'Oh well,' Natalie said, keen to take the spotlight off her friend. 'Come to mine, the work's all but done anyway, so . . .'

'No,' Tiffany said, at first so quietly that no one heard. 'No,' she repeated. This time the others looked at her. 'I can do it.'

'What's that, love?' Steve asked her.

'I can hold a meeting at my flat. You might as well know I live on the thirteenth floor of a high-rise and I've got hardly any furniture and no cups that match . . .' She glanced at Meg's table. 'Or a milk jug. But I can make tea, so if you don't mind the odd chip in your cup you can all come to mine.'

It had seemed more like a challenge than an invitation, but Natalie was pleased that Tiffany had issued it.

'Brilliant idea!' she said. 'Of course it's Tiff's turn. Thank God I say, that means I have a few more days to evict my mother before you come round – what a relief!'

Tiffany had carefully written out the address and her telephone number for everyone but Natalie, who had been there before. 'Eleven o'clock, next Tuesday then?' she said.

Everybody agreed to be there, and Tiffany was able to smile again, with a mixture of pleasure and anxiety. After all, the only other thing she'd hosted in her entire life had been a sleepover.

Tiffany had been upstairs changing Jordan as Natalie collected her things, instructed to wait for Tiff so they could leave together. Frances went to the loo (or possibly to surreptitiously clean it), leaving Meg and Natalie alone for a few minutes.

'Are you OK, Natalie?' Meg asked her out of the blue.

'Who, me?' Natalie sat up straight, as if she'd just been caught napping in class. 'Yeah, I'm fine. Why wouldn't I be?'

'You look a bit . . . preoccupied,' Meg said, with concern. 'Like you had a bit of a sleepless night too.'

Natalie hoped to God that she didn't look as guilty as she felt.

'Look,' Meg went on, 'you know that just because I'm in the middle of all of this, it doesn't mean you can't still talk to me if you need to. Has something happened with Gary?'

Natalie looked at Meg, dear sweet Meg with her tear-bruised eyes and red raw nose, and with all the pain that was weighing so heavily on her shoulders, and for a second she wanted to tell her everything. But how could she? It would be so unfair to expect Meg to deal with her problems. And besides that, Meg was offering to help a woman who didn't really exist. Maybe she wouldn't like the real Natalie at all, whoever that was.

'No, there's no problem,' she said. 'Gary and I are fine.'

'Which one?' Tiffany said as she walked into the kitchen.

Natalie looked at her. 'Pardon?' she asked.

'I mean, which Gary? It must be confusing having two Garys in your life.'

After that Natalie had left in rather a hurry with Tiffany close behind.

Finally Meg got up stiffly from the table and walked into the living room, where James had been playing suspiciously quietly for quite some time. She collapsed on the sofa, snatching him up in her arms as she did so.

'Mama, 'ook! 'Ook!' James said, pointing proudly to his work of art, which appeared to have involved permanent marker pen and her best cushions.

'I love it, baby,' Meg told him, holding him as close as he would let her before he wriggled free.

Frances hovered awkwardly in the doorway, with Henry on one shoulder. 'Do you want us to go?' she asked Meg.

'No,' Meg said. 'Look, Frances, I'm sorry I was so horrible to you. I didn't mean to be – well, I did, and it was cruel of me. But what I said wasn't true, I just wanted to hurt you. You are a good friend to me. Truly.'

Frances took a step or two into the room. 'Shall I pick up Alex and Hazel from school for you?'

Meg knew it was the closest she was ever likely to get to Frances acknowledging her apology.

'Yes please,' she said. She shut her eyes and immediately felt her exhaustion swarming in and clouding her consciousness. 'I am so tired . . .' she said vaguely.

'Shall I take the children home?' Frances offered. 'Iris and James too, if you like. I could give them tea and drop them back later, give you a few extra hours to get some sleep.'

'I think I might sleep now,' Meg agreed and then one last restless thought kept her awake. 'Robert's at yours isn't he?'

'Yes,' Frances said. 'He hasn't been back to work since . . . it all happened. Is that a problem? Do you mind him seeing the children?'

Meg shook her head. 'No, of course not. I just wonder what they'll think, seeing him there. So far they haven't noticed any difference. He's home so rarely. If they see him they'll know something is wrong.'

Frances nodded.

'I'll tell them he's been helping me with something,' she said. 'You rest and I'll bring them back after tea?'

'Ask Robert to bring them back,' Meg said, one last clear thought keeping her conscious.

'Are you sure?' Frances asked her.

'Yes,' Meg said. 'We have to start talking at some point.'

'You're sure it's not too soon?' Frances sounded worried.

'I think it's more important not to leave it until it's far too late.'

It was the last thing Meg said before she drifted off into the sanctuary of sleep.

'I know, you know,' Tiffany said almost as soon as they'd left Meg's house.

Natalie hurried on as if she could somehow outstrip the slender teenager with her speed and strength. But of course she couldn't, Tiffany was more than a match for her. She'd just have to get the whole conversation over with as quickly as possible. She took a deep breath.

'What do you know?' she asked Tiffany.

'I know that you had sex with Gary last night.'

'How can you know?' Natalie asked her, scandalised. 'Did he tell you?'

'He didn't have too,' Tiffany said quite smugly. 'You just did. It was written all over his face when he came to pick up Anthony this morning. I asked him why he was so pleased with himself and he said he couldn't tell me. I just made an educated guess that it had to be something to do with you – and I was right.'

'*Curses!* Foiled again.' Natalie couldn't help but find Tiffany's satisfaction in being right quite amusing.

'It's not funny, Natalie!' Tiffany exclaimed. 'You're totally out of order, you do know that, don't you?'

Natalie walked on briskly; as fond as she was of Tiffany she had, in her opinion at least, far more pressing matters to think about and do just now than receive a dressing down from a surprisingly prudish sixteen-year-old.

'Tiffany,' she said, with more than a hint of condescension. 'You are a lovely girl, a girl who has had more than her fair share of life experiences at a young age. But you are still only sixteen. Gary is a consenting adult and so am I. It was what we both wanted and we both knew where we stood, so really it's not as big a deal as you think it is.'

'It *is* a big deal!' Tiffany protested. 'Gary really likes you and you still love this Jack bloke. Don't use him, Natalie. You're better than that.'

Natalie stopped dead in her tracks.

'I know,' she said. 'Tiffany, look . . . it was a stupid and wrong thing to do. It's not going to happen again. Neither of us wants it to.'

'Gary would, I can tell,' Tiffany said. 'Look, you have to realise he's not just some distraction to take your mind off things or some other stupid complication to get yourself caught up in. He's been really good to me and Anthony, really good. If he gets hurt . . .' Tiffany trailed off before adding with a hint of menace, 'I don't want that to happen.'

'It won't,' Natalie reassured her. 'We made a mistake and that's all. Look, please will you just pretend you don't know? For my sake and Gary's?'

Tiffany's scowl was still quite fierce.

'I like you, Natalie,' she said, even though she looked as if the very opposite were true. 'But you really should think before you act. You rush in too fast. Actions have consequences, you know.'

Natalie looked from Freddie's buggy to Jordan's.

'I think you and I know that better than most people, don't we?' she said, with a wry smile.

'I just don't know what you want from him,' Tiffany said, beginning to walk on. 'Look at you, you've got a lovely baby, a ton of money, a big job, a nice house and you're still not happy!'

'How do you know I'm not happy?' Natalie asked her huffily. 'I've never told you that!'

'You don't have to,' Tiffany said. 'It's written all over your face.'

Jacob was still crying when Jess got in. He hadn't stopped once on the way home, even the lull of the bus hadn't sent him off. She dropped her bag and coat on the floor just inside the front door and went straight to the armchair where she put him to her breast. But he didn't want to feed, twisting his head away from her.

She felt a cold wash of panic well up from the pit of her abdomen. She touched her lips to his forehead. He felt very hot.

'Oh dear,' she said out loud to him, needing to hear the sound of her own voice calm and in control. 'Are you poorly, Jacob baby? Have you got that nasty cold? Poor you, you don't know why you feel so rotten, do you?'

Jess laid Jacob on the floor and removed all his clothes until he was down to just his nappy. And then she remembered that she had to keep his extremities warm, so she put socks and mittens on him. Still he cried.

Picking him up again, Jess went to the bathroom and took out the Calpol that Lee's mother had brought round: one of the most bizarre new-baby gifts that Jess could imagine.

'It will save your life,' Gene had told Jess as she handed it to her. 'It's a godsend.'

Jess, who instinctively did not like the idea of feeding her little baby drugs, had vowed never to use it, but now . . . if it would bring Jacob's temperature down and help him rest . . .

The label said a single 2.5 ml dose could be given to a baby aged between two and four months. Jacob was nearly three months, so she could give him a spoonful. But when she looked at him and how tiny he was, it just didn't seem right to give him drugs. Nothing else had gone into his body yet except for her milk. What if he didn't really need paracetamol, what if she would only be giving it to him to make herself feel better? She knew what Lee would do if he were here. Lee would just give it to him, but alone Jess was paralysed by indecision. Consult your doctor if concerned, that was what the label also said, and Jess was concerned.

She thought about her doctor's surgery, which was just still open and only a few yards down the road. She knew exactly what would happen. She knew the obligatory frosty receptionist would treat her like a moron and that the weary doctor would patronise and talk down to her, making her feel like an idiot for bringing her baby in with just a cold.

But she couldn't guess about giving him paracetamol. She needed someone to tell her what to do, and she needed to know that it was just a cold and not the beginning of all the more sinister diseases that had already run through her mind.

'Don't worry, sweetheart,' she told her baby. 'The doctor will sort you out.'

'You're doing everything right,' Dr Moran told her after she had finished listening to Jacob's chest. 'Keeping him cool, keeping up his fluids. His chest sounds clear. It's a bit of a worry that he doesn't want to feed, but it's not so long since his last feed and his temperature is not dangerously high. Have you got a thermometer at home?'

Jess shook her head.

'Well, you can get one at the pharmacy over the road. If I were you I'd keep an eye on him, monitor his temperature. If it goes any higher, ring me and we can decide about the paracetamol, although I would rather hold off if we can.'

Jess burst into tears. Dr Moran looked taken a back.

'It's nothing to worry about really, Ms Bergin. It's just a cold.'

'I'm sorry. It's just that you are so nice and you don't make me feel like an idiot – which has made me act like an idiot.' Jess sniffed and smiled all at once. 'Thank you,' she added.

Dr Moran smiled. 'I had my first a little over a year ago. It's much easier to talk about being a parent than to be one. I know how you feel, I know that things other people think aren't that important can seem incredibly huge and scary. And besides, you can't be too careful with a young baby. But I promise you there is no need to worry.'

When Jess got home Jacob had taken a little milk and then fallen asleep in her arms. Between then and the time that Lee got in she pressed the thermometer strip across his forehead every few minutes. So far his temperature had remained a little high, but steady.

She felt as if Dr Moran had armed her: with information, a tool and best of all the promise of backup if things got worse. The buzz of anxiety still hummed in her nerves but despite that she felt, with near disbelief, that she was coping. She was coping on her own.

For the first time in a long time she wasn't crippled with fear.

Chapter Twenty-five

Natalie stood outside her house with Freddie and wondered.

Now that she had decided to go and see Jack, perhaps she should just go and see him before she decided to do something equally decisive but entirely different, like joining an order of silent nuns in the Outer Hebrides.

Nobody knew Natalie better than she knew herself, and she was well aware that she was prone to backing out of things that were likely to be difficult and require effort.

She had improved a lot since Freddie had come along, that was for sure. Because there was no way you could tell your midwife eight hours into labour, 'Actually, I don't really like this very much any more. Can I change my mind and have a cup of tea instead?'

And tempting though it might be to leave your cater-wauling baby on the neighbour's doorstep in a basket with a note pinned to his Babygro saying 'Sorry, have discovered I prefer sleeping to motherhood', the evolutionary impulse to protect your child, even if they are breaching the rules of the Geneva Convention by keeping you up for twenty hours straight, always outweighs the desire to give them away.

Freddie had been fed and changed at Meg's. He was happily asleep in his buggy and it was quite a warm afternoon. She *could* go now.

But for some reason, as she looked up at the dark windows of her house, she felt she ought to go in and say hello to her mother. It was a similar sort of evolutionary impulse, Natalie supposed, as she let herself in and parked the buggy in the hallway, to the one that kept her loving Freddie no matter how difficult he was being. As much as she wanted to pretend she was not related to her mother and that the woman had not single-handedly messed her up almost completely, she still couldn't quite stop worrying about her. But unlike her maternal instinct, her daughterly one had no practical application at all and it was also most inconvenient.

The house was silent.

'Mother!' Natalie called out. 'Mother, are you out?'

She looked around the hallway. This time her mother's heeled boots were at the foot of the stairs. Her bag was on the telephone table and her coat on the end of the banister, despite Natalie telling her repeatedly that she should hang it in the closet in the hall.

So if Sandy had gone out she'd done so without any proper footwear, money or her coat. But then again if she had been drinking, anything was possible.

Natalie looked at Freddie, sleeping so peacefully in his buggy, and decided to leave him there for a moment rather than risk waking him.

Her mother was not in the kitchen, although there were two cigarette butts ground hard into the patio outside the kitchen window and another stubbed out in her window box. There was a full cold cup of tea, slick with that gooey lipgloss she insisted on wearing, and – surprise, surprise – an empty tumbler, still reeking of whisky.

Natalie sighed and sat down for a moment on a stool to consider the evidence. Her mum had always been a bit of a lush. She had always been fond of a drink, always had a G & T in hand when Natalie got home from school, telling her she just need a little something to 'take the edge off'.

But Natalie was fairly sure Sandy had never drunk *quite* this much. She hadn't been drunk all the time she had been here, admittedly. She had been totally sober when Natalie had left her with Freddie, Natalie was sure of it, because apart from anything else she was a different person then. A person who listened and seemed to care.

It was true, though, that almost as soon as Natalie got back Sandy had cracked open another bottle. Didn't real alcoholics drink constantly? They didn't stop for a few hours to be responsible, did they? So she couldn't be a real alcoholic, could she?

Natalie didn't like the direction her thoughts were going.

Should she worry about it she wondered. Making an active decision to worry about her mother was difficult. She knew Sandy would not be remotely grateful that Natalie was worrying about her, and if anything she would behave even worse just to irritate her. Whenever Natalie had tried to intervene in the past, Sandy had always accused her daughter of being ashamed of her, of thinking she was better than her mother and of trying to bully her into being a person she was not.

Of course, all these things were true, but that didn't mean Natalie wanted to invite the endless hassle that was inevitable if she tried once again to sort Sandy out. Sandy always told her she didn't need sorting out. It would be so much easier just to believe her. After all, it wasn't as if Natalie didn't have a few tricky situations of her own to sort out right now.

She looked up at the ceiling. Her mother was probably sleeping off her afternoon session in the guest bedroom. She decided that she'd better go and check on her and then think about going to see Jack. Or possibly vacuuming the stairs. The stairs really needed vacuuming. She hadn't done it since 2004.

Sandy was not in her bedroom. There was evidence that she had been there though. A whisky bottle with the cap off sat on the dressing table, and the bed was crumpled, the pillows stained with make-up. With a huff of irritation Natalie went to check her own bedroom, sure that her mother, like an aged Goldilocks, had decided to try all of the beds for size.

But Sandy was not in there either.

And then Natalie thought of the one place she had yet to look.

She pushed open the bathroom door. Sandy was lying awkwardly, twisted like a broken doll, by the toilet.

Natalie stood for a second, frozen, as she stared at her mother's pale face in the gathering twilight. She caught her breath and for a heartbeat she thought that Sandy was dead. And then the body on the floor groaned.

'Oh, Natalie, good. Need water, feel sick. Tummy bug.'

Carefully, Natalie hopped over her mother's haunches and emptied out the toothbrush mug to fill it with water from the tap. Crouching, she hauled Sandy up into a sitting position and propping her against the wall, handed her the mug. Sandy took a sip of water and pulled a face, like a child drinking alcohol for the first time.

'Ohhhh,' she groaned rubbing at her eyes with her knuckles. 'I must have eaten something bad.'

She looked so frail, old and small. Natalie wanted to hate her because it was so much easier than caring, but for now at least, her sense of anxiety was greater than her anger.

'You didn't eat *anything*,' she chided her mother. 'That was part of the problem. That and the almost half-bottle of whisky that you drank.'

'Eggs,' Sandy said, holding her head as tenderly as if it were one. 'I ate eggs I think. Oh God, I feel bad.'

Natalie got up and sat on the edge of the bath.

'Drink that water,' she said. 'If it stays down I'll put you to bed.'

'Thanks for looking after me, darling,' Sandy said, belching out the last word on a whisky-sour breath.

'Mum . . .' Natalie hesitated. Saying something would make her involved. Did she really want to be involved? Then again, did she really have any choice? She couldn't pretend that this wasn't happening, because it wasn't as if Sandy was safely tucked away in Spain, out of sight and mostly out of mind. She was here paralytic on Natalie's bathroom floor, leaving her no option but to get involved.

'What, love?' Sandy replied, keeping her eyes tightly shut.

'You've been drinking a lot since you got here.' Natalie tried to sound casual, as if she was merely passing comment. 'A bit more than normal. Do you drink this much in Spain?'

Sandy opened one eye and directed it at Natalie.

'I like drinking,' she said. 'It takes the edge off.'

It wasn't the answer that Natalie was hoping for.

'Mum, you're going to kill yourself,' she said, unable to skirt around the issue any longer because that would take patience, and where Sandy was concerned Natalie had none.

'I'll be dead soon enough anyway.' Sandy's voice sounded hoarse and sore. 'I'm over the hill now, past it. And what have I got? I haven't got anything. You hate me. Freddie won't remember me.' She waved her hand in front of her face as if swatting away an invisible fly. 'I like drinking, and I don't care if I die a few years earlier because of it.'

'*I* care,' Natalie said. 'I don't want you to die a drunk, Mum. I want you to sober up and die the nasty old witch that I know and love.'

Sandy made an odd noise in her throat which Natalie thought might have been laughter.

'But that's exactly it, don't you see?' she said. 'You don't

329

love me, do you? What's the point when your own child doesn't love you?'

Natalie didn't speak for a second. The last thing she wanted was for this conversation to turn into a shouting match, an argument about who loved who the least and who was the hardest done by. It was essential that she got Sandy just to think about what was happening to her.

'Look,' Natalie began. 'It's not about how much I love you. There's no excuse to turn yourself into . . .' She gestured at the pile of woman in front of her. 'This mess. One thing about you, Mum, was that you always had style. Where's the style in lying drunk on the bathroom floor at four o'clock in the afternoon? And anyway I do quite love you sometimes.'

'I never did anything right,' Sandy said flatly, tipping her head back against the wall and looking out of the window. 'Not in my whole life, not one thing right. I left home too young. If I hadn't I could have got some qualifications and a good job maybe, I was always very good at school. But I couldn't stand my father. I couldn't wait to get away from him, the old bastard.' She took a sip of the water and Natalie thought she'd forgotten it wasn't alcohol.

'If I'd got a job maybe I would have met a nice decent man, to have a proper family with. But I was too pretty. I was so lovely then, Natalie. There was no one to touch me. All the men wanted me and I wanted them to want me.' Sandy sighed as her chin flopped forward onto her chest again. 'It didn't last, though. I was already fading when your father got me pregnant. He didn't want me, he didn't want me at all. He already had a wife who was younger and prettier than me. I loved him though, your dad. I think he was the only man I ever loved and at least he gave me you.'

Natalie thought about her three-minute meeting with her father all those years ago and decided that he was not a man

330

who was worthy of anybody's love. But she had never told Sandy about her trip to find her father, and now was certainly not the time.

'I had to work hard for you, Natalie,' Sandy went on when Natalie didn't reply. 'Hard to keep a roof over our heads, you in clothes and shoes – you were always growing and I always wanted you to look nice. I wasn't going to have anyone say that my child didn't look as good as the next. I'm sorry we moved around a lot. I kept on messing things up and having to move on. But I always tried to do the best for you. I got that wrong too, didn't I?' Sandy became tearful. 'A whole life based on what? So-called friends who come and go when things get tough, no real home, love, and a daughter who "quite loves me sometimes".'

'Maybe that was a bit harsh,' Natalie offered. 'Let's say I always love you but often find you annoying. Mildly annoying. You have to admit that to come home to all of this *is* mildly annoying.'

Sandy drained the last of the water out of the toothbrush mug.

'Can I go to bed now?' she asked Natalie.

Without speaking Natalie put her hands under Sandy's arms and hauled her up, guiding her out of the bathroom as carefully as she could. Once in Sandy's room, she dropped her fully clothed onto the bed and pulled the quilt over her.

'Mum, there's no point in talking any more right now. You're still drunk and you're all maudlin. But we need to discuss this properly tomorrow. I'm not having an alcoholic as my son's grandmother. We'll sort something out, get you some proper help, get you back on your ridiculous high heels, OK?'

But Sandy was already snoring.

Chapter Twenty-six

Meg woke at just after seven that evening. She knew that her body needed hours and hours more sleep but as soon as she had opened her eyes her mind began to go over and over everything that had happened to her in the last few days, trying and largely failing to find a solution to it all. She remembered that she had asked Frances to tell Robert to bring the children back after tea, and a wave of anticipation and dread ran through her almost simultaneously.

Well, she still had some time to get herself together before he came, Meg thought. She didn't want him to see what a mess she was. She could have a shower and get changed, at least.

As she dried herself Meg looked around her bedroom. Her and Robert's bedroom. Nothing had really changed in here and yet everything had. There was still his jacket on the back of the chair. His forgotten watch, his last birthday present from her, was still on the dressing table. And there was still the impression left by his head in the pillow on his side of the bed that had remained unmade for several days now.

Meg wound her bath towel around her and picking up the pillow shook the lingering memory of Robert's shape out of it entirely, before replacing it. She sat down at the dressing table and began to brush the tangles out of her hair. It was still mainly auburn, but with a sprinkling of grey that was gradually becoming more and more dominant. Robert was always on at her to have it tinted, but she liked the silver interspersed amongst the red curls, and she felt that like the fine lines around her eyes they were part of the story of her life, a story that had always been happy until now. Perhaps it was because she didn't dye her hair that Robert had looked elsewhere.

Suddenly there was a movement behind her, and clutching her hand to her chest Meg whirled round.

Robert was standing in the door frame. He looked at her in her towel and then looked away again, as if he couldn't bear the sight of her. Meg forced herself to sit up straight.

'I'm sorry,' Robert said. 'Frances said that she'd bring the kids in an hour, that as they were all settled I should come and see you alone. She said we needed to talk and I thought she was right.'

Meg hugged her arms tightly around her.

'You're early,' she said, at a loss, confused by the feeling that her own husband in their bedroom of eight years seemed like an interloper. 'Can you wait downstairs please?'

To be so cool and so disconnected from Robert was the most difficult thing that Meg had ever had to do. As much as she hated him for what he had done to their family, as much as she loathed him, he was still the one she most wanted to see. He was the one she instinctively wanted to run to and fling her arms around and ask for comfort. When she saw him all she wanted to do was to climb into bed with him, curl up in his arms and go to sleep.

Robert hesitated by the door.

'Megan,' he said plaintively, taking a step or two forward. 'You look beautiful.'

'Robert, please,' Meg said, every nerve in her body fraught with conflict.

'But I just want to try . . .' And before she knew it he was in the room kneeling in front of her, his hands on her bare shoulders, his lips on her neck.

'No!' she cried, snatching herself away from him. She stood and took a couple of steps back towards the window. 'You just can't,' she said, unable to articulate exactly what she wanted to say. 'It's just not that easy, Robert.'

'Go downstairs,' she pleaded when he didn't move. 'Please, Robert.'

Robert stood up, at a loss, unable to fathom what had happened. He looked awful, unshaven with dark puffy eyes like he hadn't slept properly for days, and had perhaps even been crying. She was horrified to discover that the thought of him lying awake at night weeping pleased her.

'Look, just go downstairs and wait for me there,' she commanded.

He left the bedroom and hurried down the stairs and Meg braced herself to hear the front door slam shut, certain he would walk out on this humiliating situation. But it remained silent.

When she came down she found Robert sitting in his chair in the living room with the TV on and Gripper sitting at his side gazing up at him, as he stroked her, with the kind of unquestioning adulation that Meg imagined he craved, especially now.

As soon as she appeared Robert switched the TV off and stood up.

'I'm sorry,' he said, nodding at the set.

'Why? It's your house,' Meg said. 'It's your TV. You pay for it.'

'No.' Robert looked abashed. 'I mean, I'm sorry about before, upstairs. About trying to . . . I just want things to get back to normal between us, Megan. To be how they were before all this happened.'

Meg nipped at her lip. 'Before you had an affair for several months with another woman you claim not to care for, you mean?' she asked him archly.

'I thought we were going to talk, not throw accusations,' Robert countered defensively. 'Frances said you weren't dead set on ending the marriage. She said there was hope.'

Meg shrugged. 'I want there to be hope, Robert,' she said, her voice calm and clear. 'But then I remember that when you were unhappy with me, instead of coming to talk to me about it, instead of trying to work on our problems and make everything right, you thought that having sex with some tart would solve everything. And when I remember that I feel a lot less like giving our marriage another chance.'

Meg looked at him standing there in a crumpled shirt and a pair of Craig's trousers that were too short for him, and turning on her heel she walked smartly into the kitchen, Gripper close at her heels. She didn't know how long it would last, this controlled feeling of calm and composure that was keeping her steady, but she knew she had to use it while it was there, before she crumbled again.

Robert followed her into the kitchen.

'I was confused, Megan,' he said, hovering by the sink as Meg took a wine glass out of the dishwasher. 'That thing with Lynne . . . I didn't mean it to happen. We had this drink after work one night and I knew she fancied me.' He shook his head and shrugged. 'And . . . it felt good to feel that way. To feel *wanted*. You hadn't shown an interest in me like that for months . . .'

'What, since you got me pregnant with Iris, you mean?' Meg asked him sharply.

He paused, moistening his drying lips and taking a breath.

'Even then it wasn't exciting between us – you know it wasn't. It was just . . . routine. You were always so tired all the time with the kids . . .'

'Please don't tell me you had an affair because I was too tired to have kinky sex,' Meg warned him. 'And I didn't think it was "routine". I thought it was caring, gentle, loving. I didn't realise I was so dull.'

'No, that's not what I meant,' Robert said, with some frustration. 'It's much more complicated than that.' But he seemed unable to explain what the complications were just then.

'It was only meant to be a one-off thing with Lynne,' he said instead. 'But she was so into me. I liked it. I liked the way she made me feel. It was hard to give it up. I didn't want to.'

Meg took an opened bottle of wine out of the fridge and poured herself a glass. She did not offer Robert one as she sat at the kitchen table. She had to remain cool, she told herself. She had to keep detached.

If she could listen to everything he was saying as if it wasn't about her, her husband, and her marriage then she would be all right, she could keep control. And she had to keep control, because if she fell to pieces here she knew that Robert would step in to put her back together, and she knew that she would gladly let him do it. And then he would have everything he wanted without having to fight for it. Meg knew if she didn't make him fight for his marriage and his family, if she didn't make him see just how much he really wanted those things, then he might give them away again all too easily.

'Did you think about what you were risking giving up by being with . . . her?' Meg asked him stiffly. 'Or didn't you care? Did you just want an excuse to give us up?'

Robert sat down heavily at the other end of the table and patted his thigh, a gesture that would normally bring Gripper straight to his side. But although she shifted on her bottom, she did not leave her place beside Meg. Meg took an odd sort of strength from Gripper' behaviour. Even Robert's adoring dog was on her side.

'I didn't think,' Robert said, letting his hand fall against his leg. 'It seemed that our lives were so separate. I honestly didn't think you'd find out. And I always meant to end it, Megan. I never meant to leave you and the children.' He frowned and pinched the bridge of his nose. 'I *thought* she knew that but . . . she thought differently.' He leant back in the chair, his shoulders slumping like a man utterly defeated.

'That night, when I came home and I saw you sleeping on the bed – you looked so amazing, Megan. God, I wanted you so much and it was incredible, don't you think?' Meg made her face remain impassive, even though her body remembered all too well. 'It was just like it used to be,' Robert continued. 'No, better than it ever was. And it wasn't just the way you looked – it was you. It was being with you, close and intimate again, that made it so amazing.'

Meg shook her head. He was saying everything that he must know she wanted to hear, but she knew that Robert was good at that. He could make any individual feel special and important, that was his talent.

'Look.' Robert watched her intently. 'I don't know what happened or why it happened, but everything suddenly clicked back into place, and I'd decided that night that it was over between me and Lynne. I swear to you.'

Meg made herself remember the text she had read on his phone.

'You'd just come from seeing her, hadn't you?' she asked him, to remind them both of why they were sitting there.

Robert nodded. 'Yes,' he admitted.

'You came from her bed to mine,' Meg stated sharply.

'No . . .' Robert hesitated, clearly weighing up the risks of what he was about to tell her next. 'I didn't sleep with her that day. She invited me over to her place for lunch. She made a big fuss when I said I didn't think I'd be able to make it. I was weak, I didn't want her to make any trouble either at home or at work – so I went. When I got there she told me she had booked tickets for the five o'clock showing at the cinema. I could have left, if I'd tried harder I could have left and been on time for you. I knew you were waiting for me, I knew you would have cooked and dressed up. But I found excuses not to leave Lynne even after the film had ended. She thought it was because I wanted to be with her, but it wasn't. It was because I couldn't bear to come home to you and look you in the eye and lie.'

'Until you knew I'd be asleep,' Meg confirmed, wondering what inner unknown part of her was keeping her sitting in her chair erect and in control.

'Yes,' Robert admitted. 'But then I came in and you looked . . .' He half smiled. 'Very sexy in all that get-up but more than that, you looked so vulnerable and beautiful. I looked at you lying on the bed and I knew I didn't want to leave you. I knew I wanted to be with you more than ever. I made my mind up right then, before I woke you, to end it with her.'

'So if you were so sure it was over between you then why were you with her the next day, kissing her in front of everyone?' Meg asked him bitterly, as a spark of anger flared within her. 'You know, it wasn't until later that I realised that probably the whole of your office knew what was going on. I went in there with two of your children and they were all either laughing at me or worse, pitying me. Can you imagine how humiliating that feels? To be chatting to your receptionist while you were carrying on with *her* in the lobby. A very unusual way to end an affair.'

'Lynne made it difficult,' Robert said, unable to meet her

eye. 'When I said I thought it was time to call it a day she got all hysterical. She threatened to come round here and confront you. I didn't want that, I was trying to preserve our marriage not destroy it! I was trying to let her down gently so that she wouldn't rock the boat.'

'You're a coward,' Meg said quietly.

'Pardon?' Robert asked her, genuinely surprised by what he thought he'd heard.

'If what you said is true then you are a coward, Robert. You would have carried on sleeping with her even though you say you love me so much, just because you were scared of getting caught out. Gutless.'

Meg had never spoken to Robert that way in all of the years they had been together, and he stared at her as if he was looking at a woman he no longer knew. Maybe he was, Meg thought, she felt like she barely knew herself any more.

'I am truly sorry for what I've done to you, Megan,' he said. 'But please ask yourself, is it worth throwing away everything we have because of it?'

'Have you asked yourself that question?' Meg said.

Slowly Robert shook his head.

'Well, I have,' she told him. 'I've asked it about a million times since all this happened and the answer is – I don't know yet, Robert.'

She took a large gulp of wine and Gripper pushed her cold muzzle under her hand in a gesture of what Meg thought of as solidarity.

'For us to continue to be married I'll have to forgive you. Completely forgive you – and I don't know if I can do that,' Meg said dully.

Robert nodded. 'I understand,' he said. 'But I swear I'll never let you down again – I love you, Megan.'

'You'd have to prove that to me,' Meg said. 'You'd have to

never get bored or fed up about proving it to me every day, until one day I feel I might be able to trust you again.'

'I won't,' Robert assured her. 'Not if you give us another chance.'

'You'd have to leave your job,' Meg went on. 'In fact, you'd have to never go back to it.'

This time Robert hesitated.

'OK,' he said. 'But to leave so suddenly won't look good. It might be difficult to get another job. It might mean less money.'

'Then we'll sell this house,' Meg said. 'We'll get a smaller place, take the kids out of their schools. They can go to the local primary, I hear it's very good.'

'If you're sure,' Robert said. 'Then we'll do it.'

'It's the only way this is going to happen,' Meg told him. 'If it happens.'

Robert got up and walked around the table. Once again he knelt at Meg's feet, but this time he simply picked up one of her hands. She forced herself to be unresponsive.

'I'll do anything, Megan,' he said. 'I'll do anything to make things right between us, I promise. I don't want to lose you, or my children . . . I love you all so much, Megan, I really do.' And Meg watched as he bent his head and wept.

It surprised her that she didn't just fling her arms around him and reassure him then and there that everything would be all right, and she knew he would be stunned too. It seemed that she was stronger than she thought.

'I have to think about it more,' she said.

Robert looked up at her, clearly disbelieving that Meg wasn't as moved as he was.

'Really?' he asked her.

Meg nodded. 'How many months was it you were seeing her?' she asked him. 'Six at least, wasn't it?' Robert nodded regretfully. 'Well, then, I think I deserve at least as long, if I want it, to decide what happens next.'

She turned her head away from him. 'You can go now, Robert,' she said.

And it wasn't until she heard him pull the front door shut behind him that she sank onto the floor and buried her face in Gripper's fur and wept.

Chapter Twenty-seven

Sandy was still asleep the following morning.

She had slept right through the afternoon, although she must have been waking up periodically, Natalie thought, as she had got through two thirds of the two-litre bottle of water Natalie had left for her with a glass next to the bed.

Natalie didn't know how to feel about the state her mother was in.

She thought back, trying to dredge up some of the hazy and ill-formed memories of her childhood with Sandy. It did seem that Sandy had always had a drink in her hand, that was true. And she had always acted as if she were a little tipsy, but as Natalie grew older she had decided that was just an affectation, a pretence designed to make her more appealing. Still, although while Natalie had lived with her Sandy had always been distracted and preoccupied by almost everything apart from her daughter, Natalie was fairly sure she hadn't been an out-and-out drunk.

Natalie had never seen Sandy this way before and she didn't know how to handle her. She didn't actually want to handle her at all. It seemed unfair that her mother, who'd done such a ham-fisted job of looking after her, now might require some serious looking after herself.

Although her mother presented a bizarre figure in her usual

get-up of inch-thick make-up and tight-fitting clothes, at least *that* Sandy was happy with herself. The woman who had lain sprawled by the loo yesterday was a self-loathing wreck and Natalie didn't want to see her that way again. She wanted her back the way she'd always been even if it *was* desperately embarrassing, because in the end she did care about what happened to her.

So, after she had put her to bed, with an acute sense of unreality Natalie had taken two further bottles of whisky out of her mother's suitcase, took all the wine she had been unable to drink for so long out of the wine rack, gathered up the beer, vodka and even the cooking sherry and poured it all down the sink. She kept only the good wine, which she'd collected herself and couldn't bear to waste. As she locked that in the old coal shed behind as much junk as she could shift, Natalie remembered the joke she'd made about doing just that with the vodka only a few days earlier. It didn't seem very funny now.

Sandy slept on as the darkness gradually wore away into dawn, and Natalie and Freddie watched the sun rising together over the rows and rows of roof lines and chimneys, TV aerials and satellite dishes. Somewhere over those houses and streets, flats, churches and shops, Jack Newhouse was probably sleeping.

'We're going somewhere important today,' Natalie told Freddie. 'We're going to go and see your daddy. Now, I must warn you. You might not like him and he might not like you, but I think it's important to be brave and give it go, don't you? It's now or never kiddo.'

Freddie had taken the news with his usual cheerful indifference, which had made Natalie feel better. At least she could tell him when he was older that she had tried her best with his father. Whatever happened after that would not be her fault.

She sat on the edge of the bed and slid Jack's numbers out from under the lamp where she had hidden them what now seemed aeons ago. She didn't think he had started a new job yet. In fact, after everything that had happened she wouldn't be surprised if he decided to leave London again, perhaps even go back to Italy where the climate was temperate and there were no love children hanging about, or at least none that Natalie knew of. She knew she should phone him and ask him if she could come over, but she didn't want to do that.

First of all it would mean talking to him, which was an inevitability that she wanted to delay until the last crucial second because of the sheer effort of will it would require to talk to him politely. And secondly if she called in advance he might very well say, 'No thank you very much, I don't want you and your baby to come over. You're nothing but trouble.'

No, it was best to maintain the element of surprise and just turn up, Natalie thought. If he was in he'd be far too polite to tell them to leave once they were actually on his doorstep. And if he was out they could just go and wander around the British Museum until he came back. And if he was in with another woman, Natalie could take some small pleasure in breaking up the party by introducing her to Jack's son. Natalie thought it was best for Freddie and her to set off as early as possible, so that they might catch him before he went out anywhere.

As for her not wanting to have to speak to him, she'd have to cross that bridge when she got to it.

It had just gone nine when Natalie arrived at the end of Willoughby Street. She looked at the blue-painted front door that was set into the side of the Georgian building. There were three buttons. Minnie's flat was the top one. Natalie thought she saw a figure move across the window up there. Someone was in, then. A sudden wave of fear enveloped her and it took a great deal of will power to keep her feet rooted to the spot instead of running in the opposite direction.

A million thoughts rattled through her fatigued brain. What if Jack had already gone and the figure she saw was Minnie? Or worse, much worse, what if Jack had someone else in there, another woman? What if the minute she had left him on Sunday night he'd gone right out and met the next potential love of his life standing at a bus stop?

He was good at that, after all.

Natalie stood on the corner for several minutes looking at the door, frozen with fear and indecision, wondering and waiting. The bus stop she needed to return home was just down the road, and better still at this time of day there were taxis aplenty driving right by her, their friendly amber lights offering the promise of refuge and the shortest route to safety.

And then her thoughts were interrupted by a familiar voice.

'Hello,' Jack said warily. He had a large cup of coffee in one hand and a paper in the other. It might have been some kind of pastry that was in the paper bag tucked under his arm.

Natalie wondered if she looked as inexplicably guilty as she felt at being caught on the corner of his street. She was going to have to talk to him now. It was unavoidable. It would be much harder to try to sort things out with him without the use of actual words, especially considering that she was always the very worst person at playing charades.

'I'm not stalking you,' she managed to say. Her voice sounded strange in her ears, like she was listening to a recorded version of it. 'I just came to try to talk to you and then I got here and wasn't sure if I should any more.' She looked up at his flat. If Jack was here, then who was the figure she saw in the window?

Jack looked uncertainly at Natalie and then glanced down at the buggy very quickly.

'But if you've got company,' she added uncertainly, looking back up at the window.

'Company?' Jack repeated the word as if he didn't really know what it meant. He was looking at Natalie with that same puzzled expression again. He must be wondering why on earth I don't just go away, she thought, feeling almost sorry for him.

'A guest,' Natalie prompted him, hoping to stop him looking at her in that way.

'Oh!' Jack shook his head. 'No, that's Mishka, she's not a guest, she's Minnie's cleaner. She's actually a concert harpist but Minnie employs her to keep her going between jobs.' A flicker of something like curiosity passed over his face. 'Did you think I had another conquest up there?' he asked.

Natalie shook her head. 'None of my business,' she said with a shrug.

They stood there for a moment or two longer and Natalie wondered if they had now spent more time like this, miserable and ill at ease, than they had lying happily in each other's arms.

'You brought the baby with you,' Jack said, finally acknowledging what couldn't be ignored. He looked pale, Natalie thought, and she wondered if it was because of the sight of her and his progeny or if he really didn't feel well. She found herself hoping it was because of her.

'I thought you should have a chance to meet him,' she said, holding the buggy's handles so tightly she could see the whites of her knuckles. 'If you wanted to.'

'I see,' Jack said, biting at his lip.

Natalie took a deep breath. 'Jack, I think I behaved badly the last time we met and I hoped you might . . . let us come in and that we could try to . . . resolve things, somehow.' She smiled tentatively at him. 'I don't want to leave things the way that we did. It didn't seem like the right ending for us.'

Jack hesitated before nodding at last. 'I thought that too. I'm glad you came back with . . . the . . . you know – baby.'

He reached into his pocket and pulled out a key on a piece of parcel string. 'Mishka should be on her way out any minute, so you go in,' he said, handing Natalie the key. 'I'll get you a coffee. Are you allowed coffee – if you're . . . ahem . . . you know, feeding him yourself?'

Natalie nodded, repressing the urge to smile. 'I let myself have one real cup a day,' she said.

'Fine,' Jack went on. 'Well, you go in and I'll be in in a minute.' He indicated the buggy. 'You can leave that in the downstairs hallway.' He took a couple of steps before turning back. 'I meant the buggy not the baby. You can bring the baby upstairs if you like.'

Natalie nodded again, fighting the irresistible urge to giggle that only the hysterically tired and emotionally confused can truly know. She held the keys tightly in her fist, so that she could feel the metal digging into the flesh of her palm, hoping it would somehow focus her mind. At least Jack was letting them in. And he had said she could bring Freddie upstairs. It was going well so far.

Mishka was indeed on the other side of the door as Natalie unlocked it. She seemed utterly unsurprised to find a strange woman with a baby on Jack's doorstep, and Natalie couldn't decide if it was a good or a bad thing. The young woman had paused for a moment to admire Freddie so that by the time she left Natalie quite liked her, even though she was tall, slender, blonde, talented and Russian. Natalie found that she liked anyone who liked her son.

Minnie's flat looked even nicer in the bright sunshine of the spring morning. It had long sash windows that Natalie hadn't noticed before, and from the tiny galley kitchen a direct view of the museum. Minnie had to be fairly minted, Natalie thought, to own such a prime piece of property. Or perhaps she had inherited it and had lived in it all her life. The place did have that feel about it. An antiquated Formica kitchen with one of those squat cream enamelled 1950s cookers, and as Natalie nosily pushed opened the bedroom door she saw dark wooden 1930s art deco furniture that looked as good as new. The book-lined living room looked as bright and breezy by day as it had seemed warm and friendly by firelight. Natalie sat down with Freddie in her arms in the wingback chair by the now cold fire grate. Freddie was wide awake, as if he knew something important was afoot, his huge black eyes as bright as buttons as he took everything in.

Then Natalie heard the door shut downstairs and Jack's footfall on the stairs.

She braced herself. She was here to tell him that despite everything, if he wanted to be in Freddie's life she would welcome it. Whatever he might say in return she needed to know that she had given this her very best shot at success, and that for once in her life she hadn't let complacency or fear ruin everything.

'So,' Jack said as he appeared in the room, filling it up with his presence. He sort of leant around the baby, giving him a wide berth as he handed Natalie her coffee. 'Is that all right?' he asked her, looking at Freddie. 'To have a hot drink right next to him?'

Natalie shifted Freddie over onto her right knee and held her coffee in her left hand, desperate for it to cool so she could mainline the caffeine. Her mind felt fuzzy and muddled and her skin tingled with tiredness. She felt like she used to when she had been out clubbing all night, only without the booze and carefree fun. She blinked a couple of times to focus her vision and wondered if coming to see Jack after so little sleep had been the best idea. But if not now, then when?

Jack sat down opposite her on the settle, took two custard tarts out of the paper bag he had been carrying and put them on two plates on a tiny table which he positioned between them. And then without touching either one he leaned forward in his seat, resting his elbows on his knees again, and looked at Natalie.

'I'm glad you're here,' he said.

'You are?' Natalie asked him, feeing a swell of hope rise in her chest.

'Yes,' Jack said emphatically. 'Like you, I was feeling bad about what happened between us that night. It was all so intense and difficult to take in. We found out so much about each other in such a short time. I behaved badly, thoughtlessly. I didn't appreciate how my news might affect you.' He dropped his head briefly. 'I've thought about that evening a lot since then and I want you to know I'm sorry. I suppose I must have had this idea that you were sort of in suspended animation while I was away, that your life wouldn't have changed at all. But it has.' He nodded at Freddie who was staring at him in total fascination, just waiting for Jack to smile at him, when he would return the expression automatically with his wide, all-embracing grin that seemed to invite the whole world to be his friend.

But Jack did not smile.

'Your life has changed a lot,' he went on. 'And so have you. I should have realised that because I've changed too.'

Natalie felt the bubble of hope that had risen in her chest pop and melt away.

'Have you?' she asked, not really wanting an answer.

'During my illness I thought a lot about that weekend. I built up this imaginary version of you that isn't real at all.' Jack's voice was tinged with sadness. 'Do you understand what I mean?'

Natalie nodded, forcing herself to look him in the face. 'Yes,' she said with a wry smile. 'I do. I thought about you too, except I couldn't decide if you were the lost love of my life or an evil womaniser.'

'And now?' Jack asked her, with an edge to his voice that she could not interpret.

'Now.' She looked at him thoughtfully, his lean, taut features so familiar and yet so strange. This was her opportunity to be completely honest with both herself and him. Did she love him? Did she want him? Was it truly this man that she longed to be with?

The answer her heart gave her was not the one she had been hoping for, and when it came to it she found it was not the one she could share with Jack.

'I don't know,' she said instead, because it was easier. 'I can't know, can I? Like you said, we're practically strangers.'

Both of them were quiet as they let the moment pass into history.

For the first time since they had met Natalie allowed herself the thought that perhaps all Jack and she were ever meant to be to each other were ships that had passed in the night. It was a realisation that made her feel suddenly terribly sad, as a long unspoken but closely held hope was finally extinguished.

All she could do now was to try to make the best of things for her son.

'Jack,' she said, careful to keep her voice steady. 'I want to explain why I behaved the way I did. I was upset when you didn't call me after Venice. I was so sure that you would. It was a real blow to my ego and to my heart, I suppose, when you just . . . vanished. When you didn't call I thought that you hadn't liked me at all, I thought you'd used me, or maybe you thought that the expensive hotel and trip to Venice should have been enough of a pay-off and maybe it should have been.

But I let myself think it was more than that, something I *never* usually do. When I realised I was wrong, I felt like an idiot.' Natalie laughed, despite how she was feeling inside. 'I had planned to get over you and forget you entirely within about eight weeks, only after six weeks I knew I was pregnant, which did throw a massive spanner in the works.'

'Must have been a bit of a sod,' Jack said, pressing his lips into a thin serious line.

Natalie nodded.

'It was a *bit*,' she said. 'But I wasn't angry or upset about the pregnancy; I was happy, amazingly happy. I had everything in my life I needed to cope: money, a home, work, friends.' She tipped her head to one side. 'And a mother who I sort of need in a sort of unhealthy co-dependency way – but that's another story. Anyway, I knew I wanted my baby, come what may. I thought it didn't matter who his father was. I thought if I never saw you again that he and I would be absolutely fine. Only I did see you again. And I won't try to just cut you out of his life. Not if you want to be part of it.'

'It's not your fault,' Jack said slowly. 'I understand completely why you didn't tell me about him. It's probably a better reason than mine for not telling you about my cancer. While I was behaving like a coward, you were acting like a hero. I was scared but more than that,' Jack took a deep breath, 'I was embarrassed.'

'Embarrassed?' Natalie asked him, with some confusion.

'Yes.' Jack looked abashed. 'I still am a bit, to be honest, even though I've come to terms with it now. But when I met you I was just about to have a ball cut off. And I didn't like talking about it. In fact, it was my general reluctance to discuss my testes with beautiful ladies that nearly got me killed. My GP is a woman. I waited and waited to ask her about the lump. I was really lucky they caught it in time.'

'I see,' Natalie said slowly, although she clearly didn't.

'Yes, I know you think I'm an idiot but I wasn't especially rational at the time. I was worried that after the operation I'd feel emasculated, or that I'd repulse you or any woman. I thought, who'd want a one-balled man?'

Natalie tried to stop herself smiling, but she couldn't.

'I don't know how to break this to you,' she said, her mood briefly lightened. 'But a pair of testicles is not the most important requirement in a lady's list of must-haves when it comes to a prospective partner.'

'Isn't it?' Jack asked her, with a wry smile. 'Anyway, I didn't know where I'd be after the surgery and the treatment. I felt for a while that the disease would castrate me, that I'd have no sex drive. I felt weak and pathetic and I . . . I cried a lot. I realise now that I didn't know you at all, Natalie, but I did know that I didn't want you to see me that way.' He paused. 'Maybe if, *if* you had come and told me about Freddie, if I'd known that you were having my baby, things might have been different. Except the fact that we had a child wouldn't have really changed anything else, would it? We would still have been virtual strangers, still not knowing anything about each other. It still would have been one of the worst and most irrational ways to start a relationship.'

The smile that had started on Natalie's lips faded.

'That's true,' she said. For a moment neither of them could look at the other.

'I don't know what you think about me, Natalie,' Jack went on. 'But one of the things I have been for most of my adult life is a coward. I run away from things that scare me. Like the final exams in my biochemistry degree. I studied for three years, aced paper after paper but the thought of the exams did my head in, so I didn't take them. I never passed my degree. And women, it's not that I was afraid of commitment, it was more that I was afraid of making a commitment to a woman and then realising a few months or years down the line that she was the wrong one. I thought it was better to be careful. So I didn't really get very involved with anybody until . . . well, I suppose I can't really say I got involved with you.'

Jack sighed and shook his head as if attempting to dislodge a particularly unhelpful thought. 'Then there was the cancer. I ran away from that for a long time too. Didn't get it checked out for months, waited and waited for the bloody thing to go away on its own, and once I had the diagnosis, I ran away again – with you that time. And then from you; from you and how the cancer might make you see me. So you see, I am a terrible coward. I'm weak, I'm not the kind of man who could be a good father. Or at least I haven't been.' He moistened his lips. 'I've thought about nothing except you and the baby since the night you told me about him, and I realised – I've got my life back now and I don't want to live it like a coward, Natalie. I want to be brave, I want to face life and live it – the good and the bad.' Jack suddenly looked very young. 'It's just that being brave is a bit scary.'

Natalie watched him, this man she had thought of as so strong and even dashing, so dangerous to know and a real heart-breaker, and found with some amazement that it wasn't that constructed version of him that she was drawn to after all. It couldn't be, because all the feelings she had had for that distant and shadowy man of mystery were still present for this utterly vulnerable stranger. The more he told her the more she admired him, the more at last she really understood him. He was an ordinary man who'd been badly beaten and buffeted by life, and was still in recovery. He wasn't what she had thought he was at all, and yet Jack was exactly the man for her, because in the end it had been none of those artifices that she had fallen for in Venice. It had been the core of him, the heart, and that was still there.

Jack looked at Freddie, who catching his eye bounced up and down on Natalie's knee excitedly. Jack was the one adult who hadn't instantly poured smiles and attention all over him, and he was trying his best to rectify the situation by being especially charming.

'It seems to me,' Jack went on, 'that little fellow is here in the world now and he is part of me, and if you'll let me I do want to be part of his life. I don't want to run away from my son. I might not be very good at it but I'm going to try my best to be his father, the best one I can be.'

As he spoke, his words caught in his throat and he dipped his head for a moment, until the threat of tears had subsided.

'Sorry,' he said with a shrug. 'You see, once I got past the whole running for the hills impulse I realised that it is sort of like a miracle. I didn't know if I'd be able to father children after treatment. I was trying to get used to the idea of never being a father and then suddenly –' He gestured at Freddie.

Natalie smiled at him, wishing more than anything that she could just go and put her arms around him.

'Can I . . . could I have a go at holding him?' Jack asked, interrupting her thoughts. 'Can I hold Freddie?'

For a second Natalie felt her arms tighten reflexively around Freddie's tummy and then she relaxed her fingers.

'Of course you can,' she told him gently.

Jack looked nervous.

'I need to support its, I mean his head, right?' he said, looking at Freddie like he was a bundle of particularly unstable dynamite.

'Well, no, he can do that on his own now,' Natalie said, looking down at her son who was leaning forward in her lap, his arms outstretched to Jack. 'But it's usually best not to dangle him by his legs or anything like that.'

Jack's mouth twitched with the promise of a smile. 'I remember I liked your sense of humour.' He paused. 'You were joking, weren't you?'

Natalie laughed despite herself.

'Yes, I was, Jack,' she said. She was confused. She had never felt so happy and yet so sad at the same time before. It was a difficult mix of emotions to control and she felt that she might burst in the attempt.

'You know what,' she said. 'I think you are actually quite a nice man.'

'Am I?' Jack said. 'Really? Is that good?'

'It's good for Freddie,' Natalie said. She and Jack stood up together and then, finally, she transferred her son into his father's arms.

Once there Freddie's features became still as he looked up at Jack with a solemn but curious expression.

Jack looked down at Freddie in exactly the same way.

'He actually does look like me,' Jack said in amazement. 'Isn't that weird? I mean, friends and family with babies are always going on about how they are the dead spit of somebody or other and I've looked at them, these babies, and I've thought – nope, they all look the same to me. Fat, pink and squashy. But I look at him and I can see myself in him, and you too. It's the weirdest feeling. It's . . . God, it's amazing, Natalie.'

As Jack smiled down at the baby at last, Freddie's face erupted into a returning grin, and expression of pure delight.

'He smiles!' Jack exclaimed happily. 'Look, he smiles and he's a baby – does that make him advanced? What else does he do? Does he crawl yet, or talk?'

Natalie couldn't help but be warmed by his interest in her, in *their* son.

'He cries, a lot, mainly at night,' she told him. 'He poos a *lot* and he likes to try to wee in your face. He's due to start solids soon, he's desperate to crawl but hasn't quite got it yet, he can only go backwards if he wriggles about on his tummy. He smiles at people he likes and he's the loveliest, most amazing baby in the whole wide world.'

Jack nodded. 'Just as I thought. A child genius.' He took one or two experimental steps with him, and discovering that he did not drop the baby, paced the room a couple of times. Natalie sat down and watched them.

'Do you think it will be OK,' he asked her, 'you and me and him? Will it work after everything that's happened?'

Natalie looked at Jack holding their baby and she wished more than anything in the world that she could put her arms around them both and kiss them.

'We will find a way,' she said, determinedly. It had begun to feel as if things had changed between them again, as if now they had moved passed into a new phase where Freddie was the most important thing between them. And perhaps that was simply the way it had to be. Her old friend fate had put two huge great obstacles right in the middle of the part where they should have been just starting out, dating, having candlelit dinners, taking long walks in the park, spending all afternoon in bed, talking and laughing and doing all those soppy things that somehow Natalie had never managed to do. At least, not with the same person.

That part had been robbed from them both by circumstance. And now it had to be more important than ever that Jack should move on with his life, as far as possible away from the shadow of his illness. Away from that time when their lives might have been different.

'We'll be fine,' Natalie answered Jack's question, feeling her heart compress. 'I'm sure of it.'

*

A little while later Jack walked them back to the edge of Oxford Street, where they parted. He was catching the Tube down to his offices to meet his new colleagues, and Natalie planned to risk the wrath of Alice and take Freddie into work.

'Thank you,' Jack said.

He leant forward and brushed his lips against her cheek, sending a jolt of longing surging right through Natalie that nearly knocked her off her feet. It was hard to believe that something so physical, so tangible could only be felt by her and not Jack. But she had to believe it, because there was not a flicker of anything in his face that might betray that he was feeling the same way.

Natalie wondered how long it would take for these feelings to gradually fade away. She hoped she would be over it by the time Freddie took his A levels, with a little bit of luck.

'I'll see you in a few days then?' she said. She and Jack had already planned his first proper visit with Freddie on Saturday. She was to teach him all the things he needed to know to be able to look after Freddie.

'You will,' Jack replied. 'Saturday then.'

It had taken Natalie a lot of effort not to look back as she walked away from Jack and into the throng of people that the hint of spring sunshine had brought out. But walk on she had, until she was sure he wouldn't be able to see her any more. And then she had stopped and turned around and caught a glimpse of what might have been his head vanishing around a corner.

'Well, the main thing,' she told Freddie staunchly, 'is that the waiting is finally over.'

Chapter Twenty-eight

Natalie had started so early that morning on her expedition to find Jack that it seemed to her as if it should be about midnight by now. But it was barely gone two in the afternoon by the time she had got home.

Her visit to the office had been heartening. Everybody was pleased to see her and thrilled to meet Freddie. She had arrived just in time to see a walk-through of the collection that they were presenting to buyers in a few days' time, and it had made Natalie so proud that she had cried.

'It's the hormones,' she said, flapping her hands in front of her eyes before she erupted into full-blown wailing. 'I'm fine really,' she sobbed. 'Pay no attention to me, you've all just done such a wonderful job – and without me. I'm gutted!'

Alice hugged her tightly.

'Let's leave Freddie in the capable hands of ten or so clucky women and go and talk about why you're looking so sad,' she said.

'You should feel proud,' Alice said as Natalie finished telling her what had happened between her and Jack.

'Proud?' Natalie asked. 'But why?'

'Because you made up your mind, on your own, without any nagging from me to go and see him again. And it must have been so hard for you to put your feelings on the line for your sake and Freddie's. The sort of grown-up, mature thing you'd normally run a mile from if it meant you got to avoid a bit of awkwardness. And it's paid off, not exactly the way you wanted it to work, I know. But you've got Jack in Freddie's life now. Did you ever think a few weeks ago that would be possible? It wouldn't have been, if you hadn't done the right thing.'

'The thing is,' Natalie said carefully. 'The thing is that I didn't truly realise until today that I have been waiting for him, for Jack. For all these months I've had this half-arsed but heartfelt belief that he would come back for me and Freddie, and that we were meant to be together. But when he did come back it was by accident and not for me at all. And now there's this big hole inside me where the waiting and the hoping used to be and I don't know how to fill it – perhaps with misery and despair. What do you think?' She smiled weakly at her friend.

Alice looked thoughtful. 'Do you still, even after everything that's happened, have real feelings for this man? Do you love him?'

'I think I do,' Natalie said, her voice almost a whisper. 'Look, I don't know, I can't say for sure because I feel like I've only really started to get to know him now, long after the affair is over. But I know it's something serious and something strong because it lasted through a lot of knock-backs. Whenever I look at him, whenever he touches me, when I think about all he's been through or when I see him smiling at Freddie my heart beasts faster and I can feel the blood in my veins, and every part of me wants to be with every part of him whatever happens.' Natalie's shoulders dropped as a feeling of exhaustion washed over her. 'I expect that makes me insane.'

Alice laid a comforting palm on her hand. 'Maybe it's the pregnancy hormones again,' she suggested gently.

'No,' Natalie said with complete certainty. 'This time it isn't the hormones.'

'Then if it's the real thing, if you really think that you love him you have to tell him, for your, Freddie's and his sake,' Alice said.

'How can I?' Natalie asked her. She held up her hand when Alice opened her mouth. 'No, Alice, this is not the time for one of your lectures, useful as they often are. His relationship with Freddie is very fragile. It can't take any external pressure, and me throwing myself at him is just that. I can't do anything about it, not now.'

'But what if you miss your chance again?' Alice asked.

'I'll learn to live with it,' Natalie replied.

'You've changed these last few weeks,' Alice told her.

'Maybe I *have* changed,' Natalie said. 'Maybe Freddie has changed me for the better.'

'Just as long as you remember that the old you wasn't all bad.' Alice put an arm around her shoulder. 'Hey, you know what this means. Now you're going to have regular babysitting you and I can go out on the pull.'

'Mmmm,' Natalie said without enthusiasm. 'Nice idea, but I don't think I'll be ready to go on the pull for quite some time yet.'

'Who was talking about you?' Alice said.

When Natalie got home not only was Sandy awake and sober, but she had cleaned the house as well.

Natalie found her in the kitchen, washed and dressed and cooking. She looked up and smiled at Natalie as she entered the room.

'Hello, dear,' she said.

'What have you done with my real mother?' Natalie asked warily.

Sandy put her wooden spoon down on the counter and took a breath.

'I'm so sorry about yesterday, Natalie,' she said. 'I can't believe what happened. I'm so embarrassed and ashamed of myself and I just want to say that I'm sorry.'

Natalie did not move.

'Seriously, where is she? Have you abducted her into outer space for extensive tests on her liver?' she said, straight-faced.

'Please, Natalie, I'm trying to be serious.'

Natalie sat down at the breakfast bar and looked at her mum.

'Good,' she said. 'I'm glad you're being serious. Because this is serious, Mother.' She steeled herself to say what she knew she must. It was a relatively new talent, being able to face up to reality, and she thought she was getting quite good at it. 'Mum, you're an alcoholic.'

'No, I'm not, dear,' her mum said, shaking her head.

Denial. Natalie had read on the Internet that denial was very common in alcoholics.

'That proves it,' she said. 'You don't think you're an alcoholic when you drink at every single opportunity, to the point where you can't move or speak. Mum?' Natalie exclaimed with frustration. 'Come on, take a look at your life, take a look at what's happening to you!'

'You don't understand, I don't drink like that . . .' Sandy began.

'Um, excuse me,' Natalie cut in emphatically. 'I know what I see with my own eyes. Like you passed out with your head practically in the toilet.'

'I don't drink like that *normally*,' Sandy continued. 'I mean, back in Spain I have a glass or two in the evening, like I always have. I like a drink now and then. But I don't *normally* drink so much that I'm ill. It was just when I got here that I started.'

Sandy finished speaking with a little shrug and a shake of her head as if she didn't really understand it herself, let alone expect anyone else to.

'Pardon?' Natalie asked her, unable to comprehend what her mother was telling her. 'Are you saying that once you arrived in the home of your daughter supposedly to help with the care of your grandson, you thought you'd just drink yourself to death instead?' She shook her head. 'Obviously, what was I thinking? It all makes perfect sense to me now.'

Sandy took the lid of off the pan she was standing over and a waft of coq au vin lifted into the room.

'Did you find my wine?' Natalie asked her, frowning deeply. 'Because breaking and entering is a serious offence and the sort of thing an *alcoholic* does.'

'No, don't worry,' Sandy said with a sigh. 'I didn't break into the coal shed and steal your best Bordeaux. I bought some cheap stuff at the corner shop.' She held up the still half-full bottle and shook it. 'See, I haven't drunk any. I am not an alcoholic.'

'That proves nothing,' Natalie said, slightly peeved that her plan to prevent Sandy from drinking had such a large and clearly visible hole in it as the corner shop.

Sandy stirred the stew and returned its lid before turning down the heat and sitting next to Natalie.

'I don't like living in Spain,' she told her.

Natalie huffed out a sigh and rolled her eyes at this irrelevance, like a teenager who was desperate to be anywhere else but there.

'I mean, I like the warmth and the people, and my neighbours are good fun. There's this chap over the way, Keith Macbride, a Scottish fellow. Widower. Sometimes we have a drink together and do the Latin-American dance class on a Thursday evening. He's the one that's been watering my plants,' she added tentatively.

362

'You said it was a woman!' Natalie exclaimed.

'No, I said it was a neighbour, and anyway I didn't want you to think that I'd lined you up with another uncle. I know how much you hate uncles. Keith is . . . he's a comfort and I care about him.'

'So why haven't you pounced and drained him of his life force?' Natalie asked her mildly.

'I told him I couldn't be happy there with him, not the way things are with you so far away.'

'Oh God, you want to come and live here, don't you,' Natalie said, her voice heavy with dread.

Sandy shook her head. 'I'd like living in Spain, entering the ladies' golf drive and things like that, and I even think I could be happy with Keith if I could only know that things were right between you and me.'

Natalie was stunned. It hadn't occurred to her that the state of their relationship might trouble Sandy as much as it did her.

'A year I waited to hear from you, Natalie, a whole year without even a phone call.'

'You have fingers too, you know,' Natalie said defensively. 'Very useful for dialling telephone numbers. I might have been waiting for a year for *you* to phone *me*. Did you ever think of *that*?'

'Yes I did and I did phone, but you were very hard to get hold of, especially during your trip to China! Be honest, Natalie, you didn't want to speak to me at all, did you?'

'No, Mum.' Natalie's snap back was reflexive. 'I was a bit busy being pregnant by a man I've managed to fall in love with without ever really knowing him who I didn't see again after he impregnated me until a few days ago when I discovered he'd had testicular cancer. I have been a tad preoccupied with my own life. I *do* apologise.'

'The night you came back and Freddie weed in my face,' Sandy confirmed with a nod of her head.

'Yes, that night,' Natalie replied wearily, the fatigue of the day threatening to overcome her at any minute.

'And you don't want to talk about it to me, I suppose?' Sandy asked her.

Natalie's shoulders slumped and she dropped her forehead into her hands. 'What's the point of talking about it to anyone? I could talk about it for hours and hours and nothing would change. He wants to know Freddie and be his dad. That's the main thing,' she said, hoping she had made it clear that she just couldn't discuss it any further.

Sandy reached out a hand and rubbed Natalie's forearm a couple of times.

'OK then, I'll talk to you,' she said.

'Mum . . .' Natalie began to protest.

'No, just listen,' Sandy said. 'Just listen.' She paused and moistened her lips before beginning to talk. 'You have this memory of a childhood and somehow it's completely different to the one that I have. And I wonder how can that possibly be? We used to be best friends, Natalie, right from when you were a little girl. We'd make each other laugh so much, every day. Every place we went to was a new adventure. I was so proud of you, my curly-headed little girl, always so clever and full of smiles. Moonbeam, that's what I called you. And you always told me I was the best and most beautiful mother in all the world, every single day.' Sandy paused again, the smile of recollection fading on her lips. 'Then you got older and you got angry with me and you've never stopped being angry with me. And I don't know why, I don't know what changed except that I find myself feeling angry with *you*. When I'm around you I become this woman that you think I am, the woman I sometimes am – this loud obnoxious drunk, selfish and self-centred. Because when you hate me, when you're cross with me then at least you are looking at me. At least then I have your attention.'

Natalie lifted her head from her hands and looked at Sandy.

'Are you saying that you started drinking when you got here to get my attention?' She asked her mother incredulously.

Sandy shrugged. 'I'm trying to understand the way things are between us. I'm trying to work out why we make it so difficult to get on with each other. Look, I like a drink, Natalie, probably one too many here and there. And when I got here and saw you it slipped out of control, but I didn't plan it. It just happened.'

'Like throwing yourself at Gary, or was that attention-seeking too? Because you didn't seem to be thinking about Keith Macthingy very much then.'

'I was just having a bit of fun,' Sandy said. 'And anyway you threw yourself at him too, you have to admit he is pretty dishy.'

'Dishy,' Natalie said sharply. 'Dishy. That's sums it up, Mum. You're stuck in a time warp that is twenty years old. I can't believe this. I can't believe that my own mother pulled the tactics of a teenager on me to get me to notice her.'

'Didn't you hear me?' Sandy's voice rose as she tried to explain. 'I didn't plan it. On my way here I couldn't wait to see you, I couldn't wait for you to need me. I thought you'd want my help and advice. I thought we'd talk and get closer again. Like we used to. But you didn't need me, you only seemed put out that I was here at all.'

'And what about you?' Natalie replied. 'When I came in with Freddie you barely glanced at us because you were too busy having "a bit of fun" with Gary. I was hopeful, too. Hopeful that the woman coming to stay was my mum, a mother who might make me feel safe and loved for once.'

Natalie stopped herself. She had expressed out loud feelings that she hadn't truly admitted even to herself. She still felt the need – grown-up woman and parent that she was – to have her mother's reassurance that everything would be all right. And she still longed to believe her unquestioningly, just as she had when she was a little girl.

Sandy leaned closer to Natalie, her tone urgent as she tried to make her daughter understand. 'Darling, I wanted to be like that with you. I wanted to rush up to you and hug you – but there always seems to be this wall. Except for that night, the night that Freddie got me in the eye. I thought that maybe there was a moment then when the barrier was down and you were going to tell me what was happening to you. Just for a second it felt like you wanted me. Look, I know you've got all sorts of things to worry about, Natalie, I'm not blind – I just wish you felt that you could share them with me. But you didn't. I felt so hurt and angry that I had a drink and then another and another. Not a motherly thing to do I know, but a human one.' Sandy paused. 'The funny thing is that I don't think I'll ever stop learning to be a mother. There'll never be a cut-off point when I'll suddenly understand everything and know how to make it all right between us. But I *do* want to try. I *do* want things to change. I want you to be my Moonbeam again. My precious girl.'

Natalie opened her mouth but Sandy went on, holding up her hand. 'Look, I've been stupid and selfish and I am ashamed of it. Especially letting you find me so drunk. I'm sorry, Natalie. I truly am.'

Natalie looked down at the counter top. She couldn't think of anything to say. She couldn't think of anything to think. Her brain was numb trying to take in what her mother was telling her.

'You had a difficult childhood,' Sandy went on. 'You

probably went to too many schools, and I probably had too many boyfriends. Perhaps you never had a chance to feel settled and secure in one place. And you never knew your father, that's a hard thing to deal with. I know that sometimes you can miss something you've never really had just as much as something you've lost. But you have to understand, I didn't do it to hurt you, I did it because I was trying my best for you.' She smiled weakly. 'And look at you, you've turned into a very wonderful woman, which I know you think is all down to yourself but which I hope has a little bit to with me as well.'

'It wasn't that bad,' Natalie said quietly. 'I don't know, maybe it's since I had Freddie – but I've started to remember things, nice things that I hadn't thought about in years.'

'Really?' Sandy asked hopefully. 'Do you remember how we used to walk along the beach for hours, collecting pink stones? Because you only liked the pink ones.' Natalie nodded slowly. 'Or when I made you that play costume out of one of my old frocks, all purple and sparkles it was – do you remember how you loved it? And how every year until you were about fourteen I made you a birthday cake, always bigger and better and stranger than the last. Do you remember that castle cake? I made it with ice cream and it melted all over the place before we could eat it?'

Natalie kept her gaze steady on the worktop, seeing that day over again in her head. She smiled when she thought about her and Sandy covered in melted ice cream.

'And I was always there to put you to bed,' Sandy told her. 'I was there to make you breakfast, and when you got back from school. I did my best for you, Natalie. And maybe my best wasn't good enough for you, but it was all I had to give. That and the fact that I love you, so much. So I'm asking you, now you're a grown woman and a mother yourself, to try to understand that I miss you, darling, I miss my little girl.'

Natalie looked sideways at her. Sandy had said all the things that she wanted to hear, all the things that she had longed to hear for many years. But she felt so sapped of energy that it as was a struggle to respond the way she felt she should, the way she *wanted* to. If there was one thing she had learnt recently, though, it was not to let any opportunity, however slight it might seem, slip by untaken.

'It's been a long day, Mum,' she said slowly. 'I'm so tired. I saw Freddie's dad this morning, arranged contact for Freddie. It's taken everything out of me. I feel weary all over. My head hurts, my body hurts and my heart hurts.'

Sandy nodded. 'I can see that in your face,' she said gently. 'If you wanted to tell me about it . . .'

Natalie shook her head. 'I've heard everything you said and I'm glad you've said it. And I know that it's not all you, I know it's me too. For some reason, when I'm around you I become a person that I don't like very much. And I don't want to do that any more . . .' She looked at her mother, and she knew there was one last thing she had to tell her now, while she had the chance.

'I went to see Dad once, you know,' she said. Sandy's eyes widened but she didn't speak. 'I was fifteen, maybe sixteen. I'd been going through your stuff as usual, looking for make-up to steal, and I found my birth certificate. Place of birth Brighton, and the name of my dad. I know you told everybody he'd died, but although you never actually said it to me we both knew that was just a story for your public. I used to dream about him – daydreams, imagining what he would be like. Tall, dark and handsome, I suppose, all the clichés. Clever and kind and sad because he'd lost his daughter and didn't know how to find her.' Natalie paused. 'And when I saw his name, I thought that at last I had the chance to find him. So I got on the train and went to Brighton. I went to the

368

first phone box I saw and looked in the book. There were three M. Davies who could have been him. The first one was about ninety-two, the second one was very kind but said he'd never known you and that he lived with his mother and the third one . . .' Natalie paused as she steeled herself to recollect. 'Well, that was him. That was Daddy. His wife answered the door. I was a bit surprised, I didn't expect him to have a wife, and I could see kids' wellingtons in the hallway. I asked to speak to him, said I was the daughter of an old friend and . . . suddenly there he was. He wasn't very handsome, Mum, I thought he would have been better-looking. He was a bit short, going bald on top. Portly, you know. I think he had my nose, or rather I had his I suppose.

'"Hello, Dad," I said, and I remember my voice was so tiny it was nearly lost in the rush of the traffic. "It's me, Natalie. Sandy's daughter." His face,' Natalie went on, staring into the middle distance as the memory replayed itself before her eyes. 'I'll never forget it. He just looked horrified. It was a cold day and wet and I didn't have a proper coat or umbrella of course, so I was soaking and shivering. But he just stood there, staring. All he said was, "Go away, I don't want you round here. I have a wife, I have a daughter. Go away, you're nothing to do with me." And he shut the door in my face.'

'Natalie,' Sandy said, her voice low. 'I honestly didn't know.'

'How would you know, I never told you, did I?' Natalie said. 'The first man to ever reject me. I expected so much of him, Mum. I expected this amazing reunion, that he'd fling his arms around me and tell me how he'd hoped one day I would turn up. But he couldn't wait to see the back of me. I was his child, part of him, and he wanted nothing to do with me. That hurt me. It made me furious with him, but mostly with you. I blamed you for choosing that man as my

369

father. I still do, I suppose. It is still painful. I couldn't help but think how different our lives could have been. Like the other kids at school with the normal mothers, and the brothers and sisters and – the dads. Our life stopped being an adventure for me on that day. All I could see were the things that I didn't have. I blamed you. I didn't have anyone else to blame.'

'I'm sorry, Natalie,' Sandy said, her voice wrought with emotion. 'I'm sorry I got it so wrong for you.'

Natalie looked at her mother and attempted a smile.

'You didn't though, did you? Like you said, you did your best. I suppose I've always known that, but it wasn't enough to stop me from being angry. It's hard to stop. It's hard to let go of feelings I've had for so long, even if I know they don't make any sense.' Hesitantly Natalie reached out and put her hand over her mother's. 'But I want to. I want to try to stop being angry with you. I want to be close to you, Mum. I want to tell you things. I want you to tell me about this Keith Macbride and what his intentions are. But I don't think that you and I will change just like that. It will take time, and hard work probably, but we could try. We could try to start to be friends again.'

'I'd like that,' Sandy said simply.

'Mum,' Natalie said with sudden urgency. 'I'm scared. I'm so caught up in everything that's happening at the moment. I'm trying so hard to keep myself focused and hold it all together for Freddie, but sometimes I'm scared I won't be able to. That I'll go and do something really stupid and mess it all up again.'

'You're saying that because you're tired,' Sandy said, resting the back of her hand against Natalie's cheek. 'There's a bottle of milk ready in the fridge, isn't there?' Natalie nodded. 'You go to bed, darling. That stew will simmer for hours yet, it should be perfect when you wake up. You sleep and I'll watch Freddie.'

'Is it really just because I'm tired?' Natalie asked her. 'Or because I'm rubbish?'

'Go to bed,' Sandy told her. 'I'll be here when you wake up.'

'Whoopee,' Natalie groaned, but as she trudged up the stairs and fell onto her bed, for the first time in a long time she was kind of glad to know that.

Chapter Twenty-nine

Jess watched the rapid rise and fall of Jacob's chest as she lay beside him on the bed.

He didn't have a temperature, she had checked with the strip thermometer a few moments ago, and he was sleeping, although every now and then he coughed a little dry cough that made him screw up his face.

She felt the tension rise in her chest as she watched him, and laid her head gently on his chest. The speed of his heartbeat increased the rate of her own and she felt herself on the edge of panic.

Babies' hearts beat very fast, she reminded herself sternly, it's perfectly normal. But even before she had finished the thought she had called out to Lee who was in the next room watching *Soccer AM*.

'What's up?' he said when he came in a minute or so later. He was never one to respond instantly to a request to come away from the TV, unless he thought it was a genuine emergency.

'What do you think of him?' Jess asked, nodding at Jacob. 'Does he look OK to you?'

Lee knelt down beside the bed and looked at his son.

'He looks fine,' he said, a little impatiently because he was missing his favourite show.

'His heart is beating very fast,' Jess told him, even though she knew exactly what Lee would say.

'We've been through this, remember? Babies' hearts do beat very fast,' Lee repeated what she had just told herself. 'It's normal.'

'But what about his breathing?' Jess had to voice her nagging worry that not everything was quite right. 'Do you think he's breathing faster than usual?'

Lee stared for a bit longer at Jacob's chest. 'He looks the same as ever to me,' he said.

And when Jess looked at Jacob she saw that he did seem to be breathing regularly again, the dry persistent cough had stopped.

'Maybe he was dreaming,' Lee said. 'You know, like a dog?'

Jess gave him a look that sent him out of the room and back to his beloved show.

She lay beside Jacob, drawing her legs up underneath him and encircling him with the curve of her body, watching the rhythmic rise and fall of his chest until she too was asleep.

Natalie knelt on the rug in her living room with the contents of Freddie's baby bag laid out before her, together with the larger items she used on a daily basis while looking after her son.

She was trying to prepare for Jack's visit, which was less than twenty minutes away. She was trying to be organised and methodical because she thought it was better than the alternative, which involved her running around the house screaming.

So she had decided to lay out everything that Jack would need to learn about basic Freddie care, arranging all the equipment by use.

Changing mat, bottom cream, wipes and nappies.

Baby bath, baby soap, hooded towel, blanket and talc.

Bottle tops, steriliser, and breast pump. And then she put the breast pump back in Freddie's bag. He might have to give Freddie milk but he didn't have to know exactly how it got in the bottle in the first place.

Sandy leaned against the door frame, looking down at her daughter.

'Is this the way to do it?' she asked Natalie tentatively. 'Maybe you should just let the visit happen instead of trying to plan it like a military campaign?'

'Yes,' Natalie said thoughtfully. 'Yes, that would be one way of handling it, but I need to feel I'm in control of this, Mum. If I'm in control of *this*,' she gestured at the rug, 'then I'm in control of *me*.'

'OK,' Sandy said without further questioning. 'Then you'll need to show him how to dress him too. I'll go and sort out some Babygros and things before I make myself scarce.'

'Thanks, Mum,' Natalie said. Amazing, she thought, how this meaningful dialogue works so much better than trading insults and screaming at each other. It was only a shame it had taken them twenty years to work it out.

Suddenly the doorbell went and Natalie's hand flew to her chest. She held her breath.

'Are you getting that?' her mum shouted down the stairs.

'Yes!' Natalie replied in a strangled voice. Jack was early, and she wasn't nearly ready for him. She had no mascara on, for one thing, she hadn't brushed her hair since the morning and she still hadn't managed to banish her feelings of unrequited love for him to a respectable and manageable distance. Still, Natalie thought, hastily running her fingers through her hair and pinching colour into her cheeks, he'd have to be about fifty years late for her to achieve that particular ambition.

'Welcome!' she said as brightly as she could as she swung open the door.

Meg watched Frances's bottom as she cleaned the oven. She had come over when Robert had left with the three eldest children to take them out for the day, armed with a raft of scourers, degreasers and descalers.

'You don't have to do that, you know,' Meg told her. 'Even if my life wasn't in tatters I still wouldn't have cleaned it today. I'd have left it until it started to set the smoke alarm off.'

Frances's torso emerged from the oven. She sat back on her heels and looked at Meg.

'I know I don't *have* to but I *want* to,' she explained. 'Some people read books or watch TV to take their minds off things, *I* clean.'

Meg screwed her mouth into a knot. She didn't mind Frances being there, she was rather glad to see her, in fact. But not if she was going to sulk, she couldn't cope with that. A week or so ago Meg would have tried her best to placate Frances's edgy mood, to iron out her troubles as if they were Meg's fault. But not any more. She didn't feel like hedging around Frances any more.

'Are you in a mood because I haven't said that I'll take him back yet?' Meg asked Frances directly. 'Is that what's on your mind? Is that why you're here again, has he sent you to wear me down? Punishment by cleaning, yet another way to highlight my inadequacies?'

Frances stood up and dropped the nearly black scrubbing pad into the bin. She stripped off her Marigolds, threw them in the sink and sat at the table.

'No, that's not it,' she said sharply. Whatever it was that

was irritating her was gathering momentum. 'Actually I'm *glad* you haven't just given in to him. I'm glad you've haven't phoned that divorce lawyer too, mind. And it's not because you have a dirty oven, that doesn't make you a bad person. I do know that, Megan, I'm not a sociopath despite what you think.' Frances folded her arms. 'It's Robert. If there is one thing I have learnt from having my brother staying with me in my house it's that if it came to a choice between you and him, I'd choose you and I wouldn't care what Mummy and Daddy would say!' Frances finished the sentence with wide-eyed abandon.

'Frances!' Meg exclaimed with delighted shock. 'But he's your brother, you adore him! You've always said so.'

Frances shrugged. 'I know,' she said. 'I know I've always said I adore him, and looked up to him and wished I was like him. Life was always so easy for *Robert*. *Robert* sailed through at school, always captain of any team he was on. All the boys wanted to be his friends and all the girls loved him. Not like me, I only managed to get married because I was a hospital volunteer and Craig couldn't escape from me with his leg in traction for six months, and the only friends I have are the ones that you've made and I sort of latch onto . . .'

'I don't think that's true,' Meg said. 'You know Craig wouldn't have married you if he didn't love you, and as for the baby group, we made those friends together.'

'Maybe a bit,' Frances said. 'Maybe they are my friends now, sort of – but I wouldn't have ever met them if it wasn't for you. I'd be sitting at home on my own cleaning the taps until they rubbed away completely if I didn't have you. And bloody Robert moping around my house, not washing the bath out after he's had a shower, expects me to wait on him hand and foot, expects me to pity him as if none of this is his fault!' Frances smiled so tentatively and touchingly that Meg reached out and patted her briefly on the back of the hand.

'And anyway,' Frances went on, 'Robert's not Superman. He's not perfect. In fact, he's bloody well very imperfect and I'm furious with him, Meg. I'm furious with him, the . . . the – moron!'

Perhaps it was the low-grade swearing or the way her fringe trembled with fury but before Meg knew it she was laughing. For one horror-filled second she thought that Frances would be insulted and offended by her insensitivity but instead, incredibly, Frances began to laugh too, really laugh so that her shoulders shook and her fringe danced. It was a sound that Meg had rarely, if ever, heard and it lifted her spirits immensely.

'I don't know why that's funny,' Frances said after a while.

'Maybe it's not funny exactly, more just freeing,' Meg said. 'Maybe for once you said what you were feeling instead of what you thought you should say.'

Frances nodded. 'You're right,' she said emphatically. 'All my life I've stood in his shadow, looked up to him, aspired to be like him, envied him his family life, his lovely children and it turns out . . . it turns out that he is simply is a rotten old . . . PRICK!'

Frances spluttered out the last word, clapped her hand over her mouth and they squealed with laughter like mischievous schoolgirls.

'He's a bastard!' Megan cried with feeling.

'An . . . an amoeba,' Frances added, which made Meg laugh even more.

'He certainly is a spineless, gutless excuse for a man,' she said. 'With the self-control of an incontinent rat.'

For a moment Meg thought that Frances had actually

stopped breathing she was laughing so hard, cheeks burnished bright red.

'Yes and he's selfish and arrogant and . . . condescending!' she managed to get out between gulps of air.

'He's a stinking pig,' Meg hollered happily.

'A scumbag!' Frances added, the tears streaming down her face. For a while the laughter continued as they looked at each other, not needing a reason to laugh any more, needing simply to laugh.

'He's an idiot,' Meg said a little more seriously as the effects of the hysteria began to wear off.

'A bloody idiot,' Frances agreed, her giggles subsiding too. 'Someone who didn't see what a wonderful life he had until it was almost too late. Or perhaps even is too late.'

'But I still love him,' Meg said with a wistful sigh.

'Me too,' Frances added. 'The bloody, bloody prick.'

As Tiffany opened the flat door to her mother, she peered over her shoulder behind her as if she thought that Janine might have been followed.

'I thought I'd come over for a cuppa,' Janine said. 'Hope you don't mind me dropping in?'

'Of course not – but it's Saturday?' Tiffany said questioningly. 'How did you get out without Dad knowing?'

'I didn't,' Janine said, taking Jordan from Tiffany's arms and kissing her plump cheek. 'I told him, I said, "I'm going to see my daughter and my grandbaby now, do you have a problem with that?"'

'And did he?' Tiffany asked her, her eyes wide.

'He did,' Janine said. 'He's probably still shouting now, but that's all right. We couldn't go on like we have been, Tiffany. I've been your mum all your life and I'm not stopping now, not for anything. And it might take longer with your dad but we'll bring him round too eventually, I promise you. He is an idiot, but he's not cruel. He doesn't mean to be.'

'Thanks, Mum,' Tiffany said, putting her arms around her mother and her daughter.

'Now then,' Janine said, patting her daughter's cheeks lightly. 'Are you going to make me that tea?'

Steve was leaning over his drawing board when Jill brought him a cup of green tea.

'Darling, you know that I love you . . .' Jill began. Steve looked up and smiled at her, waiting for the 'but', but it didn't come. 'And you've been amazing with Lucy, looked after her so well, taken her to your little baby group – you've been just brilliant . . .'

'But?' Steve asked her. 'What have I done? Is it because I haven't been showing Lucy the flash cards? Look, Jill, I know you are keen for her to get on, but I was thinking she's only a baby after all, and maybe that book you read wasn't completely right about teaching children to read before they are one. Maybe we should just let her be a baby.'

'That's not what I was going to say!' Jill exclaimed. 'And anyway I ditched that book weeks ago. All I was going to say was that I was doing this custody case the other day, a really nasty one. A father trying to get two small children from the mother, because she was depressed and not coping very well after he left her. And I looked at her, this woman so fragile and so seriously in danger of losing her children, and I missed Lucy so much that for a second I couldn't breathe. I knew what I was doing for that woman was good and right and that I was helping another mother stand up for herself, but at the same time I realised that I just wanted to be a mother too. I wanted to enjoy the privilege of having her every day and not just for a few hours in the middle of the night. I want to take her to

379

Baby Music and swimming and all the other fun things you and that group get up to, I want to see her grow and change in front of my eyes.' She put an arm around Steve's shoulders. 'I didn't realise it would be so hard for me to go back to work – but it is, and I'm just not ready, not yet.' Jill bit her lip anxiously. 'Steve, I want to give up work and join the baby group.'

Steve looked up at her.

'Are you sure?' he asked her. 'I mean, if you want to, well, of course you can. It's just that it will be hard. You earn a lot of money. And my income is growing, but there will be quite a long gap before I make up the difference. I might not ever make it up.'

'I know,' Jill said with a shrug. 'Is it too much to ask?'

Steve shook his head and setting down his pen, put his arms around Jill's waist and pulled her into a hug.

'Don't be daft,' he said. 'How can a mother wanting to spend more time with her baby be too much to ask?' Releasing Jill from the embrace, he picked up the cup of tea she had brought him and sipped it, trying not to make a face.

'But it's not what you wanted, is it?' Jill asked him. 'You love being with Lucy too. I don't want to force you back into an office job you'll hate.'

'Actually,' Steve said thoughtfully, 'it could work out for the better. My business is picking up and if you are at home I could afford to take on more commissions. Perhaps with a bit of a push at bringing in jobs we can all be at home together, you might have to cut down on your exercise equipment and self-help books but it could work.' He set the cup down on the window sill and kissed Jill on the cheek. 'I'm not saying I won't come along to the baby group every now and then, though. I'm practically one of the girls.'

'Good,' Jill said happily. 'Thanks. Thanks for listening. If there is ever anything important you want to say to me . . .'

'Actually, there is one other thing,' Steve said rather seriously, grabbing her hand as she began to move away. 'Darling, you know that I love you . . .' he began with a slow smile.

'But?' Jill asked him, returning his smile.

'But I bloody hate green tea. Any chance of a coffee? I don't mind instant.'

Chapter Thirty

'No, his arm goes in that bit,' Natalie said as Jack attempted to get one of Freddie's legs into an arm of the Babygro.

'But how do you know?' he said, furrowing his brow. 'How can you tell arms apart from legs?'

'Do you mean on the Babygro?' Natalie asked him mischievously. 'Or the baby?'

Jack smiled sideways at her. 'Ha, ha,' he said.

It had been a pleasant and surprisingly relaxing morning. First they had bathed Freddie. It had been almost unbearably touching to see Jack holding her little boy so tenderly in the tepid water, his hands actually trembling as he supported Freddie's head and neck, clearly worried he might hurt him somehow. And it hadn't helped that Freddie had yowled his head off throughout the whole experience, only calming down once he was out of the bath, dried, wrapped in a blanket and drinking from his bottle.

Natalie had nearly embarrassed herself because she had automatically reached up the front of her top and unhooked her nursing bra, but then she remembered that Jack was watching her, and, hot with discomfort, she had hastily hooked herself back up and led him downstairs to the kitchen to show him how to warm a bottle of milk. She held Freddie for a few minutes until he had settled and then passed him, bottle and all, to Jack. The baby's eyes half closed in pleasure and contentment, one creased hand grabbing onto his ear as he sucked.

'He likes milk, doesn't he?' Jack whispered, smiling as he held his son. 'Look at him, so happy. What's that in there then?' He nodded at the bottle. 'Is that cow's milk or that formula stuff? Could I buy it from any shop?'

'Um,' Natalie grimaced, sorely tempted to lie. 'It's, um, you know, baby milk, it's my milk from my . . . er, from me.'

'Really?' Jack exclaimed, looking at her breasts with naked curiosity. 'How do you get it out of them and in the bottle, is it like milking a . . .' He stopped himself sometime after the nick of time had packed its bags and left town.

The pair of them looked at each other for a stunned moment.

'Forget I just asked you that,' Jack said. 'I actually can't believe I did. I wasn't trying to be a senseless, tactless, juvenile . . . honestly I am just . . . well, interested and very stupid. Can you actually believe that you went to bed with me? If you'd had more than two or three conversations with me it would never have happened!'

Natalie smiled, glad that he could acknowledge so easily what had taken place between them, but also reading it as a sign that he had moved on, if he was ready to joke about it. She was not ready – she was not nearly at the joking stage.

'I have a special pump,' she explained. 'I use it when I know I'm going to miss a feed. When you have him I'll put the bottles all ready in his bag, all you'll have to do is warm them like I showed you.'

'Right,' Jack said and then, 'Natalie?'

'Yes?' Natalie waited.

'This is brilliant being here with . . .'

It was then, no doubt utterly relaxed and at peace, that Freddie weed on Jack's lap.

She had vigorously attempted to sponge Jack's trousers herself while he held onto the baby, but backing away from her he offered to swap Freddie for the cloth, half turning away from her as he cleaned up as best as he could.

'Sorry,' Natalie said, for the fourth or fifth time. 'It's my fault, I forgot the nappy after his bath.'

'It's fine. I never thought I'd hear myself say these words, but I actually don't mind that he peed on me.'

She had shown him how to change a nappy next, which he had mastered with an ease that made him puff out his chest with pride. It was the Babygro that had stumped him.

'The thing is,' Natalie said, chuckling because Freddie was. 'He isn't made of rubber, you can't bend him in any direction you like, even if he does appear to enjoy it.'

Jack knelt back and looked down at the baby wriggling on the rug with one arm and one leg in the garment.

'Maybe he's grown out of this one,' he said.

'Since yesterday?'

'It's possible, I hear babies grow very fast,' Jack said, grinning at her.

She picked up Freddie and within a few seconds had him expertly buttoned into the red suit.

'He looks like a tomato. What do we do now?'

Natalie looked at the rug. She had shown him all the things she had planned. They had set a time for the visit to begin but not for when it should end. Still, if Jack wasn't ready to go that suited her, she liked having him with her, in fact she loved it. It made her foolish heart sing.

'We could take him to the park for a walk?' she offered.

His answering smile had nearly knocked her off her feet.

'Espadrilles,' Natalie said out loud before she knew it.

'Pardon?' Jack looked perplexed.

'I just wondered if you'd ever thought about wearing espadrilles,' she said slowly.

'Can't say I ever have,' Jack said, frowning and smiling all at once.

'Didn't think so,' Natalie mumbled hopelessly as she followed him out of the front door.

The daffodils were out, their bright shining heads bobbing in the breeze as Jack pushed the buggy and Natalie walked at his side. To anyone else, she thought, they must look like a couple, proud of their firstborn. As they walked on in silence she found herself smiling at every passer-by, a complicit smile that said, 'Yes you're right, we're a happy family. A happy, loving family.'

It was a fantasy that was hard not to indulge in.

'So have you got a boyfriend?' Jack asked her suddenly.

'Me, who me?' Natalie panicked. She hadn't expected him to ask her a question like that.

'I just wondered if you were seeing anyone,' Jack said. 'I'm sorry, it's none of my business . . .' but still he did not retract the question.

'I have no boyfriend,' Natalie said simply. 'No time to, even if I wanted one.'

She worried that she had emphasised her single status a little too much – she didn't want to sound desperate.

'Right,' Jack said, looking in the other direction so she could only see the back of his head. 'Well, it's none of my business.'

They had almost completed a circuit of the park when Jack suggested they found a café and had lunch. Of course they stopped at the very one where Natalie had told Meg and Jess all about her fake husband's parenting skills, and she had imagined what it would have been like to have had Jack at the birth. She never would have believed that only a few weeks later she'd be sitting with him in the same café. It was miraculous, really. She couldn't hope for better than this, it would be greedy to wish for more. Still, she did.

Jack sat with Freddie on his lap, letting his coffee go cold safely on the other side of the table as he admired the son that he found so endlessly fascinating. It was warm inside and a faint waft of baby wee emanated from Jack's trousers. He didn't seem to mind it, though.

'So, what do you think?' he asked Natalie.

'What do I think about what?' she asked him in return.

'Do you think things will work out between us?' There was a second when Natalie's heart almost stopped and her misunderstanding of the question must have showed in her expression because Jack added hastily, 'Parenting Freddie, I mean.'

'Oh.' Natalie tried to hide how much of an idiot she felt. 'Oh, well, yes then. Yes it'll work out.' She made herself smile at him. 'It will work out fine.'

'Good. Good. It would be good to see Freddie regularly. And you,' Jack said, mumbling almost into his scarf.

Sandy was sitting in the living room watching TV when the three of them got back from the park.

Natalie knew this was a moment that could not be avoided.

'Mum, this is Jack, Jack – Mum,' she said, as Jack appeared in the living room holding Freddie in his arms.

'Oh, right,' Jack said, his face blanching white. 'Oh, um, hello there, Mrs . . . Miss . . . Natalie's mum.'

Sandy pursed her lips and folded her arms under her breasts and for a second Natalie had the terrible feeling that her recently reformed mother was going to lecture Jack on the correct use of contraception.

Instead she said, 'You look like you need a good feed. You should stay for my paella.'

'Um, thanks. But I . . .' He looked at Natalie. 'Well, I could if you like?'

'Don't mind,' Natalie said, all too aware that she sounded about fifteen.

'Well then, that's settled,' Sandy said, standing up and rolling her eyes at Natalie. 'I just need to pop out to get a few bits. Give you two a bit more time together . . . with Freddie.'

It was late when Jack finally left, almost midnight.

He had come upstairs with Natalie and rocked Freddie to sleep after his eleven o'clock feed.

'I like your mum,' he said quietly. 'She's really nice.'

'Yeah,' Natalie said, thinking how stunned she had been that the three of them had passed the evening together so pleasantly. Not so long ago it would have seemed like an impossibility. 'She *is* nice, isn't she?'

She sat on the bed in silence and watched in the half-light as Jack swayed back and forth on his long legs with Freddie in his arms, trying to lull him off to sleep. He was humming something under his breath and it took Natalie a while to work out that it was a low version of 'Bohemian Rhapsody'.

'He's asleep,' Jack said suddenly, standing completely still. 'What do I do now?'

'Just lower him into his cot,' Natalie whispered. 'Slowly and carefully, try to maintain body contact with him for as long as possible.'

Jack followed her instructions to the letter and laid Freddie down in his cot.

Instantly Freddie started crying.

'Don't worry. It usually takes me four or five goes.'

387

It was actually the third attempt that was successful. Natalie held her breath as she and Jack stood side by side by the cot and watched Freddie sleep. She had known fewer moments in her life that had been so happy and so perfect and so excruciatingly painful all at once.

'I suppose,' Jack whispered slowly after some time, 'I had better go now he's asleep.'

He looked at Natalie in the half-light for a moment, as if he were waiting for her to say or do something. But she could not even dare to guess what he might be waiting for. So she waited, frozen to the spot, until he dropped his gaze and walked out of the bedroom.

At the front door Jack hesitated, looking up and down the road as if he wasn't sure which way he should go.

'Thanks for today,' he said.

'Thank you,' Natalie said.

'Natalie, look, I . . .' Jack bit his lip and rocked on his heels. 'You've made this really easy for me, you didn't have to.'

'I know,' Natalie said. 'But I wanted to, because you wanted to and because I think you'll be a great daddy for Freddie.'

Jack nodded. 'That means a lot,' he said.

'To me too,' Natalie replied.

'I'd better go then,' Jack said. He leaned forward and brushed his lips against her cheek.

'Same time next week then?' he asked her.

'Same time next week,' Natalie said. And she watched him walk down the street towards the green until he disappeared into the night. The place where his lips had touched her skin vibrated with heat.

Chapter Thirty-one

'How are things with you?' Natalie asked Meg as they arrived together for the next baby group meeting at Tiffany's tower block.

'It certainly is imposing, isn't it?' Meg said as they looked up.

'Steve will love this,' Natalie said. 'I bet you that he says post-industrial modernity within five minutes of arriving.'

Meg smiled. 'I'm not bad,' she said as Natalie pressed the flat number and they waited for Tiffany to buzz them in. 'I talked to Robert. I was very calm and quite controlled. I told him how it had to be if I was going to give him another chance. Frances has been a great help, she really has. I think somehow this has brought her out of herself.'

'And how does it have to be?' Natalie asked her as the buzzer sounded noisily and she pulled the door open, waving Meg, James and Iris through first.

'On my terms,' Meg said, holding the door from the inside for her and Freddie. 'And I told him that I'd let him know when I had decided. He cried. Twice,' she added, biting her lip as Natalie pressed the call button on the lift.

'He cried!' Natalie burst out. 'Good. I'm glad he cried. He should cry over what he's done I don't know how you can even think of having him back, Meg, I have to say it. I'm sorry – I *am* trying to understand.'

'He's behaved like a prick,' Meg said, thinking of her and Frances's name-calling extravaganza with a smile. 'But he's still here. He wants to come back. He wants me and the children, not her.'

Natalie looked sceptical as they got into the lift.

'Just don't forget exactly how much of prick he has been,' she said. 'That's all I ask. He might be crying now, but what about when he's got his feet back under the table. I really respect your values, I actually admire you, more than you can know. But you don't *have* to have him back, you know, it's not compulsory. You'd be fine without him.'

'I know,' Meg said. 'I don't feel it yet, it's still all too soon and too raw. But I do know that one day in the not so distant future I would be strong enough to be without him. But the thing is, I don't want to be without him. That hasn't changed.'

The lift pinged and the doors slid open. When they got outside Tiffany was waiting for them with Jordan dangling in her arms, impatient to be free.

'Hi,' she said anxiously. 'Thanks for coming a bit early like I asked. I wanted to know if I'd got it all right.'

'If you've got cake,' Natalie assured her, 'I don't really see how you can get it remotely wrong.'

Tiffany's flat looked very nice and she told Natalie as she followed her into the kitchen that her mum had helped her get it ready; she showed Natalie a large brown teapot containing seven tea bags, waiting to be filled with boiling water.

'My mum lent me this. One per person and one for the pot, my Nan used to say,' Tiffany said, peering into the teapot. 'Is that right, or is it one of those old wives' tales whatsits?'

'I think you need at least seven,' Natalie said. 'I like my tea strong.'

Next to the teapot Tiffany had placed two plates of Mr Kipling's French Fancies, arranged on paper napkins.

Natalie smiled.

'It looks stupid, doesn't it?' Tiffany asked her in dismay. 'You think it's funny.'

Natalie laughed. 'Don't be an idiot, Tiff. I was smiling because you've got French Fancies. I bloody love those!' She put her arm around Tiffany's slender shoulder and gave her a little hug.

'You look very well organised.' Natalie glanced into the sunny sitting room, where Meg was showing James the view. Tiffany had borrowed four dining chairs from her neighbour and had somehow acquired a red and white striped deckchair too. She had set them out in a big circle, including the beanbag, ready and waiting for their occupants. In the middle of the circle there was a coffee table that Natalie was certain she had last seen in Janine's conservatory, topped off with a white lace runner.

'So you and Janine are seeing a lot of each other,' Natalie said.

'Yeah, she's round more and more.' Tiffany wrinkled her nose. 'Is it too much that lace cloth thing? Do I look like a little girl playing tea parties?'

Natalie shook her head. 'Not at all,' she said, even though it wasn't exactly true. 'You've got enough chairs for everyone, play mats out for the babies to roll on. And cake!' She looked thoughtful. 'Actually, will you come over a bit early before my turn and organise mine for me too?'

Tiffany smiled. 'So it's all right then?'

'Of course it is,' Natalie reassured her. 'It's perfect.'

Jess was the next to arrive, along with Steve whom she had met on the bus.

'Hi,' she called as she parked her buggy on the landing outside the front door. 'I'm glad it's such a lovely day. I nearly didn't come. Poor Jacob can't seem to shake off this cold. We were both up what seemed like most of last night. He's all bunged up and can't sleep, bless him. I thought the fresh air might help.'

'Brilliant place, Tiff,' Steve added, appearing behind her with Lucy in his arms. 'This is where it's at, you know. Streets in the sky. Post-industrial modernity.'

'Told you,' Natalie said under her breath, digging Meg in the ribs.

Natalie looked round at the random group of friends that she had somehow acquired as they compared babies and chatted. It was such a relief to be here with them all. They made her feel as if she was on an even keel again, a calm sea at last, even if it was just for an hour or so; it was a break from the ups and downs of her other life.

Maybe things had gone, if not wrong, not exactly right with Jack, but there were other parts of her life that were starting to fall slowly into place. An improving relationship with her mother was one of them, and her baby group friends another. Natalie knew that now things were a little more steady she had to tell them about the real Jack and the fake Gary. It was the next, the last task on her list of brave and grown-up jobs to do. She just wasn't sure how she would ever begin to explain herself.

'There are boys in hooded tops, down there,' was the first thing Frances said when she arrived with Henry in a sling and her handbag practically welded under her arm. 'I didn't like the look of them at all.'

'Oh they're always there,' Tiff said, as she peered out of the kitchen window.

'Honestly, Frances,' Natalie said, happy to be hypocritical, 'don't be such a bigot, they are perfectly nice young men. They gave Freddie back his toy that he dropped the other day.'

It was clearly not enough to satisfy Frances.

'Well, I think we should all leave together,' she said. 'Safety in numbers after all. Or we could send Steve out in his trunks again,' she added, to general amazement. 'That would send them packing.' It took a second or two for everyone to understand that Frances had made a joke, but the instant they did there was much laughter and Frances glowed with timid pleasure.

A little while later, as they all sipped their tea, Frances leaned towards Meg, who was kneeling on the floor with James and Iris, and said, 'Robert has left his job. He phoned them yesterday and sent the letter today. He told me to tell you he hopes that makes you happy, so I'm telling you, but I told him that I thought not sleeping with another woman might have been the best way to guarantee that.'

The others in the group exchanged glances and raised eyebrows. It wasn't that Frances had changed, exactly, it was more as if she had loosened some invisible stays that had been constricting her inwardly and now she could finally breathe.

Meg's smile was fragile. 'Well, I'm happier than I would have been if my husband had gone back to work with that woman, that's for sure,' she said with a small shrug.

'I'll make certain I tell him that,' Frances said stoutly. 'But I am worried about how you are going to manage without his money coming in.'

'Somehow,' Meg said. She smiled round at the group. 'Look, you've all been so good to me, really supportive and it's meant a lot, it really has. But please, I don't want to talk about me today. I want to talk about all of you and the babies, and forget about me for an hour or two. Could we do that, please?'

She looked at Jess, who had the back of her hand on Jacob's forehead as she rocked him.

'How's Jacob doing?' she asked her.

'Not so good,' Jess said, with a little frown. 'His fever has gone, but he's so bunged up he can't feed or sleep, poor mite.'

'Looks like he's nodded off now,' Natalie said, lowering her voice. Jess looked down at Jacob. His eyes were closed at last, his lashes brushed the tops of his apple cheeks and his little mouth was a wide-open O.

'Do you want to put him in Jordan's cot?' Tiffany offered. 'I just changed the sheets this morning.'

'Um.' Jess looked down at her son, who weighed heavy in her arms.

'Oh go on, Jess,' Natalie prompted her, seeing how tired she looked. 'He'll only be in the next room, he'll soon let you know if he's not happy, don't *worry*! Give yourself that rare treat when you actually get to drink a cup of tea and eat cake simultaneously.'

Jess smiled. 'OK then, thanks, Tiff,' she said and she followed Tiffany into the bedroom.

'So,' Meg said as Tiffany and Jess came back a moment later. 'Who's got anything interesting to tell us? Steve?'

'Well,' Steve said. 'This might be my last baby group.' The women made gratifying sounds of dismay. 'Or at least my last one on my own,' he added, when he was sure they would be disappointed if he left. 'Jill is leaving work. She's going to take her maternity leave after all and I'm ramping up the amount of freelancing I do. It means we'll be feeling the pinch but we'll have more time together, and Jill will get more time with Lucy, which is what we both want. I told her that you were a great bunch of people, great friends, even if you don't respect a man's Speedos.'

'It's not the Speedos we don't respect, Steve,' Natalie teased him gently. 'It's the man.'

'Mum's going to meet Anthony properly next week,' Tiffany said. 'She's coming for tea, poor Anthony's bricking it!' She laughed. 'Dad knows and he's doing his nut, but Mum doesn't care – she's suddenly gone all hardcore. She said she told him it was about time he dragged himself into the twenty-first century and realised what a small-minded idiot he was. Dad threatened to throw her out as well, but she told him he wouldn't last five minutes without her. He knows she's right.'

'And what about you, Natalie?' Meg looked at her. 'What have you been up to?'

This was the moment, Natalie thought. The ideal moment to tell them. Here were all the baby group gathered in one place, relaxed and relatively happy. All looking like quite friendly and reasonable people. Natalie knew she had to tell them the truth about herself, if she was serious about their friendship. She had to be as honourable and as straight with them as they were with her.

'Well, actually,' she began, taking a deep breath. 'There is something . . .'

'Oh, hang on.' Jess leapt to her feet making Natalie jump. 'I need a wee, just wait a minute. I don't want to miss anything.'

Natalie closed her mouth as her friend headed towards the bathroom.

A second later a scream tore through the flat.

'Jacob!' Jess shrieked, as Tiffany raced into the bedroom, followed closely by Natalie.

Natalie saw Jacob's head as she peered over Tiffany's shoulder. For a second he looked as if he might be sleeping. But he was terribly pale, and terribly still and there was a frightening bluish tint around his mouth and nose.

'Oh God,' Jess's voice was shaking as she picked him up. 'He feels cold, he feels really cold. Oh God, oh Jacob, wake up, wake up now . . .'

'He's stopped breathing,' Tiffany said, her voice surprisingly clear and calm. 'It can only have been for a minute, if that. It was only a minute ago we put him in the cot.'

'Oh God, my baby!' Jess's cries began to reach a heart-rending crescendo. 'Oh Jacob! Jacob!'

'Give him to me,' Tiffany pleaded, but Jess held him closer to her chest.

'No, no, no, no, please no.' Jess stood there rocking Jacob in her arms, shaking her head. 'No, not again.'

'Jess, listen, give him to me,' Tiffany said, firmly. 'I went to a class about baby CPR. Let me have him. I know what to do, it's important.'

'Jess, let Tiffany have him,' Natalie urged, and as Jess released her son she collapsed into Natalie's arms. The baby's legs flopped lifelessly like a doll's as Tiffany took him, his arms swinging at his sides.

The room was silent.

'Wake up, Jakey!' Tiffany bellowed as she tugged at his arm quite firmly. 'Wake up, baby!'

'She's hurting him,' Jess whimpered, her fingers digging into Natalie's arms. 'Don't hurt him, please!'

'It's all right,' Natalie murmured, her tense and frightened tone not managing to convey reassurance. All she knew was that she remembered nothing useful about that first-aid class, and if she couldn't then why should a teenage girl?

'Right.' Tiffany's young face looked tight and pale, she took a breath. She sat on the edge of her bed, put Jacob on his tummy over her forearm and angled his head down.

She slapped him hard twice between his shoulder blades with the heel of her other hand.

'Oh my God!' Jess shrieked, struggling to pull out of Natalie's arms, but Natalie held her back. 'Stop hurting him!' She broke free and fell on her knees in front of Jacob. There was a second of deathly silence.

'Sorry,' Tiffany said quickly, and then she hit him again.

And then Jacob coughed. Once, twice. Jess gasped and Tiffany looked amazed as she hit him with the heel of her hand again, one firm bang between his shoulder blades. A thick blob of green mucus flew out of his mouth.

And suddenly Jacob was crying. He was crying hard and gasping for breath, the colour returning to his cheeks almost immediately.

'Jacob!' Jess cried and silently Tiffany put him into her arms. 'Oh my God, Jacob.' She looked up at Tiffany, tears streaming down her face. 'How can I ever thank you? You saved him.'

Jacob howled, his cry wonderfully loud in what had been total silence. One by one, five other babies who had been perfectly quiet for those few terrible moments joined in, until the flat was filled with a life-affirming din.

'We need to call an ambulance,' Tiffany said, her voice shaking. 'We need to get him checked over properly. It might happen again or he might have been starved of oxygen.'

'I'll do it,' Steve volunteered from the doorway.

'That was amazing, Tiffany,' Meg said, on the breath she felt that she had been holding in for hours.

'You saved his life,' Frances added in awe. 'You knew what to do.'

'I did, didn't I?' Tiffany's voice trembled. 'I think *I'm* going to cry now.'

Natalie reached out and put an arm around both her and Jess .

'It's OK,' she said. 'It's OK, you don't have to worry now.'

Jess snapped away from her in one sudden shocking movement.

'Don't you tell me not to worry,' she said accusingly to Natalie, her voice low with fury.

'I only meant . . .' Natalie began.

'You're just like the rest of them, you're worse,' Jess was shouting, her voiced raised above the chorus of babies. 'Always telling me I worry too much, always saying I'm overreacting, I'm being too anxious. So bloody smug and so bloody perfect. Acting like you know it all, like you know my child better than I do. Put him down in the cot you said, don't worry so much you said. But if I'd kept him with me this wouldn't have happened, if I had kept him with me he would have been safe.'

'Jess, you're in shock.' Meg touched her on the arm but she recoiled from her, cradling Jacob to her chest, his plump fist beating at her shoulder.

'Just leave me alone, all of you!' she cried, her eyes hot and dry. 'None of you know what it's like to lose a child. None of you know what it's like to hold your dead baby in your arms! I *do*!'

The others looked at each other, all horror-struck except for Natalie, who hung her head.

'Jess . . .' Meg began. 'We had no idea . . .'

'She did,' Jess said, stabbing a finger at Natalie. 'I told her, I trusted her and all she did was tell me not to worry so much.' She paused for breath and rested her forehead against Jacob's.

'Don't tell me not to worry,' she went on, the power but not the fury drained from her voice. 'Don't you tell me any more that it will be all right, because you don't know that. Nobody knows that.'

There was a hammering at the door and Steve showed two paramedics into the room.

'Jess, look –' Natalie struggled to know what to say. 'I'll come to the hospital and wait . . .'

One of the paramedics took Jacob carefully from Jess and laid him on the bed before checking him over.

'We'd better take him, to be on the safe side,' he said to Jess. 'OK, love?'

Jess nodded.

'Do you want to bring a friend?' the paramedic asked her.

'No, I don't want them anywhere near me,' Jess said. The paramedic wrapped a blanket around both her and Jacob and led them out of the flat.

'She's had a shock,' Frances said thoughtfully a few minutes later, when they had all retrieved their babies and mostly calmed them. 'And she's frightened and angry. But not at you, Natalie, she just lashed out at you.'

Natalie shook her head, holding Freddie close to her chest so that she could feel the heat of him against her skin.

'No,' she said. 'I mean, yes, she said it because she was angry and in shock but she was right, too. I *am* always telling her not to worry. I am always telling her everything will be all right. I do always treat her as if I think she's a little bit mad for not being more relaxed with Jacob. And I knew that she had lost two babies before. She's right to be angry with me. I've been crass and insensitive and told her all along that she was seeing problems where there were none. She *should* blame me.'

'Nobody could have guessed what would happen when she put him down for a nap,' Meg said. 'You couldn't see it coming.'

'Jess would have,' Natalie said with a shrug. 'If I hadn't distracted her, belittled her worries.'

'If that's what you've done then we all have,' Steve said. 'We've all let her down.'

The group didn't speak for a while until eventually Tiffany said, 'So what do we do now?'

'The only thing we can do,' Natalie said immediately. 'Be good friends, be friends who won't let her down. Go to the hospital and wait.'

They waited in the hospital cafeteria for two hours, without going to the desk or trying to find out what was happening. They didn't think it was their place to do so. All they knew was that they wanted to be there for Jess whether she knew it or not. So they drank tea and waited and they watched, waiting for a glimpse of Jess.

'Tiffany, you were amazing,' Natalie said, not for the first time. 'My blood ran cold. I just froze. I had no idea what to do. And you remembered all that baby first-aid stuff. You were incredible. So calm and in control.'

'You were,' Meg agreed. 'I'm so proud of you, which I know makes me sound like I want to be your mum and not your friend, but I'd be proud to be your mum and I'm very proud to be your friend.'

'Me too,' the others agreed, making Tiffany squirm and shift on the uncomfortable cafeteria chair.

'Wasn't that special,' she mumbled into the zip of her parka, as if she was just some awkward teenager and not the amazingly clever and brave hero that the others had seen in action a few hours ago.

'It *was* special,' Jess said, approaching the table a little warily. 'It wasn't just special, it was amazing. You didn't just save Jacob's life, you saved mine too.' She looked literally washed out, every scrap of colour drained from her face and every ounce of energy spent on her son.

The others looked at her, each of them unable to ask her how things were going, afraid to hear bad news.

'The doctors said that Jacob is stable now,' Jess said, partially answering their worries. 'Lee is with him, he arrived a while ago. He told me to come and get us a cup of tea, get some fresh air. I didn't want to leave Jacob, he's so little and they've got him in this great big cot and he's supposed to have an oxygen mask on but it's too big, so either Lee or I have to hold it as near to his nose and mouth as we can.' Jess's voice wobbled on the last word, and she looked up at the strip lighting and made herself smile. 'I mean, he's smiling and waving his legs around and charming the nurses, but I look at him and I see the way he looked when I found him and I think about how different it might have been and I . . .' She bit her lip and heaved in a deep breath. 'Lee said I needed some fresh air and a Mars bar.' She smiled wanly at the group. 'I didn't expect to see you here but I'm really glad you are. And . . . look, I'm really sorry about before, I –'

'*Please* don't be sorry,' Natalie implored her.

'I was out of my mind with worry,' Jess told her.

'But you were still right,' Natalie said. 'Who are we, who am *I* to know what you should and should not worry about? I dismissed your fears when if I had listened to them properly I could have helped you. I thought I was building your confidence but really I was helping to undermine it.'

Jess shook her head. 'That's not true. I made you feel bad about something that . . . is normal. You are normal to be and act the way you do. I'm *not*. It's not normal to constantly fuss and worry and fret.'

'But you were right to,' Meg said.

Jess pulled a chair over from an adjoining table and sat down heavily. 'I wish I wasn't. I wish that I had been wrong to worry so much. But now I do have something to be anxious about and funnily enough, now I know what it is, now I can face it and deal with it, I don't feel afraid any more.'

'What happened?' Frances asked her.

'They say that it doesn't look as if he had a cold after all. It is a bacterial thing, which in turn set off an asthma attack, his airways got inflamed and narrow. When I laid him down for that nap, mucus got lodged in his airway and he didn't or couldn't cough it out.' Jess was still for a moment, facing once again the horrific alternative reality that had been only a hair's breadth away for her and Jacob that morning. 'Tiffany did exactly the right thing. She cleared his airway and got him breathing. He's had oxygen and Ventolin and his breathing has eased now. They're keeping us in tonight and maybe tomorrow and he'll need medication and monitoring for the foreseeable future, but with the right management he'll be fine.' Jess looked as if she couldn't quite believe it. 'He's fine.'

'I'm so relieved,' Natalie said.

'The paediatrician said he'd probably had asthma for a while. She said it's quite common in young babies and that when he had that "snoring" it might have been a wheeze after all, only it stopped by the time we brought him here.' She lifted her chin a fraction. 'I knew it was something serious. I *knew* it.'

Tentatively Natalie reached across the table and laid her hand on the back of Jess's.

'Mother's intuition,' she said. 'We should have listened to you. I'm sorry, Jess.'

Jess shook her head, dismissing the need for an apology.

'They said that most babies grow out of it and that now we know, we're prepared. We've got to give him an inhaler whenever he has a sniffle. He'll have a check-up every couple of months.' Jess suddenly stifled a sob. 'I don't know why I want to cry *now*,' she said, brushing away tears.

'Relief, I expect,' Meg said. 'I feel like having a weep myself.'

'Or is it because you know that I'm hosting the baby group next?' Natalie asked her. 'That's enough to make me want to cry.'

'You're an idiot,' Jess said, although she did manage to raise a watery smile.

'Oh, much more of an idiot than you can ever guess,' Natalie said. And she made up her mind then and there. These people who had started out as random acquaintances had become her friends, the kind of friends she'd never thought she'd need or want. But over the last few weeks she had found a solidarity with each of them that was both refreshing and, yes, comforting.

She cared about them and their families and she thought they cared for her too. And if they did, then they deserved to know the stupid truth about her stupid life. No more excuses or setbacks.

The next baby group, Natalie decided. That was when she would tell them, come what may.

Chapter Thirty-two

The intervening time between the last, fateful meeting of the baby group and the day that Natalie was finally about to host it had been happily quiet and mostly uneventful. In fact, Natalie thought, the best word to describe herself, her feelings and thoughts in those days was tranquil. After the sudden storm that had swept away that bright and sunny morning at Tiffany's flat, she felt that she could see her life all the more clearly. All her petty problems and silly stories seemed utterly irrelevant and pointless now. All that mattered was that she had Freddie, and Freddie had Jack in his life.

She had even found a peaceful way of managing her feelings for Jack. She had decided to simply enjoy them quietly, secretly. She would take pleasure in his friendship and his relationship with Freddie and let her own feelings ebb and flow over her, hopeful that one day the sharp pang of want she experienced whenever she heard his voice or saw his face would be washed away and in time smoothed into a round pebble of friendship. However, she did expect this to take quite a long time, so she was hopeful that Jack would not date anyone else, let alone fall in love, for at least fifty years or so. It was a faint hope, Natalie realised, as she thought about that encounter that Jack had had with Suze in Soho Square, the one she should not know about and rather wished she didn't.

But at least knowing that Jack was interested in and even approaching other women helped her to put her situation into perspective. Otherwise his warmth, his sweet smiles, the pleasure he seemed to take in Freddie's and, yes, her company too, could have been seriously misconstrued. No, it was better like this, to admire him from a safe distance. Natalie supposed she would have to cross the bridge signposted 'Jack in Love with Someone Who is Not Me' when she came to it. Or more likely jump right off it.

Jack had called her a few days after his visit, which had taken her entirely by surprise. Why she was so shocked Natalie didn't know, but the sound of his voice so suddenly in the shell of her ear made her trip and tumble over her words for a moment.

'Um, oh? Jack!' she exclaimed. 'Well.'

'Well?' Jack responded uncertainly. 'Is this a bad time? Have you got guests or . . . a guest?' His tone loaded the last word with a meaning that she could not fathom.

'No, no – not at all – it's just that I wasn't expecting you to call,' she told him hurriedly. 'I don't know why it should be a shock. After all, I hardly ever expect anybody to call and they do and I'm not surprised then. Maybe it's because I spent so long waiting for you to call me after we got back from Venice that now you actually are here it will take me a while to adjust to you as a person contactable by telephone.'

'This is a bad time,' Jack stated, clearly taking her ramblings as a dig at their messy past.

'No!' Natalie exclaimed, perhaps a touch too desperately. 'No, Jack, it's not a bad time, it's just . . . oh look, I'm still getting used to having you around in our lives. I didn't mean to get at you. I didn't mean to say any of that stuff, I just didn't know how to say what I wanted to say which was, "Hello, Jack, nice to hear from you. How are you?"'

'I'm good,' he said. 'Work's good, I'm looking for my own place, so it's been a good few days. And you?'

Natalie paused; she wanted to tell him all about Jacob and Jess and everything that had happened at Tiffany's flat, but she didn't know if she should. It was difficult negotiating her way around this new relationship. They had been fleeting lovers, now they were co-parents, but she didn't think they could actually call each other friends yet; they were more well-intentioned acquaintances, one of whom happened to be madly in love with the other. 'It's been a busy week,' she said eventually. 'Trying to get my head in gear, you know.'

'I know what you mean,' Jack said easily. 'It is really weird, I felt nervous dialling your number. And I called because I caught myself not calling. I caught myself thinking don't phone too soon, mate, you don't want to let on what a great time you had. And then I realised that I hadn't been on a date, I'd spent time with my son and that actually I *do* want him to know how much I enjoyed spending time with him, and that I *do* want to do it again really soon and that this is no time to play it cool, even if he is just a baby and hasn't got a clue who I am yet. And I thought maybe you wouldn't mind if I called between visits to find out how he is.'

It had taken Natalie a moment or two to readjust her psyche to suit the tranquil mode she had recently adopted, because for most of the time that Jack had been talking she had let herself believe that he was actually talking about her. She had briefly forgotten that he was referring to Freddie, which made her feel first stupid and secondly self-centred. Both were traits that she had been guilty of in the past and ones she wanted very much to leave behind now.

'Of course you can call about Freddie any time you like!' she said with overcompensating, overblown verve. 'What's to stop you?'

'I don't want you to think I'm trying to take over his or your life,' Jack said. 'I mean, you don't need me hanging round you all the time, stopping you moving on . . . getting on with things, I mean.'

I do, I do, I do need you actually, Natalie had thought to herself, but she bit back the rebellious words and managed to reply dryly, 'You're right, Freddie and I do have a pile of invitations asking us to cocktail parties and premieres on a daily basis.'

She listened happily to Jack's chuckle. 'Look,' she went on. 'I want you to see him as much as possible. I really want that for him.'

'Natalie, can I ask you something?' Jack said tentatively.

'Of course,' Natalie replied on an inward breath.

'Is my name on his birth certificate?'

'Yes,' she said simply. 'It's funny, it never occurred to me to leave it off. I suppose I must have always wanted him to have something of you, whatever happened.'

'I'm glad.' Jack sounded as if he'd been holding his breath too. 'Look, I was wondering what you think. Do we need solicitors to make some kind of formal arrangement between us? Should we find out about it?'

Inexplicably, irrationally, Natalie's heart sank at the perfectly sensible suggestion.

'Well, yes, OK,' she said, unable to disguise the heaviness in her voice.

'I know what you mean,' Jack said, although she hadn't actually expressed any opinion. 'Getting lawyers involved seems a bit clinical, a bit formal. Not especially friendly.'

'But it is something we will have to do, I suppose,' Natalie said. 'Make it legal.'

'Yes, but not yet,' Jack said. 'After all, we're still just getting to know each other, right? And I won't run away. I absolutely promise you that I will never leave him.'

After Natalie had put the phone down a few minutes later she had sat for a long time and thought about everything that Jack had said. He was never going to leave Freddie, he'd said – he'd promised. And she believed him, a belief that made her rejoice for her son, but frightened her too. What if, without the benefit of distance and absence, she never got over Jack? What if she spent the rest of her life, seeing him and missing him all at once?

Now, though, the morning of the baby group had arrived and Natalie had to focus on the present. She had to prepare, to get ready for this literal moment of truth.

There had been talk about postponing it, as Jacob had come home from hospital only two days earlier. But Jess said she wanted to come, even if Jacob would be staying at home with Lee on this occasion. She said an hour or two out with her friends was just what she needed.

Natalie had rehearsed on several occasions and usually in front of the mirror, the speech that would reveal her deep, dark and murky secrets to the baby group. When she detailed the truth about her fake husband, and about exactly how Freddie was conceived (well, not exactly how), and even about her son's fledgling relationship with his still strange and worryingly wonderful father, she had to admit that her secret sounded, well, less shocking and rather more silly than she had hoped.

Still, she was looking forward to unburdening herself just the same. There was the slight risk that they might all turn on her and she'd end up with no friends at all. But Natalie had decided that there was no point in having close friends – *best* friends – if you couldn't be truthful with them.

Sandy helped her prepare for her friends' arrival by going to the shop to buy the cake.

'Do you want me to go to that lovely patisserie?' she asked Natalie. 'Get lots and lots of lovely pastries and things?'

'Thanks, but that would be far too sophisticated,' Natalie said. 'We do cake, preferably shop-bought.'

'Shop-bought cake it is,' Sandy said with a shrug, winking at Freddie as she headed out. Natalie looked at the space where her mother had been standing a moment before and found herself smiling.

Recently Sandy had been quite nice to be around. She hadn't driven her to instant apocalyptic fury for almost a week, and Natalie was discovering that if she didn't jump down her mother's throat at the slightest provocation, sometimes Sandy would have something quite sensible or interesting to say.

Occasionally Natalie found herself missing their old sparring sessions, but she was fairly sure that once she and Sandy had moved out of this intermediary stage they'd be able to fight happily once again, only this time without the great dark fear that they really did hate each other overshadowing everything. Like any relationship, the one between Natalie and Sandy would require work, effort and many small adjustments before they got it exactly right.

Similar rules applied in her attempts to manage whatever weird sort of relationship she had with Jack. He was due for his second visit the following day, and Natalie didn't doubt that it would be just as emotionally challenging as the last one. But if she could stay tranquil on the outside then she was making some progress, no matter what storm might rage inside.

Natalie was surprised when the doorbell rang a few minutes later, and supposed it must be her mother with plenty of cake but no key.

'It must be the Alzheimer's again,' she said as she swung the door open, but it wasn't her mother who stood before her. It was Gary.

'Gary!' Natalie said with an air of pleasant surprise, as if she had just remembered that he existed. He smiled at her, looking very handsome in his tight khaki T-shirt and jeans, and she wondered at the fact that she had let him slip so easily from her thoughts with that torso. How on earth had it come to pass that a skinny, lanky man had captured her heart so firmly when this one hadn't?

'I was in the area,' Gary said. 'Thought I'd drop in, see how you are and . . .' He looked down at his feet a little coyly. 'I, er, needed to talk to you about something.'

Natalie stood aside and let him in rather hesitantly, hoping that he wasn't going to ask her out again or declare his undying love for her, because she had no idea what she would say to him if he did.

'How's the wiring?' he asked her, not quite able to look her in the eye.

'Well, everything is working,' Natalie said with a shrug.

'I'm glad to hear it,' Gary said.

They stood looking at each other for a few seconds, both remembering the night they had spent together.

'You look well,' Gary said eventually.

'Thank you,' Natalie said, smiling at his non-compliment. 'So do you.'

Gary nodded, his hand on his hip. He bit his lip and looked like what he was about to say to her would be embarrassing and difficult. Natalie braced herself.

'Look, Natalie . . .'

'Gary, don't,' Natalie interrupted him, placing her fingers lightly on his lips. 'Don't say what you're about to say.' She moved a step closer and rested her hand on his forearm. 'That

410

night we had together, it was great and it meant so much to me it really did, but don't say you want more from me because I just don't have it to give, Gary. I'm stupidly in love with Freddie's dad, remember? I don't even think I could have sex with you again, even if you are a very good lover. Because I can only think about him, and I know it's stupid. And besides, you are a lovely man. A really fabulous, kind man with a really amazing body and you deserve more than to be just used for sex . . .'

Gary's face was stricken.

'Oh, don't be upset, Gary . . .' Natalie pleaded. 'There are a lot of nicer women than me, really . . .'

'I'm not upset,' Gary said, taking a step back form her touch. 'I'm embarrassed . . . Natalie, I came about the bill. You haven't paid it.'

'Oh.' Natalie suddenly felt very hot. 'Oh God.' She clapped her hand over her mouth and stared at him. And then she laughed.

'Oh my God. OH MY GOD. Come down to the kitchen with me and I'll find the bill and write you a cheque. Oh my God, Gary,' Natalie repeated as she led him down to the kitchen. 'I can't believe what I've just done, what I said to you! Of course you didn't come round here to declare your love for me. You came for a cheque.'

'Well, from what you said it sounds as if I'd have been unlucky anyway,' Gary told her, finding a wry smile as Natalie handed him a cheque. He laughed. 'Sorry, but it was pretty funny.'

'Glad to brighten your day,' Natalie replied, still able to feel the heat in her cheeks.

'Look,' Gary went on, 'the only reason I haven't tried to ask you out again is because I know how you feel about this Jack bloke. And I'm not an idiot. If you were really free, I would.'

His mouth curled into a delicious smile. 'You're pretty hot for a parent.'

Natalie and Gary smiled warmly at each other, and for one moment longer Natalie thought of that happy, easy life she might have had with him.

It was the last restful moment she would experience for some time.

'So this is Gary!' Meg's voice interrupted her thoughts. 'Oh my God, Gary, how lovely to meet you at last! When Natalie's mum said you were down here I couldn't believe it!'

Natalie whirled round and watched as her friend waltzed into the kitchen.

'How did you get in?' Natalie squeaked quite rudely.

'I let her in,' Sandy said, following Meg into the room. 'Found her on the doorstep.' She grinned at Gary. 'Hello, love, nice to see you again. I'll leave your cakes here and go back upstairs, leave you and your friends to it. If the doorbell goes, I'll get it.'

Horrified, Natalie watched Sandy disappear, wondering if she had any inkling about what chaos she had just unleashed upon her unsuspecting daughter.

'Er, hello,' Gary said. Taken aback by this woman's greeting, he held out his hand for Meg to shake but instead she grabbed it and kissed him on both cheeks. The poor man looked like he wanted to drop through the floor again.

'We've been dying to meet you for ages,' Meg gushed, giving him a little squeeze. 'I had no idea you would be here! Was it a surprise visit, Natalie?'

Natalie opened her mouth and shut it again. This was not going to plan. This was, as her mother would have told her in the not so distant past, all her chickens coming home to roost at once.

'Natalie's obviously given me a great reference,' Gary said slowly.

'Glowing,' Meg assured him with a little laugh that confused him even further, as she still held onto his hand. 'We've heard all about how wonderful you are, Gary. Every detail.'

Gary looked at Natalie in horror and Natalie looked anywhere else but at Gary. Maybe if she closed her eyes and counted to ten very quickly it would all go away.

But it didn't work, of course it didn't. If Natalie had learnt one thing during recent weeks it was that wishful thinking never worked.

Meg let go of Gary's hand at last and kissed Natalie. 'Natalie, how lovely for you to have your husband home.'

At last the penny dropped with Gary. He looked at Natalie, his eyebrows soaring skyward, his skin blanching underneath his tan.

Natalie looked back at him. 'Um . . . Well, Meg, you see the thing is . . . Gary here is . . .'

Suddenly the kitchen was filled with women, Steve and babies.

'Gary?' Jess exclaimed, going immediately over to him and kissing him. 'Well, how lovely to meet you, what a treat. When did you fly in, was it last night?'

'I . . . er, no,' Gary said. 'Not exactly.'

'Dubai, hey,' Steve said, pumping Gary's hand vigorously, with Lucy tucked under one arm. 'Some amazing design out there, incredible architecture. I'm in design myself. I find engineering fascinating. We should have a beer sometime. It must be meet-the-spouse morning – this is my wife, Jill, it's her first meeting today too.'

Gary smiled weakly at Jill, who looked as flustered and out of place amid the chatter as he did.

'A beer?' Gary said wistfully.

'Wouldn't say no,' Jill replied.

'Are you staying this time?' Frances asked him frankly as she appraised him with naked curiosity. 'Natalie does miss you, you know. I must say, Natalie, he's not how I pictured him all. I pictured him as more cerebral. When actually he's very . . . very . . . *corporeal*.'

'Ah . . . um, well.' Gary fixed his gaze on his phantom spouse. 'Anything you want to say, Natalie?

But before she could speak Sandy appeared again in the doorway.

'There's someone else here to see you,' she told Natalie with a quite outrageously obvious wink.

'What? Who?' Natalie groaned. 'Is it Tiff? I need Tiff to save my life.'

'Sorry, I haven't been called Tiff for years,' Jack Newhouse said.

'Arse,' Natalie said with a heavy sigh and then, 'No offence.'

'None taken . . . I think,' Jack said. 'You've got guests. Look, Natalie, I'm sorry to interrupt you but I really need to speak with you. I couldn't wait until tomorrow.'

Natalie looked around her at her chirping and chatting friends, and at poor Gary, who kept backing slowly towards the garden doors looking helplessly at her all the time, silently pleading to be rescued.

She looked at Jack. 'I need to say something first. Right!' she called out. 'Quiet please.'

One by one the baby group members fell silent, looking at each other curiously.

'I have an announcement. This is not how I planned to make it. I planned to ply you all with cake first and get you a bit drunk, maybe slip some cooking sherry in your tea if my mother hadn't drunk it all . . . but, anyway, needs must.' Natalie took a breath and pointed at Gary. 'This man, although he is called Gary, is not Gary my husband.'

'Husband?' Jack asked sharply. 'Did you say husband?'

Natalie thought it best to ignore him for now.

'This is Gary my *electrician* who came round to remind me I haven't paid the bill.' Natalie smiled a little sheepishly at Gary, who had his hand hopefully on the door handle.

'Oh! Oh no!' Meg clasped both her hands over her mouth. '*How* embarrassing!'

'I do apologise,' Frances said.

'Oh God, you must have thought we were mad,' Jess chipped in with a giggle.

'There's more,' Natalie said. 'There's a lot more and I'm going to tell you all about it but first I have to . . .' She stopped talking. The sight of Jack standing in the doorway took her breath away for a second.

'Jack,' she said. 'I need to sort out a few things here. Did you want to go and see Freddie and we can talk in a bit?'

'What's he got to do with Freddie?' Frances asked, with her special brand of tact-free curiosity.

'Hello.' Jack smiled at Frances with automatic good manners. 'I'm Jack Newhouse – Freddie's dad.'

There was total silence in the kitchen. You could have heard a mute mouse dropping a tiny pin.

'I told you there was more,' Natalie said with a shrug.

'What have I said?' Jack asked her.

'A bit too much just now,' she told him.

'Look, I need to know – have you got a husband?' Jack persisted, and Natalie realised that he really believed that this was possible.

'OK, well, you might as well be here for this too, why not. Mother?' Natalie looked at Sandy. 'Anyone else coming?'

'Only me,' Tiffany said as she walked into the kitchen. 'What's going on?'

'You may well ask,' Frances said.

'Right.' Natalie took a breath. 'Hello, everybody, I am Natalie Curzon. I am thirty-six and a single mother. I am not married, I have never been married. I made up a husband and called him after my electrician Gary because, oh, I don't know, it's as good a name as any. At the time it seemed easier to tell you I had a husband somewhere than to explain to what was then a bunch of total strangers that I had conceived my son on a weekend fling with *this* man –' she pointed at Jack. 'Jack Newhouse. A man who I barely knew at the time of conception and who I don't know that much better now.' Natalie paused and looked at Jack; she didn't know him well enough to be able to read his expression.

'So, you haven't got a husband,' he confirmed. She shook her head. He nodded as if the news had helped him to come to some decision. Natalie just prayed it wasn't the decision to have her sectioned under the Mental Health Act. She turned back to her friends.

'The thing is, I didn't know you then, it didn't seem important. But over the last few weeks I've got to know and love you all. I really mean that, I love you and care about you all. You have become important to me as friends, and I didn't know how to tell you what a fool I'd been. It just got harder and more stupid as time went on – every time I decided to tell you, something would happen to someone else and I'd feel like even more of an idiot. Then when Jack came back I got even more confused and muddled and it wasn't until we were all at Tiffany's, just after Tiff got Jacob breathing again, that I realised just how sad and poor I'd be without you. And if you can still bear to be my friends after all this nonsense I promise never to lie to you again, except about my age and weight which I think is more or less a given with most women over the age of thirty-five, don't you? Not that I am over the age of thirty-five . . . Anyway, you can stone me now, if you like. There's some pea shingle in the garden.'

Nobody said anything until eventually Meg asked, 'Is that all?'

'Um, well . . . yes,' Natalie said. 'What more do you want?'

'I thought you were going to tell us you were in a ménage with the electrician, your husband and this guy,' Steve said, sounding a little disappointed and oomphing as Jill elbowed him firmly in the ribs.

'I *knew* there was something more between him and you,' Jess said. 'Didn't I say, Meg? I said I knew. When we saw him in town that day she had this look on her face, she looked . . .' Jess caught Natalie's pleading glance and didn't say any more. 'Oh Nat, you idiot.'

'Does that mean you don't all hate me?' Natalie asked them.

'We think you are really rather foolish,' Frances said. 'But that was already apparent.'

'How could I hate you when you've been such a dear, good friend to me?' Meg smiled at Natalie. 'No, it was just a silly fib that didn't hurt anyone. I can't believe you didn't say something before, you silly thing. I bet you've been fretting about it all this time.'

'I have, a bit,' Natalie said. She was feeling rather foolish but extremely relieved.

'Well, at last,' Tiffany said, rather maternally, and when the others looked at her she added rather proudly, 'I knew *ages* ago.'

Gary, who had been frozen by the back door, was gradually relaxing. He looked at Jack and nodded. It was a gesture of solidarity, Natalie realised. A signal that they were both men who had survived the madness of Natalie Curzon in one way or another.

'I'll get off then,' he said, sliding open the back door. 'See you later, Tiff. Take care, Natalie, and good luck!' Natalie gave him a little wave as he closed the door, but he didn't wave back.

'Shall I make the tea?' Sandy said. 'And then all of you ladies and Steve can go upstairs to the sitting room. Natalie will just have a quick word with Jack here and she'll be up in a minute, is that OK?' Natalie had never been so glad to have her mother take control of a situation. She had never been glad of it before, in fact, and hadn't had the compulsion to hide behind her mother's skirts for at least thirty years.

'Hold on,' Jack said as everyone began to file out. They stopped and looked at him.

'I don't know any of you actually.' He looked both scared and slightly manic. 'But I have a declaration too. Why not?'

Natalie froze. She didn't know what he was going to say but she was sure she didn't want him to say it in front of everybody.

'Jack,' she said. 'Look, I'm sorry about all this . . .'

'I have to,' he said with a determined nod. 'I liked the way you spoke just now. You were very brave, I thought, and . . . admirable. It made me want to have a go. There's been a lot of ambiguity between us. A lot of things either half said or not said at all. And it's no good, not for you or me or Freddie. I want all your friends to know how I feel. But most of all I want you to know.'

'Oh,' Natalie said in dismay, looking at her mother, but Sandy just smiled encouragingly at her. 'Jack, all I'm asking is that whatever you think about me you don't let this affect you and Freddie.'

'Natalie, be quiet and let me talk,' he interrupted her.

418

'How interesting,' Frances said, taking a seat on a stool and crossing her arms. The entire baby group was listening.

'Last year was a big year for me,' Jack began. 'I had cancer and I met Natalie.' He took a breath and squared his shoulders. 'I thought the most important and life-changing thing of those two events was the cancer, but I was wrong. It was meeting Natalie.' Natalie couldn't look at him – she hung her head and closed her eyes and waited for the indictment that was bound to follow. 'Because of meeting her I now have this amazing son to get to know and be a dad to. And if that's not the most important thing that can happen to a man, then I don't know what is. But that's not all – I want you to know that I've done something much more stupid than Natalie ever has.'

'Are you sure?' Frances asked him. He smiled and nodded.

'Natalie, when I got back to London, to try to pick up my life again, what I didn't want to admit to myself was that – well, I came back for you. I was looking for you. Oh, I was trying hard not to. One day I even caught myself walking around Soho Square, because I remembered that you worked near there and I thought I might bump into you. I felt so stupid looking for a woman I barely knew, a woman who I was sure wouldn't want me once she knew . . . the things that you know now. I told myself I could meet hundreds of women the way I met you, so I walked up to this girl and started talking to her, I told her the things I told you. I tried to have exactly the same conversation as the one we had the day we met. I've never seen anyone look so bored before in my life. I didn't fancy her and she certainly didn't fancy me but I gave her my phone numbers anyway, I thought it was a hurdle I had to get over. I was wrong.'

'Suze.' Natalie murmured the name to herself, as suddenly the so-called perceived anomalies in what she thought she knew about Jack fell into place.

'I lost you. I lost you twice, once when I was too scared to show you my weaknesses, and once when I was too weak to let you know that I was scared. Scared of seeing you again. Scared of how seeing you made me feel. And when I did finally see you – you brought me to life. I tried to tell myself that our moment had passed, that we were never meant to be anything other than co-parents and friends. I said it until I almost believed it, because I didn't think I could get any luckier than I already was – a survivor and a father. I didn't think I deserved to be any luckier than that, and maybe I don't. But I don't want to be scared or weak any more, either. I have to say what I feel.'

'Say it then!' Natalie almost shouted on an outward rush of air. She took a steadying breath. 'Say what you feel, Jack.'

'I will,' Jack said, looking at her. 'It isn't over for me. I care about you more than I am able to describe. I don't want our last chance to have passed.' He took a step towards her, and the baby group looked from him to Natalie and back again in one seamless motion. 'I want to be with you, Natalie, I want to –' He seemed frustrated as he tried to find the right words. 'Look, I know you said you didn't want one but – I want to be your boyfriend!'

Natalie stared at him, open-mouthed.

'Say something!' Jack exclaimed and then, 'I'm starting to think this declaration wasn't my best plan.'

'I . . . I just didn't expect this,' Natalie managed to say at last.

'Look.' Jack took another step closer to her. 'I know it would be strange and difficult. I know we'd be the weirdest dating couple in the history of dating couples, the only one with a baby before they even get to their second date . . .'

'That *is* quite unusual,' Frances said helpfully.

'But I don't care if it's freaky. I don't care if it's a risk and if it's complicated. Sometimes complications are exactly what we need. You are a very complicated person. And I need you.' Jack took a deep breath and shrugged. 'You make my heart beat stronger than it ever has.'

There was a collective female sigh in the room.

'There, I've said it, and I said it in front all of these strange and quite scary women and that bloke, because I'm less frightened of them than I am of being alone with you and you turning me down.'

'But,' Natalie said with a tiny smile, 'we'd be mad, wouldn't we?'

'I would say so,' Jack agreed with a curt nod.

'Doomed to almost certain failure?' she asked him.

'If we always put Freddie first it might work,' Jack said urgently, taking two more steps closer to her. 'And anyway, on paper it might look like a terrible idea but here in my heart it feels like the right thing to do. The only thing to do.' Jack paused and glanced at his captive audience. 'Have I overplayed the corny romantic gesture part yet?'

'Not as far as I'm concerned,' Meg said misty-eyed, her hands clasped to her chest.

'Maybe slightly,' Frances suggested.

'No,' Natalie said slowly, afraid to blink in case she shed a tear. 'No, you haven't because I feel the way you do. I just had no idea, no idea at all that you felt the same. I never could have asked you, I would have been too afraid. You've been the strong one, the brave one. You're the one with guts. I want this, Jack, I want to be with you.'

'Will you go out with me then?' Jack asked her, smiling broadly.

'I will,' Natalie said and the two of them stood in the middle of the kitchen, in the middle of the baby group, grinning at each other.

'Is that it?' Jess asked. 'Aren't you going to kiss or something?'

'Not in front of you lot we're not,' Natalie said, smiling at her. 'And besides, we haven't even been on a second date yet.'

'Oh, who cares about convention,' Jack said decisively, and before she could move, he had closed the last two steps between them, taken her face in his hands and was kissing her. Somewhere dimly outside the feel of his lips on hers and his fingers in her hair as she wound her arms around his neck and pulled him closer, Natalie heard all her friends laughing and cheering.

'There's just one thing I want to know,' Jill asked. 'Is every baby group meeting going to be like this one?'